South of the River

By the same author

Thomas Hood: Poems Comic and Serious
Selected with an introduction and notes
Illustrated with Hood's own comic woodcuts

In These Places, At These Times
Selected poems by Peter Thorogood. Beautifully illustrated
with the author's watercolours

St. Mary's Bramber: A Sussex House and its Gardens
Five hundred years of history. Illustrated with old photographs

St. Mary's Bramber: A Pictorial Souvenir
A delightful portrait of a much-loved house and gardens
Fine colour photographs by Henry Wilson
Additional photographs by Roger Linton and Peter Smith
Nostalgic memories in prose and verse

The Complete Comic and Curious Verse
of Peter Thorogood
With over eighty humorous pen-and-ink sketches by the author

South of the River

A Novel of the Fifties

In Eighteen Episodes and over Eighty Scenes

including a Prologue, an Epilogue
and a look 'Behind the Scenes'

by

Peter Thorogood

Bramber Press

ISBN 0 - 9538281 - 8 - 2

Original cover design by Roger Linton DesRCA
Computer graphics by Tony Ketteman

Printed and bound by Antony Rowe Ltd
Eastbourne

Published 2005 by the Bramber Press
St. Mary's House, Bramber, West Sussex BN44 3WE
Tel/fax: 01903 - 816205
www.bramberpress.co.uk
email: info@bramberpress.co.uk

for
Mary and Robin

who, for very different reasons, will find
much that is familiar in these pages

Acknowledgements

The Bramber Press wishes to thank Diana Durden for her invaluable help with editing and proof-reading, Roger Linton for his cover design, and Tony Ketteman for his advice and assistance in preparing the text.

PROLOGUE: Thursday 12 February 1959

How It All Began

EPISODE ONE: St. Valentine's Eve. Early morning

A Difference of Opinion

EPISODE TWO: St. Valentine's Eve. Early afternoon

The Trouble with Millie

EPISODE THREE: St Valentine's Day. Morning

Love on Hire Purchase

EPISODE FOUR: Valentine's Day. Later that evening

The Stage is Set

EPISODE FIVE: A Saturday in April

Spring Fever

EPISODE SIX: A Saturday in early June

Paving the Way!

EPISODE SEVEN: Later the same morning

Crime and Punishment

EPISODE EIGHT: A Sunday in late June

Mixed Feelings

EPISODE NINE: Afternoon on the same day

Up to No Good!

EPISODE TEN: The next morning

Decline and Fall

EPISODE ELEVEN: Afternoon of the following day

Pains and Penalties

EPISODE TWELVE: August Bank Holiday Monday

A Day by the Sea

EPISODE THIRTEEN: Later that afternoon

Through the Storm

EPISODE FOURTEEN: New Year's Eve

A Light on the Horizon

EPISODE FIFTEEN: Early afternoon

Unexpected Visitors

EPISODE SIXTEEN: Later that evening

New Year Resolutions!

EPILOGUE: New Year's Day 1960

How It All Ended

BEHIND THE SCENES

The People Concerned

In Essex

Andrew Crawford	Market gardener. An irascible bully with a grievance
Jane Crawford	His wife. Family peacemaker. Woman with a secret
Timothy Crawford	Their son. An idealist with much to learn
Ray	Lorry-driver for Andrew Crawford & Son
John Garville	Farmer and old friend of Andrew Crawford. God-father to Timothy

At Laburnum Villas

At No 1

Councillor Joseph Gabriel Purvis	Landlord of Laburnum Villas. A social do-gooder and benefactor
Gwendolen	His unmarried daughter

At No 2

Grandpa Lawton	Ageing 'Lollipop Man' with a mission. Leaseholder and landlord to Miss Baldock
Miss Agnes Baldock	Grandpa's lodger. Manageress of the Roxy Restaurant. Spinster of means

At No 3

Bombed in the Blitz	Sole survivor: little Freddy Higgins

At No 4

Alfred Thompson	Employed at the tannery. Formerly a porter at the Borough Market. Man with a secret
Florence Thompson	His wife. Cleaning lady at the Town Hall
Mildred Thompson	Eldest daughter. Employed at the button factory
Ronald Thompson.	Schoolboy without prospects
Mabel Thompson	Baby daughter. Observer of mankind
'Smutty' Thompson	The family dog. A committed Epicurean
'Inky' Thompson	Mabel's short-lived companion

At No 5

Walter Paxton	Ex-Police-Sergeant. Retired. Amateur rose-grower
Louise Paxton	His pretty niece. Disabled by speech impediment

At No 6

Ma Carpenter	Cantankerous beldam of *The Bed of Roses*
Eddie Carpenter	Her son. Porter at Rothersey Borough Market, in the service of Andrew Crawford & Son.

Other Residents of Rothersey

Ma Donoghue	A scavenger and bag-woman
Curly Donoghue	Her son. Porter at Rothersey Borough Market and 'spiv' in the service of Andrew Crawford & Son.
Ma Blackwood	Tyrannical tycoon of 'The Lollipop Shop'
Pa Blackwood	Alias 'Legnonero'. Neapolitan yes-man, organ-grinder and illegal immigrant. Master of Beppo
Gino Polenti	Scoundrel and scapegoat
Beppo	Performing monkey. Ill-fated friend of Mabel Thompson
Councillor 'Pixie' Calthrop	Ambitious champion, Moral Re-armament Committee
Rev. Daniel Curtis	Vicar of St. Crispin's, Rothersey
Bingo Wood	Rival to Councillor Purvis
Dr. Glendale	The local doctor. Rarely comes when needed
Frank and Cynthia	Casual observers of life's little tragedies
Miss Dorothy Goodenough	Deputy Head teacher, Rothersey Secondary School
Freddy Higgins	'The triumvirate'. Ron's school pals
Teddy Rogers	
Billy Watkins	
Effie Mudd	Shop assistants at Marley's General Stores
Iris Mudd	
Lizzie Pomfrett	
Young man on coach	An outsider. Ron's 'Lone Stranger'
Priscilla (Elsa)	Daughter of teacher at Rothersey College of Art

Plan of Laburnum Villas

No. 1   Councillor Purvis and his daughter Gwendolen
No.2   Grandpa Lawton and Miss Agnes Baldock
No.3   Bombed site. Former home of the Higgins family
No.4   The Thompson family
No.5   Retired policeman Walter Paxton and his niece, Louise
No.6   Ma Carpenter and her son, Eddie

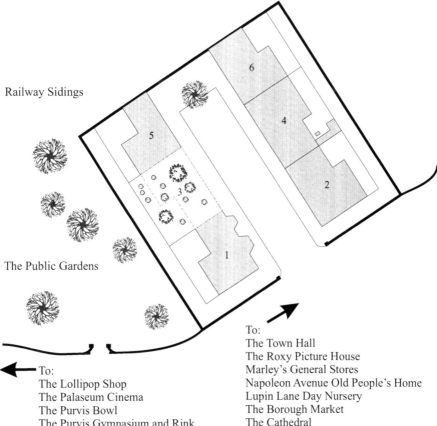

Railway Sidings

The Public Gardens

To:
The Town Hall
The Roxy Picture House
Marley's General Stores
Napoleon Avenue Old People's Home
Lupin Lane Day Nursery
The Borough Market
The Cathedral

To:
The Lollipop Shop
The Palaseum Cinema
The Purvis Bowl
The Purvis Gymnasium and Rink
The Bridge
St. Crispin's Church

PROLOGUE

Warley, Essex: Thursday 12th February 1959

How it All Began

1. Family Row

In the beginning there were daffodils. Not that it was the season for them, mind. It was just that February was a pretty lean month for Andrew Crawford, with only cabbage and potatoes to send to market. Not at all like the pea-season when the money came rolling in and you just sat back and watched it pile up in front of you — all those lovely little sixpences and shillings nestling down with the florins and half-crowns on a soft green bed of one pound notes, not to mention the crisp white fivers, large enough to pave the garden path with! Then there were the dozens of cheques that came rolling into the cash-box, all waiting to be totted up and taken into the market bank that opened each weekday morning at eight o'clock for the farmers and traders to deposit their takings.

No! February was a bad time for Mr. Andrew Crawford, with next-to-nothing in the ground that would fetch a decent price, and there wouldn't be either until the Spring crops came on. Meanwhile the men had to be paid. Didn't think twice about Andrew Crawford having to plough it all back into the business! Always wanting more pay for less work, they were, never considering for a moment the plight of the employer who gave them their holidays with pay and tickled their fancies with overtime and bonus schemes. The more you did for people, reflected Mr. Crawford gloomily one day, the more you did for them the more dissatisfied they seemed to be.

Such grievances assumed pride of place in Mr. Crawford's thoughts as he regularly took up his position at the dining-room window and gazed over the sepia-furrowed land folding away into the distance. Not a speck of green anywhere, except down on the Nine-acres where the cabbage were. All you could see was row upon row of little earth ridges stretching out into the grey winter light and merging into the bleak horizon.

Every day Mr. Crawford would watch the men trimming the hedges and ditches; every day he would wonder how much longer the old Suffolk mare could go on straining at the plough and dragging it through the rain-soaked soil; every day he would ask himself how long the rain would go on filling up the ponds and ditches to overflowing.

18

'February fill-dyke' was an old adage all too familiar to Andrew Crawford. The crops would rot in the ground and there'd be little or nothing to sell in the peak season.

It was this that made Mr. Crawford agree to the daffodil idea in the first place, but he made it quite clear to his son, Timothy, that his style of market gardening had no place for flower-selling. The whole project was scatter-brained, and directly opposed to the century-old tradition of *Andrew Crawford & Son*. He was convinced that any idea which was not his own (especially if Timothy had thought of it first) was bound to be doomed to failure. Timothy, when it came down to it, was a bit of a fool; Timothy was, and never would be, a true Crawford. All he did was waste his time playing the piano and scribbling poetry. Farming was either in you or it was not! You couldn't learn it from books. There were no two ways about it. Andrew Crawford didn't realise it in as many words, but when he told his wife that her precious son's 'daffy' idea, as he called it, wouldn't work, he was really saying that he *hoped* it wouldn't work.

As a matter of fact, the idea *didn't* work. It wasn't because, in the final analysis, it was not a good one. It *was* really, but Timothy made the cardinal error of defiantly referring to the whole affair as a 'slight misunderstanding' — so slight in fact that it changed the whole of his future from that day on! Whether it was for better or for worse remained to be seen, but, for the moment, it was definitely for the worse.

Somewhere about the middle of the month, it all happened. Tim had been hanging around in the yard the whole of this freezing February afternoon, waiting for the daffodil delivery. Ray, the lorry-driver, had joined him about three o'clock and together they stamped their boots into the frozen gravel of the yard, hugged themselves, shivered, puffed little clouds of condensation into the icy air, heads sunk into turned-up collars, fingers bloodless with wind-frost and, all the time the north wind came howling over the fallow winter fields that lay beyond the bunching-shed. By five o'clock, darkness had fallen. Still there was no sign of the daffodils. Timothy went in to telephone the station, only to be told that the flowers had already gone out on the van and that was all *they* knew about the matter!

In the warmth of her farmhouse kitchen, Mrs. Jane Crawford

poured out the tea. Timothy drank in silence, watching the blue and orange flames leaping over the apple-wood and remembering, with feelings of dismay, the argument he had had with his father about chopping down the old tree. The tree had died! So what was the point of leaving it to rot?

Andrew Crawford was one of the old school. He ran his family like a regiment — everyone had to obey or pay the price. His long-suffering wife ran the house as best she could, with the help of a twice-weekly 'daily', whilst Timothy tried to soften the burden of chores when his father wasn't looking — for fear of being branded a 'mother's boy'!

Jane had met Andrew Crawford in June 1935, at a Young Farmer's Club dance. He was a handsome young Scot, an only son, who had just inherited a five-hundred acre farm near Warley in Essex, following the death of a wealthy uncle. Andrew possessed a persuasive charm and everyone could see, as the months went by, that he and Jane would soon be announcing their engagement. An elaborate wedding at Southwark Cathedral was followed by a sumptuous reception at Frascati's. A year later Timothy was born. It was agreed to ask Andrew's old bachelor school friend, John Garville, to be god-father to the boy, and he was happy to oblige. No doubt there would have been more children on the way for Andrew and Jane but for a disastrous development that forever forged a rift between the couple — an open wound that had little chance of ever being healed.

As Andrew progressed with his business, it was clear that wartime restrictions and pressures, the terrors and dangers of air-raids, the strain of early mornings driving through London's East End to Rothersey Borough Market, were only three of the burdens that assailed Andrew Crawford. He became more irascible and unyielding as the years passed and Jane became gradually more isolated and alone. Increasingly, she and her young son were thrown together. They relied on each other for company, going for walks together in the meadows, playing piano duets in the long winter evenings and discussing the books they had read together. In short, they became almost inseparable.

It was about the time that Timothy went away to boarding-school that things started to go seriously wrong. It all began on the evening of the annual Covent Garden Association Ball at the Dorchester

20

Hotel. Jane had bought a new emerald green and silver evening dress at Marshall and Snelgrove in Oxford Street. She remembered it well because Andrew had fallen into an unwarranted rage when he first saw her wearing it. She recalled the strained silence that accompanied them all the way up to London.

Jane was a woman of very striking appearance. Tall and slim, she could make men's eyes turn even when she was wearing the most modest of dresses. The impression she made when she and Andrew walked down the steps to the ballroom was only one cause of an even wider gulf between them. Given his obtuseness, it was likely that Andrew failed to see that his jealousy was unfounded. He simply put it down to his dislike of other men trespassing on his property. But that was not the whole story by any means.

As to the running of the farm, father and son had such hopelessly irreconcilable ideas that it was to be wondered that any produce found its way to the market at all. Timothy wanted a tractor, new machinery for washing vegetables, new packaging, a new display-stand and pretty well anything new that could transform the old firm into a competitive business. His father, however, preferred to carry on with his cart-horses, his dwindling band of aged workmen and his antediluvian implements. What had been good enough for grandfather would have to be good enough for Timothy. That is how the apple-tree became such a great issue between them — a symbol of their disunity. The accumulative effect of such incidents did little to alleviate the worry in Timothy's mind that his future as a farmer was as unpredictable as his father's petulant outbursts of rage. Mention an apple to Andrew Crawford and he saw red!

Timothy and his father sat in armchairs on opposing sides of the kitchen range whilst Mrs Crawford, in her customary role as referee, leant over her scrubbed table and quietly worked at her embroidery. Talking at meals was discouraged. Timothy could remember being continually admonished by his anxious mother and told to get on with his dinner, tea or supper now and not to chatter so much or his father would give him a good telling off. There was no getting away from it, Timothy's enthusiasms were no match for his father's intransigence. He drank up his tea and went out to the yard again, only to find Ray disappearing down the lane into the darkness.

"Goodnight, Ray!" shouted Timothy.

" 'Night, Tim," said a voice dimly. "Cold ol' night!"

"Yes. Rain tomorrow."

Timothy hated weather, at least as farmers saw it — too wet, too dry, too hot, too cold. It was never right. He hated the prospect of rain the most — especially on a Thursday. Thursdays for Timothy were void of spirit, when everything was waiting for the longed-for weekend to happen — or was it simply that he hated the idea of facing up to the market at all. Customers were not always easy to deal with, still less the porters.

Half-past six! With no sign of the daffodils, Timothy went back into the house, hung up his coat and sat by the fire. His father was still slumped in his chair, gazing at the flames, between short naps. Timothy picked up the book on animal breeding he was studying for his next veterinary examinations at the local technical college and began the chapter on blood groups. A few moments passed before he realised his father was speaking to him, and the realisation startled him.

"Well, Timothy, did the daffs arrive, eh?" he said, with a tone of satisfaction at the probable failure of yet another of Timothy's misconceived schemes.

"No," said Timothy, warily "They must have been held up."

"Just as well, I should say. There's going to be a fine old frost tonight."

Timothy felt, to say the least, encouraged by his father's unexpected hint of sympathy and, though he realised that it might be a preliminary flick of the whip, he unwisely succumbed to filial self-pity, hoping his father might accept some of the responsibility himself.

"They might come yet, you know," said Timothy. "The van could be held up. It would happen on a Thursday of all days. If they come tomorrow, with the market not open on Saturday....."

"If they come tomorrow," interrupted Mr. Crawford, "it'll be your pidgin, my boy. And another thing," he went on, "I thought sending you on to college would put some gumption into you. When are you going to realise that farming is a tough business? The trouble with you is you're too mollycoddled. Too much of a 'mother's darling!'"

"Now, Andrew," said Mrs. Crawford quietly, "there's no need to go on like that at the boy. Don't be so argumentative."

"If anything," he said, ignoring his wife's motherly defence, "you're a darned sight worse now you've come home from college."

"At least I grew up," Timothy remonstrated.

"Grew up!" Mr. Crawford sneered.

"Make fun of it if you like," said Timothy. "I learnt a lot about living with people, listening to their problems. I made good friends."

"If you thought more about your work and less about your friends you'd do a lot better," Mr. Crawford scoffed.

"Look, father! I was raw, immature, muddleheaded. At least I came out knowing what I wanted from life."

"What you wanted from life! Yes, I can see that! You want a bit too much, my lad. It's about time you did something to make me proud of you. I've given you the best education money could afford, a future with the firm, and you don't care a damn!"

"Andrew!" exclaimed Mrs. Crawford. "There's no need to speak like that."

"I'll speak how I like, thank you very much," he said sharply. "Look, Timothy! You come up with these damn-fool ideas, and what happens? I end up paying the bill! They're not ideas, they're mistakes!"

"Mistakes!" said Timothy, raising his voice. "I do my best to make you see what other farmers are doing, and all you can do is sit back with a smile of self-satisfaction on your face and say that Grandfather's ideas are good enough for you so they can be good enough for me too."

Tim flung himself out of his chair, trembling with anger. He wanted to really let himself go and say what was really on his mind — that one phrase that was going round in his head like an angry wasp in a jam-jar. One day he would release it and all hell would be let loose.

EPISODE ONE

St. Valentine's Eve: Early morning

A Difference of Opinion

2. Diminishing Returns

On market days it was customary for Timothy Crawford to be woken at three in the morning. The procedure was always the same: a cup of tea in bed, a jug of hot water standing in the basin in the freezing bathroom, the aroma of toast and tea drifting up the back stairs. Timothy couldn't remember a time when it was not like this. Although his father performed this early morning ritual with unnerving efficiency, Timothy could never be sure if it was done out of a kind of inarticulate love or mere mechanical necessity. He accepted the routine unquestioningly and in the silence with which it was offered. There was no friendly 'good morning', nor was there any breakfast conversation. The second cup of tea was poured without a word. Tim came to accept his father's fondness for his own company, yet at times, in the midst of this dumb-show, some kind of veiled affection sought unsuccessfully to express itself. Translated into words, it turned to anger and argument.

On this particular Friday morning, Timothy and his father rose from the breakfast table as usual — without a word. They stepped out into the biting wind as it came pushing round the corner of the house, freezing everything in its path. The drain-cover under the dairy window was hard and treacherous under foot. Boots slithered over ice-bound puddles. In the cart-shed, Ray was warming up the engine of the lorry. It shook. It gurgled. It shuddered. It choked. It chugged and spluttered! When it finally showed some sign of life, Ray climbed down from the cab and stood with his hands pushed down into his overcoat pockets.

"What's wrong, Ray?" said Timothy, apprehensively.

Ray gave a furtive glance in the direction of Mr. Crawford.

"Them daffs don't look so clever, guv'nor. Must 'a bin left out in the cold all night."

Mr. Crawford's face set hard, his lips narrowed in the glare of the headlights. "When did they arrive?" he said, almost harshly.

"Just as I was goin' 'ome yisday night."

"Didn't you tell anyone they'd arrived?" asked Mr. Crawford.

"'Course I did! I told Master Tim all about 'em."

"No, you did not," said Timothy, sharply.

"Yes, I did and you know it," said Ray.

26

"All you said to me was something about it being a 'cold old night'. They were your very words."

"I said nothing of the sort. I said they 'come all right', and that's a fact." Ray glared at Timothy.

Mr. Crawford stood still for a moment, grim and silent. Ray watched him sheepishly as 'the master' (as the men usually called him) turned away without a word and strode to the back of the lorry, standing in the dim glow of the old oil lamp hanging on the beam above him. He stared at the daffodils.

"Timothy!" he shouted.

Ray grinned slyly. "The guv'nor's a-callin' you, I think, Master Tim."

"Timothy!" shouted the now irate Mr. Crawford. " I might have known it would come to this. Another of your cock-eyed ideas to brag about to your college friends. You might just as well take all your blasted books and throw them in the pond for all the good they do you."

Timothy looked at the forlorn frost-bitten blooms with dismay. He heard his father muttering with fury:

"By the time we get to London they won't be worth a farthing."

Timothy watched his father get into his car, slam the door, angrily rev-up the engine and drive off down the lane.

Two years of early mornings travelling up from Essex on the lorry through the suburbs of East London had immunised Timothy Crawford against the depression he felt at the sight of the endless succession of terraced houses, tenement buildings and bombed-out warehouses with their charred faces and gaping windows like empty eye-sockets. At first he had noticed them all, then grown used to them, had even accepted them for what they were and, ultimately, had become indifferent to them. Now he was thrown back on his thoughts and when he grew tired of those, he took to closing his eyes, sinking into a troubled sleep in the lunging passenger seat with its hard back. There was very little room, so you couldn't stretch your legs out and slump down into your duffel coat. Oh, no! you had to sit bolt upright, your head balancing like a ball on a stick, rolling from back to front and side to side until you felt sick with it all. When Timothy awoke it was raining.

" Just coming up towards Tower Bridge, Master Tim."

The rain was dribbling down the windscreen in indolent beads and rivulets. Timothy fixed his eyes on them in despair. Nothing was more disturbing to him than the enmity of early morning when the first light broke through the empty streets still deep in sleep. He watched a bead of rain-water trickle from the cab-roof, glistening all the way down the windscreen in the glare of the street lights.

Crossing over Tower Bridge, Timothy saw the lights of the ships berthed at the wharf below; a melancholy glow on the dark waters of the river made the raindrops on the windscreen glitter like pale sunlight on frosted window-panes. Passing Southwark Cathedral, Timothy peered at the clock.

"Nigh on four, I shouldn't be surprised," Ray said, rubbing his grey woollen glove over the side window.

"I can barely see anything through this rain," Timothy said.

"Proper 'oldin' things up, so it is, and no mistake. Ground's as wet as can be. No weather for farmers, taint, to be sure. Your father can't give 'is heart to it. It'll be the end of us, what with all this tinnin' and cannin' and freezin' and preservin' an' that."

As they turned into the Borough Market, Timothy began thinking about the daffodils again. It was not that they would make any appreciable difference to the takings — he didn't reckon on more than £50 at the most. There was no doubt this trial-run had been a failure from the start. What he was not to know was that the daffodil fiasco was to be the first of a number of unfortunate mishaps on this particular Friday morning. The flowers had suffered a punishing journey up from the Scilly Isles to London, then by rail to Essex, been bumped around on a van for most of the previous day and, after all that, had been left out in the frost, so what could you expect? Mr. Crawford would have nothing to do with them and ordered Timothy to get rid of the wretched things as soon as possible. After several failed attempts, Timothy gave them away to the Sisters of Nazareth from Hammersmith!

Ray was at his most supercilious. Contempt could be read in his hard, beady eyes. Throughout the morning, he wore a smirk of amused tolerance, which annoyed Timothy so much that he decided, should he ever have the chance, he would give the man the sack and be rid of him for ever! Then he repented. Such an action would be too much like father, like son!

Ray continued on his obsequious path with his employer throughout the rest of the morning, offering to run errands that usually formed part of Timothy's routine, going to the Post Office for stamps, doing up cotchells for what Curly Donoghue used to call 'Dandy Crawford's cronies'.

Of the two market porters in Mr. Crawford's service, Curly was known variously as 'Mr Universe' and 'Goldilocks' for his muscular frame and his shock of straight blond hair. He was the most scornful and insolent of all the market porters.

Eddie Carpenter, the second porter, a handsome, dark-haired youth, was not so mixed up as his mate, Curly, and took a much more tolerant and understanding approach to Timothy's plight. It was Eddie who appreciated the irony of the situation when the good Sisters thanked Mr. Crawford for the generous gift of wilting daffodils and presented him with a Holy Card, in pink and blue and gold, with a little verse on it about Jesus and Love. Whenever the Sisters appeared, Mr. Crawford was at his most angelic. They nourished his pride more than ever Mrs. Crawford could manage to do in her lonely Essex farmhouse.

3. Petty Cash

No sooner had Timothy rid himself of the confusion over the daffodil consignment than the more vexing mystery of the petty cash discrepancy presented itself. For weeks now, money had been missing from the cash box. Day by day, the amounts steadily increased as the 'borrower' grew more daring. Since it was Timothy's responsibility to check and replenish the money at regular intervals, it became apparent that someone who had easy access to the box was helping himself. First of all, it was a matter of a few shillings. On this unlucky Friday, the amount missing over the whole week amounted to nearly fifty pounds. In view of the row over the daffodils, Timothy decided not to mention the situation to his father until the following week.

It was Eddie's job to open up the stand in the mornings, and it was Eddie to whom Timothy's thoughts now turned as his prime suspect. Eddie was having a tough time at home looking after his cantankerous old mother. Eddie's father, old Jack Carpenter, had got himself killed over an argument with Alf Thompson, both of them porters in the market at the time. Nobody knew how it really happened. In any case, Alf left the market after Jack's death and went to work at the tannery. Mr. Crawford had taken on Eddie in his father's place, more out of convenience than compassion. Since then, employer and employed had kept their distance. Eddie invariably arrived early in the mornings, worked quietly and efficiently on the job, was always around when he was wanted. 'A thoroughly reliable worker' was the recommendation from John Garville, Andrew Crawford's friend and fellow-farmer, after he had temporarily employed Eddie when one of his men retired. Perhaps it was Eddie's quietness that Timothy was suspicious of most — Eddie trying not to be noticed, Eddie being devious, furtive and underhand.

Curly Donoghue, on the other hand, was always turning up late for work, argued with the customers, swore and fought with the other porters — quite the smart-aleck of the place, you would think! Many were the moments of resentment and frustration that Curly Donoghue stored up in his emotional black-book which, one day, would change the lives of quite a number of the people who had the misfortune to cross his path. Timothy could not bring himself to think that a man like Curly, who harboured such anger in his breast, could allow himself the luxury of such an undistinguished crime as petty theft. Timothy disliked Curly, yet, in the circumstances, it was Eddie he didn't trust.

After Curly had wheeled away the daffodils on his barrow in the direction of the Sisters of Nazareth's van, Timothy took over on the stand while his father went on his rounds. As he opened the desk-drawer to take out the cash-box, Eddie's face appeared over the top of the desk, which was high off the ground, so that his elbow was on a level with Eddie's chin.

" 'Morning, Mr. Tim. Mind if I 'ave a word with you? It'll only take a sec'."

Timothy picked up the keys and made a show of opening the cash box.

"How's yer Dad, this mornin'?" Eddie asked. "In a good mood, is he?"

"In fighting form, I should say," said Timothy, ruefully.

"I mean — is he, shall we say, friendly like?"

"Got something on your mind?"

"Not exactly — well ....." Eddie paused to rephrase his thoughts. "P'raps I have."

Without looking at Eddie, Timothy took out a thin wad of notes and a bag of coin. "Is it a problem or a confession?" asked Timothy.

"What would I have to confess about? Have you been talkin' to them nuns again?"

If Timothy had been of a superstitious nature he would have remembered that today was Friday 13th, a day considered by those people of a more vulnerable nature as unluckier than most. All he knew was that something was about to happen but he didn't know when, or where, or how.

"It's about my mum," Eddie went on. " She's bin taken proper bad, she 'as. I gets home from work yesterday dinner-time, and what do I find? Herself, sitting sprawled out on the kitchen floor. Crying her eyes out, she was, and groaning, like, and holding her side real tight. You shoulda seen the kitchen — like she busted up the blinkin' place! Table and chairs all topsy-turvy, and her 'ollerin' like the dickens! Proper smack in the eye for me, I can tell yer. ''Ere, Ma! I says. You bin doin' yer nut? A right ol' one you look, sitting on yer arse like a hen about to lay an egg!' Well stone me, if she don't give out a 'ollerin' as you never 'eard in all your born days. 'Eddie, boy', she says, 'it's me time, I knows it. It's me time!'"

"Well, the way I see it, she was none too bright, so I offers to get the ol' medicine man, see. Shouting and yelling, she was, about she didn't want no medico in her house, and she didn't want no ambulance, neither. She hadn't got nothing a good dose of cascara couldn't cure! Well, I gets her into her chair, props her up with her ol' leather cushions, and scarpers down the phone box. Blimey! In a sec' we was surrounded — blokes in blue uniforms and the ol' white cattle-truck blinking away outside. So they carted 'er off to the 'ospital."

Timothy stopped counting the money and stared at Eddie with a mixture of suspicion and sympathy.

"I'm really sorry to hear about your mother, Eddie, but what has this all got to do with my father?"

"Well, you see, Mr. Tim, I'm a bit short. Broke! I was wonderin' if you could ask yer Dad if he could lend me a couple o' quid in advance, like. With Ma laid up as she is, things are a bit tight, see?"

Eddie slouched off to unload the lorry with Ray and Curly. Timothy finished counting — the cash was short by £8 or more. A familiar voice boomed across the market:

"Timothy!"

Timothy wished his father would not yell at him in front of the porters, and especially John Garville, whom, for very good reasons, Timothy was fond of, for they had much in common.

"I'm coming," Timothy replied, his voice drowned by an early-morning train passing overhead. Reluctantly, he told Curly to take over the stand. Meanwhile Mr. Crawford was getting angry and impatient.

"TIMOTHY!" he yelled. "HURRY UP BOY!" Timothy reluctantly sauntered across to Garville's stand.

"Ah, so there you are!" said his father. "About time, too!"

"Good morning, Uncle John," said Timothy. "How's the fruit trade this morning?"

"Well, we're living in difficult times, Timothy, but you could say fine, Tim, fine," said Garville. "Oranges and lemons all the way, you might say. And how's your dear m....?"

"Where the dickens have you been, boy?" Mr. Crawford interrupted.

"Checking the petty cash." Timothy bit his lip. The words had come out on an angry tongue at the suppression of his mother's name. Instead of inciting his father, the remark played into Mr. Crawford's hands in quite another way.

"Ha!" he exclaimed, scornfully. "Petty cash? Never mind about that. If you thought about the big money more, we'd be a lot better off." Another flick of the whip, thought Timothy. A silent howl of anguish inside him expressed itself in a sudden flash of pique.

"Father!" he said in a strained tone of voice. " There is petty cash missing again this morning. It has been going on for weeks."

Mr. Crawford, who was just recovering from his little joke about 'big money', came out of his chuckling rather sorely.

"Now, Timothy!" said Mr. Crawford, with a warning note. "John has given us some oranges. Go and put them in the car. Your mother will be delighted with such a lovely present for her marmalade-making."

When they returned to the stand, a crowd of late customers was looking over the remaining cabbage, swedes, potatoes and turnips, digging and rummaging, on the look out for anything rotten at the bottom of the sack. 'There's no smell in the world more repellent than a rotten potato,' a regular customer, Miss Baldock, had complained to Andrew Crawford on the unwelcome receipt of one in her recently purchased consignment. Timothy watched the scavengers in despair. When would his father ever learn? Leaving this sight behind, they set off up the dark tunnel under the railway and came out into the bright lights of Rothersey High Street, just opposite the Express Dairy. Once seated at their usual corner table, Mr. Crawford returned to the attack.

"There's no need to take this petty cash thing so lightly, Timothy. It's a serious matter. Small crimes beget bigger ones. It stands to reason." A trace of his Scots accent broke through more noticeably when he became over-excited. "Look, Dad, I didn't want to worry you with it till I'd found the culprit."

"Very considerate, I'm sure," muttered Mr. Crawford.

"There's over £8 gone today. Apart from a break of about a week, it's been pretty continuous for a month or two. That makes over £50 missing now. I tell you — "

"Stop!" shouted Mr. Crawford.

An angry silence followed, in which only the hissing of the steam from the tea-urn could be heard. The other customers in the café obeyed Mr. Crawford's command to the last tea! They stopped eating. They stopped drinking. They stopped reading their newspapers. They stopped gossiping with their companions.

"Dad!" exclaimed Timothy. "For goodness' sake! There's no need to shout."

33

"I AM NO' SHOUTING!" yelled Mr. Crawford. "I AM VERY — [*and here he capriciously quietened his voice and hissed between his teeth as he often did when he was angry*] — I am very calm. I am very calm." All the same, he was trembling with rage and, in his usual irrational way, could not prevent himself from piling up the insults:

"You blithering idiot! What are you going to do about it, eh? How do you propose to catch this light-fingered scoundrel?"

It was clear to Timothy that his father was going through one of his fits of uncontrollable temper. At such times, all attempts by Timothy or his mother to reason with him were futile and only made things worse. The days when Andrew Crawford was a gentle, loving father were almost beyond memory. The only way was to face his anger from a position of strength, as if everything were normal — in a calm, detached matter-of-fact manner.

"I think I know who is taking the money," said Timothy quietly.

"Ah! So Mr. Sherlock Holmes has an answer, has he?"

"I know who took the money, Father," said Timothy, defiantly avoiding the gibe. "I'm not going to tell you until I have proof. You can't go accusing somebody of a crime until you know exactly who he is."

"I can't do anything, it seems," said Mr. Crawford, bitterly.

"There is such a thing as slander, you know."

"Timothy," said Mr. Crawford, with a venomous quietness and deliberation, "I would like to ask you a simple question. Who, might I ask, is in charge of the petty cash?"

" I am."

"Exactly!" exclaimed Mr. Crawford with satisfaction, "and until you find the thief, I shall see that you are personally responsible to me for the missing money, which you will have to pay out of your allowance. What with the daffodil fiasco and now this petty cash farce, I really think you had better take up some other occupation or profession."

This was exactly what Timothy decided to do.

4. Some Enchanted Evening!

"'Ere, Ed! 'Ave a look 'ere, me ol' cock. Just the job, eh?"

Curly was leaning against the coffee-stall in the market and holding up a copy of the Rothersey Gazette.

"What's up?" Eddie asked. "Picture of a luscious bird in her bath?"

"Taint likely! Always thinking about the old poker and tongs, you are! Taint healthy for a young bloke like you. Oughter get up the gym on the ol' weights and measures, mate. You want to jig about a bit. Get rid of some of that surplus energy."

"Come off it, Curly! Let's have a dekko."

Curly gripped Eddie by the arm.

"That's enough o' that lark. I aint finished reading the bloody thing."

"All right! No need to fly off the bleedin' handle, is there?"

"You can 'ave it when I'm good and ready, see?"

Eddie knew it was no use trying to get any sense out of Curly when he was in one of his moods. Always flaring up when you least expected it. No sooner had you made some harmless remark than he was lashing out at you, swearing and threatening you with his fist. Nobody, but nobody was going to tell Curly Donoghue what to do.

"'Ere you are, you twit!" Curly said, flinging the paper into a puddle. He swaggered off in the direction of the urinals, swearing at the rain. Eddie picked up the sodden paper out of the mud and opened it at an advertisement which took up half of page three:

THE PURVIS BOWL

London's Newest Bowling Alley

St. Valentine's Day

Dancing till midnite to Phil Pluckett and his Playboys

When Curly came back he grabbed the paper out of Eddie's hands again and began to read aloud:

GALA OPENING

by

COUNCILLOR JOSEPH PURVIS

in the presence of

His Worship the Mayor of Rothersey

"'Ere, Curly! Did you say Councillor Purvis?"

"That's what I said. You deaf or summink?"

"He lives in my street, Councillor Purvis."

"Whereabouts?"

"At No 1. You know, the first house on the left, opposite old Mother Baldock's place."

"I couldn't care where the old twit lives."

"Come off it! You just asked me."

"Look, I don't care, see?" said Curly, with a menacing look.

"If you knew him, you wouldn't say that."

"Oh, you make me sick. I don't want to know 'im, see? He's a bastard, see?"

"How would you know?"

"'Cos all them city blokes is bastards, else they wouldn't be where they are, would they, with their fancy clothes and their gold-plated Daimlers?"

For the sake of peace, Eddie said: "Maybe you're right," and made a point of keeping off the subject until he could get hold of the paper in Curly's coffee-break.

Down each side of the page were pictures of muscular men in white T-shirts and trousers, lurching forward on one leg, like skaters in motion, while all round them was a galaxy of admiring girls in jeans and sweaters and pony-tails.

'Wow!' thought Eddie. 'Just the job for a rainy night.'

"I would go," he said, "but I've got my Ma in hospital."

"If you turn up there again," Curly said, "she'll only send you packing."

Eddie was thinking. Bowling wasn't his line, not like dancing or a bit of roller-skating. The only thing was, he had promised his next-door neighbour, Mrs. Thompson, he would go there for his tea as Ma was laid up. The thought also crossed his mind that there might just a chance that young Millie Thompson might be around for a night out at the pictures.

"No, thanks, Curly. I got a date."

"Bring her, too. There'll be lots of birds around with all them Clark Gables there. They'll be on their knees, I tell you. I seen it all before, when they opened the Rink."

Eddie was thinking again. He didn't know Millie that well that he could take her out with blokes like Curly about.

"I dunno, Curly. Millie might not want to."

"'Ere!" said Curly, his eyes popping out of his head. "Did you say 'Millie'? Not that Millie Thompson what works up the button factory?"

"'S right!"

"Cor, blimey, mate! She's a bit of all right, she is. Gets about with the lads up the Rink. Are you coming then?"

"Okeedoke!" said Eddie, trying hard to be cheerful about it all, in spite of his misgivings.

Eddie was definitely not keen on the idea of Curly meeting up with Millie. Sex seemed to play around in Curly's head a long time before it ever got down below the waist-line. When his feelings broke loose there was usually hell to pay. Still, the Purvis Bowl wasn't at all a bad idea for a bloke with a girl like Millie, but Eddie wasn't too happy about her meeting up with Curly. No — not at all!

5. Enter Miss Baldock

As Timothy and his father crossed the road from the Express Dairy and turned into the long tunnel under the railway, they realised that all was not as it should be on the stand. Framed in the arch at the end of the tunnel was a small cameo of contention — a woman shaking her fists, Curly shouting abuse and, in the middle, Eddie, acting as referee. Mr. Crawford's first thought was that he only had to be away from the place for five minutes before things began to go wrong, whilst Timothy's thoughts were divided between an observation that his father would be smirking at the chance of proving himself indispensable, and, further, that this might be another of those embarrassing occasions when Timothy would once more be called upon to act as the firm's scapegoat.

"I won't stand for it, I tell you!" shouted the woman over the top of Curly's expletives. "I won't! I pay you good money for rubbish like this that isn't fit to feed to a dog. Seventeen years I've been a customer here, and this is the treatment I get. Last week, the Brussels sprouts were buried in mud. Now, it's the potatoes. Just look at them — it would take a month of Sundays to clean them. I wouldn't be surprised if there's mildew on them as well." The lady was as bitter as a large unmarriageable woman of forty-five might be, living in solitude in her little bed-sitting-room in the heart of the London desert.

Curly was fuming. "What the 'ell have you got to go on about? You bought the stuff in the first place. You can bloody-well pay for it, you silly ol' cow!"

"How dare you speak to me in that tone. I shall complain to Mr. Crawford. He'll have you sacked."

"Oh, yeah! Is that so?"

"'Ere! Curly boy!" said Eddie, the peace-maker. "Turn it up! Miss Baldock's one of our best customers. You didn't oughter speak to her like that."

Curly feigned a body blow, but Eddie knew that for two pins Curly would be happy to make it into a real fight, and it wouldn't be her pride Miss Baldock would lose, it would be her front teeth.

Mr. Crawford stepped forward from the darkness of the tunnel to greet her. As soon as Miss Baldock heard the soft Scots accent of

Andrew Crawford, the anger within softened to the point where she was almost apologetic for being in the right.

"Dear Mr. Crawford, I have had two sacks of potatoes from you in the last week which were more mud than potatoes. As to your turnips, they need a good bath! And your cabbage have no heart!"

"I can see you still retain your special brand of humour, my dear, even when you're upset. Now, Eddie! Fetch a couple more sacks of potatoes, check them over for Miss Baldock, and we'll say no more about it."

Miss Baldock could now afford to be superior. She looked down her little snub nose, snorted across her ample bosom, raised her head as high as an affronted spinster could, and said, sharply: "And how much is *this* little lot going to come to?"

"Gratis, my dear Miss Baldock. We don't want to lose our most charming customer, do we?" The lady purred like a well-fed cat.

"What is more," said Mr. Crawford, "we have a nice little surprise for you." With that, he ordered Timothy to get Garville's bag of oranges from the boot of the car. "There you are, my dear," he said, when Timothy returned.

"Oranges!" exclaimed the sweet-as-honey lady. "Not to be had for love nor money in these days of austerity. Just right for my marmalade-making. Well, I must be getting over to the restaurant now. We have to look after our customers, don't we, Mr. Crawford?" She was careful not to be too effusive, all the time thinking how cleverly she managed men. As a matter of fact, Mr. Crawford was thinking the same about her. Agnes considered it all a question of timing and emphasis. When you got to know a man's special weaknesses you could wrap him up in cotton-wool in no time. She took care to put on her 'happy martyr' look as she left the market.

Timothy was angry.

"Those oranges were for Mother," he fumed.

"She can have oranges some other time," muttered Mr. Crawford irritably. "How else do you think we could get rid of the woman? We can't have her spreading rumours about the place."

"Father," Timothy remonstrated, "you are always putting the blame on the customer. It's never your fault. It's always the government or people like Miss Baldock that cause the trouble. I've been telling you for weeks about a more efficient storage set-up."

"Who the dickens do you think you're talking to?"

They stood facing each other, while Ray and the porters stood over by the lorry, smoking and listening.

"I tell you, father, we are ten years behind the times. We're slowly stifling under the weight of our own inefficiency. We're being beaten in the race by people like Uncle John Garville. Look at his lettuce this morning — beautifully clean and packed in blue tissue — and then take a look at our scruffy-looking stuff. We've had it. Tradition or no bloody tradition."

"How dare you speak to me in this manner in front of the porters. I will not have it, do you hear? I don't think I need the opinion of a pianist to help me run my business. I've been farming since I was in the cradle. You and your mother have done pretty well out of it, so *you've* nothing to complain about."

Timothy longed to find the right words to convince his father of his folly.

"And another thing," Mr. Crawford went on. "Who was it who paid for all your damned veterinary books, your vacation courses, study trips abroad and all the twaddle that went with it, eh?" He stuck his finger angrily into his chest. "I did!"

"Well, you won't have to any more," said Timothy, in a voice loud enough to be heard across the far side of the market. In the midst of his anger, he remembered the mysterious sum of money deposited in a trust account at the bank for him when he was born. As far as Timothy knew, no-one had ever discovered the identity of the donor. This realisation gave him the ammunition he wanted.

"You forget I'm twenty-one now. I have a right to use the trust money now for whatever I choose to do with it. "

"Timothy! You know you are never to mention that money to me. It should be sent back from whence it came."

Timothy struggled to reason out his thoughts, to find some way of forewarning his father of eventual disaster if he did not change his ways. There was so much he wanted to say, but nothing came to him. All he could think of was the word which had been churning round in his

40

brain, rooting itself into the ground of his grievances:

"You're heading for a fall one of these days, father," he stammered, his eyes moist with emotion. "You're — oh! Father!" he said in desperation. "You're so bloody pig-headed!"

Mr. Crawford stood motionless, his lips pressed tightly into a thin pink line of contempt. Without giving any warning, he raised his hand and sent it smacking down on Timothy's ear. Timothy was stunned. His eyes suddenly filled with tears. All he could hear was Eddie's gentle voice in the distance, very far away over the plain of his despair:

"'Ere,'ere, guv'nor, steady on!'"

That was all. There was nothing more left except the long silence, his face burning, his ear throbbing with pain. He was aware that his father was starting up the car, which passed slowly by like a funeral procession, carrying away with it Timothy's hopes of a very different future than the one he was now facing. He was aware too of Ray and Curly furtively hiding behind the lorry, and he wondered if Ray realised the importance in the part he had played in the drama of the daffodils, and whether Curly had a spark of remorse over his abuse of Miss Baldock. As for the petty cash episode, Timothy was more confused than ever. In any case, these trivialities seemed now of little consequence.

6.   A Turn-up for the Books!

During the short time since Timothy had come to work with his father in the market, his friendship with John Garville had flourished, and he was happy in the knowledge that it was his mother's special wish that John should agree, when Timothy was born, to become his god-father. Garville, a market-gardener with a four-hundred acre farm near Finchingfield and a comfortable flat in Kensington, had no family of his own. He was the most amiable of men and took a great interest in Timothy's progress. He had a fine singing voice and made regular appearances in his local productions of Gilbert and Sullivan's operettas and, with the help of Jane Crawford, an accomplished pianist in her own right, had encouraged Timothy to study the piano. Author of a modest volume of poems about the countryside, John Garville had also encouraged his godson to take a practical interest in English literature and the arts generally. However it was not yet the moment in Timothy's life to devote himself to what his father referred to as 'trivial and worthless pursuits.' There was, it has to be said, hardly a day that Timothy did not steal across to the Garville stand with its glass 'box' in which sat the delightful Miss Violet Trimble, the book-keeper, who travelled up daily from Chelmsford, and always had a special welcome for the 'nice young man.' She always seemed to him to be like some exotic plant in a hot-house. She was completely unapproachable since the only contact the outside world ever had with her was a circular opening in the glass partition through which customers could pass their payments. These little pleasures, this morning of all mornings, held no attraction for Timothy, now beginning to realise the enormity of his fall from grace, as he fought back the tears and contemplated the emptiness and futility of an uncertain future.

"Come on, Mr. Tim," said Eddie. "Taint so bad as it seems. Come over the coffee-stall. It'll do you good."

Timothy let himself be guided through the piles of boxes, bags and crates — empties ready to be stacked on the lorry when Ray and Curly felt so inclined. Usually, Timothy helped them, but not today. He had finished with farming forever. He threaded his way through the staring porters. After the first sips of comforting coffee, Eddie said:

"You got a tough old man, Mr. Tim, and that's for sure."

"Well," said Tim, "we've certainly never seen eye to eye. I'm not sorry we've had it out at last. The trouble is, I'm too headstrong. I say what I think and to hell with the consequences."

"What are you going to do now, Mr. Tim? I mean, you've bin an' gawn an' done it, you 'ave! I coulda sloshed him one meself."

Timothy leaned against the counter and watched the coffee-seller in his grubby apron. It seemed to Timothy that the old man had been washing up cups since the beginning of time. As if from afar, Timothy heard Eddie's voice:

"I tell you what! How's about you an' me goin' over to see me ol' Ma up the 'ospital? Speck she could do wiv a bit o' company."

Tim was thinking it was no use hanging about the market. He realised that he needed time to measure his life up to this moment and think about what he would say to his father when he had to face him again.

"Let's go!" he said, grimly.

Beyond the particular memories of wilting daffodils, purloined petty cash, an affronted Miss Baldock, a belligerent Curly, a sulky Ray, and the fiasco over John Garville's oranges, Timothy had good reason to feel depressed.

It is occasionally at such moments as these, when we are at our lowest ebb, that miracles occur. Precisely at the point where Timothy began to lose his grasp on the last particle of hope did he discover a truth, and with that discovery, a solution which strengthened his resolve. It was a flash of insight, or perhaps courage, that comes to us in the depths of despondency, when our sensibilities are prone to the most subtle changes of spirit.

Whether it was the first impression of efficiency which permeated the hospital entrance-hall, or whether it was the methodical way in which the nurses and doctors moved about with such quiet deliberation and orderliness, Timothy did not know. In a split second, he experienced the vision of a possible path to follow. By the time Eddie came back from the ward Timothy was, at any rate, a changed person. He heard nothing of Eddie's account of his mother's senseless ravings, her swearing and wild gesticulating. All he cared about was that he had found himself a future.

"A doctor?" said Eddie, incredulously. "Well, good luck to you, that's all I can say. I wouldn't want to work in a hospital, not for twenty nicker a week, I wouldn't." He looked downcast for a moment. Timothy realised, through his excitement, that Eddie's mind was thinking along quite different lines, for he went off in search of the ward-sister. When he came back he had about him an air of dejection.

"Eddie! What news?"

"She don't look so clever, Mr. Tim. Breathing shocking, and pain in her ol' chest. Told me to bleeding well bugger off, she did. She wasn't half narked to see me. The Sister told me it was her old ticker, see. Then she started 'ollerin' and carryin' on something shockin' so I scarpered good and quick, what with her leading off at me and getting blue in the face and her eyes popping out like marbles."

"Don't worry, Eddie. She couldn't be in a better place. You certainly couldn't look after her at home."

"Well," said Eddie, "I shall have to be getting back to the market. Curly will need some help clearing up the stand." He stopped for moment, then said: "Did you ask your old man about the money?"

"Money?"

"You know, I asked you if — "

"Oh!" said Timothy. "I'm afraid I didn't, in the turmoil."

"Ah, well! I didn't mean no trouble. Thanks all the same."

Timothy, without thinking any further on the matter, took out his wallet and extracted a five pound note. Eddie took it gratefully without a word. As he was smiling at Timothy, down there in that dingy little street, the Sister in the ward above could have told him that in the short space of time which had elapsed between the moment Timothy held out the fiver and Eddie put out his hand to take it, Ma Carpenter was dead. Gone in a flash, without pain, without warning, but, uncharacteristically, in peace.

"Goodbye, Mr. Tim. We shall miss you on the stand."

"I shall miss you too, Eddie," Timothy found himself saying, but his thoughts were on the hoped-for future and not on the rapidly fading past. He accordingly felt a tinge of conscience when Eddie smiled and shook his hand, saying, with embarrassing simplicity:

"Tim, you're all right, you are!"

Both young men knew that with these words they had crossed the class divide. All former suspicions were dispelled. It was Tim and Eddie from now on.

EPISODE TWO

St. Valentine's Eve: Early afternoon

The Trouble with Millie

7. Venus Observed

Of all the houses that made up the grimy little Victorian cul-de-sac of Laburnum Villas, the most crowded was the Thompsons' at No 4. Next door, at No 6, was the Carpenter household. On the other side, at the corner adjoining the High Street, lived Grandpa Lawton and his formidable lodger, Miss Agnes Baldock. On the opposite side of the street and backing on to the Public Gardens was No 5, the home of Police-Sergeant Walter Paxton (retired) and his niece, Louise. Their house was tucked away in the corner between the high wall separating the street from the railway beyond and the charred shell of No 3, blown sky-high, residents and all, in the Blitz of 1940! There was now only Freddy Higgins left out of all that family. Destiny had insisted on his falling sick with a temperature after vaccination and having to be taken off to Guy's Hospital just when the German bomber was about to release a 'Molotov cocktail' on the Higgins home. The building had not been patched up because its owner, Councillor Purvis, was sitting pretty on his war-damage grant until he was ready to make a handsome deal for the whole close with a developer.

Laburnum Villas was a tightly-knit little community, the members of which had learned through the years to respect individual privacy by keeping gossip within the confines of the street. There was a kind of in-built loyalty, an integral part of the brickwork, that cemented this little community together. Inside may well be a seething pottage of emotional squabbles and reconciliations, illness and wellness, and a regular round-robin of domestic upsets, but there was relief for all in putting on an armour of hats, coats, overalls, raincoats, wellingtons, gloves and mufflers, and resentfully or gladly turning their backs on home-life and stepping forward into the eye of the world with a slam or a bang or a clatter or a squeaking or a whining or a scraping or a soft gliding to of the front door. Like Grandpa Lawton's chocolate 'double centres', life at Laburnum Villas had a fruity fondant of happiness around it with a bitter syrup of frustrated love inside, just enough to spoil the taste for life.

The most impressive of these little houses was Number One, with its bay windows and its twelve-foot extension built by old Purvis senior from the adjacent derelict shell that masqueraded in the old days as a newspaper shop and general stores, thus allowing a double-fronted style more in keeping with the grander residences of Napoleon Avenue. A prestigious television aerial in the shape of a large letter H was attached to the Councillor's chimney-stack and stood sentinel over the little cul-de-sac. Though as yet it had no television set to go with it, it was seen by the uninitiated to be an appropriate choice of status symbol, for Councillor Joseph Gabriel Purvis held an important position in the Borough. He lived quietly, or rather had managed to do so until this story began, cared for by his daughter, Gwendolen, a kind of seen-but-not-heard person, with no pretensions to femininity beyond her reputation for cooking and reliable house-keeping.

Joe Purvis was just fifteen when his mother and father had come to live at No 1. In those days, the house was exactly like the rest of the cul-de-sac — a small front room with a window looking directly on to the street, a small hall leading from the front-door to the foot of a narrow staircase, and beyond, the back room and the kitchen-cum-scullery, both of which looked out on a back-yard the size of a postage stamp. His first job was on a milk round, though Joe knew he was destined for better things. Through a friend of his father, he was introduced to a firm of chartered accountants who agreed to take him on at a rate of ten shillings a week. Most of the day was spent in running errands and making tea. By the time he was eighteen, he was doing small accountancy commissions. Soon he was enjoying trips out to audit the books of large shops and factories. As he was so young and energetic, he began to take a genuine interest in his clients and rarely came away from an assignment empty-handed since everyone liked to keep in his 'good books'! By the time he was twenty-one, he had passed his examinations and received a substantial emolument as a result. He then set out to find the right girl, found her, married her, settled down with her, had a child by her and thence proceeded on his road to fortune by entering public life.

Love was not for Joe a many-splendoured thing. Love was good cooking and a flair for general domesticity in a woman. Woman was made to keep the home fires burning, or something to that effect! His newspaper in the right place each morning and his slippers always where

47

they should be, by the fire, in the evening. These few simple pleasures were all he desired from a good woman. First father, then mother, then wife, had all departed this life in the hope of better things than looking after Joe Purvis. Now he was left to his own modest ambitions, whilst his daughter, Gwendolen, ministered to his every need. Nevertheless, he convinced himself that he had endured, like his biblical namesake, seven years of famine, and now he was looking forward to his seven years of plenty. It appeared, however, that dear Gwendolen was not as happy with her domestic chores as her father imagined, and had applied for a post as nanny with a family in Yorkshire.

In his public life, Councillor Joseph Gabriel Purvis had trodden the path of truth, stood up for the rights of the little man in his struggle against ever-increasing state-interference, fought fierce battles to defend civic privileges, heckled his way to fame, if not notoriety, on such vital post-war issues as the need for new hospitals, social centres, improved parks and play-grounds, and new housing projects. Realising that new developments must come in the end, he purchased for a song the whole of the little street known locally as 'Dead End' at the beginning of the war and renamed it Laburnum Villas since one of these poisonous trees eked out a pathetic existence at the blocked-up end of the street below the dark recesses of the railway viaduct. Everybody said he was mad to speculate at such a time, but fortune had proved faithful to the last.

Joe Purvis had never been one for sitting on his backside and grumbling about the state of the world. He got up and did something about it. On this particular afternoon, Councillor Purvis was to present the plans for his new housing scheme for the Borough of Rothersey to the Mayor, who gave his personal assurance that the occupants of Laburnum Villas would be among the first to be found alternative accommodation as soon as the first flats were ready in the new Rothersey Heights tower block. Councillor Purvis had his eye on a fine pent-house apartment overlooking the Houses of Parliament across the river. In his old-fashioned way he still regarded that august establishment as a gentleman of leisure might look upon his club. In former times he would have wished to be a member of this club, to be part of a vital political body of prestige and power. Yet he was not at all dissatisfied with his achievements in the so-far less sensational, less

48

scandalous environment of Rothersey in which he had resided for over forty years.

There was, however, one position Councillor Joseph Gabriel Purvis was in a mere hair's breadth of obtaining — that of Mayor of Rothersey. Accordingly, he looked round for a suitable cause on which he could peg his public prestige. In a chance conversation with Councillor 'Pixie' Calthrop, he learned that the Mayor was about to launch an investigation into the problem of juvenile crime in the borough. Mr. Purvis thereupon set about writing down details of his own campaign, which he promptly communicated to the offices of the Rothersey Gazette. His statement caused a stir in official circles when the local Member of Parliament raised the question in the House on more than one occasion, constraining the Mayor to find a place for Councillor Joe on the committee he had set up for the purpose. Whilst he was not enthusiastic to find himself sitting on a sub-committee on Corporal Punishment, a tricky subject for a possible future Mayor, he threw himself into the subject with his customary aplomb.

Councillor Purvis glowed with pride as he strode into the Council Chamber to deliver his maiden speech. The long mahogany table stretched out before him enticingly. The sensuous blue-leather blotters, the virginal writing-paper, gleaming white, lay luxuriously against the dark red mahogany, high-polished by Mrs. Thompson that very morning. There, seated in the high-backed blue leather chairs (emblazoned with the Borough coat-of-arms in gold) were social workers, fellow-councillors, representatives from the Home Office, churches of all persuasions, schools and colleges, and a number of local big-wigs, including His Grace the Bishop of Rothersey, nicknamed by the locals 'His *Dis*Grace' because of his namby-pamby views.

First to address the meeting was Bingo Wood, locally known as 'Bingo Woodn't', a *parvenu* to Council circles if ever there was one, who spent the majority of his time in blocking any advance to the Left or the Right of the political rat-race. Taking His *Dis*Grace's line of least resistance, he emphasised the need for tolerance in dealing with the young criminal:

"They are the victims of broken marriages, the offspring of indolent or drunken parents, the victims of neglect who hang about street corners, a prey to all and sundry. Surely they deserve our sympathy, not our contempt. Imagine a brother or a son of your own facing the prospect of the 'cat'. You would be savages if you condoned it. Were any of you caned at school? Do any of you remember the humiliation you suffered, the physical and mental torture? If we are to have any faith in our post-war society, shall we not put our trust in St. John and say with him that 'God is love'? Wrong cannot be cured with wrong. Not every punishment fits the crime. Ladies and gentlemen, to the introduction of corporal punishment in this Borough or anywhere else in our country I give a resounding 'No!' " [*applause from two vociferous cronies in the Public Gallery, who were to be seen with him on his periodic toadyings to the more popular part of the electorate at the "Bed of Roses"*].

Bingo Wood had played into Councillor Purvis's hands wonderfully. The lenient view was always attractive on the face of things, but give it a little thought and it starts to crack at the seams. It was, nevertheless, with some interest that Councillor Purvis noticed the burst of warm applause from the ecclesiastical and social welfare contingents and he decided to modify his speech accordingly. Since no reference had been made to any solution involving parent or school in the formation of character, the educational *bloc* remained unmoved. A short pause ensued in which the only noise to be heard was the scratching of pens on paper and the heavy breathing of His *Dis*Grace and the bumbling Vicar of St. Crispin's, who seemed more like the constellation of Gemini in their semester of sleep!

Councillor Joseph Gabriel Purvis rose to his feet.

"My Lord Bishop," he said loudly enough to waken the slumbering cleric, "ladies [*with a slight bow and a genial smile*] and gentlemen [*stressing the 'gentle'*], we are gathered together in this place [*attention of the clergy immediately caught*] to give thanks for our good sense, our religious honesty and our common belief in ultimate goodness, qualities given to us by three vital influences on the lives of every right-thinking individual — I refer to the home, the school and the church. Are we not, most of us, parents? [*the Bishop looked down for a moment, appearing to count the buttons on his frock- coat*] Are we not, my Lord Bishop [*stopped counting*], are we not so much more than parents? Are we not human beings with hearts and minds of our own? [*going down to a whisper*] Have we not the freedom to move and speak and think as we like without restricting the liberty of our fellow-creatures? Are we not therefore sensible to the feelings of those whose misfortune it is to suffer pain and anguish through the malicious actions of a selfish and wayward youth? I tell you, my friends, we must not allow ourselves to be deceived, like Mr. Wood here, by a false emotionalism. This world of ours can be an ugly place at times, full of ugly experiences, a place of falsity and intrigue and deception, a world in which the simple joys and pleasures of our childhood no longer play a part. Our children today are, plainly and simply, bored. They have lost their inquisitiveness, their sense of fun, which existed just as much, if not more, in days when we were taught to respect our parents and teachers. Today, ladies and gentlemen, our children do as they like. Our children no longer know right from wrong. And whose fault is that, I ask you? [*guilt in the faces of all present*] Whose fault is that? It is yours and mine, ladies and gentlemen [*indignant looks of 'Well, really!'*] We, the parents, the teachers, the politicians, are what is wrong with our society. We have got it all wrong, ladies and gentlemen. We have let our children down and they are punishing us for it with delinquency and vandalism."

Councillor Purvis strayed from his chair at this stage of his address, much to the surprise of the Committee, for it seemed a breach of tradition. The movement was deliberate. He began stalking up and down behind the chairs, making everyone feel uncomfortable and tingle at the nape of the neck as he passed by in his squeaky shoes. After electrifying his audience with his hypnotic footwear, he appeared almost from nowhere at the far end of the long table. Raising his hand, he pointed at the assembled company with a circular wave of the arm and shouted dramatically at the uncomprehending ceiling: "Has not our youth rejected the Sermon on the Mount? [*confused looks all round*] No, my friends! [*relief all round*] How can they reject something they have never known? [*mutterings of assent*] It is useless to talk of God to a delinquent. Look, my friends, we have to begin with fundamentals. We have to prove to this young offender that committing a criminal offence is synonymous with suffering. For this reason, I am in favour of the availability of corporal punishment as a deterrent, even if it is never, or at least rarely, put into practice. The man in the street will never be safe without it, I can assure you. Our womenfolk will never go with confidence through our streets. We only have to observe the billboards outside our local cinemas to see the shocking display of sex and violence that is forced upon us in the name of entertainment. We have only to think, my Lord Bishop, of the lewdness and crudeness of a certain novel by one of our greatest authors, once banned from our bookshelves, soon to be sold freely in our shops for anyone, of whatever age, to buy. We must not stain the primal innocence of our children. Is there not, I put it to you, a widespread delight in the literature of filth and wickedness in the magazines now on sale in our local newsagents? General access to this 'literature', if we may call it that, will have terrible consequences. It would be the ruination of our youth, ladies and gentlemen. Let that not happen in our Borough, nor indeed anywhere in our dear country [*brazenly appropriating Calthrop's patriotic phrase for his own*]. We must fight for the social order. Our youth need a new vision, new opportunities for improvement. Our new skating rink, our new bowling alleys, are a step in the right direction. I am proud to be associated with their inception. [*polite applause*] I ask you, my Lord Bishop, representatives of government, education and social services, to look to the family for your answers, and to the restoration of the basic principles of the 'three R's': respect, responsibility, and resolve. Without a sound family life and sound education we will assuredly fail our young people. This is the dilemma of our time." The speech finished amid applause and bravo's from all sides except the Bingo Wood *côterie*.

"Well done, Purvis," said the Chairman. "Damned good speech, eh? We can all go home and brood on it, old boy!"

Councillor Purvis had the satisfying feeling of having arrived under his own steam without anyone else's help. The Bishop came tripping across the room on tiptoe as if he were walking on hot coals.

"Masterly, Purvis. You did well to mention the willingness of the Church to help. It will look good in the press report."

Mr Whatever-his-name-was from the Home Office came and went out of the Chamber like an autumn leaf blown to and fro by a capricious breeze. He had not opened his mouth the whole time. In any case, Councillor Purvis was far too saturated with success to notice. As he was leaving the Town Hall, he caught sight of a familiar face in the entrance lobby.

"Well! Hello, Millie! Come to pick your mother up?"

"Oh! Mr. Purvis!" she giggled. He purred generously, glad to see Millie at this particular moment of his triumph. She gave an additional glow to his success, making him feel almost complacent. They walked out into the rain together.

"You sure Mum isn't there, Mr. Purvis?"

"Wait here, my dear, while I find out." He handed her his umbrella and skipped like a young goat up the greasy steps and disappeared through the polished oak doors, emerging seconds later with the news that Mrs. Thompson had left, at least according to the untrustworthy porter, whose policy was to plead ignorance about everything. One of those split-second decisions brought the Councillor charging down the steps, leaving all the last forty years behind him.

"Ooh! You *are* out of breath, Mr. Purvis. Come under the umbrella or you'll catch your death, you will." She held out the umbrella.

"You take it and we'll link arms." The Councillor was glad to oblige! "Ah! Millie! An old man like me!" he chuckled, flirting a little.

"Oh! Don't you give it a thought, Mr. Purvis. You and me knows one anuvver perfick! You can 'old yer 'ead up all right wiv me, you can. Anyways, it's a bit of a lark goin' 'ome arm-in-arm wiv a nob on the Council." Mr. Purvis laughed louder and longer than he had done for many a moon. Now he was deliriously happy, walking along in the rain, with pretty Millie Thompson on his arm.

Although she was almost eighteen, Millie looked more than twenty in her make-up. Her breasts were ample and her nipples stood out through her lift-me-up bra and jumper like two little round bell-pushes. Her hips were firmly rounded, revealed to advantage by her tight-fitting skirt. She had a fine pair of legs in her new nylon stockings. Joe was transported, quite oblivious of the little gathering on the Town Hall steps.

"Bless my soul!" exclaimed the Chairman as he descended the

steps in company with Mr. Whatever-his-name-was of the Home Office and the Bishop. "Well, I never!" said Mr. W.— that statement being the only one he had uttered the whole afternoon.

"Ye gods and little fishes!" added His *Dis*Grace, incredulously.

All three had stopped to stare in the wake of the 'Flog 'em and Birch 'em' supporter as he sauntered down the street arm-in-arm with a little blonde with swinging hips, in a slinky plastic mackintosh, transparent enough to show the Bishop more than he was able to take in at any one time, untrained as he was in such prurient displays of femininity!

On the bus, Millie stood close to Councillor Purvis. He found the contact between them not unpleasant. True, he was ill-at-ease. His heart was beating faster than usual. At the next stop, three more passengers were crammed onto the lower deck, so Millie had to stand with her bottom, rounded like a well-shaped pumpkin, pressing into the Councillor. Neither he nor Millie could talk. They were just wedged against each other. Not feeling in control of the biological department, through lack of practice in that sort of thing, he prayed for divine deliverance, which came with the not entirely welcome appearance of the bus-stop at Laburnum Villas.

"I feel like a celebration," said Mr. Purvis. "How about a little something to warm you up, Millie."

"Ooh! You are a one, Mr. Purvis. It'll have to be a quickie, 'cos Mum'll be wanting help with the tea."

Joe Purvis quickly unlocked his front-door, thankful that the street lamps hadn't come on yet. "Gwen'll be in any minute, anyway," he said with a mixture of relief and regret. Immediately he had spoken he knew that Millie understood his motive.

Now the dim gas-lamps came on suddenly, without any warning, flooding them both momentarily in a golden glow. A slight sense of foreboding came over him, making him shiver in the cold evening air. "Come on in, dear," he said nervously, "out of the rain." The door closed just as Curly turned into the Villas, with a barrow-load of potatoes for Agnes Baldock.

8. The Lollipop Kid

Mrs. Thompson's day started at six o'clock in the morning. Before Alf came down for his breakfast at seven, Flo always made a point of dusting the photographs on the piano in the front room. Then, she had three pairs of shoes to clean, usually some washing to peg out on the line in the backyard, and probably some last-minute ironing for Millie. Had Mrs. Thompson been a born administrator, most or even all of these jobs would have been appropriately delegated. As it was, she muddled through the work with the energy of a steam-roller, grumbling all the time, of course, because it was her nature to grumble, even when there was nothing to grumble about! Her physical exertions were counterbalanced by her mental lassitude, which produced in her feelings of frustration and general discontent, a sense of being unfulfilled, being meant for better things in life than the slavery of motherhood, and, since Alf had no respect from the children, of fatherhood, too.

Whilst Alf ate his tea in silence, she usually pottered about the yard, always in a very business-like manner, for even if she had nothing to do, it had to be done well. It was largely a nervous reaction. She couldn't bear the sight of Alf sitting glumly over his kippers, never uttering as much as a quick 'good-morning', his head throbbing like a turbine after his debaucheries of the night before. She just had to keep out of the way until he picked up his sandwiches and crawled off to the tannery.

No sooner would she hear the front-door close than she was back in the house shouting up the stairs to Millie and Ron because they were late and their breakfasts were in the oven and would be burnt to a cinder if they didn't hurry up.

Sometimes Ron was still in bed, forcing his mother to climb the stairs and literally drag the bed-clothes off him before he would stir himself into his usual sluggish morning moodiness. Getting up in the morning was just as demoralising for Ron as emerging from the Roxy after two or three hours of cinematic day-dreaming. In fact, in these early days of puberty, he found it more pleasurable to stay in bed than face the family quarrelling over the porridge and cornflakes.

"Living in our house is purgatory, I can tell you," he would complain to his friend and once-upon-a-time neighbour, Freddy Higgins.

"Purgatory! That's what it is! You only have to open your mouth and you get a clip over the ear. Stands to reason, a bloke wants to be on his own sometimes." Ron wished he could discover some secret paradise, some exotic place full of sunshine and flowers and wild animals and bright-coloured birds, a kingdom of his own, but it would have to be, for convenience, somewhere between Rothersey and Tooting Bec. In the mean time, he had to make do with his two little oases of contentment — Grandpa Lawton's and the Roxy Picture House.

As far as diet went, Mabel was a perfect little *gourmet*. Her sweet tooth encouraged her to refuse meat, vegetables and dairy products, yet allowed her to eat all manner of tarts, cakes, humbugs, toffees and lollipops. Of all the puddings Mrs. Thompson chose to make for her unruly family, tapioca pudding was one that little Mabel could not stomach. Tapioca pudding was revolting! Ever since she had had the measles and was sick all over the sheets, she had realised that she and tapioca pudding just did not mix. As soon as it came onto the table, goo-ey and rubbery, she knew exactly how to be sick all over the table-cloth. Her regular requirement was that, with the threat of refusing to eat anything at all, her mother should chop everything up on the plate just as she did for Smutty, the family mongrel. "Mabel want doggie's din-din," she would cry, referring to herself as usual in the third person. 'Well, you've got doggy's din-din, so shut up and get on with it," Mrs Thompson would reply. Whereupon, sweet little Mabel would push it all over the side of the table, much to Smutty's delight.

On the way to the Town Hall, where Mrs. Thompson was a cleaner, it was customary to stop off at Ma Blackwood's Lollipop Shop. It would have taken a month of Sundays to understand Mabel's 'colour of the day', which was as changeable and unpredictable as the English weather. When she pointed to a purple lollipop, she was handed a yellow one, which had the effect of sending her into a series of wild gesticulations until she was handed a green one because she had asked for a green one yesterday. The only way she could make these adults understand was to stamp her feet and bawl as loud as she could into Ma Blackwood's pimply face.

"Mabel wants a green one?"

"Na-ah!!"

"Mabel wants a purple one?"

"Naa-aah!!"

"A nice red one with lovely green stripes?"

The crying would stop as suddenly as it had started and there was satisfaction all round as Mrs. Thompson handed over the tuppence-halfpenny.

Mrs. Thompson was wistfully thinking that life was not getting any easier with prices going up and up and things at home going down and down. When Millie was Mabel's age, lollipops were a halfpenny each. That was in the war-time, with sweet coupons. Now everything was changed. No more rationing, no more scrimping and hoarding, no more waiting in queues at all hours to be told there was only horse-meat left at the butcher's, and she couldn't abide whale-steaks. There was no more flogging the family's clothes coupons in exchange for a few extras on the black market. But, were things any better?

Work and worry seemed to grow on Flo Thompson like warts, which, however much she tried to paint them with the solvent of day-dreams, did not seem to grow any smaller. Lines were beginning to show in her face — little thin grey wires pressed into the flesh around the mouth and eyes. Streaks of grey hair were beginning to force their way out of the scalp and crawl over her ears in serpentine pursuit of her anxious fingers as she brushed them away, in a gesture of fatigue rather than vanity.

Flo couldn't remember when things really began to go wrong — perhaps when, for no reason at all as far as she could see, Alf started to take to drink. One day she would find out the truth perhaps, but for the moment she looked down at little Mabel, sweet as innocence can be, and smiled at her dinky little face beaming at her from behind her big pink and green lollipop. Flo had a strong urge to pick her up and hug her and be inclined to accept things as they were, but she couldn't, however much she tried. At times, she wished Mabel had never been born.

Flo's feelings about Mabel were curious and complex, full of inexplicable uncertainties which as yet she could not fathom. Since Mabel was born, things had not been what they used to be. Life had suddenly become unendurable drudgery from morning to night, all

57

getting and spending, scraping and slaving. As Flo looked down into Mabel's angelic little face, she was surprised at the harshness of her voice:

"Oh! You and your lollipops! Come on, do hurry up! We've wasted enough time here as it is. I shall be late for work." She caught Mabel by the arm and dragged her out of the shop behind her.

On this particular morning, Flo caught sight of her reflection in the glass-fronted cabinet where Ma Blackwood kept her rows of sweet-jars and thought she did not look so bad after all. She still had some of the prettiness of her youth; she still retained a little of the girlishness of her courting days, though marriage and war, which sometimes she thought of as one and the same, had made a difference.

The day-nursery was a few yards down Lupin Lane, just by the gymnasium and public baths. As Mrs. Thompson passed Marley's General Stores, she made a mental note to get away from work well on time if she was to get any sausages for tea. Pushing Mabel through the gate, she 'skedaddled', as she called it. No time for messing about with kisses and cuddles at that time of day, or any time, come to that! Work had to be done, and there was no time for sentiment when there was plenty of polishing to be done at the Town Hall.

No-one knew nor cared what Mabel got up to at the nursery. It was, for Mrs. Thompson, a case of 'out of sight, out of mind'. As for the rest of the family, they were far too busy worrying about their own little problems to think about what their nearest, though not, apparently, their dearest, were doing. Whatever it was that Mabel got up to, it appeared to be far more interesting and delightful than people might have imagined. Accordingly, when her mother called for her at the end of the afternoon, Mabel indulged in what her mother called 'showing off' by stamping her little feet and screaming at the top of her shrill little voice, all to no avail, since Mrs. Thompson was always in a hurry to do the shopping for tea. Soon, Ron would be home willingly from school, Alf unwillingly from the tannery (via *The Bed of Roses*), and Millie from the button-factory.

After Mrs Thompson finished her polishing she collected Mabel from the nursery and called in at Marley's General Stores. While Mrs. Thompson moved nervously from one queue to another, Mabel was standing in the middle of the shop, contemplating the curious antics of her elders in her dispassionate, inquisitive way. As she was licking away at her lollipop with her strawberry tongue, she began staring at a plump woman in a pillar-box red mackintosh. The woman was searching for some small change in a small purse. Eventually, she discovered the vital penny and stepped on to a large weighing-machine by the entrance-door. Mabel stepped on to the machine, too. This is really fun, she thought. The penny, placed now in the slot, caused the indicator to swing swiftly up to 13 stone 10 lbs. With a look of horror, the 'scarlet' woman descended in all her glory, leaving Mabel to contemplate the indicator resting now at 5 stone 2 lbs. The woman returned to the bacon counter:

"Agnes!" she exclaimed. "My slimming tablets don't seem to be working at all. Dr. Glendale said I could eat almost anything as long as I halved the quantity on my plate."

"Dorothy!" said her also-fat friend, "You are making yourself ridiculous with this diet-business. You are the plump type and that's the end of it. Take me, for instance! I work in a restaurant, I live with food all day, and I eat hardly anything. The smell of food is enough to make me put on weight, and I'm none the worse for it."

"I must go and see Dr. Glendale again, or the boys will be making fun of me, more than they do already!"

"If you worry about what the boys think as much as that, Dorothy, then you shouldn't be a teacher, should you? Give it up! Do something else. Surely you must have discovered the truth about the children round here by now. They have no home life. Their parents don't care about them and let them run wild, like animals in the jungle. Take that Ron Thompson, for example. No proper upbringing, that's the trouble! If you take my advice, you'll assert yourself more and let them know who's boss. If we're built to be monuments then let us be monuments wholeheartedly!"

Mabel stared at the two stalwart ladies and decided that she *did* like the plump lady in the bright red raincoat. She also decided that the other of the two ladies, the one in the hat, would not be a welcome guest in her exclusive social circle.

Mrs. Thompson's voice cut through the hum of activity in the shop:

"Mabel! Mabel! Where are you! Mabel! MABEL!?!"

Miss Agnes Baldock, the unflinching manageress of the Roxy Picture House Restaurant, winced.

"Come, Dorothy! Let us escape from this appalling racket."

"Oh, my!" said Mrs. Thompson. "Miss Baldock! And you, too, Miss Goodenough, in your lovely red raincoat, an' all! Goo'night!"

"I do wish these people would not say goodnight at five o'clock in the afternoon. It is so common!" said Miss Baldock.

"Bitch!" said Mrs. Thompson, under her breath. "Thinks she's the Queen o' Laburnum Villas, the way she goes on. One of these days, she'll come a cropper, she will, and it won't be a small crater she'll make where *she* falls. Oh, there you are Mabel, you little wretch! Where have you been? [smack!] Where [smack!] have [smack!] you been? I told [shake] you [shake-shake] not to go away, didn't I?" [SMACK-SMACK!!]

Mabel began to cry. She began to cry so much that all the red and green syrup dribbled out of the corners of her mouth, ran down over her chin in little rivulets, meandering in and out of her little dimples and dripping on to her pale blue woolly scarf in nasty black spots that Ron could have learnt a lot about colour from if he had been there and not sitting with his chocolate nut crunch in a back seat at the Roxy Picture House at the time. To Mabel, now, everything began to taste horribly salt. The backs of her legs were red with being smacked. The tears rolled down her cheeks and blurred everything so much that she couldn't see the nice lady in the red rain-coat any more.

From six-o'clock on, when Mrs Thompson arrived home with Mabel, No. 4 Laburnum Villas was like a floundering ship with Mrs. Thompson as galley-slave, manacled by domestic chores until the following morning when she was released by a mutinous crew to walk the plank. Millie was next in, followed closely by Ron, provided he had left Grandpa Lawton's at his usual time, and last would come Alf, smelling of a mixture of chemicals and leather, topped up with a few pints of bitter on the way home. As today was Friday, however, it was very likely that the local branch of the 'Peace and Plenty' Movement would claim him for its own with the usual alcoholic consequences.

As life dragged to a standstill in retirement, with Alf, her husband, comatose at the tannery, Millie, groaning and sighing at her bench at the button factory, Ron, reluctant, sloping off to school, Flo Thompson was discovering that the returns for her labour were rapidly diminishing as the years raced by. The joys, the pleasures, the hopes and the loves usually associated with a happy family life had slipped surreptitiously away like pale spirits in purgatory.

It is in the nature of things that such a state of affairs could not go on indefinitely. After darkness should come the light, and with the light, new joys, fresh hopes, and unbounding love. For the moment, the Thompson family were steadily moving towards the darkness.

9. Frustration C.O.D.

Four o'clock. Curly Donoghue had messed about all day until it was almost too late to deliver Miss Baldock's sacks of potatoes, one to the restaurant of the Roxy Picture House and one to Laburnum Villas. The daylight was fast disappearing as he wheeled his barrow into the Villas, just in time to catch an eyeful of Millie Thompson's curvaceous bottom disappearing into the Councillor's comfy parlour. He stored the image in his memory for future use. So this was what Eddie Carpenter was on about! Well, Eddie wasn't the only one out to pluck a bird at the Purvis Bowl tomorrow.

Curly pulled up outside No 2, putting up his grubby thumb to press the bell under the small brass plate bearing the name: MISS AGNES BALDOCK [*followed by a peremptory: 'Ring **ONCE** only '*]. He pressed again, thumb hard on the bell, twice, three times, gyrating his hand as if he were trying to rub a hole in the wall. All the time he was thinking about the shapely form of Millie Thompson and all the time he was pressing the bell with the frustration of it all.

"**BALDOCK!**" he shouted.

Silly cow! He'd give 'er a dance one of these days. He'd make her jump. He'd see to that. The door opened slightly.

"Baldock?" he asked. He saw a pair of eyes looking through the crack..

"She aint in, son. Not for another 'alf-hour to my way o' reckoning." The old man screwed up his eyes and peered into the darkness. When he looked at Curly, he didn't like what he saw.

"Well, accordin' to my way o' reckernin', I'll leave the stuff 'ere, then. You her father?"

"Taint likely! She's my lodger."

Silly old geezer! Fancy hanging around with an old bag like Aggie Baldock!

"Where d'yer want 'em put?"

"Want what put?"

"The bloody spuds, mate!"

"You sure they're for her?"

"Well, they're not for bloody Gipsy Rose Lee, now, are they?"

"Funny!" exclaimed the old man.

"None o' your blinkin' lip, see?" said Curly.

"Money of what?"

"Bloody ol' fool! Cut the cackle."

"What tackle?"

"What the 'ell are you talking about?"

"Sorry! My hearing's a bit dicky today. You better put them out the back. She'll be in in half-an-hour according to...."

".......my way o' reckonin'," Curly chorused with a sneer. He hoisted the sack onto his shoulder and pushed past the old man, who continued to chatter away, all the time dribbling down the front of his 'guernsey'.

On the way out, Curly helped himself to a handful of *Quality Street* from a tin on the dresser. "That'll be 'alf a dollar, mate," said Curly.

"Oh, no bother at all."

"Half a dollar, I said," Curly shouted.

"What for?"

"Delivery charge, o' course! For cryin' out loud!"

Grandpa Lawton hobbled back into his room. There was a rattling of coins in a vase on the mantelshelf, during which time Curly inspected the letters on the hall-stand. He could feel no money in the envelopes. In the glove-drawer, he happened to find two five pound notes which he quickly pocketed. He'd certainly need some dosh if he was going to impress that Millie Thompson. The old man returned, holding out a half-crown in his long, bony, vein-riddled hand.

"You're welcome, son."

"I thought you said you was deaf. You're dribblin', " said Curly. Silly old bastard! Curly would like to slosh him one. Smash his blinking face in.

"You're dribblin', you stupid ol' twit! Dribblin'! "

"Yes," said Grandpa, "very middling!"

Mr. Lawton's voice trailed off and he seemed to go into a trance. Curly turned in a temper, kicked the wheel of his barrow and swore. He stood on the front door-step, staring into the rain as it fell through the circle of light which hung like a halo round the old gas-lamp on the pavement.

Curly's anger was getting well out of control as he pushed his barrow out into the High Street, in the direction of the market. Twilight had come on him without his noticing and he was risking it without lights. Suddenly, a double-decker bus came swerving round the corner from the bridge and nearly ran him off the road. Hooters and horns howled like a pack of wolves, drawing from him a torrent of obscenities, and him nigh on falling apart with frustration and anger.

10. Bitter Sweet!

At fourteen years of age, Ron Thompson was an expert at inventing excuses for his form mistress. 'Please Miss, Mum's had one of her turns.' 'Please Miss, me Dad come home drunk, he did' (*'came* home, Ronald!*') and I had to put 'im to bed.' 'Please Miss, Mabel's got the measles!' Some of his excuses he had to use sparingly. He didn't want to have to fall back on worn out clichés too often, like the one about helping a poor old lady across the street into Marley's General

Stores, all because Grandpa Lawton wasn't on duty and 'there wasn't nobody to stop the traffic.' (*"was no one*, Ronald!"). This act of chivalry took no more than a few minutes of his time, yet it apparently caused him to miss the school bus, and well, really, it wasn't worth going to school at all, was it?

Only twice in each week did Ron really want to be at school — Tuesday afternoons and Friday mornings — times when he could indulge in his favourite pastime of painting. At first, it was merely a case of daubing the paint over the paper, making something pure and white and clean into something messy and defiled. He looked upon the lesson as one glorious hour of destruction when he could let loose his muddled bodily frustrations in splashes of bright colour, splurging across the page. It was like tipping bottles of coloured inks over at random and watching something monstrous rise out of the blackness of merging greens and blues and reds.

Now, however, things were different. Ron had come to realise there was more to painting than that. There was, for example, the question of making reality out of nothing, of translating the countless fancies of his mind into visible patterns of colour, which, as they took shape, expressed his innermost longings. Unknown to himself, his vibrant splashes of red on aquamarine, of violet on yellow ochre, his sailing ships, his tropical islands, his monstrous sea-serpents, his gangling trees, were the expression of his real self, not at all the Ron Thompson other people supposed him to be.

Of all the tenants of Laburnum Villas, Grandpa Lawton was the only one who knew the real Ron Thompson, and that is why he would never say a word to anybody about the trouble over Ron's 'slight misdemeanour', destined to upset quite a number of the residents of this tiny London enclave. He would simply choose to absolve his young friend's behaviour in silence.

Between the rich and rewarding oases of his art lessons, Ron wandered aimlessly through hours of boredom and frustration. Monday was a grey waste over which he roamed through the confusing mysteries of the English language and grammar. There substantial differences between 'School English' and the Thompson lingo Ron spoke at home. Tuesday mornings brought the untold hazards of mathematics and history, accompanied by pain inflicted by one master who didn't know his own strength, and clearly believed in the Victorian method of bringing children up 'by hand'! Wednesday was a waste land, too — gymnastics with a muscular games mistress who still hadn't been replaced since the war, when the master had been conscripted into the army and later killed at Anzio. Thursday mornings were pure pleasure — nature study followed by a whole hour of painting.

On Friday afternoons, instead of sol-fa practice with the short-sighted Miss Grummidge, followed by 'English Folk-song' with a class of boys who were nothing but a gang on honkers and squawkers, he had the irrepressible urge to sample the pleasures of the Roxy Picture House. On the way, he would call in at Ma Blackwood's Lollipop Shop and arm himself with half-a-pound of chocolate nut crunch and a couple of ounces of lemon sherbets in case the chocolate made him feel thirsty. Once he was settled in to the sheltering darkness of the Roxy auditorium he felt safe. He would choose a seat in the back row in the hope of not being recognised, ready to thrill to the exploits of Tarzan of the Apes.

Sometimes Ron would sit through the whole programme again. Anything to avoid the daily dread of going home, anything to drag out his imaginary world of jungles and swamps, anything to help him escape into his world of mystery and imagination. In reality, there was no avoiding it for Ron. After such exotic images, he found it even more difficult to face life at Laburnum Villas.

Today, however, was Friday, so, as soon as he had handed over most of his codfish lunch to the school cat, he made his way, out of sight of the teachers, to the Roxy Picture House. Strolling along the pavements busy with Friday shoppers, he indulged in his customary day-dreaming. Ron......

......*swung deftly from tree to tree through the great teak forest. A hundred feet below, a lion roared a greeting. A jackal crouched in the angle of a branch. A python slithered slowly down over an unsuspecting gazelle......The young Tarzan swung down and over and up and across and down again, gripping the rope-like liana with perfect judgement of distance. High up in the lush foliage, parakeets with bright green and yellow plumage flew squawking from perch to perch, Humming- birds fluttered momentarily in a charm. The young Tarzan swung once more out over the crocodile-infested swamp and came to rest in front of.......*

........the billboard on the pavement outside the Roxy Picture House! Ron gazed at it with some surprise, coming slowly out of his dream-world into the bustle and noise of Rothersey High Street.

Grand New Double Bill

COLOSSAL   HORRIFIC

Vampire in Soho

All Star Cast

&

A Kiss In Time
The X-iest Show in Town

He stood in a daze, staring at the billboard, hardly able to cope with the idea of kisses and vampires. He thought of trying the Palaseum. Decisions had to be made if he was not to be recognised by someone from school. The commissionaire was watching him suspiciously, so he thrust his hand in his pocket and slapped his shilling piece down at the pay-box.

"'Ere! You!" shouted the commissionaire with a threatening tone. "Where d'you fink you're goin'?"

"You talking to me?"

"Who d'you fink I'm talkin' to, the Prime Minister? You being a clever sort of twit, p'raps you know what an "X" cerstifkit is, eh?"

"Certificate. You pronounce it 'certificate'."

"Watch it! Don't you tell me about the hinglish langwidge, my son."

"I aint under age, see," Ron said. "I'm sixteen, I am."

"You can tell that to the marines. Sixteen?"

"Look, d'you want my money or don't you?"

"You can go in on one condition. Keep your ugly mug out of

sight of Police-Sergeant Paxton, else I'll knock your bloody little block off, see? If he nabs you, I'll be for it, and no mistake."

Once inside, Ron settled into a corner seat in the back-row, close to the toilets, which he could escape to if any staff from the school should come in and surprise him. In the darkness of the auditorium, he couldn't see a thing for about five minutes.

While all this had been going on, Ron had missed the beginning of *A Kiss in Time*. The hero, a sort of Mr. Universe, bore some slight resemblance to Curly Donoghue — all muscle and brawn and golden locks. The girl was innocent 'sweet sixteen' and butter wouldn't melt in her mouth. With a little stretch of the imagination, she could have been Millie. When the 'kiss in time' finally arrived, it was too late for Ron to bother about, frankly. Ron was so bored that he wanted to blow a raspberry, and would have, had he not had his mouth full of nuts and chocolate and sticky toffee, churning round like so much putty. He imagined that kissing a girl must be rather like that — thick, sugary putty, and he wasn't at all sure he would like it. Nothing would have persuaded him at this time, in this or some similar place, that one day something would happen to make him change his mind.

Suddenly, everybody in the cinema was clapping with the sheer pleasure of seeing Mr. Universe united with little Miss Right, and everyone in the drab little audience would live happily ever after.

When the interval lights went up, Ron caught sight of old Police-Sergeant Paxton and his niece, Louise, sitting about ten rows down, so to be on the safe side he slipped stealthily into the toilets and locked himself in.. The lights had dimmed by the time Ron returned to his seat. He was greeted with the threatening music of *Vampire in Soho*. Soho, he knew, was somewhere 'up West', a place of mystery, inhabited by thugs and gangsters, blackmailers and their molls. Soho was also a place he was not allowed to stray into on his own. Thrusting a fruit sherbet into his mouth, he sucked his way all through the first two murders. When the vampire leaned over the girl asleep in her bed, Ron came out in goose-pimples. Fortunately, he thought, vampires only go for girls! When the monster sank its fangs into the girl's neck, Ron bit into his sherbet, which fizzed up, filling his mouth with acid frothiness. The girl was so scared she couldn't scream. She lay there without a word to say for herself — as dumb as Louise Paxton, she was. Then Ron wondered if Louise was thinking the same thing — she wouldn't be able to call out either, if anything happened to her. After the sixth murder (and the last fruit sherbet), the vampire turned out to be a cranky doctor who was conducting experiments on a frozen corpse he had brought back from Venus!

It was half-past five when Ron arrived home at Laburnum Villas. He decided to call in on Grandpa Lawton before tea-time. Grandpa's attraction was a box of Terry's 'Double Centre' chocolates and a large tin of Mackintosh's *Quality Street* assortment on the dresser in the kitchen, just for Ron. Sweets, however, were only part of the pleasure Ron derived from his daily visits. Grandpa had such a lot to talk about, the only real friend Ron ever had that he never tired of listening to.

"We're pals for life, eh, Ron?" said Grandpa one day after one of his long adventure stories.

As he reached up for the knocker, Ron had the acid taste of a regurgitated pâté of nuts, chocolate, fruit syrup and toffee that now lay like a lead weight in the pit of his stomach. His appetite for Mackintosh's delectables was decidedly absent from his mind, not to mention his mother's cooked tea, and the smack on the backside he would get from his mother for being late. All the same, he knocked on Grandpa's door and waited. When no answer came, he reluctantly made his way home.

11. The Millie Mabel Saw

The front-door slammed. Mrs. Thompson called out through clouds of blue smoke from spitting sausages:

"That you, Millie? You're late tonight, aren't you? Where've you been?"

"Round Mr. Purvis's." There was a pause while Millie hung up her coat and Mrs. Thompson took the lid off the potatoes, which were about to boil over into the frying pan.

"Mr. Purvis's? Whatever for?"

"Asked me in for a drink."

"A drink?" said Mrs. Thompson, indulging in her usual patter, repeating what everyone said to her and then posing yet another searching question: "What kind of drink?"

"Oh! Mum! Orangeade, of course."

"Orangeade? There's no 'of course' about it, my girl. Come here and let me smell your breath."

"Oh, do shut up, Mum!"

"Seems funny to me — an older man like him, in his position, asking a young girl of nigh on eighteen into his house at this time of the day, *and* unaccompanied! Was Gwen there?"

A long silence followed. Millie could almost hear her mother thinking it all out.

"Oh dear!" muttered Mrs. Thompson, scraping up the fat that had spilt on the lino when the frying-pan had gone all cock-eyed between the prongs of the gas-burner.

"Why did he ask you in?"

Millie began to sneak upstairs.

"Is there anything else you want to know?" she said irritably. "Perhaps you'd like a written statement! He wanted to give me a couple o' tickets for the Purvis Bowl do tomorrow night."

"No need to get uppity, now. A simple question requires a simple answer."

"He was celebrating," Millie said, shrugging her shoulders.

"Celebrating? Celebrating what, for goodness' sake?"

"Oh! Some speech he made at the Town Hall today. Did you know he's lived in the Borough the longest of all the councillors? Forty-five years."

"Celebrating? What with?" Mrs. Thompson asked, indifferent to the Councillor's achievements.

"Oh, Mum! I told you," said Millie, raising her voice to fit her temper. "You and your eternal questions. It's like bein' on a blinkin' quiz-programme, livin' in this house."

"There's no need to get in a huff, Millie. I was just asking, that's all."

Millie ran up the stairs in a fury and shut herself in her room.

She breathed out through her mouth into her cupped hands and then in quickly through her nose. The alcohol was making her head swim. That silly fool, Gwen! If only she hadn't mixed up the glasses!

In the bathroom, she emptied the remains of a bottle of bright red mouth-wash and swilled it round and round, gargling as quietly as she could. She began cleaning her teeth with a liberal squirt of toothpaste, her mouth filling with foam. Her eyes tightly closed, she braced herself and swallowed hard. She felt sick. Her head was swimming in concentric circles. Her stomach rose and fell on the crest of the foam, up and down like a surf-rider's. She leant hopefully over the lavatory-pan but nothing happened. A cold sweat came over her.

"Millie!" shouted Mrs. Thompson, up the stairs.

"What now?" said Millie, weakly.

"Hurry on down! Your tea's ready. By the way, I've asked that Eddie Carpenter round for tea tomorrow. His Ma was taken bad this morning. They carted her off to the hospital. I 'aven't 'eard nothing more. She could be dead for all I know."

Millie made herself rise from the safety of her bed and creep slowly back to the bathroom, where she washed away the day's layer of make-up and combed and brushed her soft fair hair. Her natural complexion, though pale now, made her seem vulnerable and to her little sister, Mabel, so lovable. Indeed, little Mabel, who shared the large double bed with her big sister, was in the unique position of knowing not one Millie but two. The Millie everyone saw during the day — Millie, the painted doll — was not at all the Millie Mabel saw.

12. Plain Speaking

For Louise Paxton, the vocalising of thought was to be found only in the silent spaces of her imagination. There, in her own intimate world of sights and sounds, she had learned to overcome solitude and surrender to the waiting hours. Quietly and patiently, she would while away the time with sewing, embroidery, reading, and the companionship of radio talks, plays and concerts. In this way, over the years, she had educated herself. Occasionally, she reminded herself that, were she deprived of her eye-sight or hearing, she should mourn life the more. Not to be able to see the colours of the flowers she tended in the small patch of garden at the back of the house, not to be able to marvel at the changing shapes of clouds, the songs of birds in the trees of the Public Gardens, or to hear the welcome sound of a familiar voice calling her name, these must surely be true deprivations. Yet she longed to fling wide her arms and flood her world with the sound of her own voice. Louise was an incurable romantic — an irony which, owing to her passionate response to life, fortunately escaped her notice.

Social activities at Laburnum Villas were limited, save for one occasion when the community spirit got the better of domestic squabbles and gave birth to the annual outing on August Bank Holiday. Louise, in common with the other residents of the Villas, could not as yet know that this year of all years was to change everybody's lives, including her own. Most of the time, however, her secret despair gripped her with claws of iron. Her sense of loneliness and isolation was stifling, sapping her very soul of its life-force, separating her from the world as if she were one of the most distant stars in the firmament.

Now, as she sat waiting patiently for Uncle Walter to come downstairs and read her the late-evening news, she was reflecting on the gentle and caring way in which he had nursed her through her recent relapse. It was sparked off by an event trivial enough in itself, but an event that had disturbed her peace of mind and filled her with a measure of renewed horror. Uncle Walter had been pruning his roses. She had heard the sound of splitting wood followed by a heavy thump. As she hurried downstairs, she saw the old man struggling down the garden, an ugly red gash across his forehead, his face streaming with blood. Instead of running to help him, she fled to her room and stood trembling by the bedside. Her thoughts went back to the day Eddie's father, Jack Carpenter, died and her mind was filled with horrific memories of a scream of pain, a mangled face, arms outstretched seeking comfort, a soul extinguished before her very eyes, and the subsequent trauma of coma and paralysis. Her recovery had been long and painful. Since that terrifying day, Louise had not spoken a single word or sound.

71

Now, the image of the mutilated face of Jack Carpenter seemed to fuse with the image of the blood-stained face of Uncle Walter, the dearest friend to her in all the world. The weeks that followed her collapse were only eased by the gentlest of ministrations by Uncle Walter, whose wounds ironically healed within a day or two. The incident taught him that still waters run deep and that things are not always what they seem in this best of all possible worlds. He knew that, in some way as yet unknown to him, Louise would have to find a cure for her condition. She would have to await the appearance of an angel, perhaps, who would miraculously restore her to health and happiness.

Hearing footsteps on the stairs, Louise froze momentarily. She clutched the back of her arm-chair till the blood drained from her fingers. By the time Uncle Walter came in she was white-faced and trembling yet her reason told her there was nothing to fear.

"Why, Louise, my dear! Are you unwell?" There was a warmth in his voice that calmed her. The old man sat with her on the green velvet sofa and began to read in the familiar, almost soporific tones of his country accent, which he had never quite lost despite his transfer to the Rothersey Police Force at the beginning of the war. He was too old to change and she was glad it was so.

The news was much the same as any other day. Uncle Walter's reading of it was, as usual, censored. She frequently found he had omitted whole sections of the crime pages and had deliberately skipped anything to do with accidents and disasters. One day, while she was dusting his bedroom, she came across an old lined notebook in which he had jotted down in the form of a diary the principal world and national events happening throughout the year — a catalogue of the violence, cruelty and stupidity of the world — which occupied his thoughts during the long wakeful night-time hours. That he should keep such things from her she recognised as one of the many smaller considerations of an aged and fond relative.

After supper, Louise sat with Uncle Walter in the glow of the sitting-room fire. She could see he had something on his mind, but it was a time before he spoke:

"I've been thinking, my dear," he said cautiously, "what we need is a lodger!" Louise frowned.

"I see you don't like the idea, but it would mean we would have someone to help out with the rent."

She felt suddenly vulnerable. In a film she had seen at the Roxy, called *The Lodger,* an innocent girl lived in fear of a sinister man who had come to live at the house. Then she thought how absurd her fears were.

"Things are getting difficult with my pension being what it is. It just won't buy what it did five years ago. Besides, you're a darned good cook. You'd be like a sister to some poor needy girl. In any case, I wouldn't want a stranger in the house till the better weather comes."

Louise had not thought of a companion. A girl her own age, perhaps?

"And another thing," went on Uncle Walter. "I'm not getting any younger. I'll be eighty this year."

He looked at her intently. Louise knew what he was thinking. The house without him would be unbearable. Life without his love and comforting presence? It was unthinkable. She realised that she was ill-prepared for any new companionship. She could not imagine herself relating to anyone else, especially someone of her own age.

"What hopes are there of you ever getting married with an old fogey like me around the place? You ought to be dancing and going out with a nice young lad to look after you when I'm gone."

Louise jumped up and flung her arms round his neck, shaking her head as much as to say: "Please don't talk like that. I know what you're trying to say. You need never worry. I wouldn't have it any other way. Don't you understand?"

"Well? What do you think?" he said, cautiously.

Louise smiled wistfully, kissed him goodnight and went thoughtfully up to her room.

13. Eddie Finds a Way for Tim

Timothy was making his way in the direction of Hungerford Bridge and thence to Villiers Street and The Strand. The emotional turmoil of the day had much affected him. He walked with heavy heart through the rain-soaked streets, his thoughts roaming over the day's events. As he was passing Lupin Avenue, he saw a solitary figure standing dejectedly on the pavement at the corner of the High Street.

"Eddie! What a surprise!"

"Well I never!" said Eddie. "Where are you off to?"

"I've booked in at the Charing Cross Hotel for tonight. I'm on my way there now. I need time to think. Mother was so upset when I telephoned. Fortunately, my father was out taking the horses down to the meadows for the night, so I didn't have to speak to him. Apparently, he hasn't said very much to Mother about our disagreement. I've been wandering around the streets all day, trying to get used to the idea of living in digs."

"You made up your mind, then?"

"Yes. I want to study medicine. I've already applied to Guy's Hospital. You know, I feel a different person since I decided what I really want to do. I feel as if I've grown up all of a sudden. Mother was wonderful about it all. She thinks she 'understands', of course, but she doesn't really know what's been going on inside me over the last year or two. To both of them I'm still a kid."

"Never you mind, Tim. You'll be O.K. Things aint never so bad as they seems."

"I hope you're right," said Tim, ruefully. In the light of the street lamp, he saw that Eddie had been weeping.

"Is the news bad about your mother?"

"I rang the 'ospital from the box over the market. She's packed it in, Tim. Ten o'clock this morning. I've just collected her things from the ward."

He gave a short sob, half stifling it. There was nothing to say. The usual empty phrases were so futile.

"If there's anything I can do to help — ," Tim said lamely.

"I've bin wanderin' the streets for hours too. Just can't bring myself to go 'ome — not with Ma not there no more." Eddie's eyes filled with tears. He shook his head forlornly as Tim put his arm round him. They stood for some minutes in silence. Then Eddie suddenly came out of his dark thoughts.

"'Ere! Just a minute. Did you say you was looking for a place?"

"Well, yes. I shall have to live near the hospital."

"Cor! I was just thinking — my neighbour, old Ma Thompson, was talking about Police-Sergeant Paxton tonight. He lives just across from me. Retired, he is, so he aint got much dough, what with his pension not much to write home about. Well, he told her he was thinking of taking a lodger, like. I reckon you'd be just right for the job. Only one thing, though — he's got a queer bit of a girl living with him. She aint said a word since — well, anyway, she had some kind of shock so they say. Always been a bit frightened-looking. Still, the old man's a good stick, if you ask me. Now, if you was in agreement, I could take you round there tomorrow morning, seeing as 'ow it's Saturday, like."

"Sounds a good idea, Eddie. It'll give me time to look around. I've got an interview at nine o'clock tomorrow. I could drop in on you about eleven. If all goes well, I'll be needing a place about June. Until then I hope I shall be staying with my god-father."

Eddie crossed over the road to the Public Gardens and made his way homewards. He turned into Laburnum Villas with a feeling of apprehension amounting almost to dread. He wondered what his feelings would be as he put the key in the front door and entered the familiar but now silent and deserted rooms. Like Timothy Crawford, he had lost someone precious, quarrelsome for all that, but someone much-loved who had gone out of his life for ever.

EPISODE THREE

St. Valentine's Day: Morning.

Love on Hire Purchase

14. A Strange Way of Showing It

By now, almost everybody at Laburnum Villas had heard about Ma Carpenter's dramatic departure into the next world. Eddie felt the weird silence that filled the house as he wandered aimlessly from room to room. He was trying hard to bring back memories of the old days before his father had been killed eight years ago, but all he kept seeing was his old widowed mother living on next-to-nothing, taking in washing, sewing for hours on end till her fingers curled up with the rheumatism. She had done it all for him and he had loved her for it. When finally she had stiffened into an invalid and had to sit about the house moping and moaning, Eddie had willingly given up his technical course and, armed with a reference from his former employer, John Garville, went to work in the market with his father's old firm of *Andrew Crawford & Son Ltd.*

Eddie hadn't felt like any breakfast. Ever since he had rung up the hospital for news and they told him his old Ma had snuffed it, a raw aching tugged mercilessly at heart. Steeling himself, he went into the kitchen, then to the stairs, running his fingers over the banisters all the way up as if he were playing a great harp. In his wanderings about the house, he would sit down, sigh, get up again, stand aimlessly about, sit down again, pick up trinkets and bric-à-brac, and all the time looking through them as if they were invisible. He wanted very much to die.

The thick curtains like carpets, the fusty old furniture from his grandad's time, with its bobbles and padded leather, the horsehair chairs, the aspidistras, the heavy Brussels lace over the windows, the antimacassars, his father's old clock, presented after he left the tannery to work in the market — paraphernalia from another age that filled him with sadness.

As he well knew, there stretched before him an agony of funeral preparations and the anguish he would suffer as he stood beside Ma for the last time in the Chapel of Rest. It had all happened before with his father — lurid memories of a badly mutilated face and tortured expression, but all that was a very different case, a part of terrible events he preferred not to think about now. His father had been gentle and long-suffering, would put up with anything for the sake of a little peace and quiet. Never grumbled or yelled about the place. No, it was always Ma who swore like a trooper and locked them out after she had been gossiping and boozing with her old cronies down at *The Bed of Roses* — talking about nothing unless it was what her old man had done or said, or not done, more like it. She would come home as drunk as a titmouse in a beer-barrel, and her, shouting and carrying on and not caring who knew neither! But now — this silence everywhere — that was what troubled Eddie.

He didn't hear the knock at first, and, when it finally registered with him, he panicked. He just didn't feel like seeing anybody this morning. When he opened the door, it was Millie, all dressed up, quite a nifty little number in her tight leather skirt. "'Allo, Ed, how are you, love? I'm ever so sorry about your Ma, Eddie, reelly I am. She was right good sort, old Ma was."

"Ta, Millie. Nice of you to come across."

They stood looking at each other in silence, and then Eddie pulled himself together enough to realise that Millie was shivering a little with the cold air.

"Come in, gel! I've just got the kettle boiling for a cuppa." He paused nervously. "If you like."

"Well, I can't stay long, mind. I got to go up the chemist's to get me home shampoo, see?"

She followed through into the front-room and waited while he brushed his hand over the seat of the best chair. He went into the kitchen and turned on the gas. As luck would have it, there was half-a-kettle of water left over from shaving so he added a bit more to make up. When he finally returned with the tea-tray, Millie said:

"Shall I be mum?

"Okeydoke!"

As she poured, dust from the cups floated to the surface. The tea was like strong Bovril.

"Ooh! no sugar," she said. He fumbled around helplessly.

"What are you going to do now, Ed? Staying on here, are you?"

"'Spect so, mate. Won't be much cop on me own though, specially without ol' Ma. She was a good'un to me, she was."

"What are you going to do wiv yerself, luv?"

"I dunno, really. Thought of going back to school again to study me old trade. I only had another six months and I'd 'a' been a fully-fledged ship's engineer, only me Dad got hisself killed. Anyway, I gotta give up the old homestead in a year with this new housing scheme coming on. The extra lolly'd just come in all right for a holiday some place, like Blackpool. I got an auntie up there, see? I might take up racing birds."

"Ooh! sounds a bit naughty." She giggled.

"No, you know. Pigeons, see? Entering 'em for the big-time. There's a lot of money in it."

"What do they do, then? The three-legged race or something?"

"Don't be daft. Fly hundreds of miles, they do. I know a bloke who sold his birds for a thousand nicker. He had a breeding hen that brought him five hundred quid." Millie gasped.

"But you aint even got the birds yet, Eddie."

"I'll get the bird if I don't do something soon."

They began laughing, and Millie felt genuinely sorry for Eddie. Not only that. He seemed to be a nice sort of bloke. Had ideas. Knew how to earn a bit on the side to make ends meet. If only he could get a break.

"You going on at the button-factory, Millie?" he asked.

"Yes, but it's so boring. The place is like a blinking skating rink, it is. All them buttons, millions and millions of them all over the floor. Get into your shoes. Red buttons, yellow buttons, green buttons, tiddly buttons, big buttons, spangled buttons, square buttons, flower buttons, ivy-leaf buttons, coat buttons, fly-buttons— the lot! The only ones we don't make are belly buttons!"

Eddie laughed and laughed, even though it wasn't really funny. Millie was nice to talk to, cosy and warm. He was more than glad she had called round. As she got up to go, Eddie did not fail to notice how she waggled her bottom to straighten her skirt.

"Thanks for tea, duck," she said. "Oh, and Mum says you're to come round to us for your tea every night, see, and not to worry about nothing, see?"

A wave of sympathy made her pause for a moment.

"Listen, Eddie! I got a couple o' tickets for tomorrow night at the Purvis Bowl Gala. Councillor Purvis giv 'em to me."

"Blimey! What did you 'ave to do to get 'em, then?" he asked with a smirk all over his face.

"Eddie Carpenter! How dare you? I'm tryin' to cheer you up, so don't take advantage. D'yer want to come or not?"

When Eddie opened the front door, Curly was blocking the way.

"Allo, Ed, me ol' cock! How's yer ol' Ma this fine morning? Didn't half give me bit of her lip last Saturday when I come round." He peered into the semi-darkness of the hall. " 'Allo, 'allo! What 'ave we 'ere?" he said in feigned surprise. "Just a bit inconvenient-like, is it?"

"None o' your lip, cheeky so-and-so, whoever-you-are!" said Millie, looking down her pretty little nose.

"It's time you learned to treat a girl proper, 'stead o' cheeking her about." She felt something stirring up inside her, and it wasn't only her heart. When Millie clapped eyes on Curly for the first time she could hardly take him all in at one go. She didn't fail to notice his film-star looks, his muscular body, his fine teeth when he smiled, and his shock of blond hair. She sidled out onto the pavement and stood half-smiling, half-pouting. Yes, she may like Eddie enough, but she wanted Curly.

"Ta-ta!" she said to Eddie. "See you tonight, then. Mum'll be expecting you for your tea. Don't worry about anything, duck. Your Ma's much happier where she is."

"Come off it!" said Curly. "Anybody 'd think the ol' gel 'd kicked the bucket."

"She has," said Millie with simplicity.

Eddie looked tearful. Curly stood fidgeting impatiently on the step. Sympathy was something he was not accustomed to giving or receiving. He began blurting out excuses.

"Er — well — er — me ol' cock," and gave a little nervous laugh. He began backing up the street in Millie's direction. He certainly didn't want to stay around with Eddie being such a mopy-dick. Eddie heard him mutter: "What you doing tonight, Mill?" and saw him slip his arm round her waist as they sauntered off together..

With the front door shut, Eddie was once more enclosed in his tomb of grief. Now that Millie had left, it was worse than before. He began wandering aimlessly about. Almost without realising it, he was

81

turning the handle of Ma's bedroom door.

The room was cold and dank. Misery welled up inside him as his eyes rested on a half-open drawer from which hung her faded old wedding dress. She must have been looking at it the day before she died. It was all creased and rumpled from being shut up for forty years. Better out of sight, it was.

Eddie moved slowly round the room fingering everything gently, trying hard to bring her back to life. He went on his journey, lightly touching her things. The room reeked of her everywhere — the bottles of liniment, the vague aroma of stale urine in the chamber-pot under the bed. Smells, yes. And tangible things, too — the hairpins, the Beleek dish that Ma Donoghue had sold her out of one of her old totting bags, the photograph of her and Dad taken on the prom at Southend, the blue woollen bed-jacket. In the wardrobe he found a couple of his old school exercise-books wrapped up in brown paper as if she had meant to take them with her. Suddenly he couldn't see anything anymore. Salt tears trickled down into his mouth. His face started to twitch. He began snivelling like the little boy he had once been and now was once again. The tears ran down over the stubble of his unshaven chin and dripped onto his hands and went splat on the brown paper parcel. He sat down on her bed and gave way to fits of sobbing, saying aloud as if she might hear: "Oh, Mum, come back to me. Don't leave me. Don't leave me here on my own. Please, please don't leave me." But the silence was only more dreadful, more chaotic. "Oh, God, help me. Help me, please," he prayed, but the silence after his unanswered prayer was even more terrible than the silence that caught at his heart after his futile words.

Sometime later, in the icy numbness that spread through him, Eddie decided he would not go to the Chapel of Rest after all. He wanted to remember Ma as she was the day before, in the hospital — raving, waving her arms about, calling everybody all the names under the sun, showering saliva over him in her rage. He had been upset, it was true, yet it was only now, in this roomful of memories, that he realised the true meaning of it all, for, although it was a strange way of showing it, she was demonstrating in her own way her own kind of love.

82

15. The Face at the Window

Laburnum Villas, with its dingy gas-lamps and grime-soaked yellowish fletton bricks, blackened by years of engine smoke from the nearby goods-yard, might have deterred anyone from ever setting foot in the place. It was not easy in the gloom of the London twilight to see the blind wall that ran right across the end of the little cul–de–sac, so that occasionally a car or lorry, swerving hopefully into the street, had to back out and, with little room to turn, could cause a traffic jam right outside Councillor Purvis's front windows, which jutted out over the pavement. At the blind end of the cul-de-sac, the solitary laburnum struggled to maintain some sense of decorum amid the drabness and air of neglect that pervaded the little street.

Tim had been buying books in the Charing Cross Road and had taken a taxi as far as the Villas. The driver was disgruntled and had to back into a stream of traffic coming round the bend from the bridge.

"I shouldn't think you blinking-well want to come round here on a Friday morning of all times, chum! Some people think we're bleeding geniuses, us taxi-drivers, the things they ask us to bloody-well do. It's murder, I tell you."

Tim looked up at the name-plate, grubby and weather-beaten: 'Laburnum Villas'. He walked slowly down past the bay windows of No 1, past the eyeless face of No 3, and crossed over to Eddie's place.

The visit turned out to be a strain from start to finish. Eddie was still too upset for visitors. Tim, for his part, was glad when Eddie suggested going round to the Paxtons to enquire about the room. Introductions over, Eddie returned to the sombre silence of No 6, leaving Tim to fight it out for himself.

"Well, Mr. Crawford," the old Police-Sergeant explained, "I'm sorry young Eddie has brought you up here for nothing. You see, we don't intend to have a male lodger. You haven't met my niece, have you? A fine girl is Louise, but I must be frank, she hasn't spoken a word since her — shall we say — 'accident'. She's a plucky young lass, but you see, it just wouldn't be right to take you, would it? It's a bit lonely for her here on her own. What she needs is a companion, someone to talk with, help her with a few jobs about the house, answering the door, doing the shopping and so on. I can't manage anything like I used to, what with my diabetes. The insulin, you see. And there's the diet, too. What we need is a young lass to keep Louise away from her depressions. Someone as would liven her up, you see."

Mr. Paxton gazed into the fire, thoughtfully. The flames flicked up into the sooty chimney in blue and green tips. Soot ignited and crept slowly over the firestones in patterns. He felt warm and at peace in this tiny room, with its faint air of mothballs and burning ash, the warmth of the fire spread over his face and temples, making him drowsy, all of which conflicted with his overriding feeling of disappointment.

"I'm sorry you can't take me. All I want is a quiet place to study. I don't even need meals. I can arrange things at the hospital most days."

"Hospital?" said Mr. Paxton. "I thought Eddie said you were in farming."

"Well, my father is. I have to admit that I shall never make a farmer, not in a hundred years. I'm afraid I'm a bit too much of a radical."

"Radical! I don't like the sound of that."

"I like progress. I like the feeling of moving forward. Not just marking time for years. Now the war's over, it is in the nature of things that they should change. Today is tomorrow's yesterday." Tim smiled ironically and looked nervously at the old man. "I told my father that once."

"That sounds as if you've had differences." He eyed Tim quizzically. Tim laughed.

"I thought you were a policeman, not a detective."

"Well, I am retired, you know. It's not so hard to tell you don't get on with your Dad, my boy. Anyway, Eddie told me something of the sort. So! You want to be a doctor."

"Yes. I'd like to work in one of the big hospitals. Maybe, to specialise. Cardiology, perhaps."

"And how interested are you in the heart, Mr. Crawford?"

"I don't understand," said Tim on his guard.

"Well, shall we put it another way, then. Have you any girl-friends? Do you like dancing and gadding about at night?"

Tim paused nervously. "Not all that much, I suppose. I like

reading, music, and so on. I don't ask for too much where my spare time is concerned. You might say I'm a bit of a lone wolf, with not so much of the wolf about me. When you've lived in the country as I have most of my life, you don't miss what you never had. Anyway, I always come up to London when I have enough money and time. I'm not one for farm-house teas and gargantuan family get-togethers."

"Not the green–fingered lad your father would like you to be, eh?"

"Well, I've had my moments. His rose–borders, for example. They're a darned sight better now than they were when he used to look after them. Not that he'd ever admit that. Not in a month of Sundays. Too darned pig-headed."

He stopped abruptly and stared awkwardly at Mr. Paxton. The fire glowed warm on their faces as they sat together in the dimly-lit room.

"I mean", said Tim, beginning again, "I mean obstinate, perhaps. Selfish and wilful as a child sometimes. You know, you're making me feel bad about him. I'm really fond of him. He has principles. He's honest and forthright, but he is afraid of himself, afraid to show love and affection. Perhaps I'll leave him to look after his own roses from now on."

"You can't beat a fine English rose for beauty," said Mr. Paxton, almost absentmindedly, for his thoughts were, for a moment, on other things. "Give me the old sorts. None of your newfangled hybrids. You can't beat the old Moss Rose and the damask for beauty. And *Crimson Glory*, soft and velvety."

Tim began to feel the old man must have been listening too much to Fred Streeter the way he was carrying on about his roses. "What about *Brazilian Wonder?*" he said.

"Wouldn't touch it. Sounds a bit foreign to me. I really love English things — English cheese, English country lanes, the roast beef of old England, and specially English gardens. No! *Crimson Glory*, that's the rose for me."

"There's no comparison, I tell you," protested Tim. There was a sudden pause — and in a flash they were laughing and the old man put his hand on Tim's shoulder just to be friendly about the whole thing.

"What suits one doesn't suit another," said Tim defiantly. He was deciding that he didn't like the place after all and the old man was being as impossible as his father. Tim got up to make his leave but Mr.

Paxton caught him by the arm and led him out through the kitchen to the back garden.

"And this," he said, "is my little patch."

The garden was neat and trim. A small narrow path of crazy–paving led to the gate onto the back alley. On each side were two smudges of grass, green after the rain, and all along one wall were bush–roses and climbers not yet in bud.

"Nigh on a hundred blooms last summer," the old man said. "Had to build up the supports for the rambler from the sheer weight of it."

As they turned back to the house, Tim caught sight of a girl's face in an upstairs window. She stared for a moment and then drew back. Tim just had time to see that she was very pretty. When he looked up again, she had vanished like a mirage.

His feelings began to be confused. Did he really want to leave home? Could he bear to leave everything behind? All the happy years of his childhood? And what about the loneliness his mother would have to endure without her closest ally? And did he really want to take on the added problem, after a hard day at the hospital, of trying to communicate with someone who had no power of speech?

"Well, sir," he said. "I must be going."

"Just a minute, my boy. What's your first name, did you say?"

"Timothy."

"Well, Timothy," the old man said, "when do you want to move in?"

"But you said — ""Never mind what I said. If you want to come then come and we'll say no more about it." Timothy realised he had no choice but to accept.

"Will Monday do, then?""All right by me, son. Though I don't know what Louise'll think when I tell her she has two men to look after from now on."

Going down the street, Tim couldn't help thinking about the girl at the window and wondered if he was doing the right thing by going to live there. He liked the old boy. The house was cosy and homely. It would certainly be a start, though the difficulty of carrying on one-sided conversations with someone who couldn't speak continued to dominate his thoughts.

All the way to the corner, he somehow felt her watching him and had an almost irresistible urge to turn round to see for himself. She is afraid of me, he was thinking. Is that it? She is scared of the world and everything in it. Was the old man really showing him the garden or was he giving the girl a chance to see and approve him. And what was all the mystery about the 'accident'? He was frankly puzzled. Her beautiful face haunted him all the way back to the Essex farm he was less and less inclined to regard as home.

16. Getting Up Steam

Agnes Baldock handed over the keys of the stores to her Saturday-evening assistant and breathed a sigh of relief. It had been a trying day at the Roxy Restaurant. One of the kitchen staff had started the day by clumsily knocking over a bowl of whisked eggs, which left a yellow viscous pool in front of the table where the salads had to be prepared. If it isn't one thing it's another, she told herself, trying hard to remember a day when she had been able to go home with her mind free of care. Keeping a hold on her staff was a constant worry. There was not much choice between a sulky, sour-faced school-leaver scratching her hair over the salads and an slapdash middle-aged mother with time on her hands.

Problems with the kitchen-girls were only the half of it. The waitresses had grown slack through lack of supervision. Only that very morning, at lunchtime, Agnes had nearly dismissed a girl on the spot for wiping a bread-and-butter plate on her bottom, the very same girl who had dropped a Kunzle Cake on the floor and, sticking the glacé cherry back on the top, served it up to the unsuspecting customer, who happened, as luck would have it, to be that dreadful Mrs. Thompson with her horrid little brat, Mabel. Had it been a person of note like Councillor Purvis — well, the girl would have been instantly kicked out on her beam-end!

A warm surge of pride spread through Agnes's ample bosom as she recalled her sally with Andrew Crawford that morning. Had she known of its effect on the life of Timothy Crawford, the flame of her pride might have been stemmed by the stream of conscience, or perhaps the scalding steam of remorse. As it was, she preferred to congratulate herself on her victory over the forces of aggression. Yes, she thought, I know how to deal with them, these men! They're just like babies. Give them sympathy and attention and they soon come smiling out of their

87

moods and sulks.

The anger of Agnes Baldock was now softened to the merest degree of annoyance as she remembered the extra sack of potatoes she had managed to squeeze out of Andrew Crawford, and a dozen oranges to boot. She reflected with some satisfaction that men were like putty in her hands. Nevertheless, her feelings at this moment were tempered by the knowledge of the deep emptiness within her. Never in all her forty-eight years in this rat-race of human endeavour, never had this void been greater, never had her heart been heavier than in these rainy days of February. Men may have been like putty in her hands, but it was like putty in the path of a steam-roller.

It was the supreme privilege of the manageress to leave her work on the dot of half-past six. It was also the duty of the girls to stay late if necessary, a duty Miss Baldock considered fitting to the inferiority of their minds and estate. At precisely twenty-past six, therefore, she put on her hat and coat, took up her spiked umbrella (a formidable weapon in case she were attacked by a sex-maniac on the way home), slipped her galoshes over her neatly-laced black shoes, and thus armed, sallied forth into her 'night of doubt and sorrow' like one of the Christian band.

The short journey home on the bus was singularly uneventful. Turning the corner into the Villas, she bumped into Ron Thompson coming away from Mr. Lawton's.

"Ev'nin', Miss Baldock."

She did not answer. He was a nasty, dirty little wretch in her opinion. She put her key in the lock unsmilingly and went in very quietly so as not to disturb the old man.

"That you, Agnes?"

Miss Baldock's mouth thinned into a pencil-line as she mounted the stairs without a word, snatching her post from the hallstand on her way.

Miss Baldock's living-room was directly over Grandpa Lawton's at the front of the house. She hung up her coat on a hanger in the special place reserved for it in the wardrobe on the landing, taking care to brush off the scurf on the collar and shoulders. Then she put her hat with its long pin, on the shelf above. Entering the room, she placed her spiked umbrella in a handy corner. Methodically, she lit the coal-fire she had laid that morning before leaving for work. Methodically, she put on a saucepan of soup of her own careful making and lit the gas-ring. Most methodically of all, she scrutinised the post, letter by letter, post-mark by post-mark. There was one from a small nephew who would shortly have a birthday and wished to remind her of the fact. Laundry bill, gas bill — if it's not bills, it's begging letters, she complained to herself. People did nothing but pay, pay, pay, and had little to show for it. Next came a long brown official-looking envelope. She was about to open it when she realised it was for Mr. Lawton. Oh, well, it could wait till morning. She wasn't going to go traipsing downstairs just to get involved in conversational inanities, so there!

Taking down the already-prepared tray from the chest-of-drawers, she put it on the table and poured out the soup. It was while she was eating some Blue Stilton cheese and water-biscuits that she began thinking about the unopened letter. What was the old skinflint doing getting official letters? Had he decided after all to take her advice and go into the Napoleon Avenue Old People's Home, where he could be properly cared for. Or had he decided to make his will? Perhaps! But then, perhaps not!

Agnes Baldock's attitude to Mr. Lawton was far from charitable. On the contrary, she was filled with resentment. After all, even though she was a cousin several times removed, she was, nevertheless, a cousin! And what had he ever done for her, pray? He had taken her in as a paying-guest (no common-or-garden lodger!) fourteen years ago. True, she was grateful at first — doing his housework for him, cooking his evening meal for him when she arrived home from the Roxy. As time passed, Agnes came to resent his dependence on her for every little thing, so that her life was no longer her own. She became a lackey. Soon she was forced to take on evening duties at the Roxy Restaurant in order not to be in the house when she was most needed. After all, why should she pay rent and do the housework as well? Being at home during the day was far worse. She was pestered with "Agnes do this" and "Agnes do that" and "Agnes do the other" until she was absolutely sick of all the come-hithering-and-thithering.

At last, when one evening the old man complained of being bored, she pointedly remarked that it was positively dangerous for a man of his age to sit about the house all day doing nothing. Why, he might pop off any moment and be found sitting in his chair, his pipe burning away in his withered old hand, and he dead as a dodo, and the house burning to the ground into the bargain. What he needed was a little routine and exercise. It was just his luck that the Borough Council was advertising for Road Safety Officers.

And so it was to be. Naturally, he had to tell a big fib about his age but he got the job on the crossing at Marley's Corner. It wasn't strenuous. He just had to stand there in the middle of the road and usher the children across. He had a nice white coat, a shiny peaked cap and a lovely lollipop sign that said "**STOP!**" in big red letters. Now, nothing could keep him away from the work. He grew to like the children and knew them all by name, and had different-coloured fruit-drops for his favourites.

When Agnes was asked to go back on the day-shift for the busy spring and summer season, she saw her neatly-arranged little world fall to pieces. She was once more faced with Mr. Lawton every evening calling up the stairs for something or other. "Agnes!" he would call out. "**AGNES!**" She simply could not face it, and this was only her first week.

While she was sitting reading the evening paper, with a hot cup of tea on the table beside her, it occurred to her that she might, without offence, unseal the envelope of the mystery letter. Hardly had she steamed it open and read the contents than she hit upon the long-awaited solution to the nettling problem of Mr. Lawton. From now on, she would set her mark at Councillor Joseph Gabriel Purvis, the landlord of Laburnum Villas.

17. Curly's Dress Rehearsal

Curly Donoghue was feeling pleased with himself. He had just come home from meeting up with Millie Thompson and he couldn't get her out of his mind. The very thought of her gave him such a sensual thrill that his whole body seemed to go out of control. He paced up and down his room with a degree of excitement and expectation he had never known before. That the luscious Millie was going to the opening of the Purvis Bowl was a dream come true. He wasn't at all guilty about doing the dirty on his mate, Eddie Carpenter. It was just a case of 'may the best man win' and Curly saw himself to be a front-runner in more ways than one now that Millie had come into his life, if not yet into his bed.

He took out his jeans and laid them over the chair. With legs astride and hands on his narrow hips, he posed naked in front of the mirror. He tensed his muscular arms, drew in his diaphragm like the male models in the Muscle Man magazines, observing with pride his long strong thighs and well-shaped biceps. The hairs on Curly's legs and arms shone like gold in the lamplight. He stroked his hands over his trim torso, caressing himself gently and rousing himself at the thought of how it would be nice to have Millie do it for him.

Opening a drawer, he took out a stack of health magazines and sat down on the bed to study them. There were several photographs of a model called Pistol.

Pistol was the ideal kind of pin up for Curly. Almost every day, Curly would pose in front of the mirror: Pistol the toreador, Pistol the Canadian Mountie, Pistol the discus-thrower, Pistol the Greek god, like the one on the advertisement for the Purvis Bowl in the Rothersey Gazette. That's the way he saw himself, striding into the Bowl, thumbs nonchalantly stuck in his hip-pockets, everybody standing back for Curly Donoghue, the champion, to have a go. And there he was, with that shiny black ball, ready to sling it down the alley, watching it ride dead down the middle to the king-pin, knocking them all for six.

The clock on St. Crispin's tower struck seven. Curly began to dress. With each garment he put on he walked over to the mirror just to keep in touch with himself. First, his skin-tight briefs with the inch-and-a-quarter hips; then the T-vest with the two-inch over-the-shoulder sleeves; next the 'shortie' nylon and wool socks and the red and black checked lumber-jack shirt. Standing on the bed, he slipped gently into his 'Quick-Zip' jeans, which he drew up over his thighs with the care of a sapper on a bomb-disposal job, checking that everything was in place to give the maximum effect. With his comb, he meticulously fingered his hair into place and gave himself a last admiring look in the mirror. He'd show that Millie Thompson what it was like to have a real live muscle-man to look up to, or his name wasn't Curly Donoghue!

18. Love on the H.P.

Mrs. Thompson was angry. What with Millie being late in, and Ron only just home from Mr. Lawton's, and not wanting any supper either, and Eddie sitting on his laurels in the front room, it was too much to put up with. Morning, noon and night she worked her fingers to the bone for the family's benefit, and what thanks did she get? The love she earned from them all was bought on the instalment plan, and it was she who had to keep up the payments. To cap it all, Alf wasn't home. Paying a call at the local most likely. A nice little crowd they were, down at *The Bed of Roses,* drinking and singing their lungs out. A regular carry-on it was. Talk about 'PEACE AND PLENTY' meetings. A pity they didn't think a bit more about the poor wives at home, getting meals that nobody wanted to eat, keeping everything hot in the oven till all hours. A nice how-d'ye-do! Now everything was ready to serve up and nobody to eat it as usual, except her and Eddie. There was no telling what Mabel was getting up to. And now that dog was scratching the paint off the back-door and whining like a winter wind.

"Smutty! Stop that, now, else I'll come out and belt you one. You'll get your supper when I'm good and ready and not before, so go back to your kennel." Smutty stopped scratching.

"S'all ready, Eddie!" she said, in a sympathetic tone, which abruptly changed to a harsh shout when she realised there was no sign of Mabel.

"MABEL!!!"

Eddie came into the kitchen as Mrs. Thompson was forking the sausages onto an old chipped dish.

"I'm ever so sorry about your Ma, luv. She was a good 'un, she was."

She went on mashing the potatoes, squashing them into a vegetable dish and patting them affectionately with the back of the fork.

"Mabel! Mabel!" she shrieked. "You upstairs?"

"Mabel aint nowhere," said Ron, pushing his way into the kitchen.

"Well, go and find her, then."

"How can I do that if she aint nowhere? Anyway, why do *I* have to go and look for her? She aint never here when she's wanted," he whined.

Mrs. Thompson turned the gas low on the tapioca pudding and turned the stewed prunes out into a dish. "Go and tell her supper's ready, I tell you."

"I hate prunes."

"Prunes are good for you," said Mrs. Thompson firmly.

A thorough search upstairs and down brought no solution as to Mabel's whereabouts. Now that Ron had done his duty, he sat himself down at the table in front of a plate of sizzling sausages and steaming hot mash. He felt sick. He very much wanted to go and blow away at his recorder in preparation for tomorrow's band-practice.

"Now, come along, Ron," said Mrs. Thompson. "Get on with your supper."

"I'm waiting for Eddie to start."

Eddie picked up his knife and set to. That was all right until Millie came down, patting her home-perm curls and flashing her silver finger-nails about. Her face was afire with rouge. She looked like the model of Diana Dors at Madame Tussaud's. Eddie didn't say much. In any case, Mrs. Thompson was worried about Mabel and went off to look for her. Now that Millie had set eyes of the handsome Curly, she was annoyed at her mother for asking Eddie round. On top of all that, she resented being asked all those silly questions over a stupid drink at old Purvis's. Anybody'd think she was a kid the way she was treated. So taken all in all, it was not a very amusing occasion.

That scratching noise began again, so Ron got up and opened the door, only to find Smutty, dripping wet and looking a picture of misery in the rain. No sooner than the door opened, the merest inch or two, than he pushed his nose through and almost immediately followed it with the rest of his anatomy. Then there was trouble. He scampered round the room, jumped up with his dirty paws, all muddy and wet, all over Millie's pink skirt, slobbering over her bracelets, and getting her generally messed up. Anybody would have thought she was being murdered the way she screamed. Eddie was frightened her face would crack into little pieces. Still, through it all, he could see she was quite a doll, waggling her hips about, brushing herself off with a damp cloth, one knee stuck forward to tighten her skirt against her thigh, and flapping her tits about like Bow Bells ringing in the New Year. 'She's a real sexy little number', thought Eddie, confidently anticipating the chance of a nice long smooch with her in the back alley later on.

Mrs. Thompson stared at her kitchen floor with dismay. It was stencilled in an intricate pattern of paw-marks where Smutty had pranced round the table, overjoyed to be out of the rain and with the smell of food in his nostrils. She grabbed him by the collar and hoiked him out into the yard, rain or no rain. She tried very hard to push him into the kennel, but he would not budge. His legs went rigid. His tail crept between his legs. He refused to go in. In Smutty's view there was no room for two. Mrs. Thompson peered inside.

"Mabel! What on earth are you doing in the dog-kennel. I've been calling you for ages. Come out at once, you naughty little girl. I'll give you such a hiding as you've never known when I get hold of you.

Do you hear me? Come out at once."

Silence. Mrs. Thompson was getting very wet. She groped round inside with her one free arm, clutching at the darkness with her rough fingers. At last she caught hold of Mabel and then there began such a squawling and a squealing that it brought the whole household to the door to see what was up. Mabel emerged from the kennel on the end of her mother's arm, struggling for all she was worth, and clutching a dead sparrow in her hand.

"You naughty [smack!] naughty [smack! smack!] NAUGHTY [smack-smack-smack-a-smack!!] little gir-irl," shouted Flo, hysterically, and shaking Mabel like a tambourine, she snatched the dead sparrow away and flung it across the yard.

"Mabel want birdie. Mabel want birdie!" screamed the little kennel-maid.

"I'll give you birdie, my girl. Just you wait."

No sooner had Mabel been dragged from her hiding-place than Smutty took up his rightful residence. Glad to be restored to his old home, he was shivering with the cold and was rather rattled to find the sparrow he had caught earlier in the day had been taken away from him.

Mrs. Thompson was convinced she had never had such a distressing day in all her life, and that the night did not offer much hope of improvement with Alf not home to supper and her arthritis coming on, and her soaked to the skin and all.

Calm once more restored, the family resumed their meal. The milk pudding and stewed prunes replaced the sausage and mash, the remains of which were returned to the oven to await Alf's arrival. Mabel, all this time, was making patterns across her potato with her knife.

"Now, do come along, Mabel, eat your food properly."

"Mabel want Smutty din-din."

Mrs. Thompson drew her arm across her aching brows, swept a wisp of hair into place, cut up Mabel's sausage into small pieces, and mixed everything into a hotch-potch of pinks and whites and browns. Even then, Mabel just picked about with it, and finally pushed it onto the floor. Ron hadn't got very far with his either and half-way through, he announced that he was going to be sick. They all jumped to their feet, plates in hand, while Mrs. Thompson rushed him up to the bathroom, where all the nuts and chocolate and sherbet and fruit-syrup and liquidated toffee and pulped-up sausage-and-mash regurgitated in a rich and gigantic effusion. Mabel came to watch, staring for all she was

94

worth at the white-faced Ron, and thought it looked like a very big Smutty's din-din that Ron had been eating. On her return to table, she was duly sick all over the cloth at the sight of the tapioca-pudding. Events had played against her this time. She was very upset indeed. Ron was sent to bed with a hot-water bottle and aspirins whilst Millie and Eddie put on their hats and raincoats and bade a thankful goodnight to Mrs. Thompson.

As they opened the front-door, they nearly fell over Alf. There he was, sitting on the door-step in the rain, beer-bottle in one hand. He was in full voice:

Red sails in the sunset,
Way out on the sea,
Oh, carry my loved one
Home safely to me.

"Come on," said Millie to Eddie, "let's go or we'll be late. Mum'll deal with him."

They sauntered off into the rainy night leaving Mrs. Thompson to her drunken husband. She stood for a while looking at him in despair.

"Get up, you rotten tyke, you. Boozing of a Friday night. Ought to be ashamed of yourself, you did. And me worrying meself sick, wondering where you was."

" 'Allo, me old dear! Peace and Goodwill to the little woman, that's what I say. Couldn't do without the ol' 'trouble and strife', could we?. Always ready to welcome you with a smile and a kind word." He took a swig from the bottle and began to sing again:

Ah, Sweet Mystery of life,
At last I've found you,
Ah, Sweet Mystery of life,
At last......'

He trailed off because Flo was dragging him into the hall, bottles and all, out of the driving rain.

"I'll give you a welcome you least expect, one of these days, Alf Thompson. It'll be good riddance and san-fairy-ann to you and the lot of 'em. Look at you! All soaked to the skin, you are. Soaked to the skin. I'll have you in bed as well, by the look of it."

She began to cry, but Alf didn't see her tears. She led him into the kitchen and took his coat off for him. As she stealthily drew the bottles from his pockets, Alf grabbed them and slammed them down on the table. He sat silent, glumly viewing the food in front of him. Then, throwing his arms into the air, he raised his eyes to the ceiling and burst into song again:

> *Oh give us a bash*
> *Of the bangers and mash*
> *Me muvver used to make.*

As she gazed at her drunken excuse for a husband, Flo wasn't sure if he realised just what a failure his life had been, just how much despair he had caused to well up in her heart — and she wondered how much longer she could go on being mother and father to a family like theirs. She knew she was losing her grip. There was Ron going his own way, and Millie didn't do anything to help matters. Far too independent, she was. As for Mabel, she was nothing but a wretched little nuisance, she was. Always grizzling and playing up. Sometimes Flo wanted to smack her so hard, just being Mabel. Mabel just didn't seem to 'belong' in the same way as Millie and Ron. No! Life at No. 4 couldn't go on as it was. Something was bound to happen sooner or later.

A pain was creeping up Flo's back and over her shoulders. Her head ached and her temples throbbed. She got up very slowly and left Alf sitting at the table, his food untouched, and the empty beer-bottles in front of him. She wearily climbed the stairs to bed. As she closed her eyes, she thought: "I'm going to have one of my turns, I know it. Please God, it isn't. Please God, don't let me have another." She was run down, that's what she was, and with the thought firmly fixed in her mind, she allowed herself the luxury of a quiet sob into the pillows.

EPISODE FOUR

St. Valentine's Day: Later that evening.

The Stage is Set

19. Oh, What a (Gala) Performance!

It was the proudest moment of Councillor Purvis's career when he declared the Purvis Bowl open to the public. There, in the presence of stars of stage and screen and well over two hundred spectators, he was aware that this was his crowning moment, the peak of his personal achievement and endeavour in the interest of the youth of the Borough. He stood up amid the applause and spoke frankly of his aims and hopes in creating a new and healthy activity to attract the young away from the streets. He had no wish to appear pompous or stuffy in front of Calthrop and Bingo Wood, who, he knew perfectly well, would have his political guts for garters if they were to succeed in their ambitious plans.

In his attempt to please all sides, he was aware that he was becoming verbose, too long-winded. He noticed the general restlessness spreading through his audience, who had not come to hear hollow speeches. He decided to play his trump card — Millie!

"Nothing could be worse than that we of the older generation should dampen the spirit of youth. I am delighted to see here this evening a young lady of my acquaintance [*hoots of laughter and wolf-whistles*] — of the very briefest acquaintance [*jeers of 'Tell that to the marines'*] — even though I have known the family for years [*shouts of 'Come off it!' and 'Oh, yeah! Tell us anuvver one!' from Curly's gang*].

" I know," the Councillor persisted, "I happen to know that she is a fine example of the typical young woman of tomorrow, a young woman I could have time for [*more laughter and hoots*] as a fervent supporter of our 'Opportunities for Youth' campaign. Here is a young girl making the most of herself [*cries of "Give us an eyeful, Millie!"*] in a difficult post-war world. That's what I like to see."

The Councillor was unnerved by his reception. He seemed not to notice the general wish to get on with the frivolities of the evening and not to have to listen to mindless waffle from officialdom about the morals of the youth of the borough.

Eddie and Curly were standing all this time one each side of Millie and, in the crush, they were pressed hard up against her, like stamps into a rubber sponge. Millie was loving it. As far as she was concerned the silly old Councillor could go on as long as he liked. Eddie, in all this close physical contact, was falling for Millie already, and, as for Curly, standing up against her with his thigh pressed hard against her bottom, well, he was in seventh heaven and very near the edge of things.

"Who was this tart" asked Curly, and was put out when Millie had to admit it was her.

So! thought Curly, beset as he was with feelings of jealousy and lust, Millie really *has* been larking about with the Councillor, after all. The dirty old man!

Eddie was getting frustrated too. Millie was taking far too much interest in Curly. After all, it was he, Eddie, who had brought her here in the first place. He wanted to tell Curly to mind his own ruddy business and stop poking his nose in where it wasn't wanted, except that Curly's nose was not the only thing he was poking up against her at that moment! Murmurs of impatience spread through the body of the hall like a virus. No corner escaped infection as the Councillor's voice rose to an almost hysterical level to make himself heard:

"Yes, my friends, the Purvis Bowl is the first of its kind in our borough and to mark the occasion I have great pleasure in asking Miss Mildred Thompson to cut the ribbon."

Whatever excitement she was feeling for Curly at that moment flashed from her body like lightning gone to earth. Her blood froze. Her legs trembled. Her arms tingled all over with goose-pimples. Her mouth opened and closed like a goldfish in a bowl.

"Go on, Millie, have a go," said Eddie proudly.

"Ooh! I can't, I can't!" she gasped. "I'd feel so daft in front of all them people. What would Mum say?"

"One Millie Thompson coming up," shouted Curly, pushing her forward and pinching her bottom.

The hubbub subsided as Millie staggered like a drunken *prima donna*, swinging her hips in her tight little skirt and toppling on her stiletto heels. At least her make-up was perfection in the spotlights! A cheer of appraisal lifted the roof. She cut the ribbon to a burst of spontaneous applause. Councillor Purvis, who had been so full of pride and joy to see his precious Bowl open at last, was now appalled by the cat-calls and the wolf-whistles from the Curly crowd.

"How's about strippin' off for us, Millie?"

"Show us a leg, Millie!"

"Give us a kiss, Millie!"

Consternation broke loose as several lady councillors attempted to leave, closely followed by the stars-of-stage-and-screen. Millie was encouraged to say a few words to save the situation.

"Ooh, I can't, Mr. Purvis. No, no, Mr. Purvis."

"Now, don't be frightened, my dear," he said, pushing her forward.

Millie simpered. Millie beamed. Millie giggled. Millie tittered. Millie danced about as if she were doing the rhumba. Millie pressed her knees together and stuck out her behind in embarrassment. Millie put up her dainty little hand, crinkled her fingers and squeaked like a mouse: "Hello, boys!" This followed by shouts of "'Ere! 'Ere!" and "Well said, gel!" Amidst the general mayhem, Purvis was pale and poker-faced as Curly performed an insulting music-hall bow that nearly split his jeans.

Eddie was furious. While the crowds dispersed to the alleys and the dancing, and the autograph-hunters assailed the rapidly-retreating stars-of-stage-and-screen, he stood leaning against the door leading to the cloakrooms. Curly came across with Millie, his arm tight round her waist. Eddie wanted to say to her: "Come on, gel! Let's scarper on our own. I go for you in a big way. I think you're a real doll!" But all he said was: "You made a proper spectacle of yourself, you did."

Millie turned on him. "And who, if I might be so bold, Eddie Carpenter, do you think you're talking to, I'd like to know?"

"Who do you think? The Queen Mother?" He had that put-down look about him. "Come off it, Millie. Prancing about like the Queen of Tarts, you were." He didn't like her cheapening herself for Curly's sake.

"Here, I don't like your tone, see?" she said, waggling her head like her mother.

"Cut it!" said Curly on the attack.

"Fancy yourself, don't you, wiv yer smart talk?" said Eddie. "Who brung Millie 'ere in the first place? Slope off." He glared at Curly, but Curly wasn't used to being talked to like that, especially by a creep like Eddie. He grabbed him by the lapels.

"You bloody little twerp. Watch out, see, or I'll have the boys onto you. You just wait!"

As if from nowhere, three or four rough-looking individuals in leather jackets and army-surplus boots arrived on the scene. Eddie was pretty sure he recognised one of them at Ma Blackwood's Lollipop Shop when he had to take Mabel round for Mrs. Thompson. He could see Millie was scared to hell, and he realised there was no use drawing blood on either side, so he shook himself free and stepped out into the rain-sodden street.

20. Venus in Orbit

Even in Alf Thompson's young days, any courting there was to be done was confined to the front room, where parents could keep a close eye on the proceedings. If you were lucky, and you were raring to go a bit further, the trick was to find a dark corner down the back alley, out of the glare of the street lamps, for a long goodnight kiss, but that was all. There was none of that hanky-panky stuff.

Millie had strong feelings for Curly but she knew exactly how far she wanted to go . On this first time alone with him, she was wary of him, scared even. He was a big lad who didn't know his own strength, and, had she realised it, his own mind. She knew he was out for the whole box of tricks and she knew she couldn't comply. Stopping at the corner of the Villas, he turned to her, smirking and playing the Clark Gable with her.

"So what now?" he said.

Millie didn't say a word. She knew what he meant and waited for him to make the first move. One part of her, the cautious part, was quite prepared to say goodnight and go quietly home to bed alone. As for the other part, what an anticlimax it would be after such passionate stirrings as she had never felt before, flooding her whole being with a new kind of ecstasy.

Millie could still feel Curly's firm muscular body against hers, and suddenly he was pulling her down the street and into a dark secluded corner of No 3, over the rubble and broken window-frames and discarded rubbish. She found herself in what had been the back-room of the house. Curly was roused. He pressed hard against her, brutally, kissing her wildly on the lips, his hands roving down her thighs and up her skirt, searching for the thing he wanted most. Millie was moaning in her desire for his strong body to become part of her. She longed for him to take her, to overpower her.

Forcing her against the wall without any ceremony, he thrust into her clumsily. Just when he thought things were going as he wanted, Millie pushed him away.

"No!" she cried. "No, Curly, don't do that." His brutality made her afraid — feelings of guilt, confused with a thousand thoughts speeding through her brain, thoughts of what her mother would say if she knew, thoughts of.....

She wriggled away from him.

"What's the matter, now?" he said harshly. "What the bloody

hell d'you think you're doing? You want it as much as I do."

"Stop mauling me about," she said almost coquettishly. "Your getting too many ideas, you are. I'm not hanging around this dirty old place for you to take what you like, and me in me best outfit."

"Go on with yer," he whispered, hoarsely.

Millie could feel the heat of his breath on her neck as he nibbled at her with his lips and the tip of his tongue.

"Wherever did you learn that?" she said softly, rising again to the bait. He didn't answer. His silence spoke volumes. She began to give herself to him, slowly succumbing to his brute strength. She had no more resistence. A jab of pain gripped her as he pressed firmly against her with his loins.

"Oh, Curly, Curly, Curly!" she cried out into the hollow roofless house and out into the night sky. Her heart thrilled as one wave of passion after another seized her, surging through her uncontrollably, Curly kissing her on the neck and lips, she groaning with the sheer pleasure of it, he being so near.

Once again, a dark unwanted thought passed through Millie's mind like a storm-cloud. In that brief moment, she was filled with fear and remorse. She began pummelling him with her fists and pushing him away from her, biting him on the lips that had recently known only passion. He started to force her again, this time more cruelly, with more lust and urgency. Her resistence spurred him on until he felt the taste of blood in his mouth. Her fingernails scored his flesh. She struggled to free herself. His passion was released in a confusion of pain and ecstasy. Somewhere inside him, something that in other more fortunate beings might be called the soul, was being torn to shreds.

In that brief moment of immobility, the distraught Millie fled from the ruined house, sobbing profusely, and telling herself that she would never go with Curly Donoghue again, not for all the stars in the sky.

After some time, Curly came out into the street and stood under the laburnum tree in the darkness. His troubled thoughts were arrested suddenly by the appearance in an upper window at No 4 of what seemed to him a vision — the most beautiful girl he had ever seen, combing her long fair hair as she sat at her mirror. He observed her for quite some time, caught as if in a trance. He realised at that moment that there existed a superior kind of beauty that for him would be forever out of reach, a beauty that had the power to make his heart beat faster and his sense of loss seem all the greater.

21. The Eyes of the Beholder

After saying goodnight to Uncle Walter, Louise Paxton went to her room. As she sat at her dressing-table by the window, she began thinking about the things she would write in her diary. She wrote down some thoughts about a play by Bill Naughton she had heard on the wireless. A group of people from Wigan were on a coaching holiday to Rome. The characters were so real that she felt she knew them all personally. The documentary style made her feel it was all so true to life. The main character, a girl, had lost the power of speech. Louise could picture her now, in the Basilica of St. Peter, awestruck by its beauty, its magnificent statues of saints and popes, and the sheer vastness of it all. Yet she could not utter a single word to describe her remarkable experience. Louise identified herself with all that happened, especially the moment when the girl came out into the bright Italian sunlight, tears in her eyes at the thought of the black wintry streets of Wigan to which she was to return.

Louise put off until the last the account of her visit to the Roxy Picture House. She was unwilling to re-live those few moments of fear, yet she knew she would sleep more soundly for writing a description of them in her diary. *Vampire in Soho* had been a harrowing entertainment, if it could be called that, for the image of the dumb girl trapped in a house of terror haunted her.

The chimes of the Cathedral clock reminded Louise that it was already late. She paused in front of the dressing-table mirror and began gently and slowly combing her beautiful long hair.

Suddenly, she heard a woman cry out in the darkness. It seemed to be quite close by, in the street below somewhere. A shiver ran through her. She had the feeling she was not alone. Standing by the window, she felt afraid, listening, waiting. Outside on the landing all was quiet, save the snoring of Uncle Walter. She tried to convince herself that she was being childish. All the same, she put out the light, pulled up the bedclothes over her shoulders and somehow knew that she was not alone. Somewhere in the night out there, eyes were seeking her out, like fearsome scavengers of darkness.

Just at that moment, Eddie, on his way homewards from his frustrating evening out at the Purvis Bowl, caught sight of Millie running across the street. He could have sworn she had come out of the bombed house at No 3, but he couldn't be sure. When he thought a little more about it he realised what a cockeyed idea it was — and him a grown man!

103

22. The House of Sand

It was well past midnight before all the occupants of No 4 Laburnum Villas were tucked up in their beds. Flo tried to read herself to sleep with a travel article about Italy in one of Millie's glossy magazines. Exotic scenes of golden sands and cypress groves and 'beautiful people', the smart young set, strolling along a river in the bright sunshine. A good-looking girl, wearing a stylish long-skirted white summer dress was laughing with a handsome youth. Flo had a dress like that once — just before the war. There was a photograph of her wearing it when she went with Alf on a trip down the Thames to Margate on the Golden Eagle. It was a day of utter happiness.... The images began slowly to fade as she drifted off into sleep.

Quite unexpectedly, in her dreams, a book, bound in orange, green and brown leather, came to her. Opening the book, she saw a picture of a maiden in a flowing white dress wandering beside a fast-flowing river, bordered by dark green cypresses

Below the cypresses and beyond the curve of the river, Flo saw a fine expanse of golden sand. She knew in her dream-state that she must reach it at all costs. With the sand she built a house and decorated it with sea-shells. Now she was inside the sandy shell of her house and she was frightened....

The clock in the front room struck a mournful two. Mrs. Thompson turned from side to side restlessly and woke up in an agitated state of mind. What with Millie coming in so late and Alf snoring his head off, she decided to go downstairs and make herself a cup of cocoa. In spite of the draining-board being piled up with last night's unwashed supper things, she enjoyed the quiet of the kitchen. She began to day-dream about all the up-to-date improvements she would like if only Alf could bring home a bonus from the tannery. A washing-machine would come in handy and perhaps one of those electric irons and a few pieces of that new G-Plan furniture and a food-mixer and some smart formica work-tops and a Ewbank carpet-sweeper and...... She began to nod a little and her half-formed thoughts began to merge with vaguely familiar images of a house of sand. Then she remembered as clear as day her strangely exotic dream.

Opening the dresser-cupboard, she took down her copy of *Gypsy Finnigan's Dream Book*, turning to the letter B. Passing by such unlikely dream images as *Bigamy*, *Bird's nest* and *Bluebottle*, she came across a reference to *Book*:

104

*A new book with a gaily coloured binding shows that
you have long cherished the desire to become an author!*

'What tommy rot!' she thought. 'It'd be a lark if I ever wrote a
book. I could tell them a thing or two, I could. How anybody could
dream about Bigamy and Bluebottles was a mystery, but what the
dickens was the name of that tree? Once more she read down the
incongruous list: *Cowslip, Cricket, Currant cake, Custard*, until she
came to *Cypress*.

To dream of a cypress tree denotes the end of a cherished hope.

The more Flo read the more confused she became. Even the
colours were conflicting. Green meant hope and high attainment in life.
Orange stood for vivid personality and a person of ideas. Brown foretold
an ordinary life led by an unambitious character content with the present.
'Content with the present! That's a laugh, I must say!' she
thought.
After all this, Flo didn't know where she was. The river meant
trouble coming. She was going to be a writer yet at the same time she
would lead a routine life, even with her 'vivid personality', and all that
twaddle. She decided to take a last sip of cocoa and go off to bed. In
the meantime, perhaps she would look up S for *Sand*. But first she had
to wade through *Sailor, Salmon, Salad* and *Salt* before getting to the
point of her dream:

> *To dream of walking on a large expanse of
> sand shows you are restless. You have a longing for
> the unattainable. You are seeking what you can never
> find. If an anemone were found in the sand, it would
> be a hopeful sign that, after a time of waiting, you
> would find true fulfilment of your desires.*

Only one thing worried Flo Thompson, as she lay listening to
Alf's snoring at her side a few moments later. As much as she attempted
to recapture her golden sands, she couldn't for the life of her remember
finding an anemone in her dream.
Sometime just after six o'clock, the whole house was awakened
by an impatient Mabel demanding attention.
"Hark at that damned kid on the piano," Alf Thompson

grumbled into Flo's unreceptive ear. "What a bloody racket! Enough to send you up the creek, it is. Saturday mornin' an' all. Cor! stone the crows! Can't she find something better to do? Go and give her a clout, go on."

As he turned over to the wall, muttering to himself, Flo stopped talking in her sleep and curled herself up in a twisted lump in the middle of the bed. Alf stuck his rear-end into her back and she woke, suddenly, with a little kick of the feet.

"Oh, Alf!" she sighed. "I was just having a nice dream. Go and tell her yourself."

Alf, grumbling and swearing, crawled across her, half asleep, and collapsed on the edge of the bed. Mabel was causing an ear-splitting cacophony to rise up the stairs and force its way into every nook and cranny. He clambered downstairs and put his head round the door of the front-room and whispered throatily:

"Turn it up, Mabel, can't you? At this hour of the morning, too."

Mabel looked as if she was going to cry. She had that bloated-cheek expression and went all water-eyes quite suddenly. She stopped playing instantly and was clearly thinking of giving quite another kind of performance as far as Alf could judge. He staggered into the kitchen, took a tin of sweets from the dresser, and returning with a handful, he thrust them into Mabel's plump little fingers.

"Now, for pity's sake, pack it in or I'll get your mother to wallop you one as you won't forget for many a long year, my gel."

Meanwhile, Mrs. Thompson, now that she had the bed to herself, had returned to her dreaming. Try as she would, she could not catch the treasured image she had lost. Two men, dressed in black, were standing before her, pushing their fingers into the sandy walls and floors, and shaking their heads and saying that she had been mistaken in trying to build her house of sand alone. It would crumble as it was crumbling now, walls toppling, floors disintegrating, and she, falling, falling, falling......falling into the swirling grey waters of the river, and all around her, the chink-chink-chink of the shells breaking up like little pieces of glass from a splintered window.

Flo woke with a start. Alf was putting a bag under the bed. He swore as the glass chinked. "Blast their little bottle-tops!" he muttered with a smile. Flo turned over.

"Alf, whatever are you doing down there on the floor?"

"What the 'ell do you think?"

106

Without so much as a by-your-leave, he climbed over Flo and pulled up her nightdress with his rough horny hands.

Afterwards, as Flo was dressing, she looked in the mirror at her drawn and haggard face, with the lines round the corners of her mouth, and she wondered about the beautiful maiden in the dream, the two men in black, and the crumbling house of sand.

By the time she had dressed and brushed her lustreless and rebellious hair into some sort of order, Alf had turned over on his back and was snoring loudly, but all that day she would not be able to get those dream-images out of her mind.

Flo sat down at the kitchen table and tried to write down her dream-memories in as logical a sequence as she was capable of. As she wrote, a host of images from the past came flooding into her mind and she began to see, through the hopelessness of her existence, a meaning to things that had been and gone forever and a deep foreboding of the shape of things to come.

EPISODE FIVE

A Saturday in April

Spring Fever

23   The Desert of Love

Saturday afternoon tea was more of a high-tea in the Thompson household and something of a ritual since all the members of the family were expected to be present. It never once occurred to any of them not to be. They had always been present and they always would be. Once the last cake had been consumed and the last cup of tea emptied down to the tea-leaves, they all felt free to move to their strategic positions for defence or attack according to temperament. The only difference being that instead of two opponents playing to win, there were five, each one fighting for his own life on the same battleground.

As the case may be, they slipped or rolled or pitched or slumped into a variety of home positions like balls in a penny slot-machine. The preliminary stage of the battle was a contest of silence, or rather, stupor. The cold war was on.

Alf, newly restored, would place himself in his favourite position next to the wireless, which he would proceed to fiddle about with, twiddling the knobs, turning from one station to another, loud, soft, full tone, dry tone, velvet tone, scratchy tone, long wave, medium wave, short wave, until heads were aching and ears singing with the mad whirl of sound filling the room — and all in an effort to track down the football results. Millie would bury her nose in the pages of *Glamour Girl* and live the life of the fashionable set. Flo would get out her knitting — bedsocks, bed-jackets, pullovers, mittens, and her special passion — babies' layettes, even though she knew of no-one who was either having a baby or who had a brother who had a friend whose wife's cousin's daughter might just possibly be in the family way.

Always in the resentful silence of the post-tea-time stupor, the contrapuntal click of knitting needles played a part in the concert of sounds created by Alf on his old wireless set. Ron would lie on his stomach, on the hearth-rug, lost in the latest issues of *Beano* and *Dandy*. Mabel was plumped into a large arm-chair and given her golly, Inky, to play with.

Inky had part of his head missing. Mabel had once upon a time tried to give him a singe and inadvertently set light to his hair. His head had melted and Mabel screamed with the horror of it all as she watched his eyes, then his nose, then his mouth slump into a congealed mess of wax. Now his hair was made up of the bristles from one of Flo's old brooms, giving him the appearance of being perpetually frightened, a sort of pasty-faced golly. Inky seemed to be the only one of Mabel's friends who could keep her quiet these days.

The really farcical moment of the afternoon would come when Mrs. Thompson returned from putting away the tea-things, to claim her chair by the fire, on the opposite side to Alf. The trouble was, Millie used to sit in her mother's chair, just to get warm. When Flo came in, confusion followed close behind. Up Millie would get, with anything but an overdose of graciousness. This was routine stuff and usually pursued its course in the following manner:

"Don't move, dear. I can sit here," Mrs. T. would say, pointing to Millie's usual chair in which Ron was now slumped.

"No!" Millie would mutter, half getting up. "Really, I don't mind."

"As I said, dear," remonstrates Mrs. T. "I don't mind a change for a bit."

"No, it's all right, Mum. Here you are. Come on Ron, move out."

"Oh, crikey! Do I have to?" says the benighted Ron.

"Oh, all right! Come on Mabel. Move out of my chair."

"Oh, for gawd' sake, don't move Mabel, Ron," says Mrs. T. "She's been screaming at me all day. I don't want her to start up again."

"O.K." says Ron, "I'll stay here and Millie can sit in Mabel's chair."

"No, really!" says Flo," I don't mind at all, really I don't. I'll sit in Mabel's chair."

In spite of all this pantomime, Millie would insist on Ron moving, and Ron would insist on Mabel moving, so that suddenly the whole room seemed to be on the move. It was like a game of musical chairs without the music, unless it was Alf's snoring.

The evening was drawing in. On this particular day it was cold and dark for the time of year and Flo decided to light a fire. The street lamps began to come on, lighting up the faces of the occupants of the little front room as if they were part of some strange *tableau vivant.*

Alf awoke with a start and gazed blearily at all the upping and downing of this wayward family of his. Like a batch of hens on a roost, they were! Through all this kafuffle Alf had missed the football results and turned off the wireless in disgust.

Once more the family settled into its familiar stupor. Ron sat gazing into the fire, thinking about his afternoon at the Roxy. Millie was knitting a violet angora bed-jacket to go with her latest lilac cotton night-dress. Flo said she thought 'violent' was a lovely colour and how it did suit her complexion, but Millie was too busy thinking about Curly. Alf was back in a troubled sleep again, his lips bubbling, giving out from time to time a low shushing sound that entered somewhere into Flo's dreaming and she was back on her golden sands again.

There was an atmosphere about the room of a Quaker meeting, each supplicant sending up signals to the Almighty, each wondering who would break the silence and rise to tell of the wonder of revelation. Only, at this moment, there seemed so little chance of such a thing happening. Just now it was the old green marble clock on the mantelpiece that brought everyone to their senses. The knitting needles started clicking again. The hot coals and ash collapsed suddenly in the grate making them all start.

"Six o'clock!" said Flo. Her voice was like a gun-shot. They all came out of their reveries. Not a word was spoken, only, in the silence, the clock seemed to be having an attack of indigestion. Five heavy thuds on a cracked bell, accompanied by an indescribable cacophony of metal scraping metal and a variety of plinkings and whirrings might have given the impression that the clock was about to vomit its innards out all over the hearth. Silence returned reluctantly to emphasise the sudden introduction to the orchestral wind of Flo's inside mixed with the staccato sounds of Millie's knitting needles.

"Did you say it was six o'clock, Millie?" said Flo.

"Oh, Mum! You said it yourself. I don't care what it is. Why don't you listen to what people say for a change?"

"I was only asking," said Flo.

Another long silence followed, ultimately to be broken by Millie:

"Can I have my programme on?"

"Oh, please don't wake him up now there is a bit of peace and quiet. I could put a hammer through that blinking wireless sometimes, I could really."

"I'm fed up with this house, I reelly am," Millie remonstrated. "Can't never do what you want. Always somebody putting their spoke in."

"Now Millie! Your Dad's having another little snooze, so do be quiet. I could just do with a bit of peace."

"Well, I don't see why I can't have my programme. I'm going to be a singer, I am, and I want to hear my programme 'cause there's a girl who won the same competition as I'm goin' in for."

Millie was hoping for some interest to be shown in her new

venture but all her mother said was:

"He hasn't had a nap like this for weeks. Must be all that beer he got through this morning."

"Did I tell you," said the persevering Millie, "this woman who interviewed me at the Roxy this afternoon says I've got a good natural voice. That's what she said. So there!" She thought: 'Put that in your pipe and smoke it!'

"I wish I could sleep like he does," said Flo, dreamily. "It'd do me a power of good. Goes right off in a second, he does. Takes me hours, and about half-a-dozen aspirins as well."

"She says if I keep on," said Millie defiantly, "I might have a chance of getting to the top. That's what she says."

"Sleep does you good, though," said Flo. "What with your Dad coming home drunk half the time, I don't wonder I can't sleep."

"And then I'd be in the money, see? And if I ever am, I won't stop in this dump!" said Millie, raising her voice. "I won't stop in this rotten house a second longer than I have to."

"I can tell you," said Flo to deaf ears, "I'm that tired, washing and ironing, and shopping and cooking. There's no end to it. Day after day, year after year, it goes on, and nobody ever thinks of me, do they?"

"I'm tired of this bloody house, I am," cried Millie. "Tired, tired, tired! I tell you."

"Tired," said Flo, "At everybody's beck and call, I am."

And so the remorseless theme and variations droned on.

"Oh!" exclaimed Millie, beside herself with the whole thing. "I'm going to turn it on whether he likes it or not."

Alf woke with a jerk and a start. Millie was twiddling to find her station, and then, quite alarmingly, the room exploded with the deafening sound of the announcer's voice.

"Turn it down, can't you," Alf shouted.

Suddenly the sensuous warmth of a female voice, cooing softly to the cool beat of a three-piece band came over the ether and Millie was in seventh heaven. Rosemary Clooney, here I come, she was thinking. Peggy Lee, Dixie Dee, who cares. She closed her eyes and slid back into her chair. But not for long. Alf wanted the racing results and uttered and spluttered his first animated remark of the evening:

"What a BLOODY ROW!"

He switched over to his own station. Millie jumped up and switched it back, flopping back into her chair and pouting at the dying embers in despair.

113

"Leave the damned thing alone, will you," muttered Alf. "I want my racing results."

"And a fat lot of good that'll do you," Millie grumbled.

There followed an incomprehensible list of names, odds, winners, losers and also-rans which Millie could see no sense in, but which Flo accepted as a suitable accompaniment to her knitting needles. This was almost the only peaceful contact she had with her husband.

"This house 'll drive me mad," Millie spluttered. "Right up the flippin' creek, it will!"

For a moment, further altercation was avoided by Ron coming to life out of an article in the *Evening Standard*.

"Dad!"

"What now?" said Alf.

"What's the meaning of uni– unilat–eral–ism?"

"What a damned silly question to ask!"

"Oh, come on, Dad. What's it mean?"

"Don't be so blinkin' lazy. Go and look it up in one of your school books."

" 'Cos it's something to do with peace. Says so here, so you ought to know. You was in the war."

Alf resigned himself to his fate.

"What did you say it was?"

"Unilateralism," Ron repeated with difficulty.

"Well, that's simple. What's the wording, as you might say?"

"It's some MP bloke. He says: 'Unilateralism is not internationalism. It is a nationalist ego gone mad.' "

"Blimey! What kind of bloody lingo is that?"

"English, soppy!" said Ron, taking the matter seriously.

" Well, who flipping well said a damned stupid thing like that, then?"

"Lord Dalton."

"Lord Dalton, eh? Well, he's a right boy, he is. Knows his kippers, he does. Yeah!"

"But what *is* unilateralism?"

"Well, let's see," said Alf, desperately, in support of Lord Dalton's argument and bitterly regretting having any kids in the first place. "Well, it's what the old geezer believes in. It's his belief, you see. When he gets up on his old plates of meat in the parliament, he says 'I believe in' – you know, this thing your was talking about. Like some blokes might get up in church and say 'I believe in God' and all that

114

lark."

"Is believing in God the same as unilateralism, then?" said the awakening young Ron.

"Well, yeah!" said Alf, at last beginning to see light at the end of the tunnel. "That's right. Clever boy, our Ron, eh Flo?"

Flo was miles away on her patch of golden sand. Ron made further use of the ensuing silence.

"And what's 'un – pal– at–able'?"

"Oh, for crying out loud!" muttered Alf. "Read to yourself, can't you?"

"But what is it, Dad?"

"I told you. Go and look it up in your books. Don't keep asking me questions."

"Will you tell me, Millie?"

"Oh, what is it," she said, tearing her eyes away from a photo in *Glamour Girl* of the luscious Elvis.

With an air of resignation, Ron said: "Dr. Edith Summer – skill said: 'Nagging is the repetition of un– pal– a – table truths'"

The mystified Millie was saved by the timely intervention of Mrs. Thompson, who said:

"If you took as much interest in your lessons as you do in the newspaper, we'd be a lot happier and you'd be able to answer your own silly questions yourself."

Ron wanted to fling the paper on the fire and start a great conflagration. Millie wanted her pop songs. Mabel wanted to scream. Alf wanted to go back to sleep and couldn't with all the racket his family were making. Flo by now had a headache and longed for some peace and quiet. Her thoughts were drifting back to her golden sands and the white dress and the two men poking their fingers into the walls of her house of sand. Now, disturbed by family discord, she wanted to cry and cry, as she had in her dream. In fact, she was on the point of doing so when Millie leapt out of her chair and switched on the centre bulb, flooding the room with a harsh white light.

"I'm getting out of this house," she shouted hysterically, "and I'm going to have a good time as I've never done before. You can all go and stew in your own juice, the lot of you."

With this outburst, she flounced out of the room, slammed the door and stomped upstairs in a fury to put her face on. Mrs. Thompson assumed her hoity-toity expression again, her thoughts being whisked around inside her head, like particles of dust in a Hoover bag. She

115

leaned forward to poke the fading embers of the fire as Alf turned up the football results to full volume.

"Is there never going to be any peace in this place?" he shouted when he realised he had missed the results after all.

Dark grey smoke crawled lazily up the chimney. All the glow in the coal had disappeared. A troubled peace was once more restored. Mabel was at last on better terms with Inky. Ron was battling with a crossword. The clock struck its cracked and mournful seven. Sometime later, Flo said:

"That was six o'clock, wasn't it? Or was it seven?" — but no-one bothered to put her right. Resignedly, she finished her row of stitches, cast off, and put her knitting away in its old cloth bag.

"I suppose I shall have to get our tea. Eddie'll be round for his usual any minute. He'll be hungry, I expect."

Her voiced trailed off. No-one was listening. No-one cared. They were far too busy working out their own problems to be in the smallest degree interested in the tedious domesticity of life at No 4. When the food was ready, they would, like zombies, obediently repair to the table to sit in their customary places. It would be something to fill in the time. After their high tea, they would go their separate ways, each one little caring what the others did. Only Flo would be left to cope with a sinkful of washing-up!

24   Desire Caught by the Tail

As far as Millie was concerned, whether it was visitors coming to tea or she was going out, it wasn't the washing and the dressing that took the time, it was putting on her face. If Millie went upstairs first you could be sure she would be the last to come down. True, her hair, her toe-nails, her fingernails, — all required the most careful attention. Never was there in the Thompson household, and not in the whole of Rothersey either, so much petting and cutting, patting and pushing, snipping and clipping, douching and shaving, combing and general tarting-up done to one human form — but her face! — well, that was a real pantomime! She succeeded with the help of innumerable powders, mascaras, rouges, lip-sticks, foundation creams, cold creams, oils and unguents, eye-shadows and toilet-waters, in transfiguring herself into an entirely different being. It was doubtful if any but her closest friends would have recognised her at all without her face on. To Miss Baldock, she appeared to be about to step on stage at the Windmill. To little brother Ron, she seemed to possess the face of a circus clown. To Curly and his mates at *The Bed of Roses* she looked more like one of the tarts on Rothersey High Street and much less easily have-able! The thick layers of creams and powders set like a mask so that nothing seemed to move except her eyes and lips.

The changes wrought to this tailor's dummy were remarkable. Eye-brows, instead of falling at the corners, went riding up on the forehead like a demon's, giving her an expression of permanent surprise. Silver-blue eye-shadow lent a pseudo-sensuous leer to her otherwise pretty eyes. Red dots in the corners bestowed the whites with a tinge of blue. The slightly drooping mouth was turned upwards to parallel the eye-brows, giving the impression that she was perpetually smiling. The colour of her skin was transformed from a natural 'peaches-and-cream' to a scorched cardboard with something of the texture of it, too. There is no doubt that this extraordinary apparition would have the desired effect on Curly and the Purvis Bowl lads if the chorus of wolf-whistles was anything to go by.

Millie, magically transformed into a pantomime doll, came downstairs in a petulant mood, not bothering to call out to her mother, as she went out, pulling the front door to with a bang and a rattle. She was wild with frustration, and reckless with it. It was timely, therefore, that a sobering 'Angel Gabriel' appeared before her in the guise of Joe Purvis, just about to put his key in the lock of No 1.

"Hello Millie! Where are you off to now?"

"Wouldn't you like to know?"

"Well, why not come in and have a drink? The company of such a pretty young lady as you is always a pleasure."

"A drink!" simpered Millie. "I know what your drinks are like! Remember?"

"Well, just a small one," he said, opening the door for her without even knowing if she would accept. She stepped in, brushing past him in a provocative way, making his heart race.

At that moment, Curly turned into the street on his way to collect Millie, hoping she would be in the mood for a bit of fun at the Purvis Bowl. He hadn't been around for some weeks as he had been a special guest of Her Majesty at the 'Scrubs' for a little spot of house-breaking. He was just in time to catch a glimpse of Millie's sexy little rump disappearing once again into the Councillor's house! Curly wheeled round in anger and made his way towards the Purvis Bowl.

Half-an-hour later, Millie emerged from No 1 and set off unsteadily towards the High Street. As she made her way up the ramp leading into the Purvis Bowl, the boys closed in on her, touching her, offering fruity suggestions as to how she might spend her evening with them. Curly soon put a stop to this wolf-play. One look and they were creeping off into the crowds as if they had never seen Millie in their lives.

"Talk about a tough guy, Curly. You're a one, if ever there was." He gripped her angrily by the arm.

"Ouch! That hurts, Curly."

"Don't you mess with me. I've seen what you get up to. I don't put up with no nonsense from tarts like you."

"What d'yer mean? 'Tarts like me'?" He led her into the hall.

"Never you mind. You'll find out soon enough," he growled.

Cool rhythms oozed through the speakers and Millie relaxed into the warm atmosphere, the hall half-filled with the early crowds of young lads and girls. With Curly next to her, something happened inside Millie. Pleasure spread through her as she felt his thigh press against her, his arm firmly round her slim little waist. The warmth of his breathing made her tingle with his nearness. They were standing next to a pillar by the bowling lanes. He pulled her to him almost brutally, running his fingers up under her hair and then down her spine and under her arms to her breasts, making her dissolve against the sheer manliness of his body. His strength and muscularity made her heart flip. His hands roamed down over her neat little bottom, sending a tremor right through her. Millie wanted Curly more than all the stars in the sky, and Curly knew it.

Suddenly, without a word, he left her and walked over to hire his shoes. When he had changed into them, he ran his hand down over his fly to make sure that everything was in place, stuck out his chest, and glanced with scorn at the Teddy-boys with their drainpipe pants and bum-freezer jackets. Bloody little pansies, he thought, with their tarty little brides. They knew when Curly Donoghue meant business. They'd better keep their distance or there'd be some blood spilt before the night was out. It did Curly a power of good to see them all ogling Millie.

Curly booked the lane for eight o'clock. He was just getting set to show the lot of them who was boss around the Purvis Bowl when he was forestalled by a small incident which put him off his stride. The crowd had suddenly been attracted by a small pimply youth in a long tweedy sweater who was playing on Curly's patch. He was throwing his pin-scuttler down the lane. He let it ride the centre as straight as a die, knocking the centre pin down dead-on and all the other nine with it. Cheers went up. Curly sneered.

"Beat that if you can," said somebody from the crowd who knew Curly. Curly strutted up, bracing himself, flexing his muscles like a boxer in the ring.

"You potty little poof!" he said. "Get back up the West End where the likes of you belong. Give over, or I'll tear the skirts off of you." The Soho whipper-snapper raised himself to his full four-foot-ten-and-a-half, saying:

"Everything comes to him who waits."

"Wait any longer and you'll get your fanny kicked in, get me?"

"Who do you think you're talking to, might I ask?" he said, rather in a Flo Thompson manner. "I've got my rights as much as you have."

"Rights or tights, you aint hanging about here no longer, else I'll bash your snotty little nose into the back of your face so you won't recognise it. Get me?"

The boy shrugged his shoulders nonchalantly and minced past Curly saying with a solicitous grin:

"Nasty spoilsport! Anyway, come up and see me sometime, darling."

There was giggling all round, and wolf-whistling, as he camped off into the bar. Curly was fit to murder.

The pins were replaced automatically and Curly took up a pin-scuttler. It was heavier than he had anticipated, this sixteen-pounder. His fingers felt too big and thick inside the holes. He gripped hard and cast away. Before he knew what was happening, he was following himself bodily down the alley and the bell was ringing up a 'foul' as he shot over the foul-line and everybody was laughing at him. As he picked himself up, he scowled unsportsmanlike at the toothy faces. He'd show them, the bastards! The pin-scuttler was returned on the under-lane. Gathering all his strength, bracing every muscle in his muscle-bound body (which did not go unnoticed by the excited Millie) he cast the scuttler away down the gleaming lane. It clattered about like an over-sized billiard ball, zig-zagging from side to side in a frenzy, and, as it reached the end, it dribbled away down the side, lethargically knocking down the end pin. Millie was laughing her teeth out.

"Ha! Ha! Hee! Hoo! Oh Curly, you are a caution. You're

119

killing me, really you are."

And there she was, doubling up and teetering, pressing her fists into her thighs and giggling for all she was worth.

"Shut up!" said Curly angrily. Millie was in stitches.

"SHUT UP! You bleeding little tart." Millie stopped dead.

"Here!" she said. "Don't you give me that, Curly Donoghue. Who do you think you are?"

He pushed her out through the rows of smirking local lads. His emotions were surging up in him like a volcano. He was mad with everybody. He was mad at the instructor with his big ideas about 'ten-four splits' and 'belly-drop balls' and 'body-English' and 'gutter-curves' — what the hell was the use of it. The bloody little twerp, showing off like that, with 'PB' written on the front of his sweater. He'd give him a belly-drop he wouldn't forget in a hurry, and as for that old bugger Purvis, he give him a ten-four split he'd remember for many a year to come.

Curly had wanted to play the 'big star' for Millie, show her a nice bit of muscle. But, no! Instead of that they'd all made him look stupid, taken the mickey out of him and laughed their bloody heads off. Three bob down the drain for a fifty-minute game that lasted five. He'd show Millie who the real Curly Donoghue was.

Millie was by stages frightened what Curly would do next, then she was excited by his brute force, then she was scared about what her mother would say if she heard about everything, then forgot it all when Curly led her through the glass doors of the *Danse Macabre Club*.

The thrill of the beat and the jiving partners on the floor swept through her as she waggled her hips about, kicked up her stiletto heels, and clung to Curly with more ecstasy than she could bear. But she could see that even by the second number he was on edge. The music was getting on his nerves. A good-looking boy began dancing a threesome with her and Curly. Millie stuck out her bottom, purred and gurgled to the beat of the drums, flicked her fingers in the air to the frenzied saxophonist's playing. The other boy started to muscle in on her. Without Millie in his arms, Curly was lost out there on the floor. He didn't know what he was supposed to do. Suddenly he couldn't stand any more of it. Anyway, who the hell *was* this guy making up to Millie? Curly swung round and punched him in the face. The youth crumpled on the floor. Amid gasps all round, Curly grabbed Millie and dragged her towards the door.

"Let go, Curly. People are looking."

"Let them bloody-well look. Bugger the lot of them!"

He got hold of Millie and shook her and shook her again like dice in a gambler's hands. Millie swore. Millie struggled to get free. Curly put his muscular arms round her, spread his hands over her back, pressed his thighs against her, and one minute Millie was swearing like a wild-cat and fighting tooth and claw, and the next moment she was kissing Curly full on the lips.

"I've got something for you," he said in a suggestive tone. She giggled and squirmed at the innuendo. He slipped a diamond ring over her finger, sparkling and flashing all the colours of the rainbow and she felt so proud to be Curly's girl at last.

"Where *did* you find this little beauty?"

"Never you mind! Let's go," he said, with his poker face.

"O.K. Curly," whispered Millie. "You say where."

In the dark of Curly's room, they undressed. He came to her and laid the whole weight of his body against her. She couldn't remember now, but she felt she had read somewhere in *Glamour Girl* that sex would be like this. As she lay under him, he put his arms round her, clumsily kissing her all the time, on her shoulders, on her breasts. Slowly, every part of her began to respond to him. A wave of ecstasy began to rise up from deep inside her, engulfed her, and she gasped as he ran his tongue over her soft white skin. Sometimes he was rough with her, hurting her so that she cried out and the pain became part of the passion. Some primitive sense of guilt at giving herself body and soul so freely made her almost wish to be absolved in some way from the inevitable consequences. Her fear soon began to melt and her whole being no longer belonged to her. A second delicious wave rose up and enveloped her as he moved rhythmically against her, groaning in his pleasuring of her. As he grew near, a long surge of ecstasy began to flow through every part of her, a long, slow unstoppable flow that enveloped her totally. In her otherwise uneventful life, Millie was at last experiencing the most beautiful and unforgettable moment imaginable, and she wanted it to go on and on and on.

It was past midnight when Millie reached home. As she turned into Laburnum Villas and scratched about in her handbag for the keys, she caught sight of her ring as it sparkled in the bluish light of the moon. She wanted so much to be in Curly's arms. A tinge of sadness passed through her like a shadow and disappeared as suddenly as it came. She could not think why it was or what it was, only that it had something to do with Curly, perhaps the sudden fit of anger, or was it despair, after he had finished with her, the almost heartless way he told her to get dressed and go home, the strange haunted look of a man with troubled thoughts. Perhaps it was only her own feelings — an emptiness, even a sense of loneliness when the ecstasy was over. Or was it, after all, a premonition?

Opening the door of No 4, she was struck by the unfamiliarity of the house and everything in it. She felt like an intruder. As she climbed the familiar stairs, it seemed to her that she was walking on alien territory.

Millie Thompson was afraid. Life now had a new meaning, a new hope. Those people she had known only this afternoon as Mum and Dad and Ron and Mabel, seemed to fall into place like the matching pieces of a jig-saw puzzle. They took on a deeper significance. She would no longer fight against them for she could no longer fight against herself. She seemed to have found the secret of her existence and cherished it within her.

25. Going Round in (Vicious) Circles

Curly flung himself on the bed and clutched at the pillows. The cold night air pinched his flesh into goose pimples but he was too pent up to care. His dream-world, which he had believed to be reality itself, was crumbling about him mercilessly. His brain was a swirling mass of confused thoughts, jumbled memories. He was searching for some kind of order out of chaos, but it did not make an appearance. All he could think of that made any sense at all was Millie, having her there next to him on the bed. The one and only ambition in his life had been to go with a woman, yet it had been the one ambition in all his twenty-three years he had feared most to achieve. Sex was to him the only pleasure through which he might escape from the dreariness of his life at Ma Blackwood's lodging-house.

There was, too, the hatred Curly felt for anybody who had a hold over him, people like Andrew Crawford and Pa Blackwood. In these circumstances, sex was his only thrill, his only panacea in his ever-darkening world. His jealousy of the other lads in the market was deep and bitter, so much so that he had made up tales of his prowess a dozen times over, like the one about the cinema-usherette he had had in the back row of the stalls one Monday afternoon at the Roxy. He had told that story so often now that he had come to believe it himself. He could look back on it as a real fact, but then, there were all too many 'real facts' about Curly's private life, as trumped up and spurious as his imitation leather jacket.

As for the diamond sparkler, he had had to promise to pay Ma Blackwood fifty nicker for it. How about that? Fifty nicker was going to be difficult to get, unless, of course, he could think of a plan. Why was it that old sod Purvis suddenly came into his mind?

At the same time, there slid surreptitiously into his thoughts the vision of the girl combing her long fair hair at her window. This momentary vision of ideal beauty had brought him as near to perfect love as he could ever be. Now a wave of hopelessness spread through his whole body and flooded his mind. He realised the unwarranted shabbiness of his life and tears came to his eyes.

In the queer silence of his room, he remembered these things and they hurt. He pressed his face into the pillow and thought of Millie's breasts, her soft skin and her body under him, the sensuous giving and taking beneath him, and, amidst the sheer physical pleasure, how numb he had felt in his heart.

The more he thought about it the more desperate he grew. Rage in his heart, he wanted to shout all the filth of the gutter into the night. War had been declared between his body and his mind. This division within him tore at his reason like jealous demons sharing a sinner's soul. They ripped into his very guts with their claws and he cried out, oh yes, how he cried out in such anguish, till his body shook convulsively.

In a flash, he was leaping from the bed, ripping at the sheets, tearing them with his fingers, tugging at the brass bedstead till it shook and swayed like a hanger in a hurricane. He smashed the mirror in the wardrobe door and watched his body disintegrate as the glass fell in fragments to the floor. He swung a chair against the bed and swung it again until it broke into a pile of firewood. He thrust his arms through the window panes till the blood flowed. He swept the wash-bowl from its stand so that it smashed against the tiles of the iron grate. Lunging and punching, he grew drunk with his own power to destroy. The room was littered with broken glass, splintered wood and twisted metal, and everywhere a cloud of white feathers floating in the air and descending like snow, till the whole room was like a battleground in winter. In the middle of it all, Curly stood screaming and shouting obscenities, blood streaming down his face and arms.

Ma Blackwood was banging frantically on the door in a

desperate attempt to make herself heard, afraid that murder was taking place under her own roof. Had she known how near she was to the truth, she might perhaps have treated Curly differently when Pa finally came and smashed the door in. Indeed, a murder *had* taken place — a bitter struggle between that last glimmer of hope that clings to lost love, and the endless wastes of despair that lie beyond. As Curly stood quietly sobbing his heart out, there was no question as to which of them had won.

EPISODE SIX

A Saturday in early June

Paving the Way!

26. Sparrow Grass!

The Thompson family never managed to gird up their loins and take themselves off to the countryside. They had never had any wish to visit Hampstead Heath and had only once been to Battersea Park when the funfair was in town and Mabel screamed the place down on catching sight of the Bearded Lady. They had no particular wish to see the purple swathes of bluebells and avenues of pink and crimson rhododendrons at Kew in springtime. Unlike Timothy, they had no knowledge of English lanes in early summer, lined with hedgerows of hawthorn blossom like drifts of summer snow, and meadows golden with buttercups. Flo could not even remember the last time she saw Rothersey Public Gardens, unless it was the time when Alf tried something on under the beech trees once. But that was almost beyond memory.

In Rothersey Market now, it was the pea season, a time of rich pickings for market gardeners like John Garville, with runner beans and marrows and radishes and lettuce and asparagus all coming on faster than you could sell the stuff. Andrew Crawford, on the other hand, without the help of Timothy's youthful vigour, was struggling to make ends meet. Ray had not proved as reliable as he had hoped and, frankly, things looked grim for the future of the farm.

All this, however, was lost on Mrs Thompson who had never bothered to shell a pea on her life and certainly not taken a knife to a fresh runner bean. It was all too labour-intensive. A couple cans of tinned peas from Marley's Stores would do just as well.

As for Mabel, well, she had other things on her mind than asparagus, a luxury which even Smutty would hardly have sniffed at had Mrs. Thompson been able to stretch the weekly shopping bill that far.

"I won't 'ave none o' that sparrow-grass!" she told Miss Baldock, who once brandished a bunch in front of Flo's nose in her superior kind of way.

On this particular June morning, the early sun would have come pouring through the windows of the front bedroom of the Thompson household had the curtains not refused to allow it to enter. Not a sound came from the grown-ups, save the occasional snort from Alf! But something was astir all the same.

Washing and dressing for Mabel Thompson were necessary but irksome preliminaries to each exciting and over-crowded day. In contrast to her sister Millie, the time devoted to these necessities was phenomenally brief. Washing and dressing were performed under

126

duress, not to assist decorum, nor to avoid impropriety, but to pander to the demands of the grown-ups. In her little pink-flowered nightie, she would jump out of bed into her Mickey Mouse slippers and run into the bathroom faster than Smutty running for his dinner. A hand under the cold tap (ugh!) and a sprinkle of cold water over her face (UGH!) sufficed for the job in hand on this particular Saturday morning. After all, the sun was shining.

On any other lazy June morning Mabel might have amused herself by quietly slipping into the bedrooms of Ron and her parents to observe their sleeping habits. Nothing interested her more that the curious nocturnal idiosyncrasies of the weird and wonderful big people.

Naturally enough, for the reason that Mabel didn't have to get out of bed to look at her, she would begin with Millie. She was right there by her side. In a way, Millie was the most satisfying subject for study. Her facial features, to Mabel's observant little eye, always appeared to have softened mysteriously in the night-hours. Everything, but everything, about Millie's face was different. It was not unnatural, therefore, that Mabel had grown to love this 'two-faced' sister.

During the day, Millie appeared to Mabel as almost diabolical. She had the look of the witch in the pantomime Mabel had been taken to see at the Brixton Empire last Christmas. Mabel didn't like this face. It wasn't real. It wasn't true to life. It just wasn't Millie. Millie's night-face was kind and lovable. Her lips were a soft pink, her eyes serene and clear, her mouth a trifle sad and forlorn, her cheeks pale, but in the chill morning air, touched with delicate rose. When Mabel saw her sister like this, she wanted to crawl over her and kiss her as a child kisses its mother — spontaneously and without warning. In the mornings of Mabel Thompson's life she adored Millie innocently and with constancy.

Mabel was intrigued by the contrast between the sweetness of her own bedroom, pervaded as it was by Millie's range of perfumes, and the stale, suffocating deserts of the other two bedrooms in the house. The rasping throatiness of her father's breathing, punctuated with wart-hog snores and grunts, reminded her of her visit to the Regent's Park zoo. It frightened her a little, but no more than her mother's twisted, tortured expression, her hair splayed over the pillow like a horse's mane in the wind, her mouth mumbling nonsense language that even Mabel couldn't decipher. There was grotesqueness everywhere in this heavily-curtained room.

Mabel did not intend this particular morning to be wasted in the idle pursuit of observing the rest of the family as they slept. As soon as she was dressed, she skipped downstairs to the kitchen, calling in at the front-room to collect a few dried-up flowers from the vase on the windowsill. These she gripped tightly in her pudgy little hand as she crept slyly out into the back-yard.

Although there was still an early morning chill on the air, the sun shone brightly on the patch of unkempt grass beside the dog-kennel. The coal-shed cast a long sharp shadow across the kitchen window. Mabel shivered and watched cross-eyed the small puffs of breath steaming from her mouth. If Ron in his turn had observed Mabel asleep, when the stains and the stickiness were washed away, he would have noticed how her little lips relaxed in sleep and softly settled into place like a miniature Cupid's bow. Now, however, those lips were pursed and full of determination. Gripping her flowers, she embarked upon a thorough search of the kennel and its precincts. Smutty lay as still as a thief in the night, as heavy as a lump of spotted-dick on the stomach. Not a hair bristled. He lay, head resting on his front paws in the twilight of his windowless abode. He knew all too well that when Mabel was around, his life was liable to change from one of quiet repose to one of turbulence and mighty movement. He was prodded and pulled and punched and pinched and tweaked and twanged until he felt the most dog-holed, dog-sick, dog-eared dog in the world. He remained quite still, following her only with his eyes, which swivelled like pendulums from side to side.

Mabel began groping round inside the kennel. Smutty was expecting the usual indignity of being eased out on all fours, but Mabel, it seemed, had no intention of evicting him from the tenancy of his dog-house. Nevertheless, he allowed himself to go heavy and limp on his sacking floor, just in case her intentions turned out to be dishonourable.

When her prodding and poking were over, Mabel stood up and let her eyes roam over the yard. The coal-shed was next. Being in the shadow, she could hardly see inside, blinded by the sun as she was for only a second or two. When her eyes became accustomed to the dim light, she saw, oddly enough to her, that the shed was full of coal. There was nothing for her in this place, not even in her father's old rush-bag of empty beer-bottles. She closed the door quietly. Then, in the shadow of the dust-bin, she found what she had been searching for.

It took a long time to prepare the grave. The ground was mushy after yesterday's rain and Mabel had to dig hard with her old wooden spoon so as to clear the twitch and weeds. At last, she managed to clear a space a few inches square on the sunny side of the kennel, and dug a small hole, pressing in the damp sides with her fingers. The sparrow lay stiff and cold on the grass. Every now and then, she glanced at it to see if it was still dead. She wanted it to come alive, but then she wanted to bury it too, so perhaps it was better that it never regained consciousness. Taking the silver paper she had taken from one of her father's cigarette packets, she gently wrapped the deceased in its shroud and laid it to rest in the little grave. Here followed a short service of nursery-rhymes she had learnt at the day-nursery, rhymes like 'Hickory-dickory dock', 'Round and round the mulberry bush' and 'Here we go gathering nuts in May', the inappropriateness of which, with their jaunty tunes and the childish abandon of the rendition, made the simple service quite a jolly affair on the whole. After filling in the grave, Mabel went indoors to the front room, and, sitting down at the old walnut piano, with its fretted front, faded green silk and brass candle-sticks, she began banging the keys down, three and four at a time with her tiny fists. It was time everybody was up!

27. Call Me Agnes!

Councillor Purvis didn't have a front-room like the Thompsons, he had a sitting-room and it was here that he ushered in Miss Baldock on this sunny Saturday morning.

"I do hope," said Miss Baldock, "you will excuse this early call, Mr. Purvis. I know you breakfast at eight, so I felt sure you wouldn't mind. You see, I have a small matter to put to you, a matter of some urgency."

"Not at all, my dear Miss Baldock. I am delighted to see you. Come in and sit down and tell me about how things are with your restaurant."

"Oh, but I haven't come about the restaurant."

"I see. But then I'm always interested in the affairs of my tenants. Always. Now are there any new developments?"

"Things are going well. We're fast becoming the busiest in the High Street." She knew the Councillor was unsympathetic to failure. "It wasn't easy from the beginning, the way things were left by the previous management. I shudder when I think of it. It is all very different since I became the Manageress."

"Yes, indeed it is, though I don't frequent the place myself."

There he was again! What on earth did he mean, 'frequent the place'? There was no cause for him to be so superior. It wasn't as if it was one of those low sorts of coffee-bars like the *Danse Macabre* with its coffin-lid tables, skeleton spoons and artificial cobwebs. Maybe the cinema was not up to much with its faulty projectors and old-fashioned *décor*. She had no liking for the gold twiddly bits over the screen and the has-been look about the grubby rainbow silk curtains that drew across after Pearl and Dean had closed their pearly gates on the advertisements. As for the out-dated recordings of Charlie Kunz and Glenn Miller, well! They were even trying to bring in that new Elvis Wesley fellow, or whatever his name was! Give her Henry Hall and Joe Loss any day! Or even stepping it out with Victor Sylvester. In any case the whole place reeked of stale nicotine and dust. No, the Roxy Restaurant, in spite of its purple walls and Egyptian-style candelabra and the view over the railway sidings, was elegant and respectable and she, Agnes Baldock, had made it so. She had turned an insipid menu into a tasty *table d'hôte*. She had replaced the slovenly post-war waitresses with smart little 'nippies' in their black and white.

Ignoring the Councillor's last remarks, Miss Baldock broke through in her blunt fashion:

"Since I modernised the kitchen and installed the *espresso* coffee-machine, Mr. Purvis, we have been able to cope with twice the number of customers. In fact we're doing almost too well!"

With these last words, she stiffened her neck, raised her eyebrows, stuck her front chin into its two companions and sucked air in through her pursed lips.

"You cannot do *too* well at anything, Miss Baldock. Economy equals efficiency, you know. Low costs and high turnover — that's the best formula for success, not forgetting the hard work that goes with it."

Was the Councillor suggesting that she, the very model of efficiency, was some sort of lazy slut? Did he really think he was the only one in the Borough to work himself to the bone? Before she could think of an appropriate reply, the Councillor came in with:

"That's the trouble with young folk today. They just don't want to work. All they want is less work and more money. The country simply can't stand it."

Miss Baldock was losing on points. Her turn to serve:

"Come now, Mr. Purvis, you can't tell me *economic* and *economical* are the same thing. The young people of my acquaintance don't know the difference. The more I think about it, the more I believe extravagance and prodigality are on the increase. It's the unwelcome reaction to our wartime austerity. Can you honestly assert that you, as Councillor for the Borough, can justify all the preposterous redevelopment schemes being proposed now, these expensive blocks of flats and all the so-called 'social amenities' you have been talking about to the local press? These schemes, in my view, are more for private prestige than the public good."

"If you are referring to the Purvis enterprises, Miss Baldock—"

"I'm afraid it's my feminine intuition again, Mr. Purvis," interrupted the defiant lady. "Perhaps you have underestimated me all these years. I know you too well. Suddenly, you have discovered that your ill-concealed ambitions have been disclosed under the arc-lamps of a woman's scrutiny. Never mind, I won't give away your secret."

Game, set and match!

That Miss Baldock had touched the quick of his nature, that she had broken down his reserve with a single word, momentarily shattered the Councillor's nerve. He had intended to refute everything if only to gain some ground for a renewed offensive. After all, why he should be so docile in the face of attack was a mystery to him. This woman had battered her ample bosom against his first defences and shattered them. Perhaps it was too early in the day for such discussions. Perhaps he ought not to have criticised her attitude to business in the way he had. He knew nothing of the economics of running a cinema restaurant, nor had he any desire to comprehend them. It was a closed book to him and he intended it to remain so.

One thing had occurred to him in the course of their conversation however. Here was a woman, he thought, here was a woman with a mind of her own. Had he not indeed underestimated her, even, perhaps, neglected her charms? Looking across at her now, as she sat perched on the edge of the horsehair sofa, plumped firmly before him in all her magnificent amplitude, he suddenly saw her as if she were one of those desirable figures in a painting by Rubens. He tried to imagine her in his arms but knew he was inadequate to the task. Still, he had to admit that his brief encounter with the seductive Millie had awakened his masculinity. Something had reminded him that the world was not all toil and hard labour, but a desirable place filled with delicious pleasures he had long since forgotten. He began thinking more about Millie and the journey on the bus — the longest five minutes of his life and so, so pleasurable. When he remembered her slipping into his arms, clutching him in the darkness of this very room....well, it seemed so long ago now. She had far too much to drink but it didn't seem to matter then. He knew something exciting had awakened in him, making his fifty odd years seem like twenty — but then that was exactly how old the young temptress looked, so why shouldn't he feel like it too? There was only one thing that troubled him, and that was his conscience. He tried not to remember the events exactly as they had occurred. He tried to concentrate on Miss Baldock. He tried to imagine her in place of Millie, and the thing that surprised him most of all was that the idea was not as unattractive as he might have supposed. Indeed, it was decidedly desirable to a degree. This was clearly something he could not have conceived had Miss Baldock not chosen to visit him on this particular morning at this particular hour.

To his surprise, the Councillor found himself speaking in a severe tone: "You are a hard woman, Miss Baldock, a hard woman."

"I am a practical woman, Mr. Purvis. I do not tally with this mollycoddling indulged in by *some* of the councillors. It is one thing to be sentimental, Mr. Purvis, it is quite another to be radical. You cannot be both without falling foul of one side or the other."

"If you are referring to the forthcoming demolition of Laburnum Villas, then you are quite wrong. Whilst regretting their passing from us, I recognise the urgent needs of the Borough for more efficient housing. I am just as proud of the Purvis Housing Scheme as I am of the Purvis Rink, the Purvis Youth Band and the Purvis Bowl. They are all my own, my personal gift to the Borough and make me a reformer of a unique kind. I'll have you know, madam, I am no mollycoddler as you call it. I certainly don't admit to being sentimental and old-fashioned. I may be over fifty years of age but I am a man, madam, a man through and through, and what is more, madam, a man who knows his own mind, a man who knows his own destiny."

Miss Baldock observed Mr. Purvis's hair wisp out at the sides with the sheer electricity generated by the heat of his rising blood-pressure. She watched him as he pounded the leather chair with his fists, and swivelled about on his behind like a weathercock in a high wind. She realised that this was her moment, this was *her* moment for a tactical *tour-de-force*, and with the assurance of Jezebel she sallied forth to the attack. Lowering her voice to the soft and gentle tones of the temptress, she unbuttoned her beaver top-coat, drew her Paisley scarf from her plump neck, leaned forward in her chair so that the Councillor was gazing directly into the shadowy warmth of her welcoming cleavage, and uttered in a conspiratorial whisper:

"Ex*actly*! Mr. Purvis, exactly! You are indeed a man of hidden gifts. How else could you have risen to such heights? Milk-boy to Mayor in how long? Forty years, is it? An achievement of no mean promise, Mr. Purvis. And how else can we humble rate-payers think of you but as a spirited and even dominant force in our midst."

She breathed heavily and paused for a reaction.

"And this is why I am here this morning, my dear Mr. Purvis. You are a man of understanding, yet without being sentimental, sympathetic when faced with human misfortune or suffering, a man determined to see justice done where justice is due."

The Councillor was only half-thinking about what Miss Baldock was saying, gratifying as it was to his pride and self-esteem. The other half was thinking that he had definitely neglected the charms of this lady and a polite invitation for a walk with him after mass on Sunday might turn out to be quite profitable, economics or no economics, and even though she was of the Roman persuasion, entirely worth his while.

"I can see," went on Miss Baldock, "that we are two of a kind, my dear Mr. Purvis. I am sure that we shall agree admirably on a small problem I would like to settle at the earliest possible moment and in the easiest possible manner."

The battle was almost won, but even at this stage, she had to be on the look out for any counter-offensive. She felt she was almost there when Mr. Purvis said: "Anything, my dear Miss Baldock, anything at all." He was still a little unsure of her, though. "You are such a close neighbour, my dear, yet I hardly know you."

"Time enough," she said, smiling encouragingly. "Time enough. I'm a busy woman, you know."

He didn't know why he should be so anxious to please but Mr. Purvis suddenly felt he wanted to do something for Agnes Baldock.

"It's a loving heart," said Miss Baldock, "that knows no rancour. That is why I have come to you for help and advice."

"Anything, my dear, anything you wish."

Without revealing the true nature of her intentions, she uncovered her plan to effect a transfer of the lease of No 2 Laburnum Villas into her own name, taking care not to mention the compensation this would enable her to claim on the termination of the leasehold. This sum, together with the small amount of savings she had accumulated over the years, would at last enable her to escape from Rothersey and open a small café somewhere on the South coast.

"Mr. Lawton is getting so frail and weak, Mr. Purvis. If only you could see him. He is quite unable to look after himself, and certainly is not in a position to run a house and take in lodgers like myself. What he needs is proper care and attention in an institution like the Napoleon Avenue Old People's Home. I believe there are no vacancies at present, but I do feel something should be done soon."

The Councillor reflected that he had come to office too late to add his name to the Purvis Retreat for the Retired, as he would have preferred to call it. But as Calthrop sarcastically remarked: "Retired what? Chipmunks?"

"The Home would be admirable," the good lady was saying, "and there, if I may say so, Mr. Purvis, your own name is a regrettable omission from the list of your own achievements."

It may have been a whim of circumstance, but Agnes Baldock was growing on Mr. Purvis, growing like a large succulent mushroom on a lonely patch of meadow.

"My heart aches," said Agnes, putting her hand to her breast, "when I think of that poor old man with no-one to look after him, what with me out at work all day. I simply can't face the idea of coming home and finding him slumped in his old chair by the fire, his pipe smoking away and he dead to the world. It would be uncharitable to allow him to go on as he is. Uncharitable."

Mr. Purvis had heard the story by incomplete instalments. He just could not concentrate. The blood was rushing about inside his head like shooting stars. All he could say was: "Anything, Miss Baldock, anything at all."

"If you are agreed then," said the lady with the plan, she rising triumphantly to her feet, "I would be only too glad to help out with the lease for a further year while Mr. Lawton is being rehoused."

"By all means," said the Councillor, adding as an after-thought: "provided Mr. Lawton is agreeable to the arrangement."

"Of course he will agree. I shall see to it."

"I shall arrange an interview with my tenant this afternoon. Should the old man refuse, I'm afraid I shall have to offer him the new tenancy, but I'm sure he will see reason after you've spoken with him."

Miss Baldock smiled him out of the room and stood beaming on the doorstep.

"Goodbye, my dear," Mr. Purvis said, with a glint of hope in his eye.

"Thank you, dear Mr. Purvis. You are so understanding." She

turned and strode manfully towards the bus-stop, halted only by the Councillor's call.

"Perhaps you would care for a stroll in the Gardens after church tomorrow if the weather's fine."

"Delighted," she said with obvious relief. "Delighted!" She paused for an instant. "And Mr. Purvis!"

"Yes, my dear."

"Call me Agnes!"

28. A Real Jazzmaroo!

Curled up into a Z-bend and clasping the sensational paper-back edition of *Love and Lucy Locket* (a special offer from *Glamour Girl)*, Millie began to feel sleepy again. Saturday morning was an every-other-week affair for her, and she always liked to follow the same routine — breakfast in bed, something to read after a fashion, and an hour or so listening to the BBC 'Saturday Club'. And here she was, trying hard to keep interested in a story about a lusty dispatch-rider and an oversexed heiress, or, as it called her, 'a lady of quality'! The novel had been headlines in the *Rothersey Clarion* but she couldn't see what all the fuss was about. She persevered, hoping to reach the saucy part of the story.

Millie dozed off. When the book fell onto the floor she awoke with a start. It was ten o'clock. *Saturday Club!* She turned on her portable wireless just in time to catch the signature tune. She picked up her copy of this week's *Glamour Girl* and began browsing through the pages on make-up until...yes...yes...it was 'The Voice' himself. She lay back on the bed, feeling delicious waves run right through her, waves of something she couldn't quite understand. She closed her eyes, sighing with pleasure, stroking her soft skin as if her hands were his hands caressing her neck and breasts.

> *Rock, rock, rock-a-bye, baby,*
> *On the big tree top,*
> *You, you, you shall be mine, baby,*
> *Beep, beep, beepidy-bop!*

After a while she climbed out of bed and began be-bopping and rocking it round the room in her bare necessities, singing, shaking her hips, flicking her fingers to the beat of the drums. When 'The Voice' stopped, she flung herself on the bed, panting and laughing by turns, her whole body alive with such a careless rapture that all caution was thrown to the winds.

"Millie," shouted Mrs. Thompson up the stairs. "It's gone ten, you know."

After what seemed a very long time, Millie picked up *Glamour Girl* and flicked to the make-up pages again. She turned to what her mother called the 'horrible-scopes' and read all about what was going to happen to Sagittarius but the forecast hardly matched the sheer physical pleasure of her imagined affair with 'The Voice'. An advertisement caught her eye:

Festival of Popular Song

Mammoth Competition

CASH PRIZES

MAYBE IT'S   *STARDOM*   **FOR YOU!**

Millie suddenly forgot all about *Saturday Club* and *Love and Lucy Locket* and horoscopes. It seemed at last she may have discovered some sort of meaning to her life. She wanted to be a star. She would settle, it seemed, for being just a starlet if it meant she could take the stage and be the idol of the boys. She wanted to sing her heart out to them, she wanted them to hoot and whistle and cry for more.

Dressing and its attendant mysteries took rather less that the customary hour. When she was ready, she sat down and wrote her fifteenth letter to 'Housewives Choice' asking for 'I'll get you tonight, baby' as rendered by 'The Voice'. She wanted it sung by him alone and not by any Tom, Mick or Barry! She wanted to hear her name over the air, broadcast to millions of fans, she wanted to sing to those millions, she wanted to impress all those 'Boys with the Voices'. She wanted to dig that crazy tom-tom. She wanted a real jazzmaroo!

Leaving the tray of breakfast things on the bed, her pyjamas spread across the floor for her mother to clear up, she picked up the novel and threw it contemptuously on the dressing-table. All that phoney sex stuff wasn't for her. She had just experienced with the sound of 'The Voice' what she mistakenly thought was the real thing. Now, she had a smile on her face, at least it could be supposed so, underneath all the make-up, and she went downstairs humming to herself.

29. One for the Band, Joe!

Once Councillor Purvis had recovered from Miss Baldock's visit, he put on his hat and coat and set off for the Town Hall. As he threaded his way through the Saturday-morning crowds milling along the High Street, his fingers curled round the smooth envelope in his pocket. The vision of days ahead in the company of Agnes Baldock seemed brighter than ever. Her visit had inadvertently awakened new feelings in him, feelings which he had long considered inappropriate to a man of lesser years than himself. Faced as he had been with such an enticing spectacle, such a backcloth of desires, such a scenery of emotions, such a high-wire of suspense, such a circus-ring of conversational gambits — such a sweet aria of love as this had brought him to realise that here, at last, he had found a woman who could sing in his own key without playing the dominant. For Gabriel, Agnes (who would never allow herself to stoop to calling him by the common-or-garden 'Joe' like the rest of the rabble of Rothersey) — yes, Gabriel, for Agnes, was truly a chromatic scale of pleasures, a tonic sol-fa of delights. He had to admit she was no Millie Thompson, yet Agnes had a mind of her own and knew how to use it. She had a strength that both appalled and excited him.

In the quiet of his office, he uncurled his fingers and took out the envelope. He had crumpled it into a twisted mess, and as he proceeded to iron it out on his blotter, he was thinking of the injustice of turning old Lawton out of No 2 Laburnum Villas. As he thought of one or two reasons why he should not (such as common-or-garden charity, for example), he could think of more reasons as to why he should. After all, was it charitable to allow the old boy to live on as he was at the moment? Wasn't it a case of being cruel to be kind? Yes, it was, indeed. Mr. Lawton was too old, too feeble to be responsible for his own welfare. At the thought of this, Mr. Purvis typed out a letter to the effect that, since the property was to be sold in the near future, he regretted that the lease could not be renewed, and advised Mr. Lawton to accept a place in the Napoleon Avenue Old People's Home as from the coming quarter. After re-addressing the lease to Miss Baldock, he walked down the gleaming corridor and knocked on a door marked: 'Councillor P.I.X. Calthrop. Social Welfare.'

"But if, as you say, Purvis," Calthrop was saying ten minutes later, "if as you say, Mr. Lawton is too old and too feeble to live on his own, then he is too old to work. I consider, in the light of the age-limit imposed at the last meeting of the Road Safety Committee, that he should be relinquished from his post as Road Safety Officer immediately."

"I did not say he was too old to work, Calthrop."

"Good heavens, man! If he can't look after himself, how on earth is he to look after other people?"

"Heaven or earth, Calthrop, I still think that is a matter for the right department to decide. We are discussing, you may remember, the possibility of getting him a place in the Old People's Home."

Calthrop's teeth were on edge. He wasn't exactly gnashing them but they gave off a little squeak every so often which sent chills running up and down Mr. Purvis's spine. Calthrop was intransigent.

"He must be relieved of his post at once, Purvis, or we shall have our children mown down before our very eyes."

"Look here, Calthrop," muttered the Councillor with the greatest restraint, "he has already had the job for three years and the children adore him. Besides, it gives him something to think about. You know what old people are like when they retire. Time weighs heavily and they die off in no time at all. If you deprive Lawton of his post you are as good as passing a death sentence on him."

"NO!" shouted Calthrop, riding his position to the heights, "no!" [*banging with his clenched fist on the desk*] "no!" [*bang*] "no!" [*bang*] "NO!" [*bang-BANG*]. His codfish eyes gyrated in ever-widening circles.

"Look! Calthrop. Mr. Lawton has to be helped out of his troubles. Dammit, man! You are supposed to be responsible for the welfare of the deprived people in the borough. He *is* over eighty you know!"

"Eighty? Over eighty!" gasped Calthrop incredulously. "You cannot allow senility to be the guide of infants. He must be notified at once, do you hear? Good gracious me! Whatever next? I shall consult

Mr. Wood as soon as I can on the possibility of persuading Mr. Lawton to move to the Home. That is absolutely final, Purvis, final."

As far as Councillor Purvis was concerned, the decision was admirable. He could not, in the circumstances, regard himself as responsible. His conscience was clear. His motives were just. If there were any doubts at all, they were chased away by thoughts of Agnes, and as he stepped out into the chill air and pale summer sun, he found himself humming into the face of the porter, and swung blissfully out through Flo Thompson's highly-polished doors, on his way to band practice.

The gymnasium, used by Curly for work-outs and muscle-building was, on Saturday mornings, the centre of quite a different kind of activity. The sound of the hard-breathing, gulping, gasping youth of Rothersey emanating from this vault during the earlier part of the week, gave place to a range of more artificial though less distinguishable animal noises. To the casual passer-by, a more exact evocation of jungle uproar could hardly have been possible, with all the hootings and hissings and wailings and trumpetings and rumblings and squeakings and grumblings that went on. The wall-bars shook like reeds drying in the wind; the horse trembled on its four legs; the ropes broke loose and samba-ed in space like giant lianas; the buck leapt into the air in surprise; the beams shook with frenzy. In the midst of it all stood Councillor Joseph Purvis. He was conducting the Purvis Band. This unlikely gang of tearaways were of a variety unparalleled in the history of music. There were little nippers on piccolos, spotty-faced teenagers with violins and cornets, puberty-pimpled youths bursting out of their ever-tightening clothes in an effort to blast away on their trumpets and tubas, and, at the back, a curious assortment of lusty louts in the timpani section. Today it was 'All together in the Floral Dance' or rather *not* 'all together' in their case!

'Fiddle, cello, big base drum,
Bassoon and flute and euphoni-UM!

Councillor Joseph Purvis was not much of a musician himself. He had hardly been able to remember how to read his tonic sol-fa, but several years with the Rothersey Operatic had given him a modicum of sight-reading and harmony that enabled him to discern the erratic flatness and sharpness of his string-players. His rare concert appearances at the Old People's Home encouraged him to bring out his old banjo and thrum away at a simplified arrangement of *Underneath the Arches*. As he was conducting the band now, his thoughts turned to the lewd behaviour at the Purvis Bowl and comforted himself that this band-practice was yet another of his social antidotes, one of those harmless physical pursuits to occupy the minds of the wayward youth of the borough. For the moment, he was oblivious of the incredible cacophony his ill-practised players were producing. For three weeks now, they had come to the gym to blow and scrape at the Councillor's command, 'just for a lark about' as one of the local Paganini's put it. In three months time, they would 'perform' their party-piece or die an ignominious death under the pen of the music critic from the Rothersey Gazette.

The Councillor was, however, not of the same mind. He would fix them with their euphoniums; he would bash them with their bassoons; he would flagellate them with their flutes; he would dig them with their drum sticks, until, instead of being what Ron Thompson called 'The Grind and Grumble Brigade', this ragbag of ruffians would, one day soon, be miraculously transported to the heights of musical sublimity as 'The Purvis Band'.

With his hawkish eye, Mr. Purvis noticed that 'Piccolo' Ron was absent, and made a mental note to complain to Mrs. Thompson later in the day. If absenteeism became the rule, the whole project would fold up and he would lose the opportunity of adding his name to yet another immortal group. Joe was not at all sure the Mayor would offer him the first Presidency of the Band. Everything depended on the success of the boys' performance at the bandstand in Rothersey Park, and this might be yet another carrot to hold in front of the prominent nose of Agnes Baldock.

EPISODE SEVEN

Later the same morning

Crime and Punishment!

31. Danger Signal

"Curly!" shouted Ma Blackwood through the keyhole. "Curly! Wake up! It's gone ten o'clock. Wake up, d'you hear? Else I'll come in there and drag the bedclothes off of yer."

Curly turned over on his face and shouted into the pillow.

"O.K. I'm up, you silly ol' cow!"

He listened as Ma Blackwood's steps receded into the back kitchen. Yes, he was up all right! and not the way she meant it either! Pressing his thighs against the mattress and clasping the corners of his pillow, he allowed thoughts of Millie to come to him, thoughts that caressed his whole body, rousing him to such an intensity that a stream of pleasure flooded through him. He remembered her soft lips and the feel of her soft breasts and the heat of her passion and her pulling away from him and her running away from him and......

"Curly!" Ma shouted again.

"Bugger off, you old bitch, and leave me be."

"Curly Donoghue! I'll come in there and drag you out if I have to. I want to clean up, do you hear?"

And there was Curly, wriggling about in the bed with his dreams and fantasies. and there she was, spoiling it all.

Far from keeping her distance, Ma took his insult as an invitation to force open the door. She tugged at the bedclothes, swearing and carrying on like nobody's business. And there was Curly, vaunting himself in all his nakedness, provoking her and calling her all the juiciest names he could think of.

"Get out of here, else I'll get the rozzers on yer," she shouted, and stormed out, banging the door behind her.

When Ma said that about the rozzers, Curly nearly split his sides laughing. He rolled about on that nobbly brass-balled bedstead of Ma Blackwood's and laughed and laughed till he cried and his belly ached like blazes. Then he turned over on his face again and bit and clawed at the pillow with rage and frustration. If he hadn't started to let his thoughts roam over that Paxton bird it could've all ended nicely thank you. Remembering what it was like to rub his hands over Millie's soft shapely body, he began to fantasise again, but that got him nowhere.

He got up and ripped the sheet down with his flick-knife. Then he slit the pillow open so the kapok oozed out onto the floor. That'd show the bloody old cow who was boss! After that, he put on his clothes and went out to look for Eddie. On the way, he couldn't stop thinking about Millie, then about that blonde girl at No 5, then about Millie, back and forth until he fair did his nut.

The trouble with Curly was that, whilst he fancied he now knew all there was to know about sex, his thoughts were disturbed by feelings strangely bordering on love — love for someone other than himself for a change. He had been brought to realise that a beautiful face in a window, distant as it was from reality, could actually mean that the object of his love did not necessarily have to be Millie Thompson.

32. The Things He Shouldn't Do

Flo left Alf to his snoring and came downstairs to get breakfast. After trying for some time to force a version of Smutty's Saturday-morning din-din of bacon and egg down Mabel's toffee-filled throat, Mrs. Thompson settled down to open the post. There was the new tenancy agreement for Rothersey Heights, which she put aside. She could never understand official documents. Anyway, whatever you did or didn't do, the result was the same, and the benefit was always somebody else's.

There was only one other letter —- from Miss Goodenough.

"Wait till that lad comes down," muttered Mrs. Thompson, as she read the solemn warning:

"I'll give him what for! Staying away from school, and me, doing my best to keep house and home together. What was it Miss Goodenough said? — 'Without wishing to upset you....' Upset, indeed! Mrs. Thompson was upset alright and no mistake. 'We earnestly beg you and your husband to exercise stricter control over the boy.....' A fat chance she had of exercising control over anybody in their house, what with Alf sozzled half the time. He didn't take no interest in the kids. He couldn't care a damn what happened to any of them. Loafing about as he was on his 'Peace and Plenty' lark. All he cared about was drink and sex (and not so much of that, neither!) He didn't want a wife, he wanted an unpaid housekeeper. As far as sex was concerned, for all the pleasure she got out of it, she might just as well be a tart off the streets, the way he treated her. It wasn't even a cash sale. She just paid for it in daily drudgery. Not one of the whole bunch of them thought any the better of her for trying against all odds to keep the family in one piece.

By the time Ron appeared, she was in a fine old tizzy.

"What's this?" she shouted, holding up the letter and waving it at him. "'S a letter, soppy!" he said, pouting, and sensing that something was up.

"You young rascal! Staying away from school, is it? I won't have it, d'you hear? I won't have it. Here's me and your Dad working ourselves to the bone to give you an 'edgerkation' and bring you up proper, and what thanks do we get for it? What thanks?"

Ron was glum over the frizzled-up bacon and wrinkled egg. He felt nothing but humiliation and resentment. He had contravened the golden rule of the criminal — never get caught out! That was what the bloke had said in *Vampire in Soho*. You always did something daft, and just when everything was dandy you got nabbed. Still, he didn't see why he should go back to school just so he could get a leathering from the old twit of a head-shrinker. He was sorry though about poor old Pudd'n-an'-Duff. She wasn't a bad old stick when it came to it; and here was Mum leading off at him.

"What the hell are you grumbling about, I'd like to know," said Ron, " I've just about had enough of this house, with all the goings-on. It's sending me flipping barmy, it is."

"None of your cheek, my lad," said Mrs Thompson in a threatening tone. "Mark my words, you'll come a cropper one of these days, the way you're carrying on. Wait till your father comes down, just you wait."

"A fat lot of good that'll do. He's useless."

Mrs. Thompson was near to giving Ron a good old swipe over the ear, at least till she remembered the words "corporal punishment" and "punishment by deprivation" as suggested alternative courses of action in Miss Goodenough's letter.

"That's enough of that. The school says you're getting out of hand. You're uncontrollable and bad-tempered and saying rude things in front of the class. Showing off most likely. I'm fed up with you. You'll go without your pocket money today."

"Oh, Mum! Why?" Ron whined.

"Never you mind why. 'Cos I said so, and that's final. Now go upstairs and fetch Millie's tray. Go on."

"Why can't she fetch it down herself?"

" 'Cos she's goin' round Eddie's place. His old Mum passed over."

"Passed over what?"

"Oh, get on with it and don't ask silly questions."

Ron shuffled out of the kitchen and went upstairs, pulling on the banisters and hauling himself up in his mountaineer mode. He surveyed Millie's room with disgust. All those bottles and pots cluttering up the dressing-table. He picked up *Love and Lucy Locket*. The cover was a bit of a lark! Some girl lying on the grass, practically starkers, and a gangster guy standing over her with his hand reaching down into his pocket, ready to shoot her in cold blood. Ron sat down on the bed to read. After several minutes he was bored stiff. There wasn't a single murder, no gang-fights, no thrills, only talk-talk-talk about soppy stuff like they did in *A Kiss in Time*. He put the book in his pocket thinking he might pass it to Freddy Higgins or Teddy Rogers, that's if he could persuade them to trade it for a set of marbles.

"Ron!" shouted Mrs. Thompson up the stairs. "What about that tray? Whatever are you doing up there?"

Suffering cats, thought Ron. Not a bit of peace in this house. Like living with the blinking Gestapo, it is.

"All right! I'm coming," he shouted back.

Before he was out of the room, his mother was upstairs and snatching the tray out of his hands, and, just as she did so, a raucous singing spread through the house. She stopped in her path, clutching the tray and closing her eyes. She hoped it wasn't. She hoped very much it wasn't. But it was! It was Alf, singing one of his father's old songs:

Keep the home fires burning......
While your hearts are yearning

"Oh, Alf, not that old First World War thing again. We know you can't get over your father getting gassed, but we have had another war since then, you know."

Run, rabbit, run, rabbit, run, run. run.
Run, rabbit, run, rabbit, run, run run....

"I don't think Dad'll be coming downstairs today, Mum," said Ron. Anyway, he thought, that wasn't going to help the pocket-money situation.

"You take this tray down," said Mrs. Thompson, "and I'll deal with your Dad. And get Mabel into her hat and coat. We've got to go to the shops."

The front bedroom was in chaos. Flo stood in the doorway and stared helplessly at Alf. He was trying unsuccessfully to stand on the bed and keep his balance at the same time. In his hand was a half-empty bottle of beer which he took a swig at and threw the bottle onto a pile of its companions on the floor.

> *We'll meet again*
> *Don't know where, don't know when,*
> *But I know we'll meet again*
> *Some sunny day....*

"Allo, Florrie, me ol' girl! Didn't reckon on getting up today. Feeling a bit choppy, see?"

She saw that desperate, hollow look. She knew he was suffering again. He stood there, swaying about like a puppet on a string, smiling inanely and staring at her with so much guilt in his eyes that it hurt her to the core of her being.

"Can't beat a bit of the ol' breakfast in bed lark, eh?"

He smiled at her a sad hopeless smile. She replied in a harsh tone that almost shocked her.

"I'll give you 'breakfast in bed lark', Alfred Thompson!"

"No need to put yourself out. I got me own this morning, see?"

He brandished a fresh bottle in his hand, waving it about dangerously, tottered, coming down heavily on one foot onto the carpet with a thick thud. Taking Flo by the waist, he began dancing her round the room, singing at the top of his voice:

> *Oh, you're a great big wonderful baby.*
> *You're the dearest thing I know.*

Flo struggled to get free, but Alf held her with such an iron grip that it frightened her.

> *You make me sigh, cry, die to be near you;*
> *Oh! Oh! Oh! you are a dear,*
> *You great big wonderful baby.*

"Alf, let go this instant. What'll the kids think?"

"To hell with the kids, me ol' gel," he shouted deliriously.

146

When your eyes begin to shine,
It makes me want to do (with a shrug)
The things I wouldn't do (with a wink)
It makes me want to do (with a hug)
The things I shouldn't do! (thrusting at her)

Alf!" screamed Flo. "The furniture! The furniture! Let me go, will you."

They swirled dangerously round until Alf put his foot against a chair-leg, toppled backwards, bringing the lace-curtains with him. Beer shot all over the walls. Vases, pots, hair-brushes, combs clattered down on top of them as they fell heavily to the floor. Out of the debris, he began to sing again as Flo got up, ruffled her feathers, brushed a wisp of hair into place, and went downstairs to write out her shopping-list.

33   Growing Pains

When Mabel Thompson had emptied half the contents of a salt-drum on Smutty's tail so that he wouldn't run away, and had a good swing on her father's combinations hanging on the line to dry, she was taken firmly in hand and dragged off on the weekly shopping expedition. Hardly were they outside the front-door before Mabel was shooting off up to the corner to have a chat with Beppo, the organ-grinder's little monkey (surely the last one left in London) and turn the handle of the organ for a penny.

Beppo was nibbling a nut on the top of the organ and staring and blinking by turns. To Mabel, Beppo was a monkey with a difference — he was just about the only friend she had besides Smutty, who was family anyway.

So there was Beppo, rattling his chain with excitement and chirping and chattering nineteen to the dozen — his eyes little black orbs of pathos, his lashes winking playfully or pathetically or slyly or distrustfully, and he all the time scratching and pinching and tweaking himself to his heart's content. Mabel loved the way the hair grew round his cheeks like side-whiskers. He reminded her of something she had seen before but she couldn't think, try as she might, where or when. One day, perhaps, she would remember. Sometimes when she looked at him,

147

she wanted to cry, or even scream, as she did when she first set eyes on him. Now, they were real friends. He allowed her to stroke him and prod him and poke him as much as she liked, and in return, she permitted him to touch her, almost affectionately, with his little black wrinkled fingers.

This morning, since Mrs. T. was behind schedule, the stop was short and sweet, so Mabel had to be very quick indeed in passing him a piece of her banana for his usual Saturday morning treat. Mrs. Thompson exchanged pleasantries with the old man while the organ shook with its labourings:

Plink-a-plink plonk plonk plonk,
Plink-a-plink-a-plonk plonk-a-plonk.

Rothersey High Street on a Saturday morning was almost more than Mrs. Thompson could stand — a streaming mass of humanity moving at snail-pace along the pavement. The crossing connecting the bus-stop on one side of the Roxy Picture House with Marley's General Stores and the Day-Nursery in Lupin Lane on the other was one of the busiest in the Borough. A slow crocodile of mothers made their way across with their recalcitrant children, just as, on weekdays, the same tired mothers dragged the same children screaming and kicking in the mornings, unwillingly to school. On week-days, pale-faced white-collar workers stumbled to their offices and pasty-faced typists tripped along on stiletto heels.

Now there were boys with sailing-boats and kites, girls clutching dolls and skipping-ropes, and old-age pensioners crossing from the park on their way back to Napoleon Avenue — everyone going back and forth in front of Grandpa Lawton's tired old eyes till it made him dizzy with it all. His feet were sore from hobbling to and fro with his 'STOP!' sign, and there was a chill early-morning breeze, unusually for June, that made him gasp and croak like an old toad. Even discounting the turn of events, nobody could have believed that this was to be his last morning on the job.

Outside the Roxy, Mrs. Thompson pulled Mabel up short in front of the crossing and waited for Grandpa Lawton to give them the signal. He was feebly trying to organise a group of children who had obviously got the better of him. They were holding hands and side-skipping round him in a circle. Mabel looked on with interest, while she finished her banana. Mrs. Thompson was looking at other things. Miss

148

Baldock, for example, who had come out of Marley's Stores laden with groceries for the weekend. They passed each other in the middle of the road right in front of Mr. Lawton.

"Good morning, Miss Baldock," said Mrs. Thompson, smiling as graciously as her nature would allow and giving a slight incline of the head just to please the illustrious Manageress of the Roxy Restaurant. Mrs. T. however, had not so much as an eyes-right from her Ladyship and Mrs. Thompson repeated the greeting more loudly, but the grand Miss Baldock passed by with her nose in the air.

"Stuck up old bitch!" Mrs. T. muttered to herself, giving Mabel an extra tug-and-a-half because she wanted to stop and watch the skipping and listen to the chanting of the children in a ditty of their own invention:

Old Daddy Law-ton,
He's got a wart on
His big nose!
His big nose.

He's got a witch in
His back ki-tchen,
There she goes,
There she goes!

They danced more and more energetically as they came to the close. Then, bursting into peals of laughter, they hopped and skipped away through the crowds in a race to Ma Blackwood's Lollipop Shop. Mabel would have liked to follow them but her mother shouted at her roughly with a "Come along, Mabel, will you?" Mabel wanted a lollipop and bawled as loud as her tonsils would let her but to no avail whilst her mother tugged at her as they began to thread their way into Marley's Stores.

All the time, Grandpa Lawton was staggering about as if he had just come out of *The Bed of Roses* after one of Alf Thompson's 'Peace and Plenty' rallies. Then, before you could say Jack Robinson, he was down. Nobody saw it happen. There he was, flat on his back on the curb, dribbling all over the pavement, his teeth chattering like dried peas in a pod, his eyes popping out of their sockets.

For a moment, people simply stopped and stared, and some gloated, but nobody thought of doing anything, so that it was some time

149

before the ambulance arrived. A crowd gathered and blocked the pavements even more. Traffic was brought to a complete halt.

"What's up with him?" asked a twisted face with a shadow of a leer.

"Epileptic, I shouldn't wonder," said his lady-companion. "Dribbling all over the place, he is. It's enough to turn your stomach, that sort of thing."

"He does look a bit dicky," said the Face, almost hopefully. "D'you think he's dying? Don't you have to put a spoon between his teeth or something. His eyes are rolling like marbles. He'll bite his tongue off, that's what'll happen."

"No, Frank! Much better to let him be," said the lady-shopper. "Might be something infectious, all that fluid coming out of his mouth."

"Tis a bit dicey, eh, Cynthie? Reckon he'll peg out if somebody doesn't do something soon."

Emergency help finally arrived accompanied by the usual wailings.

"Poor old codger!" remarked the lady-shopper. "He ought never to have been allowed to do a job like this at his age, he didn't. It's a crying shame. That's what it is." The collapsed body of Mr. Lawton was lifted slowly onto the stretcher and into the back of the ambulance without as much as a sigh. He was deathly pale and bloodless, like a piece of old meat on an ice-tray sliding into a refrigerator.

"It's a downright disgrace," muttered the lady-newscaster. "An old man like him having to work in a job like this."

"If they'd allowed him to die here and now," said the Smiler, "it would have been much better all round, I'd say."

The ambulance drew away, out of the lines of cars, lorries and scooters, amidst a chorus of honk-honking, toot-tooting, peep-peeping, gawk-gawking, ting-tinging and gong-gonging, that Mabel thought was absolutely thrilling — the most exciting morning she had had all the week.

"Mabel! Mabel!" came a familiar voice from the crowd. "Mabel!! Oh, there you are. How many times [smack!] have I told you [smack!] to keep [smack!] hold of me? [smack-a-smack—SMACK!!].

By the time they reached the corner of Laburnum Villas, Mabel's face was a mess. Tear-stains covered her cheeks. She was all at odds with the world. She was pursing her little lips, pouting, sticking out her plump little tummy in defiance, and all the time Mrs. Thompson was losing patience.

150

When they turned the corner, they came face to face with what seemed to Mabel a good excuse for bursting into another flood of tears.

Her friend, Beppo, was crying out like a baby. The old Italian was whipping him with his chain, and Beppo was biting and clawing his master with his sharp little finger-nails. Mabel howled as loud as she could because the old man was shouting in a language she couldn't make head nor tail of and Beppo was swearing and howling by turns and throwing his nut-shells at everybody who came too near. He swore and screamed at everyone, even Mabel, for all humans were the same to him. They all had two eyes and two ears like him, and arms to hit out with like him, feet to kick with like him and fingers to scratch with just like him, and he hated them all, whether they were his mean old master or the mangy-looking people who stopped to pet him, and even little Mabel, who, every Saturday morning, shared her banana with him.

When gratuitous pain is inflicted in this manner even to human beings, let alone defenceless animals, hatred inevitably follows. Beppo no longer remembered Mabel for her little kindnesses. He knew only the pain he was feeling now as the chain bit mercilessly into his flesh and he was maddened into a frenzy by this wretched little girl and her wailing.

Mabel could not forget the wound of it. It remained with her the whole day, eating into her memory till she screamed and screamed and could not stop. Then, unexpectedly, a frightening image presented itself to her — an involuntary memory of the bearded lady she had once seen at a fair-ground. She had screamed blue-murder at the time, and many times since in her worst nightmares — and now it all rose up into her little consciousness again. She could not know why, but even in the midst of her childish fears, she seemed to recognise that it all had something to do with her first sight of the bearded lady. And all the time, on this bright Saturday in March, she remembered the face of the monkey and the tears gushing from its wounded eyes, and the twisted face of the man as he leaned over Grandpa Lawton, and the strange hairy chin of the bearded lady at the circus. Mabel was so confused that she cried and cried until her jaws ached and she couldn't cry a single tear more.

"What's the matter with Mabel, Mum?" asked Ron, with a certain irritation.

"How the dickens should I know. Growing pains, most likely."

Mrs. Thompson didn't realise how right she was.

29   Check, Mate!

Ron stared at the queue that had gathered outside the Palaseum. No pocket money, he thought. What a lousy trick to play on anybody! What was wrong with being away from school? He could do a lot worse than that — holding up the bank like the guy on his friend Teddy Roger's new television set that his father said had fallen off the back of a lorry! Or perhaps he could beat up the school head-shrinker with a pair of knuckle-dusters, or kick old mother Baldock up the fanny. But being absent from school — cripes! Didn't do nobody no harm. You couldn't do no harm if you wasn't there, now could you?

The Palaseum queue stretched almost to Rothersey Bridge, and all to see *Seven Brides for Seven Brothers.* When he thought of *Vampire in Soho* he felt depressed. If it came to it, he would have to go through it all again if he wanted to escape the boredom that stretched before him. Even *A Kiss in Time* seemed more desirable than kicking around in the park all afternoon. As well as all this, he couldn't have no chocolate nut crunchy, nor no lemon sherbets. "All I want is a flipping half-a-dollar." He could blew the lot on the Roxy. It'd be worth every penny to see it all over again.

Ron dwelt on the dim prospect of an afternoon of complete boredom, and everything inside him began to sink. To counteract the onrush of depression, he began thinking how nicely he could fit himself into one of those soft plush seats at the Palaseum, watch the programme through until about five o'clock and then come out just in time to hop into the Roxy again. Six-and-a-half hours of filmic heaven, crunching his nut-crunch, sucking his sherbets, living in a world so far removed from his own, away from school, away from parents, away from Mabel and Millie — a world of mystery, sensation and fantasy; in fact, a world of sheer delight. He wanted that world so much that he was prepared to do anything to reach for it. He wanted more than anything to disappear into the darkness, to curl himself up into a ball, like the child he had been in his mother's womb. He could if he wished indulge in all manner of things worthy of being classified under Miss Baldock's sub-heading as 'getting up to no good'.

Try as he would, Ron could not drive from his thoughts an idea which had occurred to him as he was rummaging at home looking for any odd cash hidden in pots or in drawers or behind pictures. He knew, that, even if there had been any, his father would have found it by now; he could smell out money almost as well as he could a bottle of beer. No, there was nothing for it but to go round to Grandpa Lawton for some sympathy, a few sweets out of the tin in the kitchen, and a story. Perhaps he might lend him a bob or two! There was usually some small change on the mantelpiece. But what if Grandpa wasn't at home? Well, he'd have to plan a 'break-in', one like he had seen once at the Roxy.

On reaching Grandpa Lawton's he found no-one at home. Creeping round to the back gate, he peered over the fence into the patch of garden. As Grandpa Lawton always says: 'When you're caught on the spot, boy, DON'T PANIC!!! Keep calm and think of England!' All Ron could think about was that plush seat at the Palaseum. Even so, when he opened the back gate, it squeaked and squealed like a sick monkey. His heart thumped as he glanced up at the bedroom windows. The curtains were drawn over. The place looked deserted.

Ron eased his fingers into the crack under the kitchen window. Blood oozed slowly from under his nails. He sucked at them and then set to work, prising the window open with his pen-knife. The blade snapped in two. Oh, well! Fingers again. Inch by inch, he eased the frame up. The paint was smeared with his blood. Happily for him everybody's blood was the same colour. If he had had blue blood, like the Queen, the coppers would have soon known where to find him!

Heaving up the full weight of his body, he pulled himself in through the opened window. He came down puffing and blowing on the other side, leaving dirty foot-marks on the draining-board.

The house was so silent, the kitchen airless and stale. Faintly familiar odours lingered about like visitors who had overstayed their welcome. Ron felt stifled.

It was just like a *Tarzan* film. Perhaps there was a python slithering down the banisters to coil itself slowly round his body and bury its fangs into him. Or was there an unseen hand behind the door ready to strangle the life out of him. Would a mangled corpse come stiffly down the stairs and crush him to a pulp?

Ron was tingling with fear. The role of petty thief did not come readily to him. From the round tin on the dresser, he thrust a handful of toffees into the pockets of his shorts. Quietly tip-toeing into the front room, he explored the depths of the vase on the mantelpiece. Nothing. Then suddenly, a creak!

Ron's heart leapt into his mouth several times as he stopped to listen. There it was again.

CREAK!

Someone was on the stairs! Was it the mangled corpse come to

153

wreak vengeance? Ron ought to have learnt his lesson by now. That white-faced corpse he saw at the Roxy was coming down the stairs — arms akimbo, legs like a robot, its flesh a mass of scars, fingers twitching for the kill. Fear gripped Ron in a dozen places he didn't know he had! He couldn't breathe he was so scared. He began whimpering at the thought of being caught red-handed, literally in his case, for blood was still oozing out of his finger-nails. Another creak.

Creak! creak! CREAK!

Then — silence again. The house seemed loud with Ron's listening. Boom! Boom! BOOM! it went, beating in his ear-drums till it almost deafened him. It was saying: "You wicked boy! You deserve nothing but a good thrashing. You will be condemned to a lifetime of school detention. You will forced to write a hundred lines a hundred thousand times: 'I MUST NOT STEAL!' He wanted to die. He wanted Mum and Millie and Mabel and Smutty and Grandpa Lawton to come to him suddenly, all together.

A door opened and closed. A lavatory flushed. A door opened and closed. Then the creak-creak-creak on the stairs. Ron was covered in sweat.

"Is anyone there," said a voice.

"Crikey!' thought Ron. 'It's Aggie Baldock!'

In a flash, Ron was scrambling back through the kitchen window again. As he bent double to get through, *Love and Lucy Locket* fell out of his pocket and smacked down on the tiled floor. More stairs began to creak. Ron fled, not even waiting to close the window and the squeaking gate. He ran along the alley and into the back-yard of No 4.

"Ron," shouted Mrs. Thompson from the kitchen. "Is that you?

Blimey! thought Ron. She don't leave a bloke in peace for a second. She was just like that fat woman in the *Tom and Jerry* cartoons: *'Thomas! Is that you, Thomas? What is you a-doin' with your dirty black paws in ma gold-fish bowl?'*

"Yes, Mum, it's me!" he said, resigning himself to whatever fate might be in store.

"Oh, my word! Look at you. Whatever have you been up to?"

"I nearly got run over," he said lamely.

"Oh, duckie dear! you must be more careful. What with Grandpa Lawton in hospital, the roads won't be safe no more for the kiddies."Ron was far too miserable to care about such warnings. The news about Grandpa Lawton came to him as a complete surprise. That, coupled with his awareness that his mother was being sympathetic for a change

154

brought tears came to his eyes in bucketfuls. He couldn't stop them. They rolled down his cheeks in streams.

"Ah! don't cry, lovie. Won't make it any better, will it? Come here and let me bathe your knees. They're all grazed. And whatever have you done to your fingers? You *are* a mess, and no mistake."

She put her arms round him and hugged him for a moment — something she had not done in years — and not surprisingly he burst into a further flood of tears.

Ron looked down at his knees in surprise. He couldn't remember grazing himself but as soon as he saw the blood they started to hurt. His mother took out her purse and handed him a nice shiny half-crown.

"Never you mind, lovie-duck! Here's your pocket-money and a bit more to go with it. If you go to the pictures, mind you're back for your tea."

'Suffering cats!' thought Ron. 'Was it worth it? Was it blinking-well worth it? All that caper for a handful of toffees!'

* * *

Meanwhile, back at No 2, Agnes had come into her kitchen just too late to catch her mysterious intruder. She hurried out into the back garden but there was no-one to be seen. Returning to the kitchen, she noticed a small book on the floor. As she began to read its sultry pages, her expression changed to one of horror. She had never before been confronted by such vulgarity! She felt so contaminated by its lewdness that she resolved to go to confession on her way to work the next day.

EPISODE EIGHT

A Sunday Morning in Late June

Mixed Feelings

34. Louise in Love

The warm rays of the summer sun had already begun to flow like honey over the tranquillity of Walter Paxton's garden. Louise opened the kitchen door and stood on the step, breathing in the fresh morning air. In her exhilaration, she stretched out her arms towards the splendour of roses before her and smiled contentedly.

All along the high wall separating the Paxton world from the ugliness beyond, was the deep glow of *Crimson Glory*. Louise moved about the tiny lawn, feeling the turf under her bare feet. She cupped one of the largest blooms in her hands, inhaling the heady perfume, ever stronger now in the first hours of the morning. Beads of dew glinted like diamonds on red velvet against the shiny dark green leaves.

The arbour, which previously had lurched precariously to one side, now stood firm and upright under the weight of scores of small pink rose-buds, themselves ready to burst into flower in the brilliant light of the sun. From the arbour, her eyes turned to the small circular herbaceous beds, nurtured with so much care in Timothy's spare hours off from his pre-med studies at the hospital. A riot of colour lifted her heart. Below the tall pillars of the hollyhocks were delphiniums of violet and gentian blue, and below them still, the pink and silver-blue and deep amethyst of phlox, the brilliant scarlet salvia, white alyssum and the tiny star-flowers of deep blue scylla.

Louise looked once more at the newly-whitewashed garden walls, and the new green paint on the gate and the out-house, and she tried to remember what it had all been like before Tim had come to them on that bleak Monday morning in February. The little garden of No 5 had now become her secret Eden in the midst of the wilderness.

Timothy was usually away at weekends, most of which he spent sailing off the south coast. Visits to his parents became fewer as his studies at the hospital increased, and, apart from a weekly telephone call to his mother, he had no contact with them.

Louise was troubled, and naturally curious about Timothy. In fact, he was beginning to take up a great deal of her thoughts as time went on. She only had to look at the restored garden, smell the aroma of tobacco when she cleaned his room, or catch sight of his overcoat hanging up in the hall, to know how her feelings about him were changing. As she had learnt to accept him, she had come to know his ways, and her early fears had dissolved in the warmth of his friendliness, whether it was a smile or the gentle touch of his hand on her arm. She cooked for him, she washed his shirts, mended his socks, and, on occasion, when he was late for a lecture, would polish his shoes while he dashed about the house gathering up his books and notes, or fumbled about in his overfilled chest of drawers for a handkerchief. He would hastily pick up his sandwiches and rush out down the street, always turning at the corner to wave to her.

Little by little, Timothy came to realise that Louise and Uncle Walter had a closely-guarded secret. He noticed tell-tale signs during their evenings together — her occasional capricious shake of the head, a sadness that came quite suddenly across her face, even sometimes a look of sheer terror that mystified him so much that he lay awake at night pondering the cause, wondering what unmentionable memory it was that he was not permitted to share. He was troubled, too, by the inexplicable fact that, though she had never spoken a sound since the mysterious 'accident', she nevertheless had perfect hearing. He had even gone so far as to make serious enquiries at the hospital concerning the arrival of a distinguished French surgeon who had had considerable success with speech disabilities, but Uncle Walter had shown little interest, saying that it wasn't as simple as Timothy might think.

Louise listened intently when Timothy read her favourite poems to her, reminisced about his childhood on the farm, or talked about his antics at the hospital. She smiled when he exaggerated the comic side, like the student rag just before Christmas when they had shouldered red-faced Matron along the corridor singing:

Rudolph, the red-nosed reindeer
Had a very shiny nose

For Louise, their moments together were precious, though she could never give herself fully to his kindnesses. There was always an invisible barrier between them that made her hold back against her own feelings for him. For Timothy, she had a fascination which he, in his obtuse way, could not unravel. As she had no way of communicating with him, beyond her scribbled notes, there was no likelihood of their ever coming closer to each other in the circumstances. He, for his part, found her an interesting case for study which was becoming gradually more attractive to him for a variety of reasons.

However it was to be, today was Sunday, and a beautiful, warm June Sunday at that. The sun was streaming across the garden, giving a rich glow to every colour. The view from the window filled Louise with

159

feelings of pleasure and well-being. The first creakings on the stairs told her that Uncle Walter was on his way down, one step at a time instead of two like Tim. As usual the old man arrived puffing and blowing like a long-distance runner. He sat in the kitchen in his mother's high-backed Windsor chair and began to read the Sunday paper. Timothy usually took an age to come down as he disliked being read to at table, especially at the speed Uncle Walter went, stumbling over his syllables, cracking his jaw over every semivowel and forever uttering his favourite phrase: "I'll elucidate it, my dears." 'Elucidating' was one of his pet occupations. If Louise needed to know when the coal-man was coming or how many p's were there in 'hippopotamus' for a crossword puzzle she was doing, well! out would come the little pair of gold-rimmed half-moon spectacles. He would peer through them at the slip of paper from Louise's note-pad that she kept in her apron pocket for such occasions., then, glancing over the tops of his spectacles, he would drawl out his long vowels: "Well, I'll elucidate it, my dear," and almost as soon forget all about it. Sometime after, he would remember and do a little elucidating on his own, by which time Louise had either done the necessary research herself or the original query had gone clean out of her head.

Timothy's rare Sunday mornings in London were clouded by the prospect of what he called 'Church Parade'. He was 'marched off' with Uncle and Louise to the accompaniment of the matin chimes of St. Crispin's. Nothing would have pleased him more than to sit lazing over coffee and the Sunday morning papers. Going to church for Tim had too many memories of the family pew and vestry gossip. It was all so much a pretence, so hypocritical to confess a faith with which most people had lost touch. God, for him, was not the amiable, bearded old gentleman glowering down from the clouds and sighing over His recalcitrant children on earth. Everyone should be at liberty to worship his own God, and there were at least half-a-dozen in Laburnum Villas alone, and not anything as nebulous or abstract as Uncle Walter's father-figure. 'I am the Lord thy God. Thou shalt have none other God but me.' Timothy was unwilling to accept such an absolute unquestioningly. He had, buried somewhere in the religious experience of his childhood, a cloudy memory of a parable about a sower and the seed falling on stony ground, and this memory was locked away with many others in some dark and long-forgotten corner which he was disinclined to rediscover. Faith, for him, faith in God, was as unreal as the world of space-fiction.

The Sunday visits to St. Crispin's were endured more out of

160

consideration for Louise than for God. At best, Timothy did feel some lowering of spirit at the ambivalence of his thoughts as he knelt, sat, rose to his feet, sat, knelt, during the eternity of Matins. The Vicar, well past retiring age, droned feebly and inaudibly on, intractable in his belief in that benign deity sitting on the clouds in the painting over the altar; firm in his faith in a naive medieval world of angels and demons, originally and cleverly designed for a defective congregation with little or no education or sensitivity, who could only understand eternal truths in parables and pretty pictures.

Uncle Walter's stentorian tones could be heard way above the rest of the congregation as he launched into the favourite hymns of his youth: 'Fight the good fight, with all Thy might', 'Onward, Christian soldiers, marching as to war' and 'He who would true valiant be.' Tim admired Uncle's simple faith born of his country roots, and was ever more convinced that education after all might well destroy that simplicity, touched as it was with innocent charity and love, and open up whole vistas of badness in mankind.

Back at Laburnum Villas, Mabel was waiting on the doorstep to receive the churchgoers. If the truth must be known, Mabel was now all too often on the doorstep to greet them and as they now approached, she skipped off towards them, smiling, laughing, giggling with unalloyed delight to see her favourite 'uncle'. He swept her up in his arms, saying: "That's my Mabel," and swirled her round and round like a whirligig.

Louise went in to prepare the dinner whilst Tim was dragged into what Uncle Walter was pleased to call his 'Garden of Eden', where little Mabel thrust her Zoo Book into Tim's hand and furiously began turning the pages to a picture of a goldfish swimming in a bowl.

"Wassat, Nunker Dim?" she asked quizzically.

"That's a goldfish," said Tim, puffing out his cheeks like a fish: "Glob! Glob! Glob!"

He bounced her about on his knee like an India-rubber ball: "Glob! Glob! Glob!" and gave her three extra big bounces for good measure that sent her into fits of giggling. Then he read her some A. A. Milne verses about the three little foxes who lived in cardboard boxes, and added on a few Edward Lear limericks until Mrs. Thompson's head appeared over the wall:

"MABEL! MABEL!! Your dinner's ready. Come along!"

Through tears and laughter, the next ten minutes pursued their dramatic path until Uncle Walter presented the tearful Mabel with a lollipop from Ma Blackwood's shop. Thus a sticky-mouthed literary lioness was returned to the troublesome Thompson fold, her noisy little mouth closed with sweetness.

Peace once more restored, Louise, Uncle Walter and Timothy could settle down to the ritual delights of Sunday dinner with its traditional roast beef and Yorkshire pudding. After an exchange of pleasantries about the little next-door neighbour, Uncle said:

"You know, Timothy, you've quite a way with the children. You ought to get married, my boy. You'd make a fine husband for some pretty young girl — and a good father!"

"Marriage? I never think of it," said Tim as he sliced off another portion of beef and scooped up some of the gravy from the dish. "Never really have time to think about things like that. I like kids — so long as they happen to be somebody else's! Give me some peace and quiet — a good book and a good pipeful of tobacco and I'm as happy as Larry. Anyway, I'm enjoying life too much to tie myself down to anyone in particular. My father's always going on about it — carrying on the family name and all that rot. I'll come to it when I ready. Until then, I'm happy to enjoy what freedom I have. I've been tied to my family apron strings for far too long as it is."

The rest of the meal was eaten in silence. If Uncle Walter had thoughts of his own, their sole accompaniment was the chinking of knives and forks against the plates and the almost inaudible sound of water being swallowed as Timothy self-consciously took a drink between mouthfuls of the nicely tender roast beef that was currently attracting most of his attention. As for Louise, there was little she could do in these circumstances to show Timothy the measure of her love for him.

35. The Jaws of Lucifer

In the silence of her lonely bed, Agnes Baldock was lying on her back, her eyes roaming the mapless wastes of her white-papered ceiling. Like a film-projectionist, she was trying to focus a blurred image on the blank screen of her longing — imprints of another kind of life, a life moving through an unending series of projections in glorious technicolour, a life rich with satisfaction and fulfilled desires. More particularly was she now pondering the felicities of that life known only to a true lady of leisure, devoid of all the trappings of cash-desks and

162

sardines-on-toast, sluttish waitresses and insolent Teddy Boys.

As she gazed listlessly up at the bare electric light bulb, with its pink plastic shade and blue forget-me-not pattern that went black when she turned on the light, she realised that, far from living a rich pageant of experience, she was confined within the limits of a very small canvas and, what is more, one, not of ships swirling through the high seas of her desire, but motionless in a pathetic still-life that would not even make the sale-rooms.

With the advancement of years, her emotions had become a turmoil of inexpressible desires and unassailable bitterness. The acid of her frustration was at last beginning to conquer the alkali of her compassion. For Agnes, femininity had flown out of the bedroom window long ago and it would be a miracle if it ever returned. Her hair, grown stringy with lack of care, she plaited into ear-phones, a style long out of fashion. Her lips had narrowed to streaks of bitterness. Her eyes had grown hard and passionless. You could hardly say, considering her size, that Agnes Baldock was a pale ghost of her former self, but when Mrs. Thompson joked about this and everyone laughed, she was as near to hitting the proverbial nail on the head as anybody could be.

All this is, of course, true, but during the last months a change had taken hold of Agnes Baldock. No-one had noticed it as yet. It is very strange what the prospect of financial independence can do for an individual. With the chance of a lump sum from the Borough Council coupled with her own modest savings she at last had a future.

But the truth of the matter was that Agnes had been disturbed for some weeks by her almost nightly reading of *Love and Lucy Locket*. The blatantly sexual descriptions, now made by the Censor the public property of every man, woman and child who could read more than two words strung together, had opened up for her a whole world, rich with new sensations. Rooted in her mind was the picture of a woman lying on the grass, expectantly looking up at a handsome brute in leather riding-kit, standing over her like a Greek god sent from the heavens to comfort and satisfy her. The picture Agnes now painted of herself was of one possessed, painted not in one pose but in many poses that adorned the vast mural she painted in her mind as she lay looking up at her white ceiling.

Of course, it may have been the unusual heat with which this beautiful June day was blessed but it has to be admitted that no small part had also been played by that dog-eared little book she had found on her kitchen floor after that nasty little Ron Thompson had broken into the

163

house. There was no telling what he might have done if she had confronted him. A thieving dishonest wretch of a boy! When she thought about such, dare one say, 'literature' falling into the hands of the innocent, she could only marvel that some more heinous crime had not been perpetrated. Even though she had let the weeks slip by, she was determined to pin Ronald down to a confession, if only to save his soul. She would see to it that he would not be permitted to escape lightly the jaws of Lucifer.

In Miss Baldock's view, as much as in that of her friend, Miss Goodenough, such disgusting books should be withdrawn from circulation lest they fall into the hands of our innocent youth. The thought 'disgusted' her, not so much with young Ron's sexual awakening, but the unconscious revival of her own. As she reluctantly recalled her girlhood days at boarding-school, she brought to mind things which had happened and which had forever made her a sinner and a profligate. Growing older, she had come to realise the implication of such acts, with the result that she had become imprisoned in her own sense of guilt until, at last, finding no solace in her faith, had forsaken it for Rome. She made a pact with God. She confessed over and over again her wickedness and begged the Lord's forgiveness, and one blessing as a reward — that one day she would marry and thus be absolved both physically and spiritually. Alas, God had not found it in her interests to comply with her request, and she had so far been condemned to the rack of spinsterhood, living out her life voyaging over the lonely seas of celibacy.

Nevertheless, there were such things as blessings in disguise. Only recently, in the last months, she had sighted a haven, crumbling but still with vestiges of redoubt and power. It was not a case of any port in a storm, for the seas were growing calmer and her friendship with Councillor Gabriel Purvis was, one might say, less of a wet fish. Now, gazing at her ceiling-space, it became a broad seascape with a great ship surging over the waves and the blurred face of someone at the helm, someone who might just have been Gabriel, her angel in disguise, bringing light and, if not love, a mild element of romance into her life. Far-fetched as it may seem, amid all these vacillations of mood, she had grown in stature over these last months, without adding an ounce of weight to her thirteen stones.

As she was sipping her morning tea, her eye caught sight of *Love and Lucy Locket* lying, worn and dishevelled, between a copy of *Pear's Encyclopaedia* and the Catholic Breviary. She was surprised and not a

164

little guilty that she had been so undeniably tempted by a story so brash and crude. She could hardly have thought of herself in the role of the luscious Lady Lucy, yet something deep inside her allowed her to identify herself with that shameless temptress. Agnes remembered her difficulty at Confession on that bleak day earlier in the month, that fatal morning after she had read the book from cover to cover. She had called it all manner of names. It was un-Christian, diabolical, anti-Christ. It was filthy, disgusting, offensive, vulgar, loathsome. Hotness oozed from the cold print to a degree unlike any other book she had read.

Fear and envy forced her to place the blame on someone else. She had a strong suspicion that young Ronald had been the agent of the Devil, that the wicked novel had been placed before her as a test of her faith. With this in mind, she resolved upon the only course possible – she would read and resist. In the ensuing weeks 'Read and resist' were her watchwords. If, on the other hand, Ronald were by some chance to be playing the role of God's messenger, and that it had been by God's doing that this vile book had been brought to her notice, then it must be God's will that she should read it and, more to the point, resist its temptations — a kind of self-flagellation, an enjoyable punishment.

The words spun round and round in Agnes's brain. I am resisting, she told herself. I am resisting and this is my penance. She lay back on the pillows and resisted with such joy that it was not for some time that she realised an irreversible change had come about. She felt a new woman, a new more desirable Agnes. Her ceiling was revolving with new visions and sensations. She was going to surprise her friend the Councillor when she met him after Mass.

Agnes spent some considerable time giving herself a new-style home perm and getting out some long-forgotten ear-rings and a necklace that had belonged to her mother. She put on a silk summer dress with a pretty floral pattern and some smart court shoes. Her 'Angel Gabriel' was going to get a big surprise. As she was giving herself a quick spray of her new 'Fatal Fascination' perfume she remembered that she must not forget to corner Ronald Thompson about the missing money. At least *he* would be saved. She decided it would be prudent, however, at this stage, not to question him about how he came by that horrid novelette he had carelessly dropped on her kitchen floor.

36. Night and Day

Ron Thompson was bored. He didn't want to stay in; he didn't want to go out; he didn't want to paint; he didn't want to go the cinema; he didn't know what he wanted. The atmosphere indoors was hot and stuffy, but outside was worse, with the sun beating down into the backyard and Smutty panting and gasping all over everyone. Up and down like a jack-in-a-box Ron was, wandering from room to room aimlessly, mooning about the kitchen, making a nuisance of himself.

"Oh, Ron, do go out or something," complained Mrs. Thompson. "Go and play with Teddy. Fiddling about here all the time. Go on, now."

"Oh!" Ron grumbled, nonchalantly. "Can't even do flipping nothing in this house without getting torn off a strip."

"Now, then, my lad, none of your cheek. Do as I say, else I'll call your father."

Mrs. Thompson did not seem ever to notice the lameness of this last statement, nor did she perceive the inestimable sense of futility which filled Ron's inside as she uttered it. He hauled himself up the banisters in his mountaineering mode again. At the top, he caught a picture of Mabel — Mabel, covered from head to foot in her sister's face-powder. It was hanging on her eye-brows in miniature avalanches of pink snow, which fell in little light puffs onto her cheeks and tinted the ends of her eye-lashes. Ron wanted to laugh but he thought he'd set her off bawling again, and then there'd be a right old mess — all that dust and salt-water. He roamed into the front bedroom where Alf was snoring his head off after his Saturday-night out. A rush bag was lying on the floor, not very far away from several empty bottles. Ron picked it up. He had a brainwave. Devilry took charge of his pent-up energies. He was about to change Millie's appearance forever.

Meanwhile, Mabel had fingered her way downstairs, leaving a trail of powder behind her, delighted at the discovery that she too could have a day and a night face like her sister Millie. She walked, with as much dignity as she could muster, into the kitchen, where her mother was just putting the vegetables on to boil.

"'Mel me, Mummy, 'mel me!" she squealed with delight, her face thrust forward, eyes tight shut, arms splayed out like a birdling in flight.

Mrs. Thompson almost dropped the saucepan of boiling water. "I'll give you 'Smell me!' my girl. Come here this instant."

In less than the proverbial two shakes of a lamb's tail, Mabel's face, resembling the comical white face of a midget clown, was rapidly restored to its former self.

Whilst the screams of rage and humiliation were sturdily riding on the floating smells of pork chops frying in the pan, Ron was busy packing Millie's cosmetic accoutrements into the rush bag — hand-lotions, perfumes, eye-blues, pots of foundation cream, pots of cold cream, pots of vanishing cream, all did indeed vanish at magician Ron's command and were quickly transported downstairs with the deftness of a fully-trained house-breaker. The question was, where to hide it. Sneaking into the front-room, he quietly removed the ornaments and photographs on the piano and opened the lid. The reek of several pounds of moth-balls rose up, stung his nose and brought tears to his eyes. "Cor, blimey!" he thought, "this little lot'll do the world of good to that there little lot when they get together."

When Millie got out of the bath, there was hell to pay. She shouted. She screamed. She swore she'd murder the culprit if she could lay her hands on him.

Ron had never seen Millie so angry. "What a carry-on, I ask you!"

Millie was genuinely upset. It wasn't because of the heat. Not being able to find her precious make-up was only part of it. The truth was, she just didn't feel herself. In fact, she hadn't for several weeks now. She had hardly bothered about her appearance. The girls at the factory were talking about it. "What's up with Millie?" they said. She hadn't set her hair or given herself a facial for goodness knows how long, and she didn't care, either. Life for Millie just didn't seem the same anymore. One morning she had to run to the bathroom when she thought she was going to be sick. If she hadn't been going to meet Eddie for a walk and a chat in the Public Gardens, she wouldn't have worried about making herself look nice. She wanted to look nice for him, even if it was Curly she couldn't stop thinking about.

When Mabel saw Millie walk into the kitchen in broad daylight with her night face on she could have screamed, only that she was screaming anyway. Seeing Millie like this was nightmarish and grotesque. Mabel stopped crying more from the shock of it all than anything, realising for the first time how pretty her big sister was with her night face. Millie was so pretty that Mabel was suddenly all smiles. Ron laughed his head off thinking how silly girls were having two faces to cope with.

Mrs. Thompson was standing by the kitchen range clicking her tongue, shaking her head, and saying some such airy phrase as: "I don't know, really I don't!" Yet it seemed to bring everyone to their senses as they all came to table to partake of pork chops and beans. Every member of the family had some secret worry to chew over, not least Ron, who could not dispel a feeling of foreboding , some strange fear at the bottom of his stomach that told him the day was doomed to end in tears, just as it had started.

37. Monkey Business

As Agnes Baldock came down the steps of the Church of Our Lady of Lourdes, Councillor Purvis's eyes opened wide, blinked, and opened wider. It may have been because of the brilliance of her attire or simply sheer astonishment at the change. Whichever it was, it did not matter, since the effect was, to say the least, unusual. He saw that today Agnes had discarded her tweeds and earphone plaits; her hair was brushed lightly back, with the suggestion of a wave here and there. She was wearing a pale yellow suit of flowered silk, black patent leather shoes and handbag, and a broad-brimmed yellow sun-hat. No-one would have claimed that yellow was quite the right colour for Miss Baldock's ample figure, but taken all in all, she carried with her the spirit of the summer day that made our Borough Councillor proud to be beside her. Arm-in-arm, they made their way along the Sunday pavements of Rothersey High Street, nodding recognition to all and sundry as they passed.

"How about a turn in the Gardens, Agnes?" said Mr. Purvis.

"Perfect!" said Agnes in her customary serjeant-major voice.

They sauntered through the iron gates and turned down along the path past the park-keeper's lodge.

"Just look at those red roses there," said the Councillor. "What a sight!"

She screwed her eyes up into the sun and saw everything black. "Mm!" she purred. "Quite lovely, aren't they?"

"Makes you feel good to be alive," said Mr. Purvis, venturing to quote Burns:

My love is like a red, red rose
That's newly sprung in June.

168

He had to admit he couldn't remember the rest. Agnes continued:

My love is like the melody
That's sweetly played in tune.

The line perversely reminded him of the tuneless dissonances that were sometimes to be heard coming from the brass section of the Purvis Band!

"We used to sing that at school, oh dear, how many years ago?"

"I always feel good after I've been to Mass, Gabriel. The Mass is a wonderful tonic."

Councillor Purvis seemed momentarily perturbed, for a shadow passed across his face and it did not go unnoticed. They passed under the cool shade of Bushy Walk with its high elms, and shrubs in full flower

"I've enjoyed these last months, Agnes," he ventured.

She said nothing.

"It's been lonely with Gwen away in Yorkshire. I don't think she'll see the job through, mind. I can't see her as a nanny exactly. She'll miss home-life up there, all on her own."

"What you need, Gabriel, is to get yourself a wife. She could look after you properly, cook a decent meal for you as I do, and give you a little of life's comforts in your old age."

"Exactly what I... " he began and then faltered.

"What you need, Gabriel, is a good woman about the house to support you in your work. A pillar of strength she should be to you. Then you could go far. Every man in public service who's worth his salt has a capable woman behind him, especially if she has experience in entertaining and home-catering."

"Well, Agnes, that's what I was trying to say just ...."

"Now, in that direction, my dear Gabriel, the problem is easily solved."

"Problem?" said the bemused Councillor. "Solved?"

"Yes. Gabriel, solved," she said emphatically. "You and I, Gabriel. We'd make a good team."

"Team?" he said, weakly. He sat down on a bench that was conveniently beside them and began mopping the sweat from his brow.

"Oh, dear Agnes!"

"What's the matter, Gabriel?"

"Oh, nothing, my dear, nothing at all, only...."

169

"Gabriel, are you ill? Speak to me, Gabriel."

"I'm perfectly well," he said irritably. His sharp tone silenced her.

"I was going to say something of the sort myself, Agnes."

"'Something of the sort?' What's that supposed to mean?" she asked, a little on the defensive.

"It means, Agnes I am proposing to you." He took out a small square box from his waistcoat pocket and handed it to her with an air of — was it perhaps resignation, or trepidation? She opened the box and said with a tone of triumph:

"Oh, Gabriel, what a beauty! What a beauty!"

He took the ring and placed it on her finger, with the cryptic words: "Will that do?"

Agnes was suddenly filled with disillusionment, regret even. This was hardly the romantic proposal she had hoped for. What on earth did he mean — 'will that do?' The grubby little novelette crossed her mind, with 'her' lying on the grass and 'him' standing over her. It troubled her that she could think of anything so vulgar and trashy at such a moment as this. Gabriel could never match up to her image of 'him', though, believing herself to be in some way like 'her', as every woman might, she gazed down at her aging Councillor, sitting on his park bench, the natural redness returning at last to his cheeks, his grey wispy hair lightly touched by a gentle breeze, and she began to feel sorry for him. She also felt cheated out of something precious. She couldn't help herself when she said:

"It's hardly the way I had hoped."

She knew then that she had hurt him and experienced a mixture of pleasure and irritation at being so clumsy. She mollified him by saying:

"What I mean is, Gabriel, you haven't really proposed to me."

"Really, Agnes! At our ages we don't have to be sentimental, do we?"

When he finally did ask her to marry him, it came as a very damp squib and she nodded unsmilingly.

"Well, come along," she said. "We shall have to be getting home or our lunch will be spoilt. I put it on number four gas. You do remember you're having lunch with me, I suppose?"

"Yes, my dear," he sighed.

As Agnes and Gabriel set off towards the gates, something scuttled by them, stopped for a moment to scowl at them and then scoot off in the direction of the public lavatories.

"Oh" cried Agnes, cringing. "It's that nasty monkey. Shouldn't be allowed to run wild in a public place. It gave me quite a turn. Must be alive with fleas. What a horrid little creature!"

"That 'horrid little creature', as you call it, is little Mabel Thompson's best friend, I'll have you know."

"Hm!" Agnes grunted. "And she's no paragon of personal hygiene, either. That whole Thompson household ought to be fumigated."

They set off once more along the east side of the lake. A young man in jeans and leather jacket stood staring down at the water. The blade of a knife flicked and glinted in the sunlight.

"Well, well! If it isn't Mr. Donoghue. What a surprise!" said the Councillor nervously watching what Curly was going to do with the knife. "Lovely morning, isn't it? I haven't seen you about here for two or three months, now." Purvis thought for a moment. "Let me see, now –ah! yes! The Purvis Bowl, wasn't it? Back in February."

"What's it to you?"

Curly stood slouched over the water's edge, chewing gum and scowling. An enormous bubble emerged from his lips and expanded in Miss Baldock's direction. When it burst, she jumped. His jaw began moving rhythmically, up and down, up and down, in slow motion. He was standing with his hands in the pockets of his jeans, wiggling his thumbs nonchalantly.

"I aint bin around here lately, guv."

Mr. Purvis immediately foresaw the limitations of any conversation in that direction and addressed himself to Agnes. "Mr. Donoghue is a friend of Miss Thompson's, I believe."

Another voluminous bubble slowly appeared and burst in their faces. Agnes said:

"We have met before, in equally unfriendly circumstances, Mr. Donoghue and I. Are you still working for Mr. Crawford?"

"Huh! That bastard!" he snarled.

Ignoring his insolence, she said:

"And what has happened to that nice young Mr. Carpenter? I never seem to see him these days."

" 'E aint there no more. Scarpered! Aint seen 'im for a long time. Stole a lot o' money, he did. The guv'nor aint arf narked about it. Bleeding sods, the lot of 'em!"

"Mr. Donoghue! Please. Kindly refrain from such language in

171

the presence of a lady," said the increasingly frightened champion of the Borough.

"E-ooh, dee-ah!" said Curly attempting to mimic a genteel accent for the occasion. "Not in front of a lady. She aint no lady! I aint goin' to be told what to do by the likes of you."

Anger welled up inside him and he grabbed hold of the Councillor's lapels.

"Look, you creep, you aint no bleeding angel yourself, are you? You and that Millie Thompson I see yer with the other day. You bleeders are all the same, you are, with yer haw-hawin' and yer phoney ideas. Sitting on your arses up there at the Town Hall making one law for you and another for the likes o' me. Think you're God, don't you? Well, you can keep your gold-plated Daimlers and your minky molls. You're a bunch o' bastards, you are, the lot of you. BASTARDS!"

Agnes was not prepared to think about whether her newly-acquired fiancé had a gold-plated Daimler or not. "Come along, Gabriel," she said, firmly grabbing him by the arm.

"E-oh!" Curly said in an affected Oxford accent. "Bay awl mee-ans," and with a flourish of the arm and a sweeping bow he smiled the smile of an Iago as they hurried away.

"I'll get you, you creeps," shouted Curly after them. "Don't you ever speak to me like that again, see. I'm sensitive, I am."

The Councillor was transfixed for a moment. Agnes pulled him forward by the arm. She looked back to see if they were being followed. Curly was still standing at the water's edge, flicking his knife up and down in anger, the sharp blade still glinting in the hot sun.

"What a very unpleasant young man!" said Agnes.

This understatement seemed to pass over Mr. Purvis's whirring brain as he tottered out into Rothersey High Street. Miss Baldock was wondering what Donoghue had meant about Millie. As she walked along, she began to be obsessed by the thought, and would continue to be so until the mystery was solved.

38. Mixed Feelings

The transformation which had taken hold of Millie during the last month or so had to be seen to be believed as far as Eddie Carpenter was concerned. On this particular morning in June, she gave out a kind of radiance that made him feel good to be alive. She had brushed her hair into some semblance of its former self so that it fell lightly to her shoulders. It seemed so soft and silky that Eddie could hardly resist putting his hand up to stroke it — and maybe give her a kiss as well. Instead, he took her hand and led her to one of the benches along the lake-edge of Bushy Walk.

They sat together closely, Millie coyly clasping her fingers in her lap, her legs folded under the seat, while Eddie idly watched the ducks paddling by on the smooth water, ducks of mongrel bearing with mottled feathers, nondescript, doing bottoms-up and scrapping about below the surface with their bills. A cloud passed over the sun. It was only momentary, and such a thin wisp that it hardly cast a shadow, yet it was enough for Eddie to see the water go dull, turn grey. The trees seemed black and lifeless. He was touched with an emptiness, a feeling of being ridiculously small and terribly lonely. But the sunshine returned and things began to look better, especially when Millie spoke to him:

"Oh, it's so peaceful, Ed. I could stay here for ever, I could. So cool. This heat makes me feel quite queer, though. I feel proper bloated after that dinner. It aint right to eat all that greasy food at midday."

"You don't *have* to eat it, love."

"Yes, you do — when Mum cooks it and it's dumped on the table in front of you. She creates like anything if we don't eat what she cooks for us."

"Yeah!" said Eddie. "Everything in moderation, that's what I say."

" 'S all very well for you. You're a man."

Eddie certainly couldn't deny that. He just couldn't see the point of annoying Millie. Not today of all days. It wasn't everyday you proposed to a girl.

"I feel so happy here, away from everything," Millie mused. "All the kids playing and people strolling up and down as if they never had nothing to do but laze about all day long."

A few sprightly sparrows were happily flicking the muddy water with their wings and chirping, fluent and shrill.

"Proper treat it is, Mill'," said Eddie "You feeling all right now?"

"Not too bad. Must be the heat making me a bit sick and dizzy." She paused thoughtfully. "If only we never had to go back, Eddie. If

173

only something would happen and I never ever had to sit at that old work bench again."

"Must be murder up the old factory. You know," said Eddie, "you ought to have a boy-friend, Mill'. Someone as'd look after you, take you dancing, give you a bit of fun. Maybe even get spliced later on if it worked out. Have a few kids maybe."

"Kids!" she said, almost violently. "Kids? Not for me, mate. I want to get away from all that, I do. There are more than enough kids in our house, what with Ron and Mabel. And all that screaming and bawling and nagging and bickering that goes on. You ought to know, with your old Ma the way she was."

"Taint always like that, Millie. I mean, sometimes people's afraid. Afraid of themselves, like. They feel – oh! I dunno – ashamed to love somebody, let alone tell 'em they do. Frightened to let it out like it was a sin or something."

"It isn't a sin to love someone," said Millie. Her face grew suddenly serious for a moment. "Let's go. It'll soon be tea-time. Anyway, it's getting chilly, here in the shade. Let's get out into the sun, shall we?"

"Well, you're a fine one, I must say. First it's hot, then it's cold."

"Oh, do come on. You know what Mum is for worrying."

Eddie stood up and handed her white knitted cardigan, which she had been carrying over her arm all afternoon.

"You didn't need it after all," he said lamely.

She was miles away, thinking about somebody else. She half-closed her eyes, almost mesmerised by the warm breeze as it touched the surface of the water and rustled the dark leaves of the viburnum.

"Do you ever go up the market these days?"

"No, not now. Never have no cause to. Anyway, I was never one for the early mornings."

"Ever see Curly now?"

"No," he said defensively. "Not since I got the sack. Now I come to think of it, he's giv up the market stunt as far as I know."

"Why don't you go up and see him sometime?" she persisted.

"Whatever for?"

"Well, you was a pal of his, wasn't you?"

"Yeah, I suppose I was. A time ago though. Anyways, we never got on really. Too much of a smart-alick. Thinks he's God, the way he goes on."

174

"Don't you ever see him up the gym?"

"The gym?"

"Yes, you know," she insisted. "You go up there for work-outs now, don't you?"

"Stone the crows! How did you know?"

"Old Pop Purvis told me the other day. He see you going in and out. Curly goes up there too, don't he?"

"Not now, he don't. Packed it in, he has. Getting too big for that kind of stuff now he's the king-pin of the bowling alley." He bit his lip. Now he'd let the cat out of the bag!

"So that's where he hangs out," she said. She smiled triumphantly.

"Yeah! Getting proper tough, he is, with his leathers and flick-knives. One day he'll get hisself into trouble."

Millie grew silent and morose. They stopped to watch the children skipping round by the water.

"Why ever d'you go, Eddie?"

"Go where?"

"Up the gym, of course."

Eddie could not see any 'of course' about it, but he calmly replied:

"Oh! I dunno, duck. Just makes me feel good, that's all. It's something to do of an evening. Anyway, I get so blinking tied up with the old books, see? Some lah-di-dah bloke was letting off steam about this geezer called Buskin or Rustin or something. All to do with 'co-ordination' or something."

"You mean 'Ruskin', soppy."

Well! After that remark, as the saying goes in Rothersey, you could have knocked Eddie down with a feather. "Ruskin. That's the bloke. How the 'ell did you know about a geezer like 'im?"

" 'Cos I got an aunty living in Camberwell, see?"

"What the flippin' 'ell has this Ruskin got to do with Camberwell?"

" 'Cos we used to play in Ruskin Park, see? That's the name of the park, see? Cor! You aint 'arf dim."

"Leadin' off a bit, aren't you? Anyway, who cares what it's called? What's more, Curly don't go there no more."

"He never did, stupid!"

"Course he did. It was his idea in the first place."

Millie stopped, shrugged her shoulders, pouted her lips, and said:

"Would you mind telling me *what* on earth you're talking about, Eddie Carpenter?"

"The gym, of course."

"Oh, I see. That's it, is it. I thought we was supposed to be talking about Ruskin Park, or wasn't we?"

"Oh, forget Ruskin-bloody-Park, can't you? I couldn't care tuppence about it."

" 'Ere, Eddie Carpenter. Don't you speak to me like that! I didn't come out here to be shouted at, so you can be a bit more of a gent and take me home."

She started walking off towards the gates, but Eddie caught her by the arm. Near panic seized him that this might be the end of his hopes.

"Don't be like that, Mill. I didn't mean it, really I didn't. It's this heat. Makes me a bit edgy, see?"

A kind of alienation had suddenly grown up between them, and Eddie couldn't understand how he could have allowed it to happen. Try as he would, he couldn't get Millie back onto the old intimate wavelength that they had so briefly tuned into only ten minutes ago, sitting down by the lake in the cool shade of the elms.

"It's four o'clock," she said firmly. "We'll have to be getting back."

While Millie was spending a penny or two in the *Ladies*, Eddie kicked around outside, cursing himself for being such a fool as to put Millie's back up the way he had. Things might never be the same again. He found a flat stone and started to play at ducks-and-drakes, but the stone hit the water and sank instantly, leaving a series of ripples which spread over the surface into nothingness. He kicked another stone into the water with a splash and turned on his heels into the *Gentlemen's*. He was surprised to see a monkey sitting in the corner by the urinals, cracking nuts. Eddie felt self-conscious going about his business with the beady-eyed little beast staring up at him and making little crick-cracking noises with his teeth. Then he found himself being affected by the poignant, distressed look in its eyes. If only it could have talked, it would have told him what he wanted to know about several unsolved mysteries. One of the cubicles was engaged. He assumed the old organ-grinder was in there. Everything seemed very quiet.

Out in the sunlight once more, Eddie caught sight of the outline of a dark figure in the shadow of the bushes on the west side of the lake

— a tall, darkened silhouette against a background of sunlit leaves. The man was holding something metal in his hands, for it flashed when it broke into a stray ray of sunshine from the branches above. The hands moved nervously, fingers moving up and down the blade. The figure moved forward into the sun and aimed the knife at the worn wood of the bench Eddie and Millie had been sitting on only minutes ago. The blade stuck, trembling and quivering in the wood, and Eddie found himself looking straight into the eyes of Curly Donoghue and the eyes were like knives.

When Millie at last emerged from the *Ladies*, Eddie hustled her through the gate into the hotness of the dusty streets.

"What's the hurry?" she asked.

"I thought you wanted to get home, " he said, thankful for any excuse to prevent Millie from catching sight of Curly.

"Yes, but we don't have to go off at a gallop, do we?"

Her voice was softer now. She seemed more composed and ready to be pleasant.

"Well," she said, sighing, "I reelly enjoyed that."

"Enjoyed what?" He smiled meaningfully at her, but to his dismay, she was not amused.

"Your mind,"she remonstrated. "Like a sewer, it is. I can't even enjoy the simple pleasures of a Sunday in the Gardens without you making a dirty joke out of it."

She wouldn't have minded if it had been Curly suggesting it. At all events, Eddie was too anxious to get Millie home safely to worry about any misunderstanding between them over an innocent remark.

EPISODE NINE

Afternoon on the same day

Up to No Good!

39.   Peaceful Co-Existence

St. Crispin's Hall was no smaller than most church halls of its kind, with neo-gothic windows and doors and the atmosphere of a mausoleum after a funeral wake. The odour of stale food and curdled milk, remnants from the Scouts' fund-raising social last week, emanated from the poky little kitchen. The windows at the back on the south side looked on to the Public Gardens, or would have done so if you could have seen through them, for they were filled with alternate panes of pink and yellow glass, which cast a strangely mottled glow on the faces of the little group of old people seated on the hard wooden chairs, a glow which was at once inflamed and jaundiced.

About a dozen or so people had spread themselves sparsely among the first few rows of chairs, and a handful of others had settled down in isolated defensive positions. They sat or lounged or slumped or curled up in ones and twos, with the occasional oasis of faces dotted about down the middle aisle. Beyond stretched a yawning wilderness of empty chairs.

Councillor Joseph Gabriel Purvis, as Chairman, was flanked by Councillor Patrick Ignatius Xavier Calthrop (popularly known as 'Pixie') (Moral Re-Armament Committee) and Miss Agnes Gertrude Baldock (British League of Womanhood) on his right, whilst on his left sat, or slumped, the perspiring Reverend 'Daniel in the Lion's Den' Curtis, Vicar of St. Crispin's (Passive Resistence Brotherhood), and a rather purple-nosed Alf Thompson bearing a white banner announcing in large red and blue letters:

> # PEACE AND PLENTY
> # FOR BRITAIN
> # THROUGH
> # STRENGTH FAITH SECURITY

At this particular moment, Joe Purvis seemed to be seriously lacking in all three of these precious tenets. He did not feel quite himself. As he mumbled his way through to a conclusion, mild half-hearted applause broke across the sultry airless hall. He had the uncomfortable thought that the audience were clapping not for the content of his speech but because they were thankful he had come to an end. An over-filled stomach and the heady bitterness of the morning's events had taken their toll of his natural resources of eloquence and persuasiveness. He had droned on in a manner that was both wayward and inarticulate, relying unwisely on his new love as the spur to rhetoric. His stomach was burning like fire. He gulped down the sourness of his heartburn. Agnes did not appear to be the cook he had imagined her to be. All dumplings and spotted-dog. Not like his Gwen's culinary flights of fancy. Now, there was a fine cook if ever there was one. And another thing — he had missed out on his Sunday afternoon nap. He really ought to have had that, just indeed like the Vicar, who was clearly enjoying his spell of shut-eye at this very moment.

When Councillor Calthrop rose to speak, he faced a dozen pairs of eyes which looked straight through him. Out of his slumbrous stupor, the Vicar once more wiped his sweating brow and sagged into his chair like a long thin balloon with the air let out. The handkerchief slipped from his grasp and fell to the floor. It was as if he had thrown down the gauntlet of sleep and the audience had taken it up, for their heads were lolling in all directions.

Once the rampant Pixie got going, it would have taken a great deal more than a hot sultry afternoon to stop him from droning on about 'Peaceful Co-Existence'. He was a big man, burly and self-assured. Although not completely bald, he gave the impression of being so, unless you were standing close to him and could see his pale thinning hair plastered down onto the scalp. From a distance, it looked more like a grubby patch on the top of his head deposited by a passing bird. He was wearing his usual week-end attire — a neat little yellow and grey checked suit with brown and white brogue golfing shoes. From time to time, he too mopped his forehead with a floppy Paisley silk handkerchief. Strutting up and down the platform, he declaimed to his drowsy audience:

"......and I say, ladies and gentlemen, let us not forget the past and its mistakes — (*pause to allow for thinking about mistakes*) — Let us not forget the criminal acts of irresponsible politicians throughout the world. Let us not forget the lust for power and dominion of one madman over countless millions of innocent people — a scale of human degradation and cruelty the like of which the world has not seen since the rigours and terrors of the First World War."

At this point, the doors at the back of the hall swung briskly open. In trooped a rough-looking gang of youths, fresh from a drinking session at *The Bed of Roses*. At the sight of these bucolic red-faced louts, Councillor Calthrop momentarily lost his train of thought, faltered and came to a stop, whilst the rest of the audience turned round to see what was happening. As Calthrop resumed, Miss Baldock once more sank back into her chair and began musing on her life-to-be. She had dreamed for so long of being able to break away, yes, dreamed of the time when she would be able to go to the General Manager of the Roxy and tell him exactly what she really thought of his decrepit old cinema. She had other fish to fry! Now, she had handed in her notice and things were going to be very different.

The heat in the hall grew in intensity but Calthrop failed to notice the rolling eyes and twisted yawning faces of his deflated audience. The Vicar was doing very nicely — dreaming of pastures new and stipends fit for a bishop. Intermittent snores and grunts rose on the fuggish air.

".....and furthermore, let us not forget our young ones, brought up amidst the strife and anguish of a world whose earnest desire for peace was fraught with suspicion, abject cruelty and hatred. Our youth today must not be forgotten, ladies and gentlemen. Seeing them represented here this afternoon gives me hope, yes, hope for the future of our movement. Their support is vital to our success. With them we shall go forth undaunted into a future of 'Peace and Plenty'."

Calthrop paused for applause but none came. No-one seemed to realise he had finished speaking. The dozy Vicar, the pensive Joe and the day-dreaming Agnes were so comatose they might just as well have stayed at home for all the use they were. They appeared to be attending some private meeting of their own. By this time, Alf was falling round his banner with post-prandial fatigue, the pole swaying dangerously back and forth.

"Purvis!" snapped Calthrop. "Purvis! Wake up, man!"

The Councillor came out of his reverie, with dignity it must be said, and declared the meeting open for questions. Sounds of snufflings from the catarrhal occupant of a seat in the second row was all that could be heard.

A hand went up at the back.

"Yes, my boy!" said Purvis encouragingly, relieved at the chance to cover up the sound of the wheezing donkey in front of him.

"'Skee-ooz me matey! What ti-oime is it?"

"What time? Let me see. Er– what time is it?" said the

182

Councillor, taking out his fob-watch.

"Can't you bloody-well understand English, mate?" shouted the youth.

Another hand went up.

"Please. Your Warship, is this some sort o' panel game or summink?"

"No, it is not," snapped Purvis. "Please ask sensible questions."

"What does the team fink about 'Free Love'?" asked a shrill voice.

Loud, coarse laughter rang through the hall, stirring those who were snoozing to come out of their wakeful stupor. Only the Vicar was inviolable, as if turned to stone.

"Where do you keep the beer, guv'nor?" said one heckler.

"What's the panel's view on —?"

"Yes, yes, come along. Come along. Ask your question so that everyone can hear it," said Calthrop in a loud voice. The question was repeated, this time louder.

"What's the panel's view on 'avin' a nice bit o' nooky with the local tarts?"

Consternation came about through one of the snoozers who, acting from a remarkable subliminal impulse, awoke in a state of shock, and, rising to his feet in a stupor, shouted at the top of his voice:

"DISGUSTING!!"

A volcanic eruption of disapproval broke loose and spread through the hall like lava. The supporters of the League Peace and Plenty shook their fists and returned the abuse in full measure. Like a swarm of angry bees, they descended on these thugs with a threatening whoop.

"I'll deal with this, Purvis," said Calthrop. "A damnable pickle you've made of things, I must say."

He stepped to the front of the platform and spoke in a loud voice:

"I must ask you to stop this *fracas*."

"Here, you blokes," said a big muscular fellow with a scar on his neck, " he called me a f— "

"I will not put up with your vulgar wit, you oaf," shouted Miss Baldock, with a timely interruption..

" 'Ere! Did you call me a vulgar nit, you old cow?"

"I certainly did not," shouted the good lady.

Calthrop saw out of the corner of his eye that Rat Purvis and his

Roxy paramour were sidling away towards the wings.

"Come back, you cowards!" he shouted desperately. "Deserting the sinking ship, are we? Come back, I say!"

"Vulgar nit, did you say? Lets 'ave 'em, lads."

The first thing 'Pixie' felt was a blow on his midriff that sent his brussels sprouts whirling round inside him like a tornado. Over went the table and chairs. Down came the glasses and water-jug with a smash. Up jumped the defenders of the faith from the audience. Fights broke out in isolated sectors of the battle, between the gang and some of the younger League supporters. The Moral Re-Armament crowd were looking decidedly battered, and the Passive Resistence supporters sat as stiff as pokers and refused to lift a finger.

Miss Baldock felt something horrid squash into her neck. Her fingers revealed the remains of a cheese and tomato sandwich, dropped by a fleeing lady in a yellow and green woolly hat. The youth who launched this squelchy missile then smashed a chair against the wall and came at Calthrop with a leg in his hand. He fell over an amazon struggling with a fat woman in a straw hat and was well and truly winded when she threw a punch at an offending thug which hit him by mistake. It was a case of sheer bulk against *papier maché.*

Meanwhile Alf was struggling with two sturdier youths who were determined to wrest the banner from his grasp. He was equally determined that they should not. He gave one of his assailants a sharp left hook and, gripping the banner with his right hand, he kicked with his hob-nailed boots into their tender parts. Puffing and blowing at each other, vicious oaths were exchanged of increasing quality and poetic range. The banner began to sway ominously over the battle-field. Precariously, it lurched forward, remaining for a brief instant still and vertical, then came crashing down into the turmoil of heads and arms and legs.

Now a tug-o'-war ensued for possession of the banner. Three, then four, then more pairs of hands ripped it asunder in an effort to claim a souvenir. Small scraps of material with enigmatic blue lettering on floated down and were trampled underfoot. One piece read: '----**UGH**', another **'PLENTY FOR - RITA - -'** and so on. A cheer went up when a loyal defender found '**STRENGTH**' all in one piece.

Rather belatedly, the Vicar of St. Crispin's awoke out of his dreams of a more luxurious living, gazed at the disarray before him, incapable of any sensible remark beyond: "May the Lord have mercy on us!" — a sadly needed prayer for a brutally disestablished order. In his ears was the sound and the fury of cloth being rent in twain, and he wondered, seeing Miss Baldock locked in battle with an angry-looking youth, if she might not be in some embarrassing predicament before long.

"STOP!!!" he cried. "POLICE!!!"

But for all the good it did, he might just as well have invoked them to "fight the good fight" for the sound of battle calls, splitting wood, scuffling feet, grunting and groaning and as varied an assortment of swearings as you could find anywhere in the kingdom, all continued with a fearsome fury.

Calthrop was now being helped off by a supporter, as was a bedraggled Agnes Baldock, insistent on a fight to the finish. Her good Councillor was crumbling in the kitchen amidst the frugal fare of stale buns and cakes.

"POLICE!!!" intoned the Vicar more loudly, really beginning to enjoy the whole thing with a relish of a child at play. He could hardly have expected a more exciting afternoon to recount in his diary. Incitement to his flock to defend the faith at all costs earned him a smack in the eye with a ball of wet toilet paper. When he came to his senses the troublemakers were already retreating.

"Scarper, lads!" shouted the ring-leader.

In a matter of minutes, peace was restored, though judging by the upturned furniture, broken chairs, fragments of glass, a large number of ripped-off buttons of a range and size familiar only to Millie, one solitary brown shoe, a fractured flag-pole, the 'Peace and Plenty' banner in shreds all over the floor, and an artistic arrangement of intimate articles supporting 'Free Love' pinned up on the noticeboard announcing 'Recreational Activities', this was all far in excess of any little bit of vandalism perpetrated by Cromwell's troops during the Civil war, and displayed a degree of chaos unknown to the Church Hall in all its history. |

Only the smiling, starry-eyed Vicar was triumphant, full of profuse 'bravos' for his loyal parishioners. His inexplicable return to second childhood had driven from his mind any impression of the picture of devastation that lay before him. Now, however, he stopped in his tracks, sobered by the prospect of a great deal of clearing up to be done before the day was out. Alf, ever hopeful of some liquid comfort, had more than earned his pint of bitter at *The Bed of Roses.*

40. Restoration Comedy

Mrs. Thompson sat quietly knitting by the kitchen window. She gazed out into the yard, littered now with Smutty's old bones, clothes-pegs, bits of rusty iron, and as fine a collection of old discarded cupboards, chests of drawers, hutches and coops as could be seen anywhere. They housed a wide variety of useless, long-forgotten objects — rusty tin-openers, old bicycle pumps, toffee-tins of nails and screws, rubber bands matted together with age, brushes with no bristles left on them, and an old cat's-whisker receiving set. Of the many pet rabbits, tortoises and hamsters the hutches once were home to, nothing but a trace or two of a feather or tuft of fur remained.

Mrs. Thompson was expecting Alf to come home from the 'Peace and Plenty' meeting well by five o'clock. What's more, she had asked him to invite Miss Baldock and the Councillor as well. So it turned out to be rather a special tea for a number of reasons. Out came the best table-cloth with the crocheted border and the rarely-used best china. But where was everybody?

When the front-door-bell rang, Flo almost jumped out of her skin. She ran about all over the place as if her time had come to depart this life and she had to leave everything in order. She shouted to Ron to come down and find Mabel, who had been forcibly washed and dressed soon after lunch and had not been seen since. Flo turned on the gas, put the kettle on and began fussing about, looking for things she couldn't find at any price and didn't need in the end anyway. Where had she put the sugar-tongs and the tea-strainer last Christmas?

When she opened the door to welcome Miss Baldock and her Councillor, she was not as surprised as she might have been that Alf was not with them. She showed them through to the front room, settled them into armchairs and stood wringing her hands and nervously wiping them on her back-side.

"Lovely day?" she said lamely.

"Not so much as you might think," said a grim-faced Miss Baldock. "We suffered, shall I say, a small humiliation at the hands of some hooligans. Several of our members were hurt in the crush."

"Oh my gawd!" exclaimed Mrs Thompson. "Not my Alf! Is he hurt? Tell me."

" Not too badly – at least I don't think so," said Mr. Purvis.

"Oh, my GAWD!" shouted Mrs. Thompson. "What does that mean? Was he or wasn't he?"

"He received a blow between the eyes, I think. A most commendable defence, if I may say so," said Mr. Purvis. "As was that of my dear Agnes here, who tackled and laid low one of the louts by sitting on his chest until support came from our rear-guard. Most commendable!"

"That's all very well, Mr. Purvis," cried Mrs. Thompson. "But, where's my Alfie."

"He was held up."

"Held up?" said the demented Mrs. T. in a sarcastic tone. "Held up? What with? A gun?"

"No, no, no! My good woman. He stayed behind to help clear up the mess."

"Oh, very well," said Mrs. Thompson more calmly. "Tea'll be ready in a jiffy."

'Good woman, indeed!' thought Flo, all hoity-toity.

When Ron realised that Miss Baldock was in the house, he went straight back upstairs and refused to come down again. Millie was in no mood for entertaining either, especially when she knew the Councillor was actually sitting in their front-room. Her mother was bound to ask awkward questions about the visit back in the Spring, and why was it her dear innocent little girl was so sick after it.

As for Mabel, she had, since dinner-time, been out in the back-yard in her spruce clean dress and filled her panties with coal so as to help a little in the business of entertaining. She had waylaid Smutty, who had invited her into his kennel for a chat, but the heat was so intense that she decided to make it only a short courtesy call. When Mrs. Thompson found her, she was so upset at the sight of her that she broke two of her best tea-cups and had to use the kitchen ones instead.

"You NAU–ghty LI–ttle GIR–irl!" she shouted angrily, smack-a-smack-smacking Mabel, whose face was streaming with coal-black tears.

Millie was ordered to leave her pop records and come downstairs and to look sharp because wouldn't she please like to make herself useful for once and clean up Mabel before she could be made presentable enough to join the company of their distinguished guests.

"Well, Millie!" exclaimed the Councillor, his face beaming. "How are we today?"

"Not too bright," she said. "Had one of me turns."

"So you're having turns, are you? What sort of turns?"

"Ooh! Ever so queer. Fainting feelings, sick feelings, you

187

know."

He didn't know, but he tried to show some interest.

"Miss Baldock and I have tied the matrimonial knot today, Millie. That is, rather a reef-knot than a granny-knot, you understand. We are affianced, you might say." Millie did not understand the manner or meaning of his pompous announcement, but exercised a little of her feminine intuition sufficiently to exclaim: "Engaged?", astonished as she was that this unlikely couple could be so attractive to each other.

"Well, then, I suppose I ought to congratulate you."

"Mum," shouted Millie to her mother in the kitchen. "The Councillor and Miss Baldock have gone and got themselves engaged?"

"Enraged? What about?" Mrs. Thompson shouted back, still thinking of the furore at the Church Hall.

"Not enraged, stupid! Engaged!"

"Whatever for, dear?"

Millie gave up. She couldn't be bothered to make herself heard above the clatter of tea-things.

Going into the hall, Mrs. Thompson called Ron and Mabel to come immediately or else they'd soon know about it. She took in the tray of tea.

"So Millie's not too well, Mrs. Thompson."

"It's the first I've heard of it."

"Needs a pill, that's what she needs," said Miss Baldock.

Mabel appeared from nowhere, having been washed and thoroughly scrubbed. Millie slumped down into her chair and looked tearful.

"Say hello to the nice people, then," said Mrs. Thompson to Mabel, removing the green-and-purple tea-cosy she had knitted herself. The colours were rather too close to the way poor Millie was feeling at the moment and she suddenly began to feel sick again.

Reluctant Ron slouched in. Miss Baldock glared at him and he was thankful when, almost immediately, Mabel made a mess in her replacement panties, had to be quickly removed to clear the air. Miss Baldock's nose began to twitch and there were screams and tears all the way to bed for the *dear* but thoroughly disgraced little Mabel.

"Mabel's such a cry-baby, she really is," complained Mrs. Thompson. "Not 'alf so easy as our Millie was. Never heard a sound from her, you didn't. As good as gold, she was."

The way Millie felt, the gold was getting a bit tarnished.

"Another sardine sandwich, Miss Baldock?" said the hostess.

"Oh, I do wish Alf would come. Where on earth has he got to?"
The lady took two sandwiches stuck together, and commented: "They are rather big, aren't they?"
The stupid old twit, thought Ron, trying to stifle a giggle.
"Take two and then I won't have to keep passing the plate," said Mrs. Thompson. "How's your Gwen, Mr. Purvis?"
"Alas, she's gone up north to be a nanny."
"Well I never! How's yours, Miss Baldock?"
"I haven't any," said the perplexed lady.
"No, I mean your cup, dearie."
"It's doing very nicely, thank you," Agnes said sharply.
"Of course," said Flo, "it's such a trial cleaning up after them all. Worse than Ma Carpenter's parrots, they are. Now, there's a thing for you! A parrot can talk better than most people I know. One day, they was offering prizes for the parrot that could speak the clearest so Ma took her'n down the Church Hall." She began to laugh. "Oh dear! It was so funny. I must tell you"
"Oh, please, don't," protested Miss Baldock. "I do hate stories about parrots. They are always so vulgar."
"This one isn't vulgar but it's darned funny, I can tell you. They used to pick up all sorts of words from old Ma. One used to say "How's your father?" and the other would reply: "Tipping up a pint."
Flo burst into a fit of laughing but the lady-guest was unmoved.
"I must tell you," Flo went on. "Once, when the Vicar come totterin' round on the judgin' lark, he scratched his finger on the cage, sayin': "Tweet! Tweet! Tweet! Pretty Poll! Pretty Poll!" and the bird said: "Belt up and bugger off!" Flo fell into fits. "You should 'ave seen the Vicar's face." Miss Baldock winced at the predictable punch-line but for Mrs. Thompson, the joke seemed to possess an eternal kind of humour that could stand the re-telling. Mr. Purvis smiled for the first time on this chaotic afternoon.
"Gabriel!" said Miss Baldock, looking very sternly at her belovèd, instantaneously removing his smile.
"Have a date bun," said Mrs. Thompson. Then she picked up the green-and-purple cosy-covered tea-pot and hurried out into the kitchen. "I'll just go and top up."
"Well, now, young Ronald," said the Councillor. "How are we getting on at school these days?"
Ron's stomach seized up. He chewed up his sardine sandwich into a hard lump and swallowed it. It pushed its way through his gullet

189

like the blade of a sword-swallower, straight down into his rebellious inside. He went rigid and pale when Miss Baldock asked:

"Have you been doing any reading lately, Ronald?"

"Not much," he said guardedly.

"I believe I have a book of yours, haven't I?" she persisted. "Perhaps you would care to come round and collect it."

"You aint got no book o' mine," said Ron forgetting his school grammar, him doing so well and all that.

"Ronald, where's your grammar, boy? Now look here! I could hand it in to Miss Goodenough when I next see her. I'm sure she will be delighted to speak to you about it. Of course," – she paused – "You could call for it this evening!"

Not blinkin' likely, thought Ron.

The conversation turned to the topic of Curly Donoghue. Millie was intrigued to know he had been seen in the Public Gardens, but in spite of her anxious questioning she could get nowhere with the Councillor or Miss Baldock, who both began to vilify him as much as they could. At this, Millie suddenly burst into tears and ran from the room, bumping into her mother on the way, knocking the fresh supply of tea all down the hall carpet and slopping it over the wallpaper.

"Look what you've done, Millie. Just look at my carpet. Why don't you look where you're going, you silly girl. I'll never get those stains out. What a mess!"

Ron took the opportunity of skedaddling while the going was good, so the two guests decided it was opportune to make their escape, and rose in concert.

Flo's protests went unheeded and the Councillor and his soon-to-be 'lady-wife' advanced towards the front door. As Flo opened it, a green van swerved into the Villas amid an alarming chorus of hooters and horns, scattering pedestrians ambling home in the lazy heat of the late afternoon, and coming to a halt outside No 4.

The astonished and bewildered Mr. Purvis drew back into the doorway against the shock-absorber of Agnes's bosom. Everyone stared at the van as it rocked to a standstill. On the side, a defaced 'Peace and Plenty for Britain' poster proclaimed the cryptic message:

– ACE AND – LEN – FOR – RITA –

Though the whereabouts of 'Ace' and 'Len' were anybody's guess, no-one could remember getting an eyeful of 'Rita', whoever *she* was!

Alf came rolling out of the driver's seat and straight into the unwilling arms of the departing Miss Baldock. A look of terror and distaste crept over her face as the stench of Alf's beery breath tickled the tip of her nose and burnt up into her nostrils. Somehow the whole company were swept back towards the kitchen like lumps of seaweed on a tidal wave.

"How about a kiss for the bride?" said Alf, clutching Miss Baldock and stretching out his lips over the protrusive bosom.

"Mr. Thompson, really!" gasped Miss Baldock.

Alf took hold of her more tightly and began quick-stepping round the table and singing at the top of his voice:

Good night, sweetheart,
All my prayers are for you.
Goodnight, sweetheart,
I'll be watching o'er you;
Tears and parting may make us forlorn
But with the dawn
A new day is born —

"Mr. Thompson," screeched Miss Baldock, just like Ma Carpenter's parrot, "let me go this instant."

Her ample frame was being whirled round and round at an alarming speed as they fell in a heap against the chairs and the buckets and the motley collection of boots and shoes by the back-door.

"PLE-**EASE**! Mr. Thompson, **STOP!!!** Gabriel, **DO** something! **Help**! Everyone!" she gasped. As they lay sprawled on the floor, Alf sang his heart out:

Goodnight, sweetheart,
Till we meet tomorrow

He kissed her boldly and sloppily on the cheek, breathing more of his fumes into her face and eyes. Flo, who had put her hands up in horror and shame, couldn't hold herself in any longer. She burst into a fit of uncontrollable laughter and merriment so infectious that Ron and Millie forgot all their troubles and began laughing too, and doubling up

191

with delight and amusement, and thinking all the time that they had never seen anything so funny as this in all their born days.

41. How Curly Got His Come-uppance

Ma Blackwood's trade was pretty brisk on Sunday afternoons in summer. The shop was filled with a gaggling crowd of local kids all buying humbugs, whipped cream walnuts, liquorice laces, lemon sherbets, sugar mice, marzipan eggs, jelly-babies, gob-stoppers, chocolate nut crunch and her own special brand of fruit lollies. Outside, the paint was bright and new — yellow with gleaming blue edges to the windows and doors. Above the window, stretched a sign:

☺ *Ma Blackwood's Lollipop Shop* ☺

in all the colours of the rainbow. A large pink lollipop on a barber's barley-stick pole projected out over the pavement as a sign of her trade.

Ma Blackwood was a perfect angel with the kids, and they loved her — with her old rheumaticky hands and her long black dress with all the pockets, into which she frequently delved to bring out the occasional gob-stopper for her favourites, of whom little Mabel was one. Mabel was good business for Ma.

"'Allo, my little darlings," she would say to her *protégés*, "and what shall it be today? A nice sugar mouse or a chocolate bear?"

When money was insufficient, she would tut-tut-tut at them, examine the little grubby outstretched hands and say:

"Well, well! We'll have to see what we can do, won't we?"

Then she would bring out some gob-stoppers, or a handful of aniseed balls from one of the neat rows of sweet-jars on the counter, and there would be laughing and dancing down the street as the colours changed from red to purple and purple to yellow.

After six o'clock, Ma Blackwood turned into a sort of modern-day female Fagin. As soon as she had hustled the last persistent little buyer out of the shop, she put up the shutters, taking care to give a wave to the policeman on point duty, went in and locked, barred and bolted everything in sight. This done, she drew out from behind the counter some bottles of beer and shouted through the back door:

"O.K. boys! Come and get it."

The door creaked open and in slouched an assortment of scruffy-looking youths in jeans, black leather biker's boots, and rings like knuckle-dusters on their itchy fingers. It was just like the dark side of a fairy-story:

Now, all children soon come to know that the world we live in is not always as sweet as it seems [a fact little Mabel was soon to find out]. *You see, after six o'clock in the evening, not only did Ma Blackwood change her character, she changed her looks. A magical transformation took place in the shape and expression of the old witch's face. Her jaw seemed to drop, her mouth tightened up, her eyes became like slits. As for her complexion, it turned from rosy red to a muddy grey in a matter of seconds. She changed in the twinkling of an eye from the angelic purveyor of sugary delights that Mabel loved, into a greedy, vicious, toady old hag that nobody liked, not even Pa himself. To be perfectly frank, Ma Blackwood's double life was a tale that would be better classified under the heading: 'Not in front of the children'!*

Soon the counter was arrayed with a motley selection of rings, necklaces, bracelets, ear-rings, and a variety of bejewelled articles of questionable value. She took out her jeweller's glass and peered at each in turn, silently twisting each in her fingers and doing some pretty heavy breathing at the same time. The boys sprawled about the shop, watching Ma's face for signs.

"Well?" said Ma, as she picked up a lady's silver cigarette case.

A tall, lanky youth spoke up:

"Ladies' toilet up the Roxy. She come back for it just a bit too late. Helluva rumpus an' all."

"Good bit of work, Bertie boy. You're doing just fine." She picked up a sparkling bracelet. "Well, come on, lads, which of you is it?"

A boy in drainpipe trousers and sporting a quiff of hair in the very latest style announced with pride:

"Off an old gel having a dekko at the monkeys up the zoo. I coulda wet meself laughing at the old bird telling people to watch their purses."

There was a burst of laughter but Ma soon shut them up and said

193

scornfully:

"Paste!" she sneered.

The boy looked sour and dangerous and might well have given her a good going over if she hadn't been Ma Blackwood. As he went to take another swig of beer, she snapped at him:

"And not so much of that rat's poison, either. Costs me a deal of dollars and well you know it."

She picked up a pair of pendant ear-rings.

"What's this trash, eh?"

"But Ma! Genu – ine Mayfair, that is," said a spotty-faced youth. "Real Berkeley Square stuff, with nightingales on!"

"Who said you could do these classy jobs, eh? Big-head! Stick to the streets you know. I thought I was running an outfit for small-time pick-pockets, not for gang of smarties of the likes of you."

With that, she threw the offending articles across the room at him. "I'm warning you," she said angrily.

The boy picked up the ear-rings and crept back into his hole in the corner.

"You little squirt, you! Don't you give me any more lip. May be one day, you'll learn what's worth it and what aint. Just because it sparkles don't mean nothing. All what glitters aint always gold and mind you don't forget it. The tricks of the trade need a bit of savvy. It's not all just bravado. Where's Curly today?"

"Aint seen 'im,"said Scarface. "We was uvverwise engaged!"

"And what were you up to?

"We," he said with a glint in his eye, "we," he said, "was having tea 'n and crumpet with the Vicar."

Ma went red with rage. Her blood-pressure rose to several notches short of bursting-point.

"I'll kill you lot. I keep on telling you – KEEP AWAY from them sort o' places. I don't want no trouble with the coppers. I don't want none of you up in court."

"I see Curly hangin' around the Public Gardens," said Gino. "Wavin' a flick-knife about the place. I see 'im talking to that fat old bird from the Roxy.

"I never 'ad no faith in that boy," said Ma. "Got a kink somewhere. One of these days he'll come a cropper, he will. Owes me fifty nicker for that diamond sparkler I give him for that tart of his. A bit of a smarty-boots, he is, if you ask me. I tell you one thing — he's losing his marbles, poor sod! He might be a good-looker and he thinks he's God's gift to women but he's gotta be careful else he'll find himself in the clink, and us with 'im."

A door slammed. Ma motioned the boys to get back out of sight just in time for Curly to see her move some beer-cans off the counter.

"Well! Look what the wind's blown in. And where 'ave you been, Billie-boy?"

"Around," said Curly, defiantly chewing at some gum.

"Nothing like a simple answer to a simple question. So I'll ask you again. What have you been up to, Curly?" He blew a bubble of gum at her.

"Look here, I aint the sort to be mucked around with, not by nobody. Where have you been?"

Curly knew she meant business.

"Over the Gardens," he said sullenly.

"Oh, how nice!" she said menacingly, picking up a jack-knife from under the counter. "Havin' a kip in the sun, were you, Goldilocks?"

The gang laughed and jeered. Curly's face set rigid. He knew what Ma meant and he didn't like it one bit. He lurched forward and grabbed her by her fat neck.

"You bleeding ol' cow," he yelled. "I'll do for you, I warn you!" Only the feel of cold steel of Ma's knife against his ribs stopped him from doing her an injury. He drew back, fuming.

"I'm telling you, Ma. Never speak to me like that again. I'm a big boy now."

He stood back, panting like a lion ready for the kill, but Ma was too quick for him. She turned on him:

"And I'm telling you, your dirty little life aint worth the flick of a knife to me. You're useless, you are. I don't trust you, Curly. You've got a brain like a goat and kinky into the bargain. You've got something badly wrong inside of you. You're weak in the head, you are. You're plain bonkers, matey! Well! Hand it over. What have you brought me?"

Now, it can definitely be said that, as this Curly business proceeds to get out of hand, this tale is definitely not one that should be told in front of the children! In fact, not even in front of respectable grown-ups, whoever they may be! It does not give a good impression of human nature. In fact, it would seem a slight on the animal kingdom to say that these ruffians had anything in common with any other species than reptiles as far as the citizens of Rothersey were concerned

"Come on what have you brought me, eh?" said Ma.

"Sweet Fanny Adams to you. D'you know what that means, you ol' tart?"

"Don't you dare use that kind o' lingo with me. Where were you yesterday?

"Up the Dilly."

"Posh, eh? Pickings thin, were they?" she sneered.

She wanted to rouse him, to make him really long to have another go at her. He was ferocious, a snarling tiger and she was the tigress, spoiling for a fight, for every tussle she had with any of her boys had something of the mating game about it.

"You know what you are, Curly Donoghue, you're a bloody pansy and you don't know it. Well, you do now, don't you? You know now."

Something went click in Curly's brain. It set in motion all the stirrings of his subconscious. His blood boiled with indignation and unbounding hatred for this fat lump of flesh that was Ma Blackwood, fat and quivering like a jellyfish as she smiled at him viciously, remorselessly, making him want to wipe that silly smile off her face, to stop her eyes from looking at him with such scorn. He whipped out his knife. Ma heard the flick of the blade as Curly lunged at her.

"Boys!" she shouted. "Give it to 'im!"

Out from behind the counter and the stacks of sweet-jars came the gang, like a flash. Curly reeled, almost drunkenly, towards Ma Blackwood. His reason had been cruelly twisted out of shape. The whole weight of his body was behind that blade and Ma was certainly thinking she was about to experience her last moment in this life. An almost primeval cry came from his lips. But the gang were onto him in seconds, like a pack of wolves. A hefty boot kicked into his solar plexus and he was suddenly down, on the floor. He tried to get up but another boot sank into his groin and he yelled out in pain. Another boot smashed him in the teeth and blood ran down his chin. He managed to get to his feet and they came at him from all sides, punching, kicking. Blood streamed out of his nose. Another fistful and his eyelid was torn and the blood blinded him. He struggled to free himself, hitting wildly into the air with his fists, gulping, groaning as blow on blow smashed into his muscular frame. He went down with a crash, grasping the glass-fronted cupboard full of boxes of the delicacies Ma was so famous for. Spikes of glass spurted and splintered the floor. The boys stood panting with excitement, in an almost sensual frenzy. Curly was gasping on the floor, gripping his groin and groaning.

Ma Blackwood had been looking forward to this little scene for some time. She had enjoyed it, every minute of it, as she watched the boys going about their handiwork, so silent, never uttering a word, just the quiet panting, groaning, cries of pain, scuffling of boots, and Curly lying on his back, passive as a young girl, the boys letting him have it with their boots and fists. It seemed to Ma Blackwood like an elaborate orgy, the lust of wolves fighting for the favours of the female. In reality, it was the bloodlust of the pack turning on its own number.

"That'll do, boys. He's had his bit of fun."

The gang stood back to survey their handiwork, stunned by their own power, exhilarated at the sight of Curly lying on his back in a pool of his own blood.

"Let's get inside, boys. It's supper-time. As for you, Curly, you'd better get yourself cleaned up, if you know what's good for you. And by Gawd, don't you ever defy me again. I'm warning you. I want that fifty nicker in my hot little hand by the end of the week or you'll be having a repeat performance. I'm telling you, your name won't be worth the paper it's written on. I'll have you skinned alive. D'you hear me?"

With that, she slammed a bottle of beer down on the counter and went through to get the boys their supper.

42. Ron's Black Sunday

"Well, Ronald," said Miss Baldock as she squeezed herself into Grandpa's Lawton's favourite chair, "I am delighted that you have seen sense at last."

Ron was quite naturally downcast and ashamed. He stood awkwardly, his hands clasped nervously behind his back, his knees perceptibly shaking.

"I only wanted to see Grandpa. Really I did."

"A mighty peculiar way of doing it, I must say, and an absolute lie into the bargain. You know perfectly well, as you did at the time of the theft, that Mr. Lawton was in hospital, so how can you stand there and have the face to say such a thing. Now, tell me the truth or I shall have to speak to Miss Goodenough about you when she comes to see me at the restaurant tomorrow ."

Ron remained silent.

197

"Don't forget," said the indefatigable seeker after truth, "don't forget I can prove you entered my house for an illegal purpose, and I shall make no bones about letting your father and mother into the secret if you defy me."

"I never did, Miss Baldock. You aint got nothink on me, you aint. My Mum knows I was at band practice up the gym. You ask old Purvis."

"Ask who, Ronald?" she said, shocked at his apparent lack of respect.

"Er – Mr. Purvis, ma'am. Sorry!"

"That's better. A modicum of civility goes a long way when you try. Now! Councillor Purvis thinks you were somewhere else, Ronald."

"Well, he's flipping-well wrong, then," said Ron, defiantly.

"Ronald! Now let us be truthful about this. You were *not* at band practice, were you?"

"I aint got nothin' to tell yer. Leave me alone."

"'I aint got nothing?' What kind of English is that? I'm afraid you are not going to get very far in life if you can't speak your own language properly. Ronald! Why did you break into my house? And what about this?"

She brought out from behind her chair, the ill-fated copy of *Love and Lucy Locket.*

"Have you ever seen this before?"

"I never seen it in me life."

"Ronald! Correct your English, please."

"Sorry, Miss Balcock."

"Baldock, Ronald, please."

"Sorry, Miss – er – I keep forgetting."

"English, Ronald!"

"I have never seen it in my life before."

"There we are. You can do it if you try. You say you were at band practice. How is it then that your name is not ticked on Mr. Purvis's register of attendance? Don't forget you are the only one who plays the recorder and the piccolo, and you weren't there, Ronald. What more proof do I need?"

"You don't 'cos I was!"

"You was, "began Miss Baldock, forgetting herself, " — you were what?" she asked, hoping for better grammatical skills.

"Oh, for cryin' out loud!" said Ronald in despair.

"Not only that, my milk money went missing at the same time.

Mr. Lawton would have paid the milkman with it if he hadn't come a cropper in the High Street and been carted off to hospital."

Ronald's eyes suddenly filled with tears at the thought of Grandpa Lawton.

"Ronald, you can't blackmail me with blubbing. I shall get your father to make you repay every penny."

"Dad won't do anything, I can tell you. He's hopeless."

For once, Ron was rather glad his father took so little interest in him.

"Then I shall resort to more drastic measures. I shall go straight to the Police Station and report you and you will be sent away to prison. You've heard of Borstal, I suppose? You won't like that, I can tell you." She spoke of it with such authority that Ron could have believed she had personal experience of the place.

Ron began to whimper — in short, sharp staccato sobs at first, then his face screwed up into nothing and tears streamed down his cheeks.

"Oh, no! Miss Baldock. Please don't send me away. Please, don't send me away."

How could he tell her that he missed his friend, Grandpa Lawton, so much? There was just no-one to talk to now. All he wanted was to sit in Grandpa's chair (at present capaciously occupied by the enemy) and wait for him to come home again. Ron didn't mean to break in but she would never believe him in a hundred years.

"I shall not hold my patience much longer, Ronald," said Miss Baldock, trying hard not to be affected by the show of remorse, for she was a fair woman if nothing else.

"Why did you take the money?"

"I didn't take any money. I didn't. I didn't." He burst into another fit of sobbing. "It was that 'Goldilocks' feller took it."

"Which fellow?"

"Him what brought the spuds and oranges."

"A likely story!"

"It's true, I tell you. I was here with Grandpa Lawton when he came. The money was on the dresser when I went to get some toffees. It was there and then it was gone, I tell you."

"So it was Curly Donoghue," said the half-believing Miss B. "I really don't know what to think."

"Eddie Carpenter'll tell you. He knows, he does, 'cos he told my Dad Curly stole money from work as well."

199

"Stole from work?"

"Yes, almost every week money went missing and Eddie got the blame. He was letting off steam about it to my Dad. He got the sack."

"Does Mr. Crawford know about this?"

"Who's he for a lark?"

"The gentleman Mr. Donoghue works for."

The whole story was too bewildering, yet, thought Agnes, anxious now to believe in Ronald's hard-won innocence, there might possibly be some grain of truth in it. If only she had known in February, she might never have had the argument with Mr. Crawford, Eddie might never have been falsely accused, Timothy Crawford might never have left the market and broken with his father, and though she could not know, Louise might never have found someone to fall in love with. Certainly, poor Ron could have been saved the worst gruelling interrogation of his life. Miss Baldock was happily oblivious of all these injustices, else she might have felt a further need to confess to Father O'Flagherty when she was next at mass. But tomorrow was Monday and she resolved to pay a visit to the market then instead of on Tuesday, as was her original plan.

"Now, run along Ronald. We'll leave the matter as settled, shall we?" An unaccustomed softness came into her voice. She began to feel she had treated little Ron rather harshly. "Now you can forget all about it. Here's the book. Mind you return it to Millie, otherwise I shall have something more to say. Do you understand?"

"Yes, m'm," he replied, almost inaudibly.

She led him gently to the front door, her arm round his shoulders, in an almost motherly way.

"Miss Baldock," said Ron a little shyly.

"Yes, Ronald."

"When will Grandpa come home?"

"I'm sorry to say I do not think he will come home again, Ronald."

She was suddenly embarrassed at the thought of explaining the intricacies of her plans.

"He's critically ill and he may have to go away."

"Is he going to die? Is Grandpa going to die?"

"We all have to die sometime, Ronald. He's suffered a lot with his broken arm and fractured hip. Now, with pneumonia on top of it all, he is better off where he is."

"Yes, but is he going to die? Will he get better soon?"

"At best, Ronald, he will have to go to the Old People's Home."

"Please don't let him die, Miss Baldock," said the poor boy, beginning to sob again.

Agnes looked down at his tear-stained face and suddenly knew that he would somehow hold her responsible if the old man did pass into the next world and she felt her conscience troubled in the matter.

"Ronald, dear boy! It is God's will that we should die when we do. It is not for us to choose. If Grandpa makes a reasonable recovery, you must ask the Good Lord's forgiveness for abusing his friendship in the way you have."

"Yes, but what if he dies and I never see him again?"

"If we cannot confess our sins to God, Ronald, then we have to live with them for the rest of our lives. You will have to do the same."

That night, as Ronald curled up in bed, he couldn't get away from the thought that he had grievously wronged his good friend, Grandpa Lawton; that he had irreparably damaged something that was so precious, so vital, so full of love and companionship. He must go to Grandpa. He must seek him out wherever he may be and tell him everything.

Remembering Miss Baldock's words, he took certain decisions in consequence. Whether they would make any difference at all to what he had done, for what's done cannot be entirely undone, he could not know. Everything was a matter for conjecture.

Ronald closed his eyes, turned over on his side, and cried himself to sleep for the first time since he was a baby. He was beginning to know the pain of growing up at last.

EPISODE TEN

The next morning

Decline and Fall

43.   Curly's Grand Performance

On the Monday morning after Miss Baldock's revealing interview with Ron — a warm sunny morning, with a clear sky, an almost imperceptible breeze blowing from the south-west and pushing puffs of lamb's tail clouds before it, a morning, one likes to think, as one rarely finds anywhere but in England at this time of year — Andrew Crawford stood in his grandfather's old high desk counting through the petty cash. His expression was pale and drawn, his cheeks sallow and his eyes had a weariness about them. With Timothy no longer by his side, he was feeling the strain.

The new deal with the hotel and restaurant trade, together with the building of the new glass-houses for the tomatoes, Andrew Crawford reluctantly had to admit, had boosted profits no end even if it had been Timothy's idea. On top of that, it was the pea season. The scarlet runners and lettuce weren't doing too badly either. And as for the resplendent red-sticked rhubarb, there was an absolute run on it!

Timothy could, of course, know nothing of this since he had not made an appearance in the market for months and he certainly did not intend to go anywhere near home for a very long time.

The moment after Curly had gone to breakfast, Miss Baldock arrived.

"Well! Well!" crowed Mr. Crawford in patronising tones. "Quite a surprise to see you here on a Tuesday morning, my dear. You're looking very bonny, so you are." He made a rapid appraisal of her new image and patently approved.

"I thought I'd get in before the Wednesday crowd," she said. In fact, Friday was her usual day in spite of the hot weather, but she had come looking about for Curly.

"And how's the Restaurant coming along these days?"

"Well, Mr. Crawford, nobody's going to the cinema much while this heat-wave's on, especially not with our old-fashioned air-conditioning. A great demand for salads at lunch-time, so I do like them to be crispy fresh. Nothing so off-putting as a limp lettuce or a wrinkled over-ripe tomato that squirts in your eye when you try to cut it. People are getting fussy about their food these days. Anybody'd think there'd never been a war on."

"I can see you're a great one for quality, Miss Baldock. You should have a little place of your own."

Although the idea registered in Miss Baldock's mind, she had

204

more pressing business to settle.

"And how is Mr. Donoghue these days?" she asked.

"Donoghue! Ah! Now there's a useful lad for you! Swears like a trooper and works like a Trojan. I can forgive anything if a chap works hard and really earns his pay, Miss Baldock. Now, my son was never one for throwing himself into things. Too much of a dreamer. Timothy's a good lad, no doubt. But he's not cut out for a real man's kind of life. A bit of a sissy when it comes to hard work. He'll regret leaving the firm the way he did. He's forfeited his birthright all for the sake of his stupid pride. My driver, Ray, has taken on much of Timothy's work. It's a change to have a touch of loyalty around. Mark my words, one of these days Timothy's bound to come crawling back, begging me to take him on again."

Miss Baldock couldn't help thinking what a sorry state of affairs it was that led Mr. Crawford to think of his son as being in the same league as any young lad picked straight off the High Street.

"I don't think you'll find he'll do that, Mr. Crawford. He's too determined to succeed in his chosen profession. And he has his eyes on a pretty young lady."

"Oh, has he indeed? And how would you know?"

"I know because he is lodging with one of my neighbours."

Andrew Crawford looked as if he was about to explode.

"Is he indeed?" glaring at the startled lady. He shouted right into her face:

"WELL, I DON'T WANT TO KNOW!"

After a pause to compose herself, Miss Baldock continued:

"I went to see Mr. Carpenter last evening. He lives in the same street too, you know."

Crawford grunted disapproval and went on counting his petty cash.

"Huh! It seems quite a nest of criminals in your precious little street, if you ask me. He'll have to be taught a lesson, that lad. The young scoundrel! I trusted Eddie more than my own son. They all go wrong sooner or later, don't they?"

"Eddie is a very nice lad," said Miss Baldock.

"I know what you're trying to say, but there was only one individual who could have stolen that money — Eddie Carpenter. Always hanging about behind my back. Either Timothy is lying to save his face or suspicion rests with Eddie. I'm not blaming my son except that he bungled the whole thing. It all points to Carpenter being the guilty party. He was in financial difficulties when his mother was ill. Doesn't it seem odd to you that no money has been missing since?"

"I shouldn't be too hasty in your judgments, Mr. Crawford. We are all fallible, you know."

"What do you mean, woman?" said Crawford, growing red in the face. "Are you trying to teach me how to run my own business now?" He glowered down at her from his perch and said curtly:

"If it's peas and lettuce you'll be wanting, I'll thank you to give your order and be off ."

Miss Baldock pursed her lips and bristled.

"I'll take a bag of peas, a box of lettuce and a dozen punnets of tomatoes. Book them down. I'll settle up at the end of the week. Now, as I was saying," she said firmly, "things are not what they seem, Mr. Crawford. You can't go on turning a blind eye to the bare facts of the case, now can you?"

"Look here!" he said defiantly. "What are you getting at? Are you trying to implicate me. I'll please you to keep a civil tongue in your head – and a silent one at that!"

"I – AM – NOT," said Miss Baldock, raising her voice, "I am not trying to implicate *any*body who is truly innocent."

"Well who the devil d'you think it is, if not Eddie Carpenter?" shouted Crawford in a frenzy.

"Mr. Donoghue!" She drew herself up to bosom-battle stations.

"Dammit, woman! What the hell do you mean by coming down here poking your nose in?"

"There's no need to be offensive, Mr. Crawford. I happen to know just a little more about your affairs than you give me credit for. So, before you go setting the blame at someone else, you'll do well to listen to what I have to say."

"Is that a threat, woman?"

"I must ask you not to address me in that uncouth manner. It does you no credit. You know my name. Use it!" she said, as the flame of justice flared within her.

"Mr. Crawford! I am in possession of information which I must verify and you are the only man who can help me. I, too, have had money stolen and, small as the amount is, I intend to track down the thief. Other reputations are at stake, Mr. Crawford, besides those of Eddie and your much-maligned son. I, too have only two suspects and they are not the same two as yours. I interviewed one last night. The other I intend to interview this morning."

"The other?"

"Mr. Donoghue."

She stooped, half-expecting an outburst. Instead Mr. Crawford went even redder in the face and began fidgeting with his pencil.

"It so happened," Miss Baldock continued, "a neighbour of mine, Councillor Purvis, had been to lunch. After he left, I went upstairs to rest for an hour. Suddenly, I heard a noise outside. First, a dustbin being moved, then the kitchen window being forced open. As I had drawn all the curtains, I peeped through just in time to catch sight of someone getting into the back part of the house. I thought of confronting him, but I was afraid of being attacked. I stayed upstairs, listening. I let him roam around the downstairs rooms. After a time, everything seemed quiet again, so I crept down only to find the kitchen window open and dirty foot-marks all over the draining-board. Finding no-one, I went upstairs to fetch my umbrella. When I got downstairs again, I found a book, lying on the floor. It had fallen out of the intruder's pocket. This was his silly little mistake, Mr. Crawford. Every criminal makes one, you know. One day, I shall find out who the owner of that book is. The thief turned out to be Alf Thompson's son."

"Yes! Yes! Yes! This is all very well," muttered Mr. Crawford. "Alf Thompson's son, eh? I must say *that* doesn't surprise me. But what has all this rigmarole got to do with me?"

"Patience! Mr. Crawford. "Patience! A virtue you could do well to cultivate, in my view. Now, where was I? Well, I have at last managed to interview the boy and I wouldn't have bothered if it hadn't been for my concern for his welfare. He gave me certain vital information about your petty cash thieving."

"Oh, he did, did he? Well, I'll be bound! I told you Carpenter was to blame, didn't I?"

"One moment, Mr. Crawford. I haven't finished. You had a pretty big row with your son over the thefts, is that not so?"

Crawford grunted a grudging assent.

"Then listen to me, Mr. Crawford. Mr. Carpenter was worried about the disappearance of the money. He had, on two occasions at least, seen it being actually removed. "

"There you are, you see. An accessory to the fact. I knew he had something to do with it all along."

"He was worried about the matter, " said Miss Baldock.

"Huh! I bet he was!" said Mr. Crawford with an ironic smile.

"Doesn't it surprise you," said Agnes, "that there was no cash missing between 25th February and the end of March? Six weeks with no thefts at all."

"Even the most hardened criminal in the country gets frightened off for a spell," replied Mr Crawford, "but he soon gets back on the game again. He can't resist it. It's his life-line."

"Yes, Mr. Crawford, but has it ever occurred to you that in that very week, one of your porters was off sick? Mr. Donoghue, to be precise. You see, he was not off sick. He was in prison."

"In prison?" said a very surprised Mr. Crawford. "Whatever for?"

"Housebreaking. It seems surprising that you do not take more of an interest in the sometimes nefarious activities of your employees."

"Housebreaking! Prison! But how on earth do you know?"

"My fiancé is a Councillor for the Borough of Rothersey, Mr. Crawford. One of his tenants, a retired police-officer, remembered reading about it in the newspapers at the time. Now you may also remember you made a gift of oranges to me after I had complained about some potatoes I had bought from you. Mr. Donoghue delivered one of the sacks to the Roxy restaurant and one to my house What is important is that it was Donoghue who took the money from my kitchen, not the boy who climbed through the window."

"I can't believe it," muttered Crawford. "I can't believe it. I won't."

He pounded his knuckles into the desk-top.

"It seems," said Miss Baldock sharply, "you won't believe anything anybody else says, either. Perhaps you would like to check those dates with your son. And this time, perhaps you'll be a little more diplomatic with him. You might have the decency to call on Mr. Carpenter and apologise, too. More to the point, you might care to have a word or two with the villain of the piece and see what he has to say for himself."

"I can't believe it," Crawford muttered to himself.

Miss Baldock left him standing ensconced in his high desk and threaded her way through the maze of boxes and crates, stacked ready to be loaded onto the barrows.

Mr. Crawford gazed at her receding expanse of back and swore he would never serve her again as long as he lived. Damn the woman! Coming here with tittle-tattle about what was no bloody business of hers.

Try as he would, Andrew Crawford could not chase the virus from his system. It multiplied until his whole mind was inflamed with the injustice of his actions. A persistent memory came back to life, pushing itself insidiously between his other thoughts – the memory of a day in February when he had lost control of his jealousy and his pride. He was too proud now to feel guilty over misplaced trust, yet he knew in his heart of hearts that he *was* guilty of something perhaps more heinous. He turned suddenly white. Then, just as soon, his face flushed with anger. He trembled as his heart began to thump.

"Curly!" he yelled across the market. "CURLY!!!"

Curly, who was sauntering casually back from breakfast, looked at his master with spite written all over his face. Curly did not like being shouted at by anybody, especially the likes of Andrew Crawford. If anything, Curly slowed rather than quickened his pace, stopping to light a Woodbine as a gesture of defiance. Then, he looked up into Mr. Crawford's bright pink pudgy face and knew just what he'd like to do with it.

In his turn, it was not unnatural that Andrew Crawford was wondering what someone had done to Curly's face. Curly's face was hardly a face at all. It was distorted into curious shapes, lumps protruded from normally neat curved surfaces, inflamed lumps that now perforce remained unshaven and grotesque and formless, angry purple bruises that rose out of thick weals slashed across the flesh. He looked like a feather-weight champion after a heavy-weight fight, only Curly was not exactly a feather-weight as Millie knew only too well! His left eye was half-closed and an angry purple gash showed just above the swollen lid.

"Did you call me with your sweet voice, guv?"

Mr. Crawford was too perturbed to ask about the injuries. He wheeled round and spluttered into the mess that was Curly's face:

"I'll have none of your blather, laddie. You're going to tell me the truth and nothing but the truth. We're going to have a nice little chat, you and me."

"A little chat?" said Curly mimicking Crawford's soft Scottish accent.

"Yes!" spat Mr. Crawford. "Yes! About the petty cash thefts."

"Petty cash, guv'nor?"

"You know what I mean. Don't stand there and say 'petty cash' as if butter wouldn't melt in your mouth. You know perfectly well what I'm talking about and don't you deny it."

"Oh, I do, do I?"

"Look here, Donoghue, I have reason to believe you have been

209

dishonest with me and I intend to get to the bottom of it."

Crawford was going to say that he had always been a hundred per cent behind Curly right from the start but, no, he looked into the face of Curly Donoghue and knew that belief had disappeared for ever.

"Honest, guv! Now what a thing to say," Curly said, with a menacing grin.

"Now, listen to me, Donoghue. I want to have your explanation as to how that money was misappropriated. I want to clear the matter up once and for all."

Crawford's face was nearly purple.

"Money? What bloody money?" said Curly with a curl to his lip.

Curly would have had a better answer ready if he hadn't been so mutilated by his so-called friends in the Polenti gang. Somehow, he just couldn't get his brain working this morning.

"The money you stole," shouted the demented Mr. Crawford.

"P'raps you didn't count it proper, guv."

"What drivel! Do you realise, Donoghue, that on the last occasion £5 was stolen from the box. In the end, there was over £150 missing. "

"A hundred and fifty quid, eh!" said Curly, with a low whistle, an irritating tone of false sympathy and a smile that could kill a viper.

"You sure of it, guv'nor?"

"I think I have had enough mathematical education to prove, Donoghue, that I *can* count up to five," said Crawford, drawing himself up to his full height and pointing an angry finger.

"Now, I'm warning you, Donoghue. I shall not let the matter rest till I find the culprit. So you'd better give me a satisfactory explanation. You're not straight, Donoghue. I can see it in your face."

This must certainly have been true if Crawford was speaking in the strictly artistic sense, for a Hieronymous Bosch or even a Salvador Dali at his most surrealistic would have found it a challenge.

"Either you tell me where the money went or I call the police, and from what Miss Baldock tells me, you wouldn't like that, would you? Another little chat at the Station and a nice invitation to stay with them for a year or two at the tax-payer's expense?"

"Anuvver? Anuvver? What d'you bloody-well mean?" Curly was boiling up inside.

"What I say, Donoghue. Don't you understand the Queen's English? I know you've been inside."

"All right! So I have. What's it to you?"

"No money was missing in the time you were, as you call it, 'sick'. What a coincidence!" said Mr. Crawford, with contempt.

Curly was looking dangerous now.

"Look here, you bastard!" he yelled. "Who the bloody hell d'you think you are? I'll do that Eddie Carpenter when I see 'im. I'll slit 'is guts out, I will."

He glared at Crawford with such hatred that it was surprising the older man didn't crumble to dust. Curly wanted to smash the old bugger's face in. Curly wanted to screw his fists into his fishy little eyes until they were grey pulp at the back of his head. Curly wanted to slash his knife over Crawford's fat throat till he couldn't breathe. Curly wanted to kick him in the crutch till he howled for mercy. Curly wanted to....

Mr. Crawford stepped down from his high desk and stared into Curly's face.

"And furthermore, Donoghue," he said, "how do you explain the disappearance of Miss Baldock's milk money from her kitchen on the morning you delivered the potatoes? I cannot have my porters thieving from my customers' very pockets."

Curly stared at Mr. Crawford with an expression of utter confusion.

"Come now, Donoghue! I can't wait all day. If you don't give me an answer I shall be forced to turn you in, do you understand? It is my duty. And I'll tell you another thing. You're sacked, Donoghue!"

Curly cried a cry that went echoing through the girders high up under the bridge overhead. He seemed to lose control. He began to lurch and sway with anger and frustration.

"Your duty? Your duty?" yelled Curly. "You lot are all the same. Always thinking about your duty. You bastards! Just as long as it's some other poor bloke as pays for it in the end. You think just because you dole out the cash of Fridays you're flipping God. You think you can do what you bleeding-well like to poor sods like me. You think you've got the whip-hand, mate, but I'm telling you straight, you aint. 'Cos it's the likes of me that the likes o' you can't do without. It's a flippin' police state, that's what it is, and I'm bloody sick of it. Sick of it."

"Now that's enough of that talk, Donoghue. I didn't ask you for a speech on social reform. Now come on, out with it, I say."

"Out with it?" yelled Curly, now lost to all reason. "Out with it? I'll learn you a lesson you'll never forget as long as you live. You bastard! You BLOODY BASTARD!!!"

With a vicious sudden movement, knife clenched in his fist, Curly lunged forward. Mr. Crawford saw the momentary flash of the blade flick out its gleaming tongue. His face turned ashen. Curly's fist thrust against him and a cry of pain rang out over the Cathedral close, threading its way among the empty crates and boxes, and on into the dark recesses of the arches.

Curly felt the blade resist the toughness of Crawford's coat and then slide smoothly into the fleshy paunch. One! Two!! Three!!! Curly couldn't stop. He just went on stabbing the blade into the crumpled, seemingly lifeless body of Andrew Crawford. In a flash, Curly snatched a wad of notes from the petty-cash box and deftly slipping his hand into Crawford's inside pocket, pulled out a wallet, fat with the day's takings. Then he scooted off, up into the shadows of the tunnel and out of sight, leaving behind him Crawford's limp body, lying in the damp warmth of its own blood.

44.   Faces in the Mirror

The night had been hot and muggy. Millie had awoken with a troubled mind and the memory of having to get up and take a blanket off the bed. She remembered feeling stifled and how she stood by the window slowly breathing in the night air. In the comfort of darkness, she had experienced a sensation of indescribable loneliness and futility. It had been as if she were sailing silently through space with no human being for millions of miles around. She might have been one of those Russian space-dogs gliding round and round the earth, with a fate as man-made as a tin-opener and with less point to it. She felt that dog had about as much idea of where it was heading as she had then — there at the window by herself, desperate and alone in the dark. That Mabel was sleeping the untroubled sleep of angels agonised Millie, made her aware of the countless forces at work in her own mind and body, bringing up from deep down inside her a strange sense of bewilderment which sent swirling movements round and round in her head until her eyes were swimming. Then, she felt herself falling.....falling.....falling.....

When she came to, she was cold and shivery. She was lying spreadeagled on the floor of her bedroom. Only a faint breeze ruffled the curtains. As she struggled to recover herself, she could see the gentle wafting of the curtains willing her to come back to reality. Now in the bright morning sunlight, her eyes ached and an overpowering feeling of nausea joined forces with her despair. If only she could end it all. If only....

Millie crawled back into bed just as Mrs. Thompson came in with a cup of tea and a digestive biscuit. She was far too preoccupied with getting Alf off to the tannery and Ron off to school and herself off to the Town Hall to notice anything unusual about Millie's face.

Millie leaned back on her pillows and was thankful for the warm tea, glad that her mother hadn't noticed her fainting fit. Suddenly it was nine o'clock. At first, she panicked and got into what her mother called 'a regular tizz'. She should be at her work-bench at the button factory by now, and here she was sipping tea in bed as bold as a duchess. She turned on *Housewives Choice,* lay back on the pillows, closed her eyes and drifted off into a dream-world of song, broken only by her cup-and-saucer tipping over on the sheets, sending dregs of tea spitting in little brown spots all over the pink nylon sheets. Her inside turned a lethargic somersault when she heard the announcer saying:

And now, calling Miss Millie Thompson of Laburnum Villas, Rothersey. Hello, Millie! How are we on this lovely bright morning? Now, Millie, you say you have written fifteen times for your request and have never had any luck. Well, Millie, your luck's in today, love. Thank you for the super-duper card with the red-silk heart embroidered on it and all the lovely little bits of white lace round it. Now Millie your request is for 'Love me tender, love me true', which you want me to play for your sweetheart, Curly Donoghue. Hello Curly wherever you are! Well, let's hope you're listening right now because here's 'The Voice', the fabulous Elvis, singing just for you:

'Love me tender, love me true.....'

A turgid mixture of joy and melancholy brought back memories which would have been better forgotten. She was wounded, body and soul. Her fate was sealed and Curly had made sure of it. She loved Curly more than anything in the world, but she loved alone and she knew it. When she looked in the mirror and saw an image of Curly

213

reflected somehow through the moist of her eyes, the image was thrown back at her, cold and as untouchable as the reflection of her face in the glass of her dressing-table mirror. Her song had come to an end.

"Millie! Millie!" shouted Mrs. Thompson up the stairs. "It's twenty past, you know. You'll be late, my gel, you will. It won't be my fault if you get the sack. I can't afford to have you lazing about the house all day waiting for something to turn up. I gotta get meself off in a jiffy. I don't intend to lose my job as well, you know."

Millie could hardly see to comb her hair. The tears came thick and fast. When she looked again in the mirror she saw only the image of hopelessness.

"O.K. Mum!" she said, trying to put on a token of a face at least.

When she came back from the bathroom, Mabel, who had been up and dressed in no time at all, was climbing all over the bed, bouncing up and down on the old springs to make them squeak. Millie powdered her nose and ran a lipstick she had borrowed from her mother lightly over her lips. To her workmates she had let herself go 'something shocking', but to little Mabel, she was beautiful. She felt only love for her big sister as she stared at her now. Millie's hair fell lightly around her temples and ears, her lips showed a softness and a sweetness that certainly sent Eddie into raptures whenever he set eyes on her. Mabel jumped from the bed and flung her little dimpled arms round her big sister and giggled with happiness and delight. She expected Millie to do the same to her. Instead, Millie put her arms round Mabel, practically hugged the breath out of her, and burst into a protracted fit of sobbing.

45. Tim Thinks Again

By the time people came running to get Ray, who was lazing about the coffee-stall with the other lorry-drivers, Mr. Crawford had sunk into a coma. John Garville had already come rushing over and was now holding, cradled in his arms, the slumped mass of almost bloodless flesh that was Andrew Crawford. He waved Ray off to Guy's to seek out Timothy and to call for an ambulance. Ray went off puffing and blowing to carry out the toughest bit of work he had had to do all morning. He began running because he knew very well from the look on the Master's face that it was a matter of life and death.

Timothy came quickly to the scene. Pale and shaken, he stood helplessly by and saw, to his dismay, life ebbing away. When the ambulance arrived, he watched his father being laid gently onto the stretcher and carefully lifted into the back. A doctor was giving an emergency blood transfusion on the spot. Timothy stood as if frozen in time, with the terrible thought that it was touch and go as far as his father's life was concerned.

Never in all his life had Timothy felt so wretched, so useless, so helpless. Perhaps more than this, he realised the futility of the way things had turned out and a faint but growing awareness of how much he owed to this near-corpse, lying there lifeless, it seemed. This thing, which now could no longer speak, give orders, shout abuse, be mean or unforgiving — this was his father, a father he could no longer recognise. This thing, devoid of its personality and possibly its life, that could no longer have any influence over him, unexpectedly brought tears to his eyes for the first time since that ill-fated day in February. He caught a brief glimpse of his father's old high desk and on it the petty cash box that had been his downfall and the painted board on the front of the desk that proclaimed: *ANDREW CRAWFORD & SON.*

Timothy knew that life suddenly had changed, that his ambitions and dreams were under threat, that he had now reached another crossroad with no sign-post to guide him. Like the eponymous figure of *Child Roland to a Dark Tower Came*, the stark poem by Browning that he had been recently reading with Louise, he had also journeyed along an unknown path, perhaps had travelled falsely, perhaps had taken, like the knight, the uncertain way that led him to the dark tower whose meaning he could not know. Was it false ambition? Or a broken promise? Or perhaps a betrayal? He felt a dark kind of suffering growing within him and he wanted to escape from it, to return to the way things were, to happier days when there was love and the companionship of home. But he also knew in his heart of hearts that it was all in the balance, an almost irretrievable dream. Was there such a thing as divine mercy? As he had watched his father receiving life-giving blood, he asked for proof of that mercy.

Before Timothy set off for the hospital, he found himself being somehow drawn into the Cathedral. Once inside, in the stillness, he stopped beside the Shakespeare memorial for a moment. Involuntarily, he rested his hand on the head of the reclining figure, now shiny with the touch of thousands of 'pilgrims' to this place. The coolness and smoothness of the stone comforted him, gave him something of that

215

inexplicable strength it had given to so many other worshippers to this literary shrine.

In the chancel, the choir began rehearsing an anthem, the sounds of which spread like an ethereal voice and wove itself round the carved stone columns of the nave, reaching out to his heart and filling him with a multitude of confused thoughts and feelings. He began to feel something more was required of him than prayer. Whatever kind of faith he would have to find in himself must begin with his own feelings, his own understanding of the way. Hadn't he been told at school how God's world worked for good in spite of the evil around us. He knelt down in one of the pews and began to pray, self-consciously at first, and then fervently. He not only prayed for his father's life to be spared, but he prayed also for his soul to be freed from guilt. He did not mind how faint the voice might be, but it must, above all, be unmistakable.

46.   An Appointment Made

A long steel paper-knife shaped like a dagger, with Arabian designs in red, gold and black, lay on Councillor Purvis's breakfast table. He picked it up, gazing idly at its curved scimitar blade and was reminded of events and people he would have preferred to forget if only memory would allow him to.

He struck the knife into the flap of the first envelope. It was a letter from Gwen to say that she was not happy in Yorkshire and had decided to return to London at Christmas, provided her family were able to find another nanny for their three brattish children, who were at present plaguing her night and day with their tricks and tantrums.

Mr. Purvis was both pleased and disturbed; to have Gwen home again would be a fine addition to his domestic comfort. She was an excellent cook and housekeeper. Her pies and preserves could only be spoken of in superlatives. What better than a woman to whom he owed nothing but a roof over her head and yet she would perform all the tasks of an unpaid housekeeper, and, what is more, actually enjoy it.

There was, however, the question of Agnes to be considered. How, for instance, would the self-effacing Gwen stand up to the ebullient Miss Baldock? Would she fade herself to nothing and creep about the house like a frightened mouse? Would Agnes turn into a

Baba-Yaga and make his home, as in the Russian fairy-story, a sort of hut on hen's legs? Mr. Purvis could see that it was all very well to be engaged and go on living in separate houses but when, after twenty years of celibacy, he introduced another wife into his bedchamber, shamelessly and deliberately, right under his daughter's very nose, and she herself pretty-well on the shelf at thirty-five, and he almost sixty. 'Well!' as Agnes would say: 'Whatever next!'

Then there was the question of his hoped-for election as Mayor of Rothersey. With all his achievements in the spheres of social welfare and sports in the Borough, everyone said he was a 'dead cert for the mace and chain'. Everyone *said* so. But did they *think* so? Well, what did it matter? The Councillor *knew* so.

Ought not, then, a man of his calibre, and future Mayor of Rothersey to boot, be capable of adjusting, from the level of the dinner-table, to the heady heights of the nuptial bed? Why, of course he could. Gwen might come home whenever she pleased. What better than a daughter, versed in all the branches of domesticity, yet was, like all good well-brought-up young ladies, rarely to be seen and never heard. Well, hardly ever! When Gwen arrived home again, the door-knocker would be brightly polished, the door-knobs like little gleaming suns; meals would be served regularly and with a minimum of fuss, and the whole house would be a bright as a new pin. All this would allow his dear Agnes to attend civic functions and assist with entertaining celebrities in the Mayor's Parlour.

This conclusion reached, the Councillor now opened the second letter, which put him in an even better mood for the day. It was from the Secretary of the Napoleon Avenue Old People's Home informing him that a place could be made available for Mr. Lawton as soon as he left hospital. A dark thought clouded Mr. Purvis's feeling of well-being, only briefly, as he reminded himself of the last report on the old man, who, said the doctors, was showing signs of weakness generally, and the situation looked grave. However, his trust in Agnes and all she stood fair and square for drove the thought from his mind. Agnes knew best.

Unknown to the Councillor, however, he was shortly to become the victim of the scandal-mongering Curly, who had waited until the time was ripe to reveal to Ma Blackwood some 'interesting' information about the Councillor's supposedly sexual relationship with an under-age girl. The fact that Millie was not quite 'under-age' did not trouble him. In this case. The truth could be stretched to suit the situation.

The third letter was in an unknown hand and quickly drained

any sign of colour from the Councillor's cheeks. He read it once. He read it twice. He read it three times. He stared at it, mesmerised by the scrawling primitive script. It was signed: 'Monkey-Face'. It urged him to remember a particular day in February when he was seen taking a young girl into his house for immoral purposes, and he would no doubt recall entertaining the same 'local tart' in April last, and that this local tart was going to have a kid by him, and that he'd better watch out else there'd be trouble. A number of strong Anglo-Saxon expletives were carelessly sprinkled about the page like tea-stains, and just as ineradicable in the Councillor's confused mind. The letter suggested, quite rudely, that he would be 'fit for the knacker's yard', 'dead meat', and other such butcher-like phrases. Worst of all, an association with the men's lavatory in the Public Gardens, a building which happily did not for once bear his name, was to say the least unwelcome. He was to go there at three o'clock this very afternoon and place a sealed envelope containing fifty one-pound notes on the window sill over the urinals. The letter ended with the questionable and no doubt unconscious rhyme: "If you want to be a flipping mare, you'd better flipping-well be there." In other circumstances, the spelling of 'mayor', might have done justice even to Ronald, but the Councillor was *not* amused. His world had, in a matter of minutes, come crashing down about him like heavy hailstones on his balding head. His cup fell out of his hand and broke into pieces on the tiled hearth. His fingers felt suddenly inert and flabby. From his light-hearted optimism of a few minutes ago, he did a power-dive into the depths of despond. Panic ran through him like a virus. Marriage and mayorships were annihilated from his mind by the force of his shame and possible public exposure. What he was feeling now was, alas, only a fraction of the dread and anguish he was to feel later in the day. He — Councillor Joseph Gabriel Purvis, militant upholder of the birch, champion of youth, propounder of 'Peace and Plenty', idol of the helpless and down-trodden, self-styled improver of public morality — was now a figure of ignominy and ridicule.

But what to do? Should he rush to the arms of his beloved and weep on her ample bosom? Should he confess to her that he had, indeed, entertained Millie? Should he solicit Calthrop and do what Millie might have referred to as 'spilling the beans'? Should he reveal the blackmail incident to Millie? No, that would be going too far. But had he not gone too far as it was by asking her into his parlour in the first place?

Yes, and what would dear Agnes say about this little kettle of fish? Would she break off their engagement? What would Calthrop have to say to it all? No doubt, he would be as unctuous and over-bearing as usual, delighted that he would stand a better chance of promotion with Purvis out of the way. Pretty shrewd was Calthrop! No, for the moment Purvis decided to keep Agnes and the Town Hall out of this business.

When the Councillor had tied everything together again in his brain, he began to realise a number of salient factors in the case. Firstly, he was, after all, totally innocent. This realisation came almost as a shock. The very fact of his being accused of such lewdness filled him with guilt and shame. Yet, he *was* innocent, whatever Agnes or Calthrop believed. Secondly, he certainly remembered inviting Millie in for a drink one Saturday evening in April. However, the offending note was not in Ron's handwriting. All this added up to one thing — the identity of the blackmailer was more than likely to be Donoghue, the market porter. Mr. Purvis recalled, too, that Police-Sergeant Paxton had read of Donoghue's conviction earlier in the year. At last things were falling into place. He would put on his hat and nip across the road to have a quiet chat with Paxton, a man surely well versed in local police matters. Indeed, the Councillor dearly hoped that no legal proceedings would be necessary.

Louise came smiling to the door and ushered the Councillor into the musty front-room. He felt uneasy in the closed atmosphere of this little room and was accordingly relieved when Louise led him through the kitchen into the bright little patch of garden and disappeared into the house again.

Old Walter Paxton settled himself into his chair and sat listening, not unsympathetically, to the Councillor's confession, so haltingly and shamefacedly told. Gently sucking on his pipe, Mr. Paxton reflected for a while, his sharp old eyes lost in thought as he gazed at his roses. At last he spoke and the advice he gave drove straight through Mr. Purvis's shrivelled heart like a pickaxe through soft loam. Of course, the Councillor was innocent but that did not alter the fact that he was being blackmailed. Nor was there any proof of his innocence in the opinion of a scandal-loving public. Nobody ever really believed a victim of blackmail was wholly innocent, even if he was proved so. People always wanted to believe the worst. It allowed them to feel self-righteous. They took a vicarious pleasure in the misfortunes of others. Such is contemporary morality.

This, in essence, was what the old man said to the Councillor, whose self-esteem by now was smarting like iodine in an open wound. The only course to take was to go the police, tell them the whole story and face the consequences. They would respect his wish to remain anonymous. He would become the mysterious 'Mr. X' in the case. But he must go now, quickly, while the proverbial iron was hot. The gang had made an appointment and the appointment had to be kept. If Mr. Purvis refused to go, it would be the old man's bounden duty to report him to his old Force. It was a crime to withhold information and he didn't intend to start doing so now.

When Councillor Purvis left that rose-filled garden of Walter Paxton, he was a man with a heavy burden and a dark future. His mood of profound gloom contrasted ironically with the bright June sunshine. He walked slowly, full of dread, in the direction of Rothersey Police Station. Once on the steps, he faltered, like a man on the brink of disaster, reeling wildly in that brief instant when the dread of the unknown future meets the despair of the known past. Those fatal words of Walter Paxton's whirled round and round, urging him on against his own volition: "The matter must be elucidated, Councillor Purvis. An appointment has been made and an appointment must be kept."

47. How to Catch a Councillor

If it had come to the point, Agnes Baldock would have openly admitted to a strong dislike of Andrew Crawford's bombast and pretentiousness. He lacked self-control, was proud and obstinate, wanting in compassion and what little love he had for his fellow-beings was cloaked in sackcloth of guilt, dour and humourless. Yes — openly she would have admitted these things. Inwardly, she would equally have been prepared to admit that he still held some of that old attraction she had once felt towards him. Here was a man who knew what he wanted from life and intended to get it, whether or no. Miss Baldock preferred her menfolk to have ideas, especially if they coincided with her own. She liked to be able to tell a man's ideas just by looking at him, and, with Andrew Crawford, she could read him like a book.

She realised how foolish she had been in expecting him to notice her reference to her 'fiancé'. It had passed right over his head without registering its name and address, so to speak. As for the argument over the stolen money — well, she might just as well have been talking to a brick wall for all the good it had done. She had expected Crawford to be rude and mulish. Now, if it had been that nice Mr. Garville, well, that would have been another kettle of fish. Always so courteous, especially to a lady of quality like herself. Never a sharp word in all the seventeen years she had been dealing with him. Handsome too! Tall and manly. She wouldn't have minded a try at him, but somehow she found him mysteriously unapproachable where affairs of the heart were concerned. Pity he was such a confirmed and dedicated bachelor! Still, Gabriel would do, was better than nothing — and she had had plenty of nothing for far too long!

Agnes prided herself on her tough, bulldozing techniques which she found far more effective than some of the namby-pamby methods some women of her acquaintance used. She reflected on her altercation with Andrew Crawford and was satisfied to think she had won the day where he was concerned. Of course, it was all a matter of time, but time was a commodity in short supply in her case. Whilst she was quite prepared to sit back and wait for a response, she could not wait for ever. Alas, since Andrew Crawford and Garville were both scratched from the marriage race, there was nothing on the horizon that really matched her desires. Her greatest fear was ending her days in loneliness and solitude, living her life out on an emotional wing and a prayer. In Gabriel Purvis, she had made a supreme compromise, had followed the dictates of reason rather than romance.

Agnes turned out of the market, with its narrow alleys and byways, into the less suffocating warmth of the High Street. A slight breeze caught her hair, caressed it momentarily and, thinking better of it, passed on, leaving her flushed and unprotected in the hot rays of the late morning sun. She ambled aimlessly by the Town Hall, looking up with surprising disinterest at the gross neo-gothic façade and the highly-polished oak doors swinging to and fro. It was all so unbearably unromantic, yet to Agnes, so unreal too. She called to mind a scene in a French novel she had read in her youth in which an oversexed young couple made passionate love together in the upper window of the Town Hall while watching the Mayor deliver a speech to the crowds in the square below. She remembered being shocked when one of her horrid little friends had inked out the 'B' in the title on the spine to read: *MADAME -OVARY*. The schoolgirl joke seemed very tame now as she looked up at the plain windows of Rothersey Town Hall. There was nothing transcendent about them, nothing that could excite passion or even romance.

Whilst Agnes had no wish to be cheated out of marriage, it was the idea of it that appealed to her more than the institution itself. The more she thought about the practical side of so-called wedded bliss the less she cared for the idea. She was inclined to call the whole thing off — only twenty-four hours after the initial entanglement. Being the woman she was, she put aside these musings. Though she resisted the thought that she had been rash with Gabriel on their Sunday-morning walk, the thought was persistent and harried her troubled mind all the way to Marley's Stores.

In the middle of the crossing stood a large rotund woman with a 'STOP!' sign gripped firmly in one hand, whilst with the other she grasped the bloodless hand of a reluctant child, almost dragging the defenceless little creature across the black and white stripes, impatiently, irritably. A number of children ran past her, ignoring her protests and sticking their tongues out at her in defiance. The woman's white coat billowed out like the sails of a galleon as she marched, *gauleiter* fashion from kerb to kerb. Agnes was reminded that this strong-armed female was the replacement for frail Mr. Lawton and tried to take more kindly to her.

Agnes turned into Marley's Stores to buy a tube of tooth-paste. True, she had a tube only half-used but she desperately wanted to talk to somebody, and who better than Lizzie Pomfrett, the girl on the bacon counter? Lizzie was so excited by the news of the engagement that she went round telling the story to all the other girls — Effie Mudd in ironmongery and her sister Iris in toiletries.

Unpredictably, an urge to confess came over Agnes to go to Our Lady of Lourdes and tell Father O' Flagherty everything. From there, she went on to the Roxy, where she told the cinema-manager, who told the kitchen staff, who told the four dumb waitresses, who were so dumb they recklessly spilled the beans to all the lunch-time regulars.

Back at Marley's, Lizzie was saying: "Fancy an old bag like her catching a Councillor!"

"Yeah" interrupted Iris. "A bit of a baby-snatcher from all accounts. He's been seen about with that Millie Thompson."

If it is a failing of human nature to gossip, then it must be said that the general feeling in Rothersey was one of good-will rather than rancour, though the mistaken rumour that Joe Purvis was getting spliced to a nubile young girl thirty years his junior caused certain scandal-loving sections of the community to believe he had got her in the family way, which in turn accounted for the untruth spread around about a 'shot-gun wedding' at the Registry Office.

Since Agnes moved in what she liked to consider superior social circles, she was unaware of this infamous tittle-tattle. She swung through the chromium-plated portals of the Roxy Picture House, her heart was once more restored to its former pride and joy, soon to be greatly inflated by the excited whispers of clientele and kitchen staff. It was at that very same moment that Councillor Purvis swung through the doors of Rothersey Police Station, his heart filled with foreboding.

48. Outing for Gino

"Come on! Up with you!" shouted Ma Blackwood, shaking Pa's shoulder. "It's high time you was about, you lazy tyke! There's work to be done. The shop's been open these two hours or more."

Pa turned over and blinked into her face, sleepily sucking his dry, yellow tongue back into some kind of reasonable state.

"Mamma mia!" he groaned, rolling over and pushing himself up on his elbow.

"Che ore sono?"

"Time you was up. Time is money round 'ere and don't you perishin' well forget it."

"Agh! Money! Money! Money! Is all you tink of, I tell you. Ever'ting is money. I tell you what we do in Napoli when I was kid. We lie in sun and kiss all di girls and drinka di vino. We no work. Is all you English tink of. Work, work, work! Money, money, money! And what 'appen to love, eh?"

"Cut it out, Pa. I'm warning yer, see? I aint goin' ter stand around here wasting my time. I say time's money and I means it. Can't you hear the tannery hooters going it. Blimey! Anyone'd fink the Jerries was comin' again, the way that siren goes on wailing. Up and down! Fair turns me all of a shiver, it does. Your breakfast's on the table, so get up and quick about it. You gotta go over the park, so get a move on."

Ma began flicking the duster over the furniture, making a good deal more dust than there was before as far as Pa could see.

"What you doin'? You make bloody blitz on Poppa."

223

After she had finished raising the dust, she began laying down the law. Pa assumed his customary hang-dog expression.

"Look here, you old bugger," she said. "You're getting as lazy as sin."

"Ha!" laughed Pa. "Ha! Don't seem old sin is lazy around 'ere." Ma ignored him.

"I'm all worked up about that Curly-boy. Bit of a fancy type, if you ask me. One o' these fine days, he's gonna come a cropper. He's a cocky little sod!"

"Never did like that boy, Poppa didn't," said Pa, pensively. "Un vero delinquente! He make a big-a mistake one day. You see! An' we all end up in de clink."

Pa pushed back the bedclothes and sat up on the edge of the old brass bedstead. Then he stood up gingerly and began scratching himself all round his midriff, scratching for all he was worth through his grubby old combinations.

Ma looked down at them, sniffed with scorn.

"I don't know how you wear them things in this weather. You stink like a polecat. You're a disgrace."

"Well, I tell you something you no like, you old cow! We pretend we marry when I come from Napoli, with the false papers. You get me permesso to stay one month and I stay here ten year and nobody know. Well, I tell you, I wish I back there, where I belong."

"Belt up, will you, you old goat! You get out there in those Gardens. What I want is information. Keep your ears open, see? You know our trade. All you gotta do is to find out things. Keep the boys up to date with what's goin' on. This morning, I want to know what that Curly-Boy is up to over the park. With him on the run there's no telling what'll 'appen. He can't break cover. The rozzers 'll 'ave 'im in no time. Left a message with one o' the boys. He's goin' ter leave fifty nicker for the diamond ring I give 'im for that tart of 'is on the window-sill in the Gent's lav and I want you to be there to see that everything's hunky-dory, see? I promised 'im a couple of addresses in Ireland as part of the deal. But if he finks I'm goin' over the park, he's got anuvver fink comin', 'cos I aint. He wants to do me in for good an' all and 'e aint gonna get the chance. I'm sending Gino over instead. He don't understand no English as can give 'im away. And he knows he'll be getting a one-way ticket home if he don't play it right. There aint no flies on that Curly, mind. So watch out! He's a crafty one. He got a lesson he won't never forget, but he's angry, that boy, and by angry I

224

mean dangerous. He's scared too, and when a bloke is both, watch out! There'll be fireworks, I tell you."

With that speech over, Ma left Pa to complete his not over-elaborate toilet and went off to clear up the boys' rooms, especially Curly's in case she found some useful clues.

Downstairs in the shop Gino was trying hard to be nice to the customers. On the premise that the customer is always right, he was battling with a small girl who seemed to know what she wanted but whose vocabulary was even more wretched than his own. He shrugged his shoulders at the tall young man with her and said:

"Mamma mia! What you like, bambina?

Such a question was impossible to answer. Even Mabel did not know. She studied the rows of sweet-jars and pointed to one of them. It was accordingly delved into by Gino's grubby fingers, sweets extracted, only to be rejected.

"Deez ones?" he smiled, inwardly fuming like a little Macchiavelli, and thinking all the time he would like to take this little Mabel and throw her into the lake.

"No! No! No!" she cried irritably.

"Madonna mia! Santo Dio!," he shouted into Mabel's pouting little face.

"Mabel want lolly. Uncle Tim. Mabel want lolly," she screamed.

As far as Gino was concerned, this 'Uncle Tim' was a bit of a 'cretino'.

Some time elapsed before Mabel decided on which colour she preferred today, so that, by the time Ma Blackwood finally poked her nose round the corner, Gino was in a frenzy of frustration.

"Now, look who's here. My little pet!!" said Ma, as if she was talking to a chimpanzee. "How are we today, my little darling?"

She delved into her big deep pockets and brought out, as if by magic, a nice purple sweet for Mabel and peace was restored once more.

"Right, Gino, my lad," said Ma suddenly, just as Mabel was skipping out of the shop hand-in-hand with Uncle Tim. "We're closing."

Gino thought *(all' italiano)* she was going clean off her rocker! Closing up the shop at half-past twelve?

Up went the CLOSED sign. Up went the shutters. Down came the blinds. In the semi-gloom, Ma turned and faced the handsome youth.

"Now, Gino, my boy! Before you go over the Park — let's 'ave a little action, shall we?" She chuckled. "Bel lavoro, eh?"

Gino did not pretend to misunderstand her. He resigned himself to his fate. She came towards him and put her ample arms round him, saying: "We'll have a bit of fun now, shall we, amore mio?

"Si, signora," he sighed, without the slightest grain of enthusiasm.

49. Flo in a Flutter

"Hallo, Smutty, old boy!" said Tim sadly, as he gave him a pat and a stroke. It was rewarded by busy tail-wagging and a double exhalation of warm breath on Timothy's palm, as much as to say: "What a blessing you've taken Mabel in hand. At least I can have the kennel to myself now."

"Hallo, Tim," said Mrs. Thompson. "You're back then!"

Tim wondered if she thought he was some kind of mirage the way she asked such idiotic questions. In a sense, he *was* a kind of vision for the Thompson household — a vision of a richer existence they had somehow been denied — the moneyed classes with their cars and their big houses — and one thing Flo did not know anything about — the time to enjoy one's blessings.

Flo had the idea that rich people did nothing but sit on their laurels and wait for the money to come rolling in. Rich people never got up at six in the morning, never had to do the washing on Mondays, and never had to put up with their children bawling at them at all hours of the day and night. All those men on the buses and tubes in the mornings, with their bowler hats and rolled umbrellas and carnations in their button-holes — they were the lucky ones. They were the people at the top who travelled with *The Times* and hadn't a care in the world. She couldn't see what they could be reading about — page after page of pointless print. Rich people, according to Flo, seemed to have nothing to worry about and nothing to think about. Money did it all for you. All rich people had to do was to sit back and down a plateful of roast beef and greens with a pint of the best and everything in the garden was lovely.

Mrs. Thompson had to confess that she did not really like Timothy. All right! He was well-mannered, yes, but he was a bit too much of a clever-clogs to her way of thinking. Too blinking keen to

226

come round and gloat over their misfortunes. Besides, he was getting too close to Mabel, fussing, fondling, cuddling the way he did. And here she was trying to get on with her rinsing and wringing.

"So you're back, then?" she repeated with some irritation and wishing he would go away and leave her to get on by her own sweet self! With an effort, she brought herself to say: "Ever so nice of you to take our Mabel off my hands for a bit."

"Only too glad to help, Mrs. Thompson," said Timothy.

Anything, he thought, to get away from thinking about his father over at the hospital. The emergency operation should be over by now. It was, they said, very touch and go. He had lost so much blood. Either way, whether his father came through or not, Timothy would have to wait around until his mother could get up to London, and that would not be before the three o'clock train arriving at Liverpool Street Station.

He watched Mrs. Thompson rubbing out the smalls on the scrubbing-board, her face wet from the rising steam.

"Hot weather to be washing today," he said.

"Mondays is Mondays, that's all there is to it. My mum always did her washing on Mondays and her mother before her, so I don't see why it should be any different for me."

"Doesn't Millie ever help out?"

"Her?" said Mrs. Thompson derisively. "That'll be the day! Anyway, she's so touchy lately. All them buttons is getting on her nerves, that's what I think. Our Millie ought to take a 'oliday, only she'd be bored to tears. She likes the dancing and jigging about up at the Bowl, larking about with the boys till all hours. If you ask me, she's going to get into trouble one of these days. And she won't be told. A proper little tartar, she is, when she wants to be. Still, taken all in all, she's a good girl really."

While Timothy and Mrs. Thompson were idly chatting, Mabel went out to have her own little chat with Smutty, who only wished to be left alone and least of all wanted to enact a polite *thé-dansant* with extra prods and pinches from Mabel's sharp little finger-nails. He dragged himself up ponderously, eyes swivelling apprehensively from side to side. Then he vacated the cool darkness of his kennel for the heat of the midday sun. He slumped down on the sparrow's grave and began panting furiously, his pink tongue lolling with the heat. Mabel, as it happened, had long since forgotten her darling sparrow and cared little for Smutty's irreverence. She crawled into the doggy darkness of the kennel and squatted there like a pagan queen among the bones and relics

227

of her realm.

The atmosphere in the Thompson household had the semblance of being all peace and tranquillity, yet, tensions lay under it like molten lava ready to erupt. Mrs. Thompson continued to moan about her daily drudgery in her house of sand. Mabel seemed to be planning some dramatic scene, with all the histrionics she could muster. Millie was clearly out of sorts, with the growing realisation of a dreadful truth about herself which one day she would have to face up to. Alf was fretting over a dark secret he didn't want to talk about. Ron was disturbed by his fear of being publicly disgraced over his break-in at Grandpa Lawton's. In short, the Thompson family were living in an atmosphere of secrecy and fear.

As for Timothy, quietly sunning himself on the kitchen step, nothing could alleviate the feelings of dread at what seemed the inevitable outcome of the disastrous events of the morning. Now, as Mrs. Thompson thrust her head into a cloud of steam, Timothy sought to say something, anything as long as it kept the conversation going, but Mrs. Thompson was far too preoccupied with her own problems to be bothered with visitors on a morning such as this. Maybe she did resent him. Maybe she *did* find him a nuisance calling round to see Mabel so often. Maybe she *would* prefer him to keep out of their way. The truth of the matter was that, just at this moment, Timothy could not help being interested in the curious mystique that surrounded Mabel Thompson's world. He saw in her a small but expanding ripple of genius on the dark labyrinthine tides that troubled Laburnum Villas.

Drama was part and parcel of the Thompson way of life. There was one performance at least on every day of their lives, with the occasional *matinée* thrown in for good measure, usually a solo by Mabel in which she could hold the stage for as much as an hour at a time. When the final curtain came down and they all tumbled into their beds, there was an uncanny silence about the house as if ghosts from the past were about to take over and put on a show of their own. Dreams and day-dreams were part and parcel of this unhappy state of affairs in the Thompson household, but what happened now was no dream.

Into the midst of the piles of shirts, vests, night-dresses, pyjamas, socks, into the midst of the dank smell of steam and soap-suds, staggered a very pale and frightened-looking Millie, assisted by a friend from the button-factory. As soon as she sat down, Millie burst into tears. Her mother looked up, vague and uncomprehending, brushed a wisp of hair back with her soapy fingers and then panicked in her usual

228

Grand Guignol manner. Amidst tears and steam, she succeeded in understanding that Millie had been taken "real bad" at work, and what a to-do it all was, with the girls all of a dither and not knowing what to make of it all, and them slithering about all over the buttons — trying to get Millie out into the fresh air of the damp, soot-laden Rothersey High Street.

The first thing that Timothy did was to rid themselves of the garrulous companion.

"Oh, don't go, Effie," cried Millie. "I don't want to be left alone with this lot."

Effie was sent packing in spite of protestations and the front door firmly closed to snoopers, nosy-parkers, and other local busybodies.

"Oh, Mum!" groaned Millie. "I do feel bad, I do. Got a terrible pain."

"Never mind, dearie!" said Mrs. Thompson. "I'll get the doctor."

"I don't want no doctor," cried Millie. "There aint nothing wrong with me. I've just got a pain, that's all."

Ron was dispatched to fetch Dr. Glendale. He was found to be away on holiday, suffering from a touch of the Trossachs.

"You wouldn't 'ave a pain if there wasn't nothing wrong," said Flo. "Could be your appendix."

"No, please, Mum! It's just the heat. All them machines, the noise of 'em. I couldn't stand it no longer."

"That's all right, dearie! Now you go and lie down and rest yourself, there's a good gel. I'll bring you a nice cup o' tea in two shakes of a lamb's tail."

Millie collapsed on the bed in tears. When her mother came up, she sat down and put her arms round her daughter — an unpremeditated act of compassion which embarrassed her, making her draw her arms away suddenly. The situation was worsened by Millie falling against her mother and holding her so tightly that Mrs. Thompson winced with pain.

"Oh Mum! Oh! Mum! I feel awful."

"P'raps you ate too much for your supper last night," Flo said.

Slipping out of the room, she crept downstairs, leaving Millie quietly weeping on the pillows. In the kitchen, she confronted Timothy.

"I don't know what to make of it, I really don't. All that carrying on. I mean, what's she bin up to, I like to know?"

229

"She may have pulled a muscle. Could be strain at work. How old is she? Eighteen, is it? How regular have her monthlies been?"

"What a thing to ask, I must say!" said the distracted mother. "'Taint my affair!"

"Don't upset yourself, Mrs. Thompson. I'll go up and see how she is."

Ten minutes later, he came downstairs.

"I can tell you, Mrs. Thompson, it's not appendicitis. She needs plenty of rest."

"Am I going to have to be saddled with her at home?"

"She'll be all right, Mrs. Thompson. Don't worry. Everything's quite normal."

"Well, I 'ope so. I can't take any more. I really can't."

"Look here," said Timothy hotly. "Millie needs a bit of love and care. Wait till the doctor comes and he'll be able to tell you what to do."

"What about her work? She gives me a bit every week, you know. Oh, dear! What's Alf going to say?"

"Hang her work!" said Tim, irritably. "And to hell with what Mr. Thompson's going to say. If only Dr. Glendale had been here!"

"Him! Huh! Silly old fool! He couldn't cure a flea."

After an hour the duty doctor arrived, a feckless young man who fussed round Millie like an old woman. This was obviously his first confinement. A light barley soup was prescribed, and plenty of rest.

" Well," said Flo, " I never had no rest, nor no refinements, or what ever you calls it, when I had my kids."

As Timothy walked back to the hospital, he realised how much he had to learn about dealing with the Mrs. Thompson's of this world, the tolerance, the patience that would be expected of him in the future by hundreds of people coming to him with their problems and ailments. Nevertheless, he was as sure as anybody could be that, before the year was out, Mrs. Thompson, whether she liked it or not, was going to be a grandmother.

EPISODE ELEVEN

The afternoon of the following day

Pains and Penalties

50.   An Appointment Kept

The Palaseum clock struck its tinkling half-past two as Curly slipped through the gates of the Public Gardens and slithered down into the shadows of Bushy Walk. He vanished into the thick foliage of the laurels and leant against the trunk of an elm. He was breathing heavily, short gulps of the grimy air regurgitated in the heat of the day from Rothersey's docks and wharves and the belching smoke of the barges as they passed by under the bridge.

Shortly afterwards, Pa Blackwood appeared from the direction of the shop and crept swiftly into the Public Lavatories to secrete himself in a place where he could observe the arrival of Councillor Purvis with the fated fifty pounds blood-money.

Curly was not in good shape after his ordeal at the hands of Ma Blackwood's boys. He was dirty and unshaven. Sweat streamed down over his stubbled cheeks. His brain reeled with a confused of thoughts. The truth of the matter was that, for once in his life, Curly Donoghue was scared. He was on the spot. After what had happened at the market he knew what it was to be on the run, not able to show as much as a finger in public, let alone his face. And not a soul to help him, except, if his luck was in, maybe Ma Blackwood, and she wouldn't lift a finger of hers to help him unless he paid over that fifty pounds, and in double quick time! He knew she would not stop at just a punch-up next time. He knew that, with Pa Blackwood as her spy, he was never going to get away without paying up on the nail. Ma was dangerous. She had 'connections' who could make a bloke's life a misery. All he needed was a break, just enough cash to get the hell out of it — Ireland maybe, him and his old bag-woman of a mother — yes, he could pick her up out of the dirt and take her away from all the squalor and the hopelessness, back to the green land of her fathers.

Now Curly caught sight of Gino, hovering about like a frightened fly on the path leading out of Bushy Walk towards the public lavatories. Getting him to write the threatening letter to Purvis had been a walkover. Even with Gino's limited skills in English, the idea was worth it if it kept Curly out of the blackmailing racket. He didn't intend to get himself put in clink for nothing. 'No-one, but no-one's going to stitch me up on a blackmail job,' he told himself.

Thoughts of what he had done to Andrew Crawford broke in suddenly, and hatred made him forget for a moment his main purpose. 'That bastard!' he muttered aloud, and followed it with a few of his

232

favourite obscenities. Then thoughts of his father came into things all of a sudden, confusing him even more:

My old man was the biggest skiver you could ever meet, going off, leaving him and his old Ma to make it alone.......and Ma was just the same in the end. What happened to her, eh? Leaving me to fight it out on me own. I aint never seen 'er to this day, and I don't want to, neither. I mean, leavin' me like that. Livin' on a bombed-site. And me only a nipper at the time, eating out of other people's dustbins, trailing round the streets till all hours picking up anything we could lay our hands on. I mean, what kind of a mother is that, eh? She don't care if I'm dead and I don't give a damn about her. Women's all the same, if you ask me. You can't trust 'em. As for that Millie Thompson, now there's a bloody little tart for you. She's been laid by just about every bloke in the Borough, including that creep, Purvis. Anybody could see she's in the family way, and her going out with that twit, Eddie Carpenter.

Right in the middle of all this, Curly was interrupted by the appearance of Councillor Purvis, frail and frightened as he furtively looked around for signs of the mystery contact for whom he was to leave the packet of fifty crisp green pound notes (all carefully marked by the police!). Almost immediately behind him walked a short pudgy little man, wearing a tartan tie and horn-rimmed spectacles. Mr. Purvis slipped into the toilets with a self-conscious air that betrayed his state of mind. The little man followed. After a few moments, which seemed like an hour to Curly, Mr. Purvis emerged once more into the hot sun and went off in the direction of the Band-stand. Almost immediately the little man rushed out, wildly waving and calling after the Councillor:

"Excuse me," he cried. "I say, you there! You've forgotten your parcel!"

Purvis stopped and faced him with a look that would have frozen most people to ice.

"We do forget things, don't we?" said the irritating little man. "We must be more careful, mustn't we? What would the wife say if we got home without our little gift. Anniversary, is it?"

Incapable of speech, the wretched Mr. Purvis managed to force a smile.

"Lovely weather, isn't it? Just the right time for a stroll, if I may say so," said the intruder. "Lived in the district long?"

"All my life, pretty well," said the Councillor, in a discouraging tone.

"Now, isn't that nice! I've only just moved here, you know. The wife too, of course. Mustn't forget *her*." He gave an absurd little giggle. " Couldn't leave the little woman behind, could we?"

Purvis was casting furtive glances towards the toilets.

"Yes," went on the intruder. "We've rented a nice little house in Lupin Lane, just near Rothersey Secondary School, you know. The roof of the gym just shuts out the view of the gas-works. We like it. Lovely to see the youngsters playing. Makes us feel young again just to listen to them. Of course, Cynthie, — that's my wife — I always call her Cynthie, but her real name's — "

"Yes," interrupted Mr Purvis. "But I'm afraid I really must go....."

"....Cynthia," persisted the little man, "but it sounds so formal, don't you think? Well, anyway, Cynthie just *loves* London. Well, after thirty years in Worthing, we just got fed up to the teeth. Howling gales in winter — blown inside out on the prom — wheelchairs by the dozen in summer — stinky-poo's from the seaweed in the hot weather — we just thought it was time to up and out before it was too late. I had a little drapery store, you see, and you can't sell up just like that, can you, without having plans? I said to Cynthie, I could never be like those poor souls up the road, living on public charity. No! We've got our little nest — and our little nest-egg — not much, mind, but enough to have our little Sunday treat out when we want to."

The Councillor was by now distraught beyond measure.

"Am I keeping you?" asked the little man. "I mean, I've got plenty of time. Now you look quite a spry old feller to me — for your age! Where do you live?"

"Well, I — "began Mr. Purvis.

"No!" interrupted the Irritant. "Not the Old People's Home! We must be neighbours. Now, we ought to arrange a little party of the oldies one afternoon. Do you play *Snakes and Ladders* or *Ludo*? Maybe a bit of whist?"

At this point, Mr. Purvis lunged forward towards the packet and grabbed at it. Ten minutes to three and an appointment had to be kept.

"Oooh!" said the little man. "Snatchy-snatchy! Now, we must ask nicely, mustn't we!"

The Councillor's brow puckered and his face was flushed with frustration.

"Now, come along, my man! I haven't time to mess about here. I have an assignation."

The Irritant looked as if he was festering for a fight but let go of the packet more from astonishment than anything.

"Well!" he muttered through thin little lips. "Cynthie will have something to say about this."

Mr. Purvis was, by this time, hurrying off towards the Public Conveniences, leaving the intruder with the impression that a weak bladder was indeed a direful and distressing complaint to be saddled with.

Meanwhile, Curly was beside himself with rage. He pounded his fists into the tree-trunk. At that moment, Gino appeared, hoiked out on the end of a plain-clothes man's arm. He was fighting him off and shouting blue murder in a rich stream of Italian expletives. Councillor Purvis followed, hoping against hope that he would not be recognised by any passing colleagues.

With this, Curly burst into a stream of obscenities and tore at the bark of a tall birch with his nails, tore at it till his fingers bled. He pummelled the wood till the pain shot up his arms. As the plain-clothes officers hustled Gino and the Councillor into the police-car, Curly wanted to cry out and shout abuse at them, but he dared not. Instead he kicked brutally at the tree-trunk, ripped down a branch half-fallen, tearing the soft green and silver bark from the wood, like the skin of a ripe banana. He crushed the wood under his boot and began to kick violently through the undergrowth and on through the herbaceous borders, trampling on the plants, grubbing them out with his boots.

Inside the toilets, Pa Blackwood was still keeping a watch, though unseen by Curly, who took out his knife and scored through the paintwork, back and forth, up and down and across again, until the tiled floor was sprinkled with a fine speckled carpet of pale blue flakes of paint. He turned towards the door marked 'Engaged' and kicked it, rattling the lock furiously, and banging on the door.

"What are you doing in there, you dirty swine?" he shouted.

As he stepped out into the sunlight, a monkey scampered across in front of him, sat down by the begonia-bed Curly had helped so effectively to destroy only minutes before and started to scratch itself, all the time watching Curly till he felt its eyes running through him like spears of hot steel. He flung a stone at it, causing it to scamper a few yards off where it sat squeaking and scowling among the red geraniums.

For some reason, Curly remembered Crawford lying in a pool

235

of blood. He gave a low moan, then, in a mad rush of fear, he made his way in the direction of the bridge. He'd have to get in touch with one of the big Soho fellers north of the river, else he'd be up in front of the beak quicker than he could swing a monkey!

51. Louise's Secret Garden

The very gloom in which the house at No 5 had been cast was itself sufficient evidence of the sympathy which Uncle Walter felt towards Timothy and the near-tragedy of the morning's events. Once the initial moments of panic and horror were over, the normal routine returned, but with subtle overtones of conversation that belied the apparent calm, only disturbed momentarily by Timothy's return from the hospital with the news that his father had not regained consciousness and there was little hope of his doing so. The gloom pervaded the little house remorselessly, pushing into every corner. Louise began to feel for the first time in her life that the house was crumbling about her under some great and unavoidable avalanche.

"Well, Tim, my boy," said Uncle Walter, gravely, "we can only wait, but you have our love to help you along."

A silence ensued, as if they were already mourning a great loss. Something, it is true, had died, something intangible, something none of these good people could pinpoint. Finally, Uncle said, in a tone that suggested the continuance of a remote conversation carried on in another world beyond their own grieving:

"And how's our little Mabel, today?"

"Mabel?" said Timothy, absent-mindedly. "She's doing fine. We're really getting on like a house on fire. She's really opening out like a flower, that little girl. She'll end up on the stage one day — a real little actress."

"Well, if she's changed at all, it's due to you, my lad. You've quite a way with the kiddies. You'll make a good father when you get round to it."

"Now, Uncle! Don't let's start that all over again. You know very well I'm not interested in getting married. I have to meet the girl of my dreams yet, anyway."

Mr. Paxton laughed good-humouredly and said:

236

"All right! All right! Keep your hair on! No need to get so hot under the collar about it."

There was a twinkle in his eye, betraying a hidden allusion that did not escape Timothy.

"Well, one thing we can say," the old man went on, "Mabel has the cheeks of *Crimson Glory* about her. A real little picture of health and happiness, and a sight better than that sister of hers. Any fool can see what's up with her."

"How did you know, Uncle?" Timothy asked.

"It's not difficult to see, is it? Anyway, we had a visit from the — shall we say — 'other half' this morning."

"Good God! You mean the father?" said Timothy, who had come to no great conclusions on the subject.

"How did you get to know about it, Tim?"

"It was when I brought Mabel back from the sweet-shop. Mrs. Thompson was doing the washing and suddenly Millie burst in and there was a bit a hysterical scene. I went up and sat with her for a few minutes. I knew then what it was. They were all in such a state but I couldn't tell them. I had to wait for the doctor."

"I can't imagine Mrs. Thompson getting anxious about anybody," said Uncle. "She's always so wrapped up in her own troubles, if you ask me. No wonder her husband seems to have taken to the bottle."

"Luckily, I prevented a real scene from developing, in the absence of Dr. Glendale. Apparently he's done a Harry Lauder and hit the 'high road' to bonnie Scotland for a fortnight. So we're waiting for the locum. I'm not so brilliant when it comes to dealing with hysterics, unlike my mother. Thank God, she is so capable when it comes to a crisis. No matter how bad things are, she keeps a calm exterior and a cool mind even if she's twisted up inside with emotion. I wish I could be like it too, but I broke down when I saw Dad lying there in a coma. Mother put her arm round me. She spoke no word but I knew she was desperate by the look in her eyes. When we got outside, the Sister told me to think of Mother's feelings, so I took hold of myself and everything was all right. Then I felt bad about breaking down in front of her. Almost selfish. Anyway, I'm going to make up for it tonight and take her out for supper somewhere in the West End. Lyons Corner House — the Brasserie, perhaps. There's a good pianist there — he plays all her favourite tunes. We'll be able to have a good talk about things." He paused for a moment and frowned as if a shadow came across his thoughts.

"Uncle! I have something to tell you before Louise comes in. I had a letter today about this new operation they are considering at the hospital. You remember the French surgeon I spoke to you about? Well, it seems that he would be prepared to see Louise and talk to her about possibilities. If there is a need to operate, then he would make all the arrangements. I also went to see a very able psychiatrist who specialises in trauma, who tells me there may be some deep-seated problem that could be unravelled without too much pain. He mentioned hypnosis as another possibility. What do you think?"

"I don't know, Tim," said Uncle Walter, guardedly. "I'm suspicious of a lot of these newfangled treatments they've brought out since the war. As far as I can see, they're more likely to kill than cure."

"Uncle! Please, at least, think about it. Louise is young and beautiful. I want so much to help her. You will think about it, won't you?"

"You know, Tim," said Uncle, "I've a feeling you're going to make a good doctor when it comes to it, but you may find another path in the end. Sometimes the path we have already trodden is the path we can best follow. Still, I do notice a certain expertise when you carve the Sunday roast! Butcher to surgeon in three easy lessons, eh?"

They laughed together and Louise came in and beckoned them into the garden, where she had laid tea. The warm late-afternoon sun shone over the little rose-garden and made them feel relaxed as they settled into their garden-chairs.

"Louise, you have beautiful hands," said Tim, as Louise poured out the tea. "You ought to be a pianist. Or a ballet-dancer."

She smiled with pleasure and waited for Uncle Walter to answer for her.

"Or a surgeon," the old man suggested with a chuckle. "Or a painter, perhaps. She's a real artist, is my Louise. She sews and embroiders like an artist. She cooks like an artist. She suffers like an artist."

The remark seemed not to affect her beyond her making an enigmatic glance in Uncle Walter's direction, but it was almost too brutal for Timothy's liking. But then he told himself that he hadn't yet learned to gauge her sensitivity as Uncle had. The old man still droned on:

"And sometimes she even looks like an artist, especially when she brings me my tea in the morning, her hair all over the place and her pale, undernourished cheeks. Like something out of one of those romantic operas, she is."

Louise smiled at Uncle Walter's teasing and put her hand on his arm to show her appreciation.

"Now, just look at her, Tim. She'd make some lucky young man a wonderful wife."

Louise withdrew her hand suddenly and her smile faded into a frown. She picked up Timothy's cup and nervously replenished it, held out the sugar bowl to him and raised her eyebrows as if to say: "Are you taking sugar today?" though she knew perfectly well Tim never had sugar with tea unless he had lemon with it. In spite of this obvious attempt to foil Uncle's sally, the remark hovered over them all for a moment and then darted out of sight like a swallow in flight over the treetops. The matter ended abruptly as Louise lifted the muslin cloth away from the table to reveal a large bowl of strawberries and a jug of cream beside it. Timothy gasped.

"Louise! You *are* a wonder after all."

She tried to mould some words with her lips, but Timothy was still finding it difficult to lip-read. The sibilants were the worst. Was she saying *said* or *shed*, *shirt* or *church*? As for *cab* and *gap*, *tap* and *dab*, they were indistinguishable. Gradually, he was learning to watch the pressure of the lips and their roundness or narrowness. Now, as she moved her lips, he thought how pretty they were, so soft, so delicately tinted, and they seemed to be all the time saying to him: "I love you." He turned to Uncle in a panic and said:

"I can't understand, Uncle. What is she trying to say?" Then he bit his lip. Sometimes, every word he spoke to Louise seemed to hold some embarrassing overtone.

Uncle's bright eyes watched her re-form the words.

"She says: "That's enough, you!" It's as good a thing to say to a young man who doesn't know a birthday treat when he sees one!"

"You mean, " said Timothy, "well.....Louise. Why didn't anybody tell me?" There he was again, using all the wrong words. How it must hurt her so.

The only gift he could possibly give her in the circumstances was a light kiss on the cheek. Almost immediately, he regretted it. He blushed. She blushed. Uncle said nothing and watched the young couple eating their strawberries and cream.

As soon as he could, Tim excused himself on account of his projected outing with his mother. He fled up the steps into the kitchen

239

and disappeared into the shadowiness of the front hall. Then the front door banged shut.

Louise sat for a while, looking round at Uncle's flowers and the white-washed walls that enclosed them and her and Uncle in their intimate, silent world. She wanted to fly out of it like a butterfly escaping from a net. She longed to be able to confide her secret to a sympathetic listener, someone who would have to be special enough to confide in, someone she would have to love first before she could open her heart. To Uncle Walter, her eyes spoke more unhappiness than the silent movements of her lips. Had Timothy cared to peer more deeply into those eyes, he might have discovered the secret garden of her emotions. It was certainly there, like Uncle's precious roses, in all its colours. She recalled a medieval poem Timothy had read to her about a garden and a rose, a lover and a beautiful damsel, and the gate to the garden was called 'Love'. So far, Timothy was wandering in a maze of bypaths, and it seemed unlikely that he would ever discover the true way through to Louise's secret garden, unless — as Uncle Walter dearly hoped – a means could be found to open his eyes. Something — it was difficult to envisage exactly what— something *had* to happen to break the mould — something dramatic and vital that would change their lives forever. How this might be no-one could possibly imagine, but happen it must, if Louise was to share her secret with Timothy.

52.   A Chip off the Old Block!

On his way through the back streets to the river, Curly was startled by the crash of a dustbin-lid close by. As he passed, he saw an old crone rooting around for scraps, throwing out old rubbish in quest of food and fag-ends. He was surprised when she stood up and spoke, still holding a grubby piece of rag in her wrinkled hand.

"And what'll the likes o' you be doing in these parts?" she said in her rough Irish.

It took Curly a second or two to realise that this pathetic old woman was his mother. When he did, he changed into another Curly, a Curly from way back, in the time when they lived together in a shack on a bombed-site, a time when he had to scrimp and scrounge for anything as long as it kept body and brain working, and he had needed brains to

240

live like that, did Curly Donoghue. Over the years since he had left her behind him and struck out on his own, he had not needed help from anyone, least of all her. But now? Well, she seemed heaven-sent, a murky apparition moving about in the gloom of his subconscious come forward into the air and materialised before his very eyes.

"Have you no tongue in that head o' yours?" she said brusquely, yet with undertones of affection.

Curly stammered out his words as if he were at a confessional.

"Where you bin, Ma?" he said in an anguished whisper. "I aint seen you for months,"

His tone was one of mild reprimand, the kind a child makes in protest at some inexplicable action of its elders.

"So it is you, is it?" she said quietly. "And a fine old mess you're after getting yourself into. And now you turn up like a bad penny just when you're in a bit o' trouble, so you do. There's a bad streak running right through you, young feller, and to be sure I don't know where you get it, unless it's from that slitherin' old bowsey of a father o' yours."

"Taint likely!" said Curly truculently. "I didn't never see nor hear of him. Not that he aint to blame for leaving us both in the lurch."

"And what in the name o' all that's holy !" said Ma Donoghue, "would I 'a' done with him if he'd have stayed, I'd like to know. Him swearing about the place, an' forever boozin' down at Barney's Bar. Always in the courts, he was. And mean, he was. Why, 'tis so mean he was, that one, if he had two watches he wouldn't tell you the time. And a liar too, he was. Arrivin' home drunk as a lord, breathin' his whisky-breath all over you. 'Ah, 'tis your old hubby come home to you,' he'd say. And he after coming straight from the courts for stealing, and picking pockets. 'Sure!' says he, 'sure, wasn't I comin' home with me creel o' turf and wasn't I goin' straight as a dye for Barney's Bar for a sharpener, when I ups and meets with a representative o' the strong arm o' the law! And didn't he up and send me to the courts for doin' nothin' at all, at all.' Always romancin', so he was. That's your father for you. An' him cheeking everybody like the good-for-nothin' he was. 'So you've come home,' I says to him, and him been put away three whole weeks an' all. 'An' so I have,' says he, 'an' can you spare me a penny for me trouble?' That's your father for you. Yes, Curly, you got the badness from him, just like I said. And a poor dribbling lump o' humanity he was. And us living on a London bombed-site! 'There's plenty o' bogs round the place,' I says — Council ones at that! Why don't you go to one o' them for a change?" And by all that's holy, if he didn't kick the bucket in one of 'em, behind locked doors, as it were. That's your father for you, Curly. And as far as I can see, you're headin' in his direction in double quick time."

Curly's head was a whirling mass of memories that jerked his brain back and forth like a yo-yo. They filled him with waves of melancholy and remorse till his head hung low with the humiliation of a lifetime.

"Don't be like that, Ma," he said meekly.

"Ah! Stop your blatherin', boy!" she shouted in a capricious burst of anger. "Get out o' me sight before I start me yellin'."

"Aw! Shut your face, you bloody old cow!" he shouted back, suddenly with the old frustrations rising to the surface.

"You was never no good for me. Who was it put me out on the streets? Who was it taught me all the tricks o' the trade? Who was it got me mixed up with Ma Blackwood's gang? I'm in trouble, I am, good and proper. And whose bloody fault is that, eh?"

"Trouble or no trouble, you'll be getting no help from me, " she said, turning her back on him. "I got me own troubles."

He grabbed her arm. She glared at him with bright eyes. She seemed suddenly to be a pathetic figure more in need of *his* help than he of hers, as she stood there in her tattered old coat tied together with assorted pieces of string. Her wrinkled yellow face and rough hands were testimony enough to a hard life lived out of necessity rather than joy, but in the dim glow of the street-lamps such things were barely visible save the brightness of her eyes, which shone like two jet beads in the darkness.

53.   A Time of Waiting

The water bubbled up in the saucepan. Mrs. Thompson tossed in an Oxo cube, some chopped-up turnip, carrot, onion, and potato. So much for the old fogey of a locum whose prescription was for 'a little light homemade vegetable broth' to bring Millie to her senses again. Flo would have much preferred to serve up something really tasty like a tin of Heinz tomato soup.

Monday night was oddments night anyway, but Mrs. Thompson had not a scrap of faith in the doctor's diagnosis, let alone his crazy prescription. Whoever heard of having broth on a summer's evening like this, for example? The man must be mad, or leastways incompetent. Still, Millie had to have soup and Millie was going to get it, good and proper. Quite the little madam, she was!

One way or another, there was going to be hell to pay before the day was out. Mrs. Thompson knew it as surely as she was at that moment spooning out the contents of two tins of baked beans into a saucepan. She put them over the flame. Then turned opened a tin of pears and plopped them into a Pyrex dish on the table, next to a dish of Bird's custard. She heaved a sigh as she caught sight of the basket with the day's washing, all waiting for Wednesday's ironing.

Yes, there's going to be hell to pay today! The question was, who was going to pay it? What with Alf and Ron not home, Mabel as quiet as a mouse (which was never a good sign) and Madam Millie out for the count upstairs — it was promising to be a stormy evening.

When that old fool of a doctor told her what was wrong with Millie, Flo had ten fits.

Millie never said nothing about her monthlies — the shame of it! What would everybody think? — her having a kid and not even spliced. The little hussy! Coming home here and blubbing all over the place, pretending butter wouldn't melt in her mouth. It was all very well to be sorry after the damage was done. And what about her poor mother having to look after her! It had been difficult enough asking for the afternoon off, but to ask for the week off, well! With her being part-time at the Town Hall and Millie being off sick there was going to be peanuts coming in for the housekeeping. Millie or no Millie, baby or no baby, Flo Thompson was going back to work whether anybody liked it or not. Millie, queening it upstairs, would just have to look after herself. She got herself in this mess so she could get herself out of it. Ron could do a bit of the looking-after for a change. It would keep him out of mischief, stop him messing about with that painting lark, making a muck-up of the furniture with his pots and brushes. Why on earth couldn't he be normal like other kids and help his mother more? Then there was Millie's silly nonsense over the pop-singing lark. Never came to anything! Just fizzled right out like everything else anybody ever tried to do in their house. Life was one round of toil and trouble from start to finish, without even as much as a break or a breather. What was life anyway? You came into it with pain all round you, and screaming and howling to get back out of it before you'd seen five seconds of it, and you went out of it with pain inside you almost too much to bear, and

243

in between? Well! — it was just hell let loose!

Into the midst of Mrs. Thompson's reveries burst the doggy-smelling Mabel, who had emerged from the kennel dragging a pathetic-looking Inky behind her. She was very annoyed; she had made the discovery that Smutty had cannibalistic tendencies. One of Inky's hands had been gnawed off completely, and all the pink wax of his little arm, gored by Smutty's angry molars. There was plenty of dried-up old bread in the back of the kennel so why couldn't Smutty have gnawed on that instead of making mincemeat of poor Inky? Mabel had missed Inky for days and days, and now, here he was — battered and disfigured almost beyond recognition. It was clear that he would have to be washed and very carefully treated for his wounds.

Mabel crawled out of the kennel and shook a dimpled finger at Smutty, whose ears went straight back and practically tied themselves in a bow with the shame of it. He lowered his head and stood looking up at her with guilt in his eyes and half-expecting a pinch and a poke. As it was, she ignored him, turned her back on him, and went into the kitchen, whilst Smutty slithered back into his kennel.

Opening the dresser drawer, Mabel took out a box of matches.

"Mabel!" said Mrs. Thompson sharply. "Put them matches back else I'll give you a clip over the ear. Do you hear me? Your asking for it, my gel. What do you want with the matches anyway?"

Mabel stared at her mother bending over the saucepans and knew perfectly well that, in the twinkling on an eye, her mother would have forgotten all about the matches.

Precisely, Mrs. Thompson did forget all about the matches and began checking the washing, putting it all in piles, ready for tomorrow's ironing, whilst the wily Mabel quietly slipped through the hall and into the front room, closing the door behind her with an expert regard for silence. Sitting Inky in one of the green armchairs, she deftly lit one of the candles in the brass candelabra defiantly attached to the piano. When the flame had grown and melted the wax, she grasped the candle in her pudgy little hand and in her best professional manner coined from the girls at Marley's hair-dressing saloon, she began putting some shape and style into Inky's bedraggled hair. However, Inky, being a boy, had to be subjected to the same treatment as Ron — short, back and sides and a singe to finish up with. She replaced the candle, rather shakily, in its holder and set to combing and snipping, all the time carrying on the kind of platitudinous conversation about the weather, the state of the lollipop trade and the latest news about Smutty's indignities.

Mabel was not at all herself. She was a smart little hairdresser with a new customer who was drinking lemonade and reading all the latest gossip under the drier. She applied the candle flame for the singe and, in less time than she could say 'Ink –', his hair was ablaze. Then his little coat. Then his smart little trousers. Then his little socks and shoes. Then, most horrible of all, his little flesh-coloured limbs began to melt and smell very nasty indeed. Now the seat of the chair caught fire. Mabel began apologising profusely to her customer, saying that, if he would kindly continue sipping his lemonade, she would have everything under control in a jiffy.

When all was lost, she took him up, the horrid sight that he was, and banged his smoking head on all the chairs in the room, one by one, and so every chair received its scorching and dab of molten wax that immediately took flame. By the time she reached the window Inky had crumpled irreparably into a mass of nothingness, just molten wax and charred innards and, most terrifying of all, flames darting out of his head. Fire swept up the lace curtains in a sheet of flame and printed a grotesque black face on the ceiling as if by magic, and the shapeless shreds of curtain hung disconsolately from the scorching-hot metal rod above.

When the flames had died down and disappeared, Mabel, conscious of being the perpetrator of great events, took up the shapeless lump of wax that was beloved Inky, carried it out ceremoniously, closing the door on the bitter fruit of her misfortune and began making arrangements for yet another funeral.

If Smutty had thought about things a little more, he might have realised that he was rapidly becoming the unpaid curator of Mabel's little cemetery. Indeed, by the time supper was ready, his kennel rose out of 'The Dumps' like a miniature 'Chapel of Rest', surrounded by the tombs of Mabel's luckless friends.

With the passing of Inky, Mabel was to travel yet another step in the painful process of growing up. She began to realise that, in some obscure way, she was responsible for a death, a death that was to bring only loneliness and a sense of loss. Now, she had only Smutty left to talk to. There was no Inky, no Beppo, not a friend in the world. So she stood in the middle of 'The Dumps' and cried bitterly till the tears rolled down her chubby little cheeks and drenched themselves on her wax-spotted pinny. But much worse was to come.

"Oh, for goodness' sake, Mabel!" said Mrs. Thompson. "Whatever's the matter with you now? Look at you! All dirt and muck, and just before supper, too. You're a very [smack!] naugh- [smack!] -ty [smack!] lit- [smack!] -tle [smack-smack!] girl [smack-a-smack smack!], you are [SMACK! SMACK!]."

Mrs. Thompson was particularly on edge this evening, not least because Alf and Ron hadn't come home yet. Doubly irritated by Millie's constant demand for attention, she had taken it all out on Mabel. When Ron did finally show his face, she was in one of her moods.

"And where have you been, I'd like to know," she shouted angrily. "Come and sit down immediately, d'you hear me?"

"Cor!" said Ron, raising his eyebrows in protest. "What have I done now?

"None of your cheek, my lad. I've just about had enough of things for one day. Where've you bin."

"Playing hop-scotch."

"Huh! I should think you want your brains tested, messing about in the streets at this time of the day."

"Why?" said Ron in a hurt tone.

"Don't ask me why. Get on with your supper. Larking about like that."

"Crikey! Proper old sour-puss, you are. Can't never do nothing without you saying it's blinking-well wrong. A proper old grumble-guts you are."

"I'll give you 'grumble-guts', my lad. Anymore of that and I'll tell your father when he comes in."

"If he comes in, you mean."

"Now, that's the last time," Mrs. Thompson warned, giving Ron a box round the ears. "Don't be so cheeky. Get on with your tea and stop talking so much."

"Cripes! Anybody'd think it was a church, the way we go on. Why is Millie's coat on the dresser, anyway?"

" 'Cos she had to come home from work, that's why."

"What's up with her, then?"

"Never you mind."

"Is she in bed or something?"

"Oh!" said Mrs. Thompson impatiently, "yes, she is. She's not well. Now get on with your food, will you?"

"Is she going to have a kid?"

"Will you stop asking so many questions," said Mrs. Thompson desperately. She went on with her sorting and piling, delving at arm's-length into the laundry-basket. "If you must know, she is!"

"Yippee!" he cried, clapping his hands with glee. "Does that mean I'm going to be an uncle?"

"I s'pose it does, son. I hadn't got round to thinking about that side of it all."

"Cor! The blokes at school won't half be jealous. Me! An uncle! And you'll be a granny and Mabel'll be an auntie. She'll be the youngest auntie in the whole of England."

He paused for a moment. The smile faded from his lips. Then he said, with a serious expression that he normally only assumed with Grandpa Lawton:

"Mum!"

"Oh, what is it now?"

Ron, the half-innocent, was testing the ground.

"How do babies get born?"

"Oh, do shut up, Ron. I'm tired. I've been washing all the afternoon and cooking and running up and down stairs after Millie, and now you have to keep on pestering me with questions."

"Billy Watkins told me it was naughty to have babies."

"Now, be quiet, Ron. Don't be rude. It's none of your business how Millie got it. Anyway, she aint had it yet."

"Which man tried with Millie, then?"

"Be quiet! You're not supposed to know about them sort of things at your age."

Mrs. Thompson felt near to tears but she held firm in spite of the ever-present fear that her house seemed to be crumbling around her. She longed to be free of it all, free of Alf, free of Millie, free of Ron and Mabel, free of the Town Hall, free, free, free.....

She sat down and cut some bread, only half aware of what she was doing. The gleaming blade of the knife cut through the crust so smoothly. She had given it a good sharpening that very morning. Dark thoughts began to roam through her mind about the pointlessness of her life.

The front door banged to as Alf came rolling up the hall. Ron jumped up, thinking it would be best to get out of the way while the going was good, what with his father drunk as a fish and his mother in a tizzy.

In the hall, Alf leaned dizzily against the wall.

"'Allo, Ron, me ol' son."

"Hallo, Dad! Hey! What do you know? You're going to be a grandad!"

"I know, I know," Alf muttered drunkenly. "And Millie's your Aunt Fanny! Tell me another!"

""It's true, Dad. Millie's going to have a baby."

With that, Ron ran past and out into the street, slamming the door firmly behind him. The old green van stood lurching into the gutter. On its side should have read:

THE LEAGUE OF PEACE AND PLENTY
FOR BRITAIN

---

which some bright spark had transformed with a few deft dabs of black paint:

THE - - ACHE OF PErCE AND - LEN - -
FOR - RITA - -

---

and the Vicar of St. Crispin's warning slogan:

✝ THE LORD IS AT HAND ✝

---

had been miraculously translated into the cryptic:

- HE - ORDerS A - sHANDy

— clearly the handiwork of the triumvirate, who had not the slightest regard for other people's property. Ron skipped gaily off up the street to join the perpetrators of these literary masterpieces, Teddy Rogers and Freddy Higgins, and trounce the local girls at a another game of hopscotch.

By the time Alf had reached the distant haven of the back-kitchen Ron's parting sally had managed to creep into his addled brain, and once there, it exploded with violence.

"Flo!" he yelled brutally. "Flo!"

"Oh, so you've got here at last, have you? About time too. Look at you. You're as drunk as a titmouse."

Alf lunged into the bowels of the back kitchen and bawled:

"What's this I hear about Millie?"

"Now, Alf. Sit down and have your supper, will you? It's been on for hours, you not bothering to come home and get it. There'd be a tidy old rumpus if you came home one day and found I wasn't here no more, now wouldn't there?"

"Answer me, woman!" Alf hissed, looking dangerously close to hitting her.

"Oh, for goodness' sake, don't carry on so. Your supper'll be getting cold. Millie's all right."

"I'm asking you, my gel. Is she going to have a kid?"

"Well, if you must know, she is!"

Alf swayed dangerously. He staggered over a chair, trying desperately to work things out in his brain. For an instant, he looked dead into Flo's eyes and she knew there was no going back. There was no trying to undo what could not be undone. This was the moment she had feared ever since her dream of the house of sand. Now it was to finally crumble. Now she was to sink with it into the swirling waters of that darkening dream-river.

In a flash, Alf took up the kitchen-knife she had only seconds before had been using to cut the bread, he uttering oaths and abuse, foul and incomprehensible mutterings filled with slobber and spit. Flo cried out as he turned back into the hall, brandishing the blade wildly.

"No! Alf! Alf! No! No!" screamed Flo. "Please, Alf, no!" She rushed at him, tugging wildly at his coat, trying to restrain him with all her strength, but, in his mindless rage, he pushed her in the chest, brutally, and she fell sobbing at the foot of the stairs. By the time she had mustered enough strength to follow him, he had already reached the bedroom door.

Millie was sitting up in bed with a tray of supper things on her lap. She looked pale and pretty with no make-up on, her silky fair hair dropping loosely over her shoulders. Already aware that all was not right, she looked up, startled as Alf burst into the room. Horror spread through her as she saw the knife gripped firmly in her father's hand. She screamed out loud and shrill.

"You bloody little whore! So you're going to have a kid, are

249

you?" spluttered Alf. He rushed at her murderously, knife gleaming in his hand. With the other hand, he grabbed her hair, tugging at it violently as she struggled to get free. He began cutting and hacking at it, while Millie continued to scream and struggle. Such a strangely biblical reaction could only be explained by the existence of some deeply-seated *malaise* in Alfred Thompson's deeply disturbed mind, some hidden aberration that had been festering beneath the surface, guilt perhaps for some sin of his own making. Millie's tray went crashing to the floor. When Alf had strewn the bed and carpet with her hair, he stopped, breathless and confused in the sudden realisation at the excess of his violence. Millie lay back on the pillows, sobbing, her head a grotesque chopped-up mass of hair, sticking out in all directions. As she caught sight of herself in the dressing-table mirror, a pained yelp escaped from her lips and she recoiled in terror.

"You'll not stay in this house, my gel. You're no daughter of mine. Not no more, you're not!"

Millie burst into a fit of hysterical screaming as he staggered out of the room.

To say that Mrs. Thompson's heart was filled with grief would be understating the situation. She was cast down among the devils of her own making, or rather, Alf's making, and she at last was constrained to admit it.

"Oh! Alf! What have you done to our Millie?"

She stood in the doorway, helpless and terrified. Her home, which until now she had thought of as being firm and inviolable, was now in ruins.. An emotional earthquake had struck and the tremors would be felt through many houses in the little street.

Upstairs, Flo saw the travesty that was before her, gazed almost uncomprehendingly at her stricken daughter, went to her with all the love she could muster, took her in her arms and wept. Millie turned her head away from her, her eyes staring yet unseeing.

Mrs. Thompson stood up, moved away towards the door, glanced at her wayward child and slowly descended into the hell below stairs. She saw Alf sitting at the kitchen table, with his head in his hands. He was silently weeping, though she had the impression that he was thinking of himself more than Millie.

Flo slipped slowly into the front room to get away from it all, only to be faced with the blackened, charred remains of the chairs and curtains. On the floor were the burnt remains of a photograph, the last vestige of her love for Jack Carpenter — a picture taken with her and

Alf on an outing to Southend-on-Sea. Now that memory was erased for ever. She leant against the wall of her house of sand, felt it falling, grain by grain into the fast-flowing river of her dreams. All that remained to her now was a time of waiting. She felt her head suddenly begin to go round uncontrollably. She was afraid it might be a stroke. Just as the thought came to her, she fainted.

54.   Decline and Fall

It may be argued that it was the greatest mistake of Councillor Purvis's life when he decided to have the whole business of Millie Thompson out with the calculating Calthrop. The incident remained forever printed on the mind as one of those inexplicable turning-points in our lives when, at last, we are compelled to face the reality we have for so long preferred to ignore. Years after the event, Mr. Purvis was to recall the shame and ridicule he endured at the hands of his principal rival.

As he stepped into the office, Joe Purvis thought that this particular evening must be the most beautiful, the most enjoyable of all the early summer, and he reflected on the happy state of the occupants of Laburnum Villas and compared their happiness to his own misery and dejection. He considered its irony and pondered on the ways of the world that allowed a man at the peak of his career to be cast down into the pit at a single stroke.

As might have been expected, Councillor Calthrop, champion of the Moral Re-Armament Committee, made the most of his opportunity. He ranted, he raved, he paced to and fro, with his hands behind his back, fingers twitching with indignation. While he declaimed on morality, Councillor Purvis came to know what a very terrible indignity it is to be called a hypocrite. It is the worst form of humiliation. There is nothing like it in all the scale of human feelings, nothing so completely degrading. To be an integrated human-being is one thing, but to be classed as a public fraud, or indeed a fraud of any kind, was to suffer death to the soul, not to mention one's self-respect.

No! Councillor Purvis would remember this moment as long as he lived. Here was Calthrop waving his arms in the air, using this earnest confession as a sparking-plug for all the petty jealousies he had harboured in his plump frame in over twenty years of service in the Borough. Councillor Purvis was debased to the coinage of a common-or-garden clerk. He was the scapegoat for all the myriad instances when his fellow-councillors had, from time to time, confronted Calthrop with their objections and their superior suggestions. If the Police had not informed this pompous, portly little councillor of the press leakage, Councillor Purvis would never have been thrust into the disastrous predicament in which he found himself.

"I don't deny," said Calthrop, "that blackmail is a very serious affair, but there is usually some cause for it, don't you think? It means that one individual has rooted out the dark secrets of another and used them to his own ends, Purvis. But first, Purvis, there must be a dark secret. Yours has proved to be thoroughly base and low, Purvis. Indecent assault is a punishable crime, and the fact that such a crime has been committed by an upholder of public morality in the Borough will not go unnoticed, in the Borough."

The last words were ominously intended to shed light on the rivalry between these two principal candidates for the Mayorship at the coming election.

"Yes, Purvis, you have been irresponsible for a man of your position in society. Socially, professionally, morally irresponsible. You must take the consequences."

Here, at this point, Calthrop's tone changed from headmasterly reprimand to one of insult and condescension.

"You, see. Purvis! Your public mask conceals the face of a criminal. Now isn't that right?"

Pointing a fat but defiant finger at the dispirited Purvis, he said in his thin-lipped way:

"I intend to see you pay for it, Purvis. I shall see you grovelling in your own dirt before I'm through with you. I'll see your name scrubbed off the books, so I will. And as for your stupid little plans to reform the Borough, I'll see them into the ground. You don't suppose I've been sitting here on my backside in this office just twiddling my thumbs, do you? Don't think I haven't been making my plans too. It's the likes of you who build up a nice little public image for themselves that come a cropper in the end. Make no mistake about that, my fine fellow."

Calthrop had worked himself up to a frenzy. All the hatred he had ever felt towards his rival now spewed out like venom, and reason now began to lose its way.

"I'll see you out with both fists, Purvis. I'll kick you down those stairs as hard as my boots can kick you. Just because you were brought up in the Borough doesn't give you the right to dictate to those of us who weren't. Nothing is going to give me greater pleasure than to put the final nail in your sad little coffin."

Purvis winced. He was stunned and mystified by the intensity of Calthrop's acrimonious outpouring. He found it difficult to believe that such bitterness had lain dormant for so many years. Who, then, had been the real hypocrite? Many indeed were the ways of ambition. For a brief moment, Councillor Purvis felt almost sorry for Calthrop. He remembered that, when it came down to it, this was just a brush between colleagues. A pacifier by nature, he was of the opinion that personal enmities, if they had to exist at all, must be brushed aside in the interests of the community. It was all to do with a sense of proportion, of justice, of right-thinking.

"Look here, Calthrop, you really have no right to — "

"I have every right," shouted Calthrop, now almost puce with anger.

"My dear fellow," said Purvis, in a huff, "the Police instructed me to discuss this matter *in camera*. I see no reason at all to take any action at this stage. After all, I *am* innocent, you know, until such time as I may be proved guilty. You are pre-judging the case. You are far too impetuous."

"Impetuous!" shouted Calthrop, stopping in his tracks. Then, hissing like a viper: "Impetuous-ss-ss! I am not interested in your perverted views, Purvis. I am interested in the plain facts of the case. Now that it's all spread like ordure across the nation's newspapers, I see no reason at all to beat about the bush. You, Purvis, must resign. You must get out. Save the name of the Borough before it is too late. You are *kaput*, my dear feller. I am sorry, but facts are facts. It's goodbye to you and your futile reforms, and goodbye to the Mayorship."

"I say, Calthrop, steady on. We're all human, you know. We all have our little moments, don't we? Take you, for instance!"

"Take me! How dare you? We are not talking about me. We are talking about your seamy little affair with a button-maker."

"I'm innocent, I assure you. I only asked her in for a drink and the glasses got mixed up. How could I help it? Anyway, at the time, it did not seem such a dreadful thing to have happened. I can't turn the clock back."

"A nice kettle of fish, I must say. The drinks were mixed up,

253

you say? Very convenient, *I* would say. Quite the lady-killer, aren't we, Purvis? Do you suppose a court of law would believe a word of it?

"Court of law? You don't think it would ever come to that, do you?"

"Good heavens, man! It's all been in the newspapers about the arrest of Gino Polenti and your disgraceful involvement in the case. You can't avoid it. Some action will have to be taken if the public interests are to be protected."

"But what will people say? My tenants! My colleagues! My fiancée!"

"Considering that one of your own tenants is involved in this murky business, I should think that the Council, the Clergy, your sycophantic followers, and every tomnoddy in the Borough will all have plenty to say. I think, as far as your colleagues are concerned, you may take my views as representative."

Fears came rushing into Councillor Purvis's already over-crowded brain, through which now emerged a mystery that had been troubling him.

"Do you realise, Calthrop, a whole lot of things tie together in this story. I can see you are sticking to your mixed-up view of things. Listen to me! Firstly, the authorities don't believe Gino Polenti wrote that note. At least, he did write it but someone else dictated it. Who? Then again, was it Polenti's gang that broke up the 'Peace and Plenty' meeting? I remember, when I and my fiancée were taking our stroll in the Public Gardens yesterday we met Donoghue, looking highly explosive! Waving a flick-knife about and swearing at people. Now he's on the run. It's odd, isn't it? With the police on his heels so soon, and me getting the blackmail note the very morning when he goes and stabs Andrew Crawford? The police are completely satisfied that Polenti's English is not up to writing that note. What is even more interesting, Calthrop — and perhaps you will get this firmly fixed in you head as a leader of public morals — there is the possibility that, right under your nose, there is a vicious gang at work in the Borough that is going to undermine all *your* little reforms as well! The vice-squad is on to them and before long you are going to look pretty silly."

"Tommy-rot!" Calthrop snapped, not quite sure of his ground. "Vice in Rothersey? You must be mad. This is a good working-class area except for the bottom end of Lupin Lane. You can't tell me we're turning into another Soho!"

"Nevertheless—and I'm telling you all this in secrecy, mind!—

254

Polenti is being held in custody and has already been charged. They are hoping to put the gang off the scent for the time being. With a bit of luck, Donoghue will turn up again. The police are already combing the clubs in the West End."

Councillor Purvis was beginning to see himself in the light of a public hero. This might, after all, be his big chance to prove himself worthy of the position of Mayor of Rothersey. Together, he and Agnes, would brave the storm of public protest and rise above it to cloud-capped peaks of glory, or so he hoped — at least until Calthrop broke through his musings like nut-crackers through a walnut.

"You will have conveniently forgotten, no doubt, my words spoken at your disastrous 'Peace and Plenty' fiasco, yesterday. I quoted an example of a 'public figure' who had lead thousands to their doom through his irresponsible policies. Now, I may say with confidence, you have succeeded in adding another to the infamous list. I also remember, with peculiar irony, the passionate plea you made for freedom of action just so long as it doesn't limit the liberty of others. I should say you have confined Miss Mildred Thompson pretty efficiently, one way or another! It is a pretty good example of what you called "the glamorous extravagance of sex and violence" in modern society. Your words speak through your deeds, Purvis. You were caught in the act by three members of the Committee as they left the Town Hall."

Mr. Purvis raised a trembling hand in protest, thwarted by Calthrop's vicious eloquence.

"Purvis! It's only natural that you should wish to justify yourself in the light of the accusations made against you. They haven't been made in court as yet, but, mark my words, Councillor, they will be! They will be! If you take my advice, you will get out now, Purvis. Resign! Pack your bags. Get out while the going's good. Get your property deal through and leave the district. Skip off out of it, Purvis. Your days as a Councillor in the Borough of Rothersey are numbered. Good riddance, *Mister Purvis!*"

55. Ron Comes to Terms

The Gardens were deserted save for a few isolated couples canoodling under the shadows of Bushy Walk.

The evening sky was the palest blue above the black silhouettes of the trees, blue merging into orange and then to green and yellow. The scene reminded Ron of a book of fairy-tales he used to read, with illustrations of blue-turreted castles rising into pale green and orange skies seen through the black frame of forest. He thought he would like to paint a picture like that one day, but not now. He was far too miserable for that. All he needed was for one person to take an interest in him, someone he could depend on, who would give him the chance in life he longed for.

As he passed through the gates into the High Street, he felt the heat of the sun-warmed pavements against his cheeks. He would have been the happiest lad in Rothersey if he never had to go home again. All he wanted to do now was to roam about the dusty streets by himself.

At first, the idea of wandering down to the riverside attracted him. The boats would be beautiful and mysterious as dusk drew in. He could see them sliding under the bridge, their funnels flat on their backs, and the silent figures of the bargees, quietly smoking their cigarettes and dreaming of distant seas and more exotic shores than Rothersey Reach.

To Ron, the Bridge was the frontier to his knowledge of what lay beyond the sprawling area of factories, warehouses, Victorian villas, small shops, railway sidings and docks that made up the Borough of Rothersey. Ron had never ventured beyond it on his own though he had often wished to.

Ron's greatest regret was missing the Coronation procession. The whole school came back with tales of troops of horse guards in scarlet cloaks, streets decorated with bright banners and bunting, bands marching in the Mall, princes and princesses in their carriages, the Queen smiling from her golden coach, the cheering rain-soaked crowds, and the festive street parties. All this, and he had had to go and catch a bad dose of flu that put him flat on his back, shivering with a fever and moaning at the injustices of a life that wouldn't allow him to be present at one of the greatest events in his life. He remembered how trapped he felt as he gazed from his bedroom window at the brilliant display of fireworks that lit up the night sky.

Ron had always kept to the south side of the river. Now, the way things were, he had half a mind to run across and disappear into the maze of streets beyond Blackfriars, to wander round St. Paul's, Ludgate Hill, and Fleet Street with all the newspaper offices. He fancied taking a look at Trafalgar Square and Buckingham Palace. He might even catch a glimpse of the Queen. Then, as night came, he could creep through the Soho streets, which his mother had warned him not to go anywhere near on pain of death. "I'll kill you, if you do!" she had told him once, in a phoney threatening tone. If *Vampire in Soho* was anything to go by, Soho was certainly not the place for him.

Ron started thinking about Grandpa Lawton and how much he had missed him in the long weary weeks after the accident. For since that day, Ron hadn't a friend in the whole world like Grandpa. And after the talking-to Miss Baldock gave him, he had not been near No 2 Laburnum Villas. He sensed that a strange death had taken place where once was warmth and friendship. Life was not the same anymore, and Ron was afraid it would never be the same again, even if Grandpa did come home. Was Miss Baldock sure about Grandpa getting better? If he died.....?

Ron strolled miserably past the Roxy Picture House. He had no money. The bill-boards purred enticingly at him:

IT'S COLOSSAL   IT'S STUPENDOUS
IT'S SENSATIONAL

The Adventures of Robin Hood

IN GLORIOUS TECHNICOLOR

also showing

THE BLACK HOLE OF CALCUTTA
Full Supporting Programme

'The Black Hole of Calcutta', thought Ron. It'd be like home from home!

"Starting in ten minutes, sonny," said the Commissionaire hopefully.

Ron shrugged his shoulders and thrust his hands deeper into his empty trouser-pockets.

"Walk up! Walk up! Come along, sonny! Let you in half-price.

257

How about that? Not so many customers today with this heat."

Ron walked by without a word or a glance.

"Little bastard!" muttered the gold-braided, sweating, red-faced, recently-retired school caretaker.

"Dirty little...." he hissed through his teeth, smiling at a woman who was eyeing the billboards. "Programme starting now, madam. Nice and cool inside."

When Ron reached the Town Hall, he could see, in a large window on the first floor, a burly man pacing up and down the room and talking all the time to a tall, grey wispy-haired man. Ron was pretty certain it was Councillor Purvis. The bright polished brass door-handles at the main entrance made him realise that even his mother was capable of doing something well. A pity she didn't polish the ones at home like that.

As Ron stood disconsolately looking up at the great neo-gothic frontage of the building, he felt a hand on his shoulder, and it made him jump out of his skin, or nearly.

"Well, my boy! And what are we doing out in the streets on our own at this time of the evening, eh?"

"Hallo, Mr. Curtis, sir. I was just wondering if —"

"Yes, my boy! Wondering what?"

Ron was put out. Why was it that grown-ups always interrupted what you were saying and never seemed to let you finish a sentence?

"Oh, nothing," he said lamely.

"We look a trifle sad this evening, don't we? And on such a fine evening too."

Ron remained silent and brooding.

"Now, what's the matter, eh? Bored with our holiday already, are we?"

"A bit. Never did like half-term. Keeps you at home too much."

"Ah!" exclaimed the Vicar. "When you have to go to school you don't want to go, and when you have to stay at home you wish you were back at school again. I really don't understand you youngsters. Anyway, Ronald, Miss Goodenough tells me you have got on well this term. She says you're top in Art and second in Maths. Now that's just fine, isn't it?"

"I s'pose so," said Ron sullenly.

"Aren't your mother and father pleased with you, now?"

"Never told 'em."

"Never told them? Why on earth not?"

"Wouldn't be interested if I did. They don't know nothing about maths and stuff like that."

"Maybe they don't, Ronald, but do *you* know anything about bringing up a family and cooking and washing clothes? Do you know about working in a tannery, and all about dyes and chemicals?"

"No!"

"Well, then. You cannot expect others to know all about your own work, can you?

"S'pose not."

They were ambling along in the direction of the Market. The Cathedral clock chimed solemnly in the distance and sent a chill of loneliness, almost like cold steel, through Ron's turbulent despairing thoughts.

"Tell me, Ronald. What do you want to be when you grow up?"

"Oh, I dunno, really. Engineer maybe."

"An engineer, eh! Well, that's a fine career for a good lad like you. If you go on working well at school, you might get a scholarship when the time comes."

"A scholarship!" said Ron, beginning to show a tiny spark of interest. "Do you really think so?"

"I don't see why not. Everybody has a future and it's up to you to make the most of it. What branch of engineering ?"

"I want to build ships, maybe. No, maybe I just want to get on a ship and go to Africa and build dams and things. Anyway, to do something really big. And maybe see other countries, too, and maybe go lumber-jacking in Canada or New Zealand, or building railways in South America, or maybe even oil-drilling or diamond-mining."

"My goodness! That's a lot of maybe's," chuckled the Vicar. "Well now, I don't think somehow you'll have time in one life for all that, but it's good to have ideas, my boy."

The Reverend Curtis was not entirely surprised at Ronald's outburst of enthusiasm. He had always suspected that something more lay hidden beneath the layer of *gaucherie* that covered Ron's real self.

"You certainly seem to know a lot about it all."

"Well, you see, I used to talk it all over with Grandpa Lawton, see? He went out to New Zealand, he did, tree-felling, he did. And he fought in the Boer War and got all kinds of medals for bravery, with coloured ribbons on 'em. I always used to go round and talk to him, I did. Now, there aint no more talking 'cos he aint there no more."

259

"What about your Dad? Can't you talk to him?"

"Him! He's always drunk. Whenever he sees me, he just clips me one over the ear-'ole."

"Dear me!" was all the Vicar could say.

Quite suddenly, without warning, Ron asked:

"Is Grandpa going to die, Mr. Curtis?"

"I don't know, my son. He was very seedy last week. We didn't think he would last the night through."

"Are you going there now?"

"That's right."

"Can I come with you?"

"Well," said the Vicar guardedly, "I suppose you may. I would have to ask the ward-sister. Last time I was only allowed to stay a few minutes. It is rather late in the day for visitors now. I'm allowed in because one or two patients sometimes like a brief session of prayer before they rest. Still, if you really want to see Mr. Lawton I will have a word when we get there."

"Will Grandpa die?" said Ron, anxiously insistent.

"We don't know, Ronald. He may, by the grace of God, recover his strength. There is nothing like the power of the human will to survive."

"How?"

"By the help of the doctors and nurses, the wonders of new medicine since the war, but especially by having enough faith in God's will."

"What is faith?"

"Faith is when you believe in something so strongly that you will never allow yourself to be influenced by the opinions of others."

"Well," said Ron thoughtfully, "what is God, then?"

"God is Love, just as St. John said."

"Well, if I believe very strong like, believe in 'Love' so as nobody'll ever anymore make me feel any different, will Grandpa get well again?"

"Possibly, Ronald. If you believe hard enough."

"How hard?"

"As hard as you can, my boy. With every fibre in your body, with your whole heart, with all your thoughts bent on prayer."

"Like prayers at school?"

"That's right, only, this time, all by yourself, at home, kneeling by your bed before you go to sleep."

260

The two united souls passed through the swing doors of the hospital, those same doors that Eddie and Timothy had entered in their turn, with similar feelings of dread.

Ron was frightened by the cold white tiles and the long corridors with sad-faced people sitting on polished wooden seats, and trolleys of shiny surgical instruments, the strange smell of ether and antiseptics and detergents, and the cold empty laughter of the nurses. A pang of fear ran through Ron from head to toe. He held back until the Vicar turned and took his hand, saying:

"Come along, Ronald. You do want to see Mr. Lawton, don't you?"

Another long tiled corridor, then up some stone steps and through yet more swing doors into the ward. The Sister came to greet the Vicar, who whispered to her in inaudible tones. She nodded conspiratorially, put a hand on Ron's shoulder and guided him along the ward.

They came to a bed curtained off from the rest. Ron stood at the foot, frightened and feeling very much alone. Grandpa lay quiet, so still, like one of those marble effigies in the cathedral Ron had heard about. The old man had grown thin, so thin that Ron could hardly recognise his old friend whose face now was drawn and yellowish, so emaciated that Ron felt his heart beating with a kind of emotion he had never known before. The grey stubble of Grandpa's beard glistened in the light of the lamp overhead. An unbearable feeling of fullness in Ron's chest made him gasp. He felt a pressure on the muscles of his throat, a twitching of the nerves in the corners of his eyes. All he managed to whisper was:

"Grandpa! Grandpa!"

There was, however, no sign that Grandpa had heard this small voice calling him. He lay so still and seemingly lifeless. Tears ran down Ron's cheeks, tears of loneliness, tears of love, tears of remorse. He wanted so much for Grandpa to live. He found himself mumbling wildly:

"I didn't mean it, Grandpa. I didn't, honest. I didn't think you'd mind me sitting in your chair and having one of my toffees from your tin. 'Cos it was like you was there with me all the time. I didn't do nothing wrong, Grandpa. Please say it was all right. Please say it was all right, Grandpa, 'cos I didn't mean no 'arm, honest I didn't."

The old man lay motionless, as if he were deaf to Ron's words. Ron turned back down the ward, weeping silently, afraid of attracting attention. The Vicar was still chatting to the ward-sister as Ron passed them. He retraced his steps along the unfriendly corridors, the only sound, the clip-clop of his heels on the polished parquet floor. Two men in white coats went by him, wheeling a patient back from the operating theatre. All Ron saw was the long pale face and the closed eyes, as if in the long sleep of death, and he remembered Grandpa lying there so still in the ward.

Out in the street, Ron hardly noticed the traffic or the people. As he passed the Town Hall he did not see the lights were out, nor did he cast even a cursory glance at the Roxy bill-boards. Entering into the strife-torn house at No 4, it seemed to Ron that he was crossing a battle-ground strewn with corpses, a territory of despair, of hopelessness and futile dreams. He crept up the creaking stairs to his room. As he undressed and stepped into his pyjamas, he tried hard to think about what Miss Goodenough used to say in Scripture lessons. It was difficult, because he had never really listened to that sort of stuff very much. Then he thought about what the Vicar had said, and suddenly Ron remembered something – something which suddenly mattered to him—a large motto the class had had to paint in letters of purple and gold. It read:

$$\mathcal{B}elieve\ and\ thou\ shalt\ receive$$

Ron remembered the words because he could never understand why 'believe' was spelt differently to 'receive'. 'God is Love' — that's what Mr. Curtis had said, so if Ron believed hard enough in 'Love' and prayed to 'God', as Tim at this very moment was trying to do, he might just be sure of receiving a reply by the next post.

Ron knelt down by his bed and tried to recall the words of the Lord's Prayer. He tried, he tried, and he tried again. The jumbled, half-remembered phrases came to him as through a haze, but they seemed all the more poignant in their inaccuracies, like some almost meaningful yet mysterious mantra that seemed to be more of a direct line to God than any prayer he had ever heard. He prayed with his whole heart and mind, so earnestly that, when he finally climbed in between the sheets, he fell asleep as soon as his head touched the pillow.

EPISODE TWELVE

August Bank Holiday Monday

A Day by the Sea

56.   Point of Departure

The indicator on the oak-cased barometer in Councillor Purvis's hall pointed to 'Fair', wavering slightly but strengthened by the latest weather reports on the BBC firmly announcing 'bright periods' and temperatures rising to the eighties.

Accordingly, as on countless other August Bank Holidays, the rain teemed down in solid sheets, deluging the gutters of Laburnum Villas with enough water for Mrs. Thompson's washing days for a whole year. A sudden squall in the night had blown the Councillor's precious television aerial askew so that it leaned ominously over the footpath below. Yet, rain or shine, this was the one day in the year-to-year routine of the Villas, when every single tenant forsook worry and troubles, locked and bolted their doors on them.

This was, after all, to be a special treat, rain or no rain, for it was the last Bank Holiday outing this little band of life's voyagers would be taking from Laburnum Villas. By this time next year, there would be only a heap of rubble where once was hope, love and joy in small measure, and a surfeit of despair and indifference.

Apart from old Ma Carpenter, six-months deceased, and the now-ailing Walter Paxton, who had suffered a serious decline in health over recent months and was in no condition to leave his bed, the party was much the same as in previous years, for Louise had been persuaded to join in spite of her uncle's indisposition. Timothy, the only outsider in the whole affair, had decided to drive his mother down in the car to spend a few days with his father, who was about to finish his period of convalescence in Hove. Timothy, ever hopeful of a sea-change, was confident of enjoying a few hours' sailing on the coast.

The coach was a thirty-seater, the rest of the space being occupied by several buxom little typists from the Town Hall, two or three likely lads from the tannery, and a dumb waitress or two from the Roxy Restaurant, not forgetting Iris and Effie Mudd from Marley's General Stores, and Lizzie Pomfrett on the bacon counter. Some of the invited guests and friends were, however, notably absent, unwilling as they were to brave the downpour.

When the coach backed down the little cul-de-sac, everybody appeared on their doorsteps in the face of an inclemency sufficient to dampen the most stubborn of spirits. The driver took one look at the motley crowd and, raising his eyes to a very wet Heaven, muttered: "Oh, Gawd! What a bloomin' shower!" and slipped quietly away to find some culinary comfort at Miss Trencher's English Breakfast Rooms in the High Street, a haunt of a whole *côterie* of market traders.

The clouds swept low over the little street, shedding gloom everywhere. Water streamed from gutter-pipes, gushing out over the pavements, splaying delta-fashion across the flagstones, streaming into the bubbling, gurgling drains. Slate and grimy yellow brick gleamed blackly in the tarnished silver light which, from time to time, broke through the almost solid weight of dull grey cloud.

At half-past eight, doors began opening one by one to exhale an assortment of curiously-clad trippers — dressed, that is to say, for summer, yet overcoated and mackintoshed for winter. Besides carrying a variety of sun-tan lotions, sun-glasses, sun-shades and swimming costumes, the inveterate travellers were dressed for the occasion in raincoats, plastic raincoats, rain-hats, Wellingtons and galoshes. Everything and anything waterproof covered an otherwise sun-worshipping community, setting forth, as it seemed, into the unknown wastes of Tooting Bec and beyond, like dedicated explorers, fortified with a few bottles of best brown ale and a couple of hot-water bottles to boot. Such is the tenacity and stoicism of the English traveller.

First on the coach was Ron, in white beach-shorts and a bright blue and yellow check shirt. His blue school raincoat was slung carelessly over his shoulders at his mother's orders. He flung it off, shook the rain out of his sandals, tossed his swimming trunks on the rack above, and, taking out a tattered copy of *Beano*, he spread it out on his knees and was soon absorbed in the adventures of 'Dennis the Menace' and 'Roger the Dodger'.

Eddie came next, raindrops dripping from his ears, raindrops dripping from his eyebrows, raindrops dripping from the end of his nose. An old khaki army cape protected his new cream whipcord pants from Cecil Gee's and a smart, as he would have it, 'snazzy' navy-blue T-shirt from Millett's in the Strand, if you please!

" 'Allo, Ronnie, me ol' cock. How are we this luv'ly mornin', eh?"

Ron was far too taken up with the exciting escapades of Dennis and Roger to hear.

" 'Ere!" Eddie exclaimed. "Aint we on speaking terms then?"

"Oh, it's you!" said Ron, grudgingly. "Got your swimming togs?"

"Of course, I 'ave, guv."

"I haven't had a single swim in the sea this year," said Ron.

265

"Cor! Luvverduck! You don't have to go to the sea for a swim, the way I see it, matey. There's enough water round here to fill a couple o' full-sized baths."

"Who wants to swim in a bath?"

"All right! All right! A bit jumpy, aren't we, this morning?"

Ron went on reading, while Eddie made his way to the back of the coach to bag two corner seats for himself and Millie. He appeared to shake several pints of rain onto the floor, folded his cape and sat down to read yesterday's edition of *The Sunday People.*

As the rain pattered persistently on the roof of the coach and streamed down over the windows, Louise climbed on, looking every bit as pretty as a film-star. She was wearing a transparent plastic raincoat and hood, under which could be seen a sleeveless cotton frock with a spray design of flowers over the bodice and round the hem of a full skirt. She carried an Italian basket with a green lining. Ron sat with his eyes glued to his comic in the hope that Louise would not choose to sit next to him. She made him feel awkward, embarrassed, tongue-tied as she was. He just could never think of anything to say to her. What was the point if you couldn't get an answer? Everything had to have an answer, or so his maths master said, and *he* ought to know. Ron couldn't help swivelling his eyes round, Smutty fashion, to catch a glimpse of her as she combed her long fair hair into place. If only she could speak, he could like her. She always smiled at him, like Tim and old Mr. Curtis, like Grandpa Lawton. They were all in a class on their own as far as Ron was concerned. Maybe even Eddie, too. But Louise couldn't speak so how *could* he get to know her?

Just at that moment, to Ron's dismay, the Vicar came tottering round the corner, skating about on the shiny pavements like Mr. Winkle on the ice. He clambered aboard, gasping and wheezing and coughing and spluttering with an asthmatic vengeance. Putting out the handle of his large black umbrella, he hooked it on the chromium hand-rail and hoisted himself up with a series of clutchings and scramblings and wrenchings and clenchings that made Ron all twisted up inside.

"Well!" gasped the Vicar, breathing hard into Ron's face. "If it isn't young Ronald! And how are we today?"

Ron quickly put his comic on the spare seat next to his just as the Vicar lurched forward to claim it.

"And how's your mother?"

"All right."

"And your father?"

266

"All right," said Ron more quietly.

"And little Mabel?"

Crikey! thought Ron. Is he going to go through the whole blinking family?

He began scrapping about on the floor, pretending to look for a non-existent pencil. He came up with a stray sixpence and an old bus ticket — and five grubby fingers!

"Well! Well! Well!" the Vicar went on.

"Here we go!" Ron muttered defiantly, his head between his knees. "Everything in triplicate!"

"Are you keeping this seat for someone?"

"Yes," lied Ron.

"Oh!" said the Vicar, looking quizzically at his young prey. "Well, never mind. I'll sit here until whoever you're saving the seat for turns up, shall I?"

The reverend gentleman struggled out of his raincoat. Ron wanted to knock his Anthony Eden on the floor and trample on it, he felt so frustrated. Sharp little pricks of discomfort on the back of Ron's neck made him wince — a shower of raindrops fell from the brim as the Vicar put the hat on the rack above.

"Now, where were we? Ah! Yes! Yes! Yes!" he said, and went off into a lengthy account of the trials and tribulations of some people Ron couldn't care less about who had just moved into the district from Worthing.

"The poor souls came to London to get away from the wind and the rain and just think what they've run into. They've only exchanged the smell of rotting seaweed for the stink of rotting fish! Their house backs on to a fish-and-chip shop! Such bad luck, don't you think?"

Ron grunted. This was not going to be a good day as far as he could see. The Vicar persisted in droning on. Five more minutes and they'd all be for the off, and then perhaps the old 'parson's nose' would start twitching at somebody else for a change.

Almost simultaneously, the doors of No 1 and No 3 opened to expel a be-tweeded Miss Baldock and a clearly agitated Gabriel Purvis. They marched and tottered respectively to the centre of the road. Ron thought they were going to salute each other, military fashion, but they turned and advanced on the coach, looking very much like Nervo and Knox about to tap out a two-step in the old music-hall style.

Mr. Purvis had to stand back some way to allow Miss Baldock to prise herself in through the coach-door. She was the wedge and he

267

was the crow-bar! He pushed her, he pulled her, until at last he managed to ease her into position in her one-and-a-half seats. She permitted the Councillor to dovetail himself in as best he could.

"Well! Well! Well!" said the Vicar, craning his neck round. "And how are our little love-birds this morning?"

Agnes grimaced, shook her feathers in irritation and chirped tartly: "Only as well as can be expected, Vicar."

"Well! I'm bound to say it is not the best of days to venture forth from our little love-nest, is it?"

"What does he think we are?" muttered Agnes to her fiancé. "Anyone would think we lived in an aviary the way he talks. Silly old fool!"

"Well, it's all a matter of temperament, isn't it?" Mr. Curtis persisted. "It all depends on ourselves, what we feel inside, how much strength we have to resist the outside world. No matter what the weather is like, if we are happy in ourselves, then we shall be happy, rain or shine. I always think of the great G. K. Chesterton in one of his essays where he says: 'I shall love the English climate till I die, even if I die of the English climate.'

The Vicar tittered merrily into Miss Baldock's acidulated face, saw that she was not amused and resumed his third degree on Ronald Thompson.

A cold draught suddenly blew up the capacious skirt of Agnes Baldock.

"Get up and close the door, Gabriel. It's absolutely freezing in here. The sooner we start the better, as far as I'm concerned. I thought we were supposed to leave at 8.45."

"We are, my sweet. A minute or two to go yet."

" A minute or two! I shall be surprised if we leave before ten o'clock at this rate. No sign of the driver and half the people not on the coach yet." 'Half the people' meant the Thompsons.

At a quarter-past nine the driver finally appeared, in a strangely devil-may-care frame of mind, after indulging himself by sinking a full breakfast of bacon, two eggs, sausages, mushrooms, baked beans, and a large mug of strong tea.

"Mornin', ladies and gents. Luvly wevver fer ducks!"

Looking at the glum faces, he shrugged his shoulders and lit up a Woodbine.

Common little man, thought Miss Baldock. He's only the driver, after all. Some people didn't know their proper station. *She*

268

knew perfectly well how to behave before *her* superiors, though she had to admit she hadn't any.

"Where *is* everybody? Oh, really!" she exclaimed. "I knew we wouldn't leave on time. I knew it!"

"But Agnes," said Mr. Purvis, "it's only just a quarter past the hour."

"Nonsense, Gabriel! Your watch must be wrong."

"My watch is infallible, dear. It never goes wrong."

"Nothing is infallible, Gabriel."

"Ah!" said the Vicar. "How true! How true! How true! We should all be a lot better off if we realised that we poor mortals are only fallible."

Miss Baldock could not understand the logic in which a man, or woman for that matter, could be better off by gloating over his (or her) imperfections. It was the philosophy of the hopeless. Happily, Agnes had been allowed by fate to rediscover her hopes and even a tiny part of her youth. The thought of her forthcoming marriage brought sunshine into this cloudy day. It sweetened her and, laying a podgy hand on Gabriel's wizened wrist, she smiled the smile of complete possession.

"Warm enough, dear?" she purred, tucking him into the seat like a baby in a cot. "Mustn't catch cold, must we now?"

Her captive's reply was drowned by the groaning, swishing noise of the door sliding back, letting in a blast of cold air which exploded into Miss Baldock's skirts again. The screech of Flo Thompson's voice sent a short sharp shock through everybody's nervous system.

"I told you we was leaving at a quarter-to-nine, Alfred Thompson. I told you to get up when I called you, didn't I? What with no breakfast and your face all cut about from shaving, you look a proper old mess, I must say. Millie," she screamed. "MILLIE!! DID YOU LOCK THE BACK DOOR?!!!"

"No, mum. I forgot," she said in a pathetic voice. She had not made a good start to the day what with being sick in the wash-basin.

"Well, go back and do it then. You've got a head like a sieve, you have. I dunno, I really don't. Who'd be bothered with kids, I ask you? Now where's Mabel?"

She thrust her head back through the door and shouted almost into Miss Baldock's face: "MABEL!!!"

"Mabel is not here, Mrs. Thompson," said the agitated-beyond-measure manageress from the Roxy.

"Not here?" reiterated the desperate earth mother. "Are you sure?"

Miss Baldock rose to her feet, crushing her affianced one to a pulp against the metal arm of his seat, and boomed at the agitated Mrs. Thompson:

"NOT HERE! DO YOU NEED IT IN CHINESE AS WELL?"

"Ooh! I say," said Mrs. Thompson, shocked by this sudden outburst. "Keep your hair on!"

Everybody started to laugh.

"I do not wish to be told what to do with my hair, Mrs. Thompson," said Agnes, angrily. " Now, please ask Mr. Thompson to locate your daughter and allow us to get on the road. We are already ten minutes after the scheduled time of departure."

The Vicar had a very practical suggestion! Could Mrs. Thompson go and look for Mabel and bring her back post-haste? At that moment, Miss Baldock's tweedy behind did a power-dive into the seat. Simultaneously, Mr. Purvis attempted a vertical take-off, but thinking better of it, remained rooted to the run-way. He was immediately impaled by his beloved's twin-turbined jet doing a pancake landing on top of him. She touched down with the finesse of a load of exploding TNT. The coach shook wildly, heaved into the gutter and wobbled to a standstill. Mr. Purvis, like an old Tiger Moth, chugged away to a final splutter and all was silent once more.

At last, Mabel was found. A resounding smack brought her howling out of her hiding place in Smutty's kennel and screaming right into Miss Baldock's ear, as she was lifted over heads, knocking our lady's hat for six. With her hat perched precariously on the back of her head, Agnes looked more like a docker's mate on a spree. Alf, however, did not reappear.

Millie followed her mother, Eddie waving to her from the back and pointing to the empty seat beside him. She made it plain that she was in no mood for company and sat down in a window seat on her own. Mrs. Thompson plumped herself down in a muddle of lunch-packets, wet raincoats, spades and pails, a box of elastoplast in one hand in case of accidents, and a bottle of aspirins for any chance of a headache.

"I told you, Gabriel," said Miss Baldock, "we would be behind time. I told you so." Turning her head slightly and raising her voice to a heavily audible level, she said: "If *some people* took a *little more trouble* to arrive when they're sup*posed* to arrive, *other* people could be *half-way* to *Bright*on!" Ron was surprised that, for once, he had to agree with the old frump.

Emerging from her hard-boiled eggs, rock-buns and flasks of strong tea, Mrs. Thompson returned an eye for an eye by saying that if *some people* had kids of their *own*, they'd *know* how to *bloody-well* shut their *traps* and *mind* their *own bloody business*! So *there*!

The situation was saved from developing into a first-class row by the driver starting up the engine. The coach shook itself into a rumble and had passengers jogging about in their seats in no time. Music burst forth over the loud-speaker, momentarily deafening everybody until the volume was adjusted, and even then, ears were singing with the force of the initial thunder of sound. The coach moved slowly off into the rain, only to be stopped by Mrs. Thompson screaming over the top of the music.

"Here! I say! Driver! Stop! Stop! My Alf aint on."

Miss Baldock was beside herself, happily for Mr. Purvis only in the figurative sense of the expression.

"Really! Really!" she said, furiously fidgeting. "Really! **Really! REALLY!"**

The coach once more jerked to a standstill. Mrs. Thompson began frantically trying to wipe the rain off the window — from the inside! Then she stood up with her burden of lunch-packets and pails banging into Miss Baldock's head and gave orders for the door to be once more opened. Alf swung on with half-a-dozen bottles of stout in his arms.

"Carry on London!" he shouted, oblivious of the contention within. The driver once more started up. This time, no sign of life from the engine.

Suffering cats! thought Ron. What now? Everybody began to have a strong urge to rush for the door and go straight back indoors.

"Come along, my man!" said Miss Baldock. "We can't wait here all day, you know."

"Look, madam," shouted the demented driver, "praps you'd like to get out and bloody-well push if you're in such a bleeding hurry!" — which choice of epithets was, at the risk of being pedantic, hardly sanguine in the circumstances. He sat back in his seat in a bolshy way and glowered at her. Everybody thought he had gone on strike. He had a nasty attitude of 'shirt' about him.

The Vicar of St. Crispin's came forward with sweet conciliation and all was well again.

Up got the driver and set to cranking the old bus into some sort

271

of motion, and all were relieved when at last they turned out of the Villas into the High Street.

The rest of the party were picked up outside the Roxy. They poured into the coach in a rush of wet plastic, squeaking Wellingtons, rubber water-wings, string-bags pulling on coat buttons as the girls scrambled for spare seats. They pushed, they fought, pressed their way through, calling to friends to come and join them and generally scattering the whole interior and its occupants with a copious quantity of rain they had managed to collect at the bus-stop. It was like a mass-christening at St. Crispin's!

A young man suddenly appeared as if from nowhere. He was good-looking, of average height, with clear grey-blue eyes and neat in his appearance. Effie noticed him first and her heart flipped. He was sitting motionless on his own near the back of the coach, spoke to no-one and stared all the time through the window. Nobody could recall how he got on the coach in the first place and nobody could quite place him. Mabel had to be restrained from climbing all over 'the nice man', as Flo called him. Agnes thought she had seen him sometime or another in the Roxy Restaurant, but she couldn't be certain. Ron was convinced he must be that actor he had seen in a comedy film a few months before about a doctor. Dirk somebody. Dirk B.....? Was it at the Palaseum? No! Oh, well! It would come to him sometime. But the strange impression just would not leave him alone. Millie couldn't fathom it out at all but she did have an uncanny sensation in the nape of her neck, as if he were staring into her very soul. Lizzie fancied she'd seen him lurking round the confectionary shelves at Marley's Stores that day back in June when old Mr. Lawton had his accident. But she couldn't be sure. Eddie was pretty certain he had seen him exercising up at the gym sometime or other but he couldn't think when. As for Alf, peering through a beer-haze, he was inexplicably reminded of an evening visit to *The Bed of Roses* back in June after the 'Peace and Plenty' do. He was getting morose in his cups about poor old Jack Carpenter dying, when he noticed a young man he only half-recognised standing at the bar. All in all, nobody could be sure of anything.

After a time, the mysterious young man seemed to merge into the background. Every now and then a head would turn to see if he was still there. In the general gloomy half-light, not a soul on the coach could really be certain he would still be there when they looked round again. After a time, nobody really bothered about him. The best thing was to forget the wretched fellow and concentrate on the outing to

272

Brighton.

Ron was thoroughly fed up with it all. Grown-ups seemed to be the most asinine beings imaginable. A silly clottish lot of gumps, that's all they were! Here it was — half-past-flipping-nine! And they'd only got as far as the Roxy.

Once more, the intrepid band started off and turned up Napoleon Avenue.

"'Ere!" said Ron, "why are we going up here? Taint the way to Tooting."

"I know," replied the Vicar. "Wait and see!"

"Cor! Luvvaduck!", cried the thoroughly dispirited Ron. "I could've walked to Brighton and back in half the time! I wish I'd never come, that's what I wish."

They pulled up outside a large double-fronted Victorian residence with a grey slate roof and tall windows.

"Whatever are we stopping for now?" asked Ron irritably.

"That's what we're stopping for," said the Vicar, proudly and pointing to the front door.

Ron peered through the window at the wide porch. Some people were gathered there, huddled in the doorway.

"Why, it's Grandpa!" cried Ron, jumping about like a frolicking flea. "It's Grandpa! It's Grandpa!"

He waved his hands in the air, trying hard to attract the old man's attention.

"Grandpa! It's me! Ron! It's me!" he shouted.

When the old man waved his stick at him from the porch and came gingerly down the ash-covered drive to the coach, Ron could not believe that life could be so good after all.

"Now, my boy," said the Vicar, with a twinkle in his eye, "I think you'd better have that seat you've been saving for 'someone', don't you? I'll go and sit with Miss Paxton."

The extent of Ron's happiness could be measured only by the degree of annoyance and embarrassment Miss Baldock was feeling. Mr Lawton, much to everyone's surprise, had recovered sufficiently to be discharged from hospital and was now settled in his new surroundings at the Napoleon Avenue Old People's Home. Miss Baldock had congratulated herself on successfully keeping Ron away from his old friend whom she considered in her wisdom to be a bad influence on the boy. Her day was ruined, not so much by the exasperating delays of departure, but by the presence of old Lawton and by the insistent

273

pricking pins and needles of conscience over her acquisition of the lease.

Even though the coach carrying the little band of day-trippers was now trapped in a long line of stationary cars and double-decker buses converging on the Elephant and Castle junction, Ron, quite undeterred by the inclemency, and implicitly following the Vicar's earlier dictum that "it all depends on what we feel inside", was bouncing up and down on his seat with the excitement of it all. The prospect of a day by the sea was indeed a happy one, and to such happiness was added the joy of once more being united with Grandpa Lawton.

57. Florid Romance

Ron was oblivious of the rain in its role as arch-spoiler of his day out. But now, here they were, marooned again as they inched past a traffic island surrounded by a chaos of cars, all trying to push one another out of the way and none having much idea of where they were going.

"Where are we now, Grandpa?"

"Tooting Bec."

"But you said we was at Tooting Bec ages ago."

"No, I did not. I said it five minutes ago."

"Bet you it wasn't."

"Oh! You youngsters! Too impatient by far. Why, when I was a boy, there weren't any of these jet aeroplanes and rockets and things. You just had to go on Shanks's pony if you couldn't afford the train. There were none of these ocean-going vessels like they have nowadays. It's not half as romantic. The year I went out to New Zealand — why, I sailed in a windjammer, my lad."

"Cor! Grandpa! One of them with big white sails, and mutinies, and the captain walking the plank, and slaves in chains, and —"

Grandpa laughed affectionately. "No, no, no," he said, shaking his head like a Chinese idol, "but we did have great white sails billowing in the wind — and in the Indian Ocean there's plenty of wind, I can tell you. We used to lie on the deck, flat on our backs, and gaze up at the sails, watch them straining at the masts, creaking on the ropes. When we got tired of doing that, we'd hang over the sides of the ship and search for sea-snakes."

"Sea-snakes!" said Ron, his eyes popping in all directions.

"Sea-snakes, yes! Long coiling things with fierce eyes like Chinese dragons. Many was the poor devil to get dragged under, even along the coasts. Once had a mate went swimming close to Madras. You know, where the curry comes from, hot enough to make you drink up the whole ocean in a single gulp. Made your tongue hang out for weeks, it did. That's Indian curry for you."

"Yes, yes!" said Ron urgently, "but what about the sea-snakes?"

"Sea-snakes?" said the old man, knitting his wrinkled brow.

"Oh! Come on!" said Ron impatiently. "Yes, sea-snakes. You was telling me about sea-snakes. What are they like? I mean, do they swallow you all in one go? Do they poison you with their fangs?"

"Well, there were sharks, too," went on Grandpa.

Ron gave up.

"We hove to in the Solomons that year. Had my first meal with a cannibal. Way up in the hills, it was. Three days trek through the rain forest, all steaming with the heat, too. Rose up from the ground like mist. Felt almost as if I was in the pot with all the onions and turnips myself!"

"Cannibals?" said Ron, gaping. "Do you mean man-eaters?"

"Man-eaters are tigers. These were real men eating real men. Mind you, it was like a sort of religion, you understand. We didn't know they'd chopped up one of the tribesmen just for Sunday lunch — and all served up on a dish of yucca leaves, decorated with fruit and flowers."

"D'you mean they actually cooked him in a stew-pot?"

"Yes. With a liberal sprinkling of salt and pepper, of course."

"But isn't it bad to eat people?"

"I suppose it is, son. But a man's got to eat *some* meat, and who wants to eat snakes and lizards — they do eat them as well, as a delicacy, mind. But a nice loin of human or a bit of rump — well, I mean to say, you wouldn't say no if you were starving up there in the jungle. Anyway, it aint legal to eat humans now. Things have changed a good deal since my young days. They probably get a regular supply of corned beef, nowadays."

"But weren't you ill? Didn't you want to be sick?"

"What ever for? Tasted real good. Couldn't tell it from a nice juicy joint of veal. Anyway, we didn't know it was man-meat until after we'd had our coffee."

"Were you ever sea-sick, then?"

275

"Ah! Well! That's a different kettle of fish altogether. Seasick? I should say I was. Dozens of times, crossing the Indian Ocean. Rough as Old Harry, it was. And there'd be man-eating sharks lurking about looking for any choice tit-bits that might happen to go overboard. You could see their dorsal fins cutting through the waves like knives."

Ron was tingling with delight. It only needed Grandpa to untap Ron's imagination with his tales of heroism in exotic climes for Ron to be transformed into another being. His face was a picture of wonderment and adulation. To him, it was like being a personal friend of the heroes he had met with time and time again at the Roxy. *Really* riding the high seas in search of prehistoric monsters, *actually* struggling in the coils of a giant anaconda, *actually* braving the stratosphere and discovering life on the moon — not that Grandpa ever laid claim to an actual moon-landing as such! ·

Ron hated it when Grandpa stopped talking. Just as he hated it when the film came to an end at the Roxy. There was that devastating hush that spread through the audience as the lights went up and people started to rustle their sweet-papers and seats started squeaking and banging with everybody deciding it might be advisable to make for the *Ladies'* or the *Gents*. And all that was left for him was home, and thoughts of what Miss Goodenough would say tomorrow, and what excuse he could think up this time. As for his mother, working away in the kitchen, and never a good word to say for anybody, and Millie, moping about the place, looking largely like an interrupted dream. Talk about misery!

Then there was Mabel. A proper little lollipop kid, she was. It was always Ron who had to take her up to Ma Blackwood's, Ron who had to sit her on the toilet, Ron who had to pull her out of the kennel by the pigtails. No wonder she regarded him as 'the enemy'. She had probably hated him ever since the day he twisted her arm when he'd been a plain-clothes cop arresting a lady killer! Or was it a pirate-captain torturing a captive maiden? Of course, Mabel would never understand that, as far as Ron was concerned. Why should she? Nobody ever understood anything in their house. So why should Mabel be any different to the rest of them? Yet, there were times when Ron knew Mabel was different, and sometimes it surprised him to think that his mother and father could produce a daughter who had a passion to bury everything she loved and act out her childish fantasies. As well as that, they had a son who wanted to do nothing but play the piccolo and paint all the time.

No! Nobody understood anything. His father could never give a straight answer. He always hedged round a question so that you didn't know if he had answered it or not at the end. Old Purvis always said Alf Thompson would make a good member of Parliament. But Ron couldn't come to terms with the thought that perhaps his father really didn't know anything about life at all!

How could you have any respect for grown-ups if they went on like that all the time? There was his mother getting all her words wrong. Ron remembered the time when she mentioned about wanting some of "that tubercular furniture". Old Pudden-an'-duff called it a 'malediction' or something. Seen like that, Ron considered his mother was not very well educated, and he once told her so to her face, for which modest service he received a sharp clip round the ears. Ron believed that, in their household, you only got punished for telling the truth. Whereas old Grandpa Lawton — well! — you could say what you liked to him and he didn't mind a bit. In any case, Ron never had any reason to pick him up on his grammar.

"Well, go on, Grandpa. Go on!"

The old man had now reached Australia!

"Well — we landed at Perth. Just like the Mediterranean it was. All oranges and lemons, and sitting in the sun, and lovely warm nights. Real luxury after rolling about the oceans for months on end. Perth, " he mused. "Yes!" he sighed. "That's where I got mixed up in a fight."

"A fight?" said Ron, bouncing about again.

"I got pretty badly hurt, too," Grandpa added for good measure.

"Cor! Where? I mean, how? Was it painful? Did you bleed? Did you nearly die?"

"Well, that was what made me so bad with pneumonia after my accident, you see. I got stabbed in the chest. The old war-wound, you see, flared up again."

Here he trailed off again into a quiet musing of his own, and it was some time before Ron was able to revive the old man's flagging inspiration to something of its former originality. Ron need not have worried for he was soon immersed in a flood of stories about gang-fights in the docks, strange rites performed in the Chinese quarter in Rangoon and exciting discoveries hundreds of feet under the Java seas.

If being cuffed over the ear might be called an expression of affection in the Thompson home, then Ron had ceased to appreciate it. He had moved slowly and painfully away in the direction of the illusory film-magic of the Roxy and the web of mystery and imagination that

277

Grandpa Lawton was able to weave for a young mind starved of adventure. When the time came, as eventually it had to, for Ron to get up out of his cinema seat or leave his comfortable fireside pew next to Grandpa Lawton, Ron's heart was like a grey winter afternoon. There was only the dreariness of Saturdays and Sundays to be spent in the company of parents who never answered questions and never listened to what you were saying, and rattled on about nothing for hours on end. In Ron's whole life, nothing was equal in dread and despair to this unbearable home-coming.

Grandpa was now tree-felling in New Zealand, his last port of call.

"Oh, I know you climbed up to the top of the tree, but what happened then?"

"Well, we were about a hundred feet up, see? We used to start lopping off branches — "

"A hundred feet?" gasped Ron.

"Well, that was nothing, my boy. There were trees twice as tall. Great big fellers, they were. We used to climb them like a couple of monkeys on a stick. Of, course, I was a big chap in those days. A big strong feller like Eddie."

"Well," said Ron, frowning, "how is it you've got so small, Grandpa?"

Mr. Lawton paused for a moment, perplexed.

"Oh," he said ruefully, "sickness and old age make you like that. You go on losing weight all the time. Sort of go into decline. Bones get brittle and nobbly."

Ron felt it was very strange that a man could grow up and then grow down again.

"Well, do people grow smaller when they get old?" said Ron.

"Not exactly. Some people do kind of fade away, but not entirely. You know what the song used to say: 'Old soldiers never die, they only fade away!' Some people die big and some people die small. It's in the nature if things,"

"Go on about tree-felling. What happened when you were at the top of this tree? I want to go to New Zealand, and sail in a clipper and watch for sea-snakes."

The old man went on with tales about forest-fires round the camp, and camp-fires in the forest, but he never did get back to telling Ron what happened at the top of that tree. Now, Ron was listening to the story about how the forest caught fire and all the animals came running and scurrying out of the undergrowth to escape the sharp tongues of flame and the intense heat, and how, in the evening, below star-studded skies, the lads sat down for a meal and a sing-song in the glow of the camp-fires, and slept soundly in rough blankets till morning.

Ron found himself looking over his shoulder at the young man no-one knew, who seemed to have been listening to every word, though he was still staring out of the window, deep in thought. Ron was sure he had seen him before, perhaps at the Roxy. But then, this 'Lone Stranger' (as Ron began to look upon him), did he not bear a vague resemblance to one of the inspectors who visited the school last term? But then, no! Not really.

Grandpa's voice broke through Ron's musings.

"Yes, my boy! Those were the days. Give me life in the open air every time. But you can't go doing all those things now. That's all dead and gone. There's plenty you *can* do, though. What about yeti-hunting in the Himalayas, or crossing the Antarctic snows, or reaching for the moon, even? That's what you must do, laddie. 'Reach for the moon, and finger the stars,' as the poet says. Now, where did I read that?"

Ron was pretty sure he could never reach the moon. As for fingering the stars, well, he wasn't going to be the one to get his fingers burnt! In any case, what did it matter? A whole day stretched ahead of him — a whole day to spend with his very best friend in all the world.

58. Four Characters in Search of an Author: Scene 1

Boy is in love with girl, who is in love with ......it's the old story, the tangled web of emotions that binds people together and yet keeps them for ever apart. A mother, a father, a daughter, a young man..... here they are seated on stage, ready to open their hearts to anyone who will listen. They are incapable of listening to each other because they have no way of breaking the mould of their relationships, no meaningful words to release their pent up feelings. There is only fear, guilt, frustration, resentment, incomprehension, and an overriding sense of hurt.

The scene is a coach on its way from London to Brighton. It is summer. It is also raining and overcast. The young girl and the young

*man are sitting as far apart as possible because they want to be near
each other, only they cannot give in to it. There are too many barriers.
It is the same for the mother and the father. Their love has died a death,
perhaps many deaths, and they have made a terrible truce, many times
over. They too have to break the mould, before it is too late.*

*All four characters are, in a sense, searching for a miracle-
worker, more articulate than themselves, who might discover for them
how to express the secret language of their souls, bring them closer
together, release them through the power of the spoken word from the
dreariness of their lives they are now disposed to contemplate as the
coach bumps and rattles along the road on its way to the seaside of their
dreams. Occasionally, we see their faces contort into some appropriate
semblance of speech. Lips tremble, noses sniff and twitch, faces affect
the shadow of a smile or a grimace or a scowl or a frown or a sneer or
a teeth-baring grin. From time to time they all affect a sigh peculiar to
each. Sometimes they even shed a tear or two.*

*At present they are caught in a time warp. They are wanderers
in an emotional labyrinth in which they have lost the life-saving thread
that will lead them back to the happiness they have all but forgotten.
What is about to happen to our four helpless and solitary souls can only
come about if this 'author' they seem to be searching for can somehow
unravel the turmoil of their thoughts. Perhaps only then can they
emerge once more from darkness into light.*

*In the process, Alf and Flo, Eddie and Millie, find themselves in
a confessional frame of mind. One by one, they seem to focus on the
silent stranger. Perhaps he will understand. There is surely no more
sympathetic listener on a long journey than a lone, defenceless
travelling companion.*

Eddie

Do you know something? This 'ere ol' blunder-bus is giving me
the gip, matey. 'S me own silly fault for sitting over the blinking
wheels. Bumps you about like a jack-in-a-box, it does. Just my flippin'
luck to be left up the back here on me lonesome. I mean, it'd be a bit of
all right, eh? Millie and me sitting back here all cosy like in the
corner.......

Blimey! We're just passing the old Brixton Empire. That takes
me back. Me ole dad used to be a regular there. Used to laugh 'is 'ead
off at Monsewer Eddie Gray and 'is antics. Not to mention Flanagan

and Allen an' co. Max Miller an' all, and Tessi O'Shea. I'm sure he fell for Marie Lloyd once. Had bit flair, did my ole dad.........
Funny, you know! Millie having a kid like that. Fancy springing that on a bloke. Fair floored me, I can tell you. There she was, one minute prancing and dancing about like Diamond Lil, and the next — well, blow me! I mean, how can you tell the difference, eh? All tarted up, and a face on her so as you wouldn't know her from Adam — well, you know what I mean! That was Millie one day, see? And the next? All her hair in such a mess as you've never seen. Stands to reason, a bloke's gotta notice something aint right. And when I goes in and sees what's been going on in their house, well — you coulda stoned me!
'You aint 'alf a bunch o' kippers,' I says, acting it up a bit, see? 'Aint you lot got no know-how? Aint you got none of the live-and-let-live? All right! So Millie's bin and gone and done it good and proper. So? What's done is done. You can't put the clock back. Aint she your own flesh-and-blood? If you want to go and take it out on somebody, take it out on the bloke what got 'er into trouble in the first place. I mean to say — going up there, carving her about. Your own daughter! 'Taint right, I tell you. Getting yourselves all worked up like that. Don't you lot realise you coulda done her in good and proper,' I says........
Well! That did it. Just about saved Millie. She coulda been a gonner, sure as I'm sitting here. But I tell you, it still don't alter the fact that Millie's goin' to 'ave this kid. Cor, blimey, mateys! Now, there she is up the front seat, all on her lonesome. It don't make sense..........

Millie

Oh! This rain gets on my wick! What a day for a trip to the coast! Reminds me of the time I bumped into old Mr. Purvis outside the Town Hall. It fair pelted down, it did. Never haven't liked rain since that. Sends me right down in the dumps, I can tell you. All that eternal dripping and dribbling, and mud splashing up your stockings. Who'd 'a' known it was August Bank Holiday! Woulda done a sight better staying at home on me own. Only, then Mum'd have to stay at home as well and she'd send me potty with her nagging. They can't leave me alone for five minutes. Say they don't trust me. Honest! The way she goes on. Taint normal. Always asking questions. Questions, questions! Where've you been? What d'you do that for? Who were you with? Why are you so late? Questions, questions, questions! I can't stand that kinda carry-on. I can't really.......

281

As for Dad — well! Don't think we ever had a real conversation in our lives. Sometimes I think he's lost his flippin' tongue, the way he goes on. I'd like to know what sort of a father he's supposed to be. I'll never forgive 'im for what he done to me. Never! Frightened the livin' daylights out o' me, he did, with that knife in his hand. I feel such shame. It makes my heart ache with it all. The shock I got when I looked in the mirror and I see what he done to me. Doesn't bear thinkin' about. Now I can't bear anyone to come near me. Not even touch me, neither. I can see Mum now, standing there as helpless as a new-born kitten, crying, crying, and letting on so. Mind you, we both thought Dad was going to kill me. He would 'ave if I'd 'ave let on about who the father was. I woulda bin cold meat, I can tell you. After that, it took all it could take not to pack me bags and get out of the place forever. But I didn't have no strength left. It just knocked the stuffing right out of me.......

Now we've all gone back to the same old routine, only things is not what they used to be. Never will be. There's Mum still with her fighting-irons on just the same. Dad's gone back on the drink again. Worse than before. He's got a real problem. Sometimes I think he knows something I don't. Some sort of secret, like. Well, he'd better not try on any of his old tricks down in Brighton, else I'm leavin' home for good. And that's final!.......

Alf

When I wake up after a kip I feel real bad. Me stomach's all of a turnover. And as for me arms and legs — well! All of a quiver, they are, like I was scared out o' me wits or something. Me head's like a bleedin' roundabout, whirling round so fast people look rubbed out and smudgy, like one of the ones in that painting Ron done, over at the school.

Cor, blimey! There was me dribbling all over it. Wiped it off of it wiv me sleeve, I did. Well—I mean to say—how was I to know it'd go all blurry. A bit o' spit couldn't do no harm. But hey presto! The faces all went into a helluva mess, I can tell you. Made me laugh, it did. Ron wasn't 'alf wild. Never spoke to me the whole week. And all 'cos this 'ere painting was s'posed to be pinned up for some prize-giving or something. Wasn't half a carry-on, I can tell you. Him blubbing all over the place. Cor! anybody'd o' thought I'd done it on purpose. But I ask you — you can't 'elp accidents, now can you? Instead o' saying sorry,

282

I upped and gave 'im a clip over the ear. Then I saw the look on his face. As if I'd torn his heart out. Now, why the 'ell did I do that, eh? And I tell you something else — along comes this johnnie from the Art School and tells 'im how original the painting is and would Ron like to put it in for the blinkin' prize!.........

My Ron's a clever boy, mind you. Honest as they come, too. He'd never do anybody down without feeling sorry afterwards. A bit of a chip of the ol' block, if you ask me. Sort o' knows what's right, even if he don't do it the way he wants to. You know, I always mean to go and have a parley wiv 'is teacher. But you know what it is — what with keeping me job goin', and the ol' 'Peace and Plenty' lark of an evening — well — there aint much time for that sort o' caper......

Thinking of this 'Peace and Plenty' outfit— now, there's something as really matters. I mean to say, if you've got a boy growing up, what sort of a future has he got, kowtowin' around with the local kids, gettin' 'isself into bad ways, turning 'isself into one o' them Teds? I mean, taint right, is it? A father's gotta do something for 'is kids one way and another. Get the world straight a bit. Blow some o' the ol' cobwebs away before some other ol' bugger blows us sky high........

Now, old Ron, well — he don't want to work hard at school and get prizes and things if he's goin' to end up fighting a war, like ol' Jack Carpenter and me. He's a right good lad, is our Ron. Oh, I know he's always larkin' about up the Roxy, but that don't do 'im no harm. No! Ron's just a kid with ideas. Some of 'em may be bad for all I know — maybe most of 'em, but he's gotta learn the hard way. Like it says in the papers, as long as the good'uns win in the end and the bad'uns get what's comin' to 'em, well — everything in the parlour's lovely......

Flo

'Pon my soul! Never get nothing but rain, rain, rain, the whole blinkin' year round. Who wants to go sloshing round Brighton in galoshes in the height of summer? What on earth made me come on this trip in the first place, I'd like to know? Just because we've bin goin' to Brighton every Bank Holiday since the year dot don't mean to say we have to play muggins this year an' all, now does it? I mean, just look at it! Pelting down, it is. And 'ere we are only passing through Purley. You won't catch me setting foot outside this coach, I can tell you. I shall stay here and have me sandwiches in the warm. None o' that traipsin' about in the wet for me, catchin' me death!........

283

Oh, I do wish I hadn't come, I do, really! I could 've stayed at home and done a bit o' mending. Even got done with that pile of ironing, too. After all's said and done, Mondays is Mondays, and there's no two ways about it. There's still mouths to be fed. Talk about a woman's work is never done! In our house, you could go on for twenty-four hours a day and never get through. Drudgery from morning to night, that's what it is, and no thanks for it, neither..........

The way they all go on you'd think I wasn't there most of the time. Running about after 'em like a blinkin' flunkey, doin' this and doin' that and doin' the other. Mind you, I'd soon hear about it if their shoes wasn't nice and shiny, or their tea wasn't ready just when they happened to feel like it. You can bet your bottom dollar somebody'd have something to say. Not one of 'em ever stops to think of the 'undred-and-one jobs I have to get through in the day. I mean, 'taint fair to expect me to do more 'n I'm doing now, is it? Stands to reason, they couldn't want no more done for 'em, leastways, you think they wouldn't. But up they come with something or other to pester me with. Never a dull moment with that lot, I can tell you.........

Eddie

Lovely gel, Millie is. Fair did me nut when I see her come out that day without her makeup on. I didn't catch on who it was at first. She looked sort of different —her eyes and mouth most of all. They was — I dunno—kinda soft and sad, like. Full of a kind of grief, that's it. Her eyes— well —they was so— sort o' deep and vulnerable, like. Well, when I see 'er like that, I can tell you, matey, it was love at first sight. 'Cos I never see her before like that —not really—what with all that muck plastered over her dial........

Alf

Funny how me own flesh-and-blood can be so different — as chalk from cheese. I mean, you'd never know Ron and Millie were brother and sister, not the way they carry on. Millie? — well, she's out on her own, she is. Never took no for an answer, even as a kid. I tell you, she's too bloomin' independent. Does what she wants to and to hell with anybody else. Never says a blinkin' word from one day to the next as isn't a grumble or a grouse. It's always something I've done or her mother's done, or nine times out of ten, hasn't done!..........

284

Then again, there she is, our Millie, always up to some game or other, knowing full well she can no more play it her way than the cow that jumped over the moon! Take that pop-singing lark. Well, I mean to say, what a fiasco, eh? Drove us nearly potty with her croonin' and warblin', she did. It all fizzled out like everything else she tries. She aint never bin satisfied with her 'ome life. Always got to go one better than the rest of us, and then she comes a cropper!..............

Pity she never said no to that bastard what give her the kid. I'd do him good and proper if I could only lay my hands on him. I ask you! A young girl like Millie! It aint right. Not only that. What about all the neighbours, eh? Chirping like sparrows on a dung-heap, they was. I s'pose I shoulda told the gel the facts o' life. But somehow she seemed to know more 'n I did, and that's saying something! Funny thing is, she seemed to be always our little gel. Never seemed to grow up. Like our little Alice in Wonderland, she was. Leastways till she started all this make-up lark, painting her face like a Japanese doll. She was no sight for sore eyes, I can tell you. One thing though — our Millie's a smasher when she's not smarming that stuff all over her face. Never knew old Alfie-boy's daughter could be so pretty. She'd do just nice for some feller as needs a wife. Trouble is, who'd have her now and have to take on some other bloke's kid. What the hell can you do, eh? If you go to the police you only get your name in the Sunday papers, and the scandal'd kill ol' Flo ....

One of these days, though, I mean to have a real talk with Millie. Get down to basics a bit. Catch up on all the time we never spoke to each other. I keep trying to talk to her, but — I don't know what it is — I just can't find the right words. She aint easy to fathom, mind. Anyways, now she won't have none of it. And there she is, the baby on its way, and me wanting to talk to her, just so as I can let her know how I really feel, and then we could......Oh, to hell with it! What's the bloody use?..........

Eddie

Crikey! That was a right bump, that was. Felt the springs sticking up me jumper just then! I'm not exactly the fleshy type, you see. Not like old Mother Baldock! Now there's a one for you. Always belly-aching about something! I never know what to make of her half the time. The way she used to lick old 'Dandy' Crawford's boots was nobody's business. Still, she aint such a bad old stick when you get beyond the face-value bit, though as faces go she aint quite the one that launched a fousand ships! Used to give me a good tip at Christmas though. More than Curly ever got, I can tell you. Always taking the mickey out of her, he is. Never lets her alone. Mind you, he never let anybody alone once he'd got his claws into 'em. Always ready for a punch-up is Curly. He's a real queer sort o' bloke. Takes hisself too serious. If you played a joke on him he'd as soon give you a couple o' black eyes!

Of course, he's got the body all right with all those work-outs up the gym. He taught me a thing or two about the ol' muscle-power. A regular Mr. Universe, he is. Biceps as big round as my calves. Going up the gym regular-like with' 'im, even little old Eddie's had to throw out his T-shirts. Sometimes I get to doing a bit o' sparring with 'im, but he gets a bit vicious when he's roused.......

Well—what can a feller do, eh? All that liftin' and shiftin' up the market's helped me put on quite a bit o' muscle. I could take Curly on any day. Let's hope I never 'ave to. He's dangerous, is Curly. You can see the veins stand out on his biceps like nobody I know. When he tenses up and pulls in his stomach inside of 'im and pushes out his chest—well!—he's a blinking Johnny Weissmuller! Nigh on pulled my arm out the other day in the market when he was larkin' about showing off in front of the other fellers. A regular Tarzan he thinks he is! When he done that, I thought, blimey! I'd better get a bit more brawn on me if I'm goin' to join up. No use being a whippet when you have to size up to some o' these matelot-boys. Taint no good havin' a set-to in the old Casbah if you aint got a touch o' the Stewart Granger about you!. Well, I mean, stands to reason, don't it?.........

Flo

You know, that Tim Crawford's a much nicer sort o' bloke since he's been living with the Paxtons. Couldn't stand the sight of him at first — him with his prissy ways and la-di-da accent. But I tell you something — he's a perfect gentleman, he is. Speaks to you as if you're really somebody. He's got ever such nice manners. Knows ever such a lot about everything — art, politics, and all sorts. Not like our Ronnie, the lazy little devil! I never know what he's getting up to half the time. Skivin' off from school. Hangin' about the street-corners with his pals, gettin' up to no good, I shouldn't wonder. I can't understand what the hell they teach 'em in these 'ere schools. It's all very well Miss

Goodie-Two-Shoes writin' to me and complainin'. Why don't *she* do something about it? *She's* in charge, aint she? I mean what the hell are schools for if they aint for keeping kids in order—*and* for keepin' 'em from gettin' under my feet!........

As for Mabel — well! Glad to be rid of her up the Day Nursery for an hour or two. Worried sick, I was, that day when she went off on her own. Nearly run over by a damned great lorry in the High Street, she was. Said she was looking for her monkey-friend. Beppo aint it? Well, what a caper it was. Had to get the little rascal into Marley's and sit her on the counter. There she was screaming the place down and her little knees all torn and bleeding. Lucky she wasn't killed, that's what I say. I ask you! Running into the road like that without as much as an eyes right. 'S just asking for trouble. If they 'adn't taken old Lawton off the crossing job there would'nt be no accidents.......

To tell you the truth, I don't understand Mabel, I don't really. She gets up to some queer old tricks at times— burying things, and that. All 'cos she 'eard us talking about Jack Carpenter's funeral. Little blighter, she is! Don't never show no sign of life while we're chatting, but she's listening all right. With all ears. Doesn't forget anything. Then, suddenly, it all comes out. You never know what kids are picking up when you talk, do you? She's just like old Ma Carpenter's parrot. I mean, they pick up any old thing and blurt it out about a week later......

But life aint bin the same since Mabel set fire to our front-room. It sort o' killed something in me, it did. When I see that room all burnt to a cinder, well! — I could have cried meself sick.........

D'you know, the first time I saw that room was on my wedding-day. Alf's Mum and Dad, well — they lived in the kitchen day in, day out. So we 'ad no cause to ever use the front-room 'cos me and Alf, we did our courtin' in the back alley or up at the Roxy in the back row. So that old front-room never changed from one year to the next, nor has it since. That is, till Mabel mucked it about. Won't never be the same again......

But it aint the chairs or the curtains I miss. Not even the old piano. It's that photo of my Alf. I loved that picture. When he was all young and lovely. Ever so 'andsome, he was. Strong and manly, he was. Fair bowled me head over heels, he did. How he made love to me, with such passion. O' course, we never went all the way in those days. I do miss the old Alf, the Alf I used to know in them days...........

That photo was all I 'ad of 'im an' me and poor old Jack Carpenter. I used to go in there of an afternoon, and there they was, looking at me out of the old frame, my Alf with that handsome smile of his, looking young and fresh as the day he asked me to marry him. Always enjoyed our Saturday afternoons, sitting doing me knitting and gazing at his picture. Now, I aint even got that. Just the memory, and you know what happens to that after twenty years or more!............

Millie

Ron should never have told Miss Baldock about what Eddie said. And Eddie should never have told me about what Curly did, neither. I mean, how can I do anything about it? I ask you! If Curly *really did* take that money from Crawford, then.......... I coulda sworn Eddie was havin' me on. If I hadn't met Mr. Purvis that night, he wouldn't 've given me that ticket for the Purvis Bowl and Eddie wouldn't 've bin able to take me and I wouldn't 've met up with Curly. And maybe, Curly wouldn't be where he is now, wherever that is! If I hadn't bought that *Love and Lucy* book and Ron hadn't left it over Miss Baldock's place........ And if she hadn't poked her nose in where it wasn't wanted, Curly would have most likely been free as a bird now.............

What a mix-up, eh? Just goes to show you, you never know what you're doing most times and what it's going to lead to, do you? Just a casual remark and in a jiffy your boy friend's put in the nick. .... Oh, I do feel sleepy!....... I often wonder though..............just supposing Eddie did take that money after all.......just supposing.........then Curly would never have had that row with Crawford and he wouldn't be on the run like he is...........just supposing.............

Alf

.........woke up just now and caught sight of a signs for Redhill and Three Bridges so I've no blinkin' idea where we are, to be honest......

I was just thinking about Eddie. Now, there's a boy for you. A real fine lad. Got principles, he has. To tell you the truth, I was hoping he and our Millie would..........well, never mind now. That's the thing with me — I build up hopes, get ideas, and then — boom! All blown to bits. I can't help regretting it — may be Millie might just have got fixed up with Eddie if she hadn't been with this other feller. Eddie's a clever lad. A bit like our Ron in some ways. He's not only got brains, neither.

288

He's got brawn too. I never seen such a change in anybody in my life as there is in Eddie. He's grown real handsome. He'd make a girl a good husband sometime. I just wish it was going to be our Millie. I haven't forgotten how he gave up his studies and went to work just so as he could keep his old Ma going with a pint or two. And him only a kid at the time. Any boy as'd do that is fit to be a son-in-law o' mine. But there you are, you see. Fate, aint it? His old Ma never appreciated him anyway. Always nagging, she was. Specially after old Jacko packed it in. And her always tight as a bob-tailed tit up at *The Bed of Roses*.....

Funny how it all started between me and her — seeing as how I felt so bad about Jacko's death. Somehow, there was Flo nag-nag-nagging away at home, and there was Ma twiddlin' her thumbs in the corner of the bar looking like death warmed up. Well, what can you expect in a situation like that? We went together a time or two, 'cause we both felt bad about old Jack, see? We'd sit it out till closing-time and then I'd 'see her home' like. Old Jack wasn't much cop in the bed department. Most likely felt the same about Ma as I do about Flo. Never give 'er enough o' the old slap-and-tickle — not that I'm exactly a Valentino! But I do know how to give a woman what's needed. I should think she was a bit over the top for Jack, though, the way she used to go at it. Crikey! It was like it was a bout of all-in wrestling with her. I used to think her old brass bedstead was going to give way underneath us. Mind you, I like it a bit physical meself. I used to get real roused when she was in what you might call her fightin' mood. Talk about the battle of the sexes! ....

You know, you can go on doin' what you're supposed to be doing never realisin' what's what till years later. Haven't you ever 'ad that feelin'? What I mean to say is — you go on doing something, or not doing it as the case may be, and you go on like it for a long time — well, you know — like me giving Flo a goodnight kiss, for instance, or me clipping our Ronnie over the ear, or me wanting to talk to Millie — and I never can't do it 'cos I aint got the guts to. You go on puttin' things off, forgettin' things, 'cos you can't bear to remember 'em, putting things off till tomorrow, and tomorrow becomes the next day, and the next day becomes next week, and so on and so on. I mean, you just go on and on, and then it's too late to do anything about it. Or maybe you go on and on so much that you do something you wish you'd never done in the first place, like Millie.........

In our house, I only 'ave to open my mouth before somebody's 'avin' a go at me. Always takin' things the wrong way, they are. First it's Millie, queening it around, then it's Flo shoutin' her head off, or it's Mabel bawling into the back of my neck. My head's at bursting-point with it all till I can't stand it no more. I just 'ave to clear off to *The Bed of Roses* for a pint or two.......

Our house is like the cockpit of Europe, I can tell you. Everybody's scrappin' for the same bit of territory, like the Frenchies building the Maginot line, and the Jerries marching into Poland. Well, I mean to say, it's too much for a man to put up with, aint it? Then there's the family teas on Saturdays, all of us crammed together like sardines in a tin. Calm before the storm, it is. The silence really puts me on edge. 'Cos that means we're all crouching low in the trenches waiting for the first salvo. Meanwhile, we're all 'avin' heartburn with all the waitin' for it. There's Flo clicking away with her needles, Ron with 'is flippin' crosswords, and Mabel as quiet as a sniper on the watch. Everybody's a target in our house! Then suddenly, when you're least expecting it — BOOM! BANG! and the battle's on! Our house aint a 'ome, it's a bloody battlefield!...........

I can't tell you what the silence is like when I get home from the pub. I can hardly bring meself to put the key in the door for fear of making a noise. Then there's the gropin' bit – feeling my way along the passage, dribblin' round the furniture in the kitchen, everything swimming about like there was a deluge, no movement that wasn't round and round and round. And what do I come home to, eh? Bloody tapioca puddin' and prunes!.........

There's always Flo sittin' there with a funny look all over her face. Watching, staring, givin' me an old-fashioned look as much as to say: 'Look what the wind's blown in!' She just sits and stares. Never says a blinkin' word. Her brain's goin' round though – all the time. Never stops thinkin', she don't. She can read me like a book. Knows exactly what I'm thinkin', she does. So there aint no need to talk, you see. We can just sit there on our backsides in that room for years and years and nobody says a bleeding word. We just go on and on sitting there, thinking, thinking, thinking till it comes out of our ears.............

O' course, nowadays, she's turned into a regular old nagger. But back in our courtin' days, when we were walkin' out, well — she was quite a gel. Never ever let you go too far, though. I had to mind me p's and q's , I did. Mind you, the more she never let me, the more I wanted to have her. And she played on that most likely. To look at her now, you'd never think it, sittin' there all washed out. What a sight! She's just let 'erself go. Never tarts 'erself up and when I get a bit raunchy like, she won't have none of it. Just pushes me off of her, like she's all froze-up. I can't help thinkin' of the good old days, me an' her courtin', doing what come natural-like. Havin' a kiss in the alley at the back of our house, or havin' a bit of a snog on the bench in Bushy Walk...........

Sometimes I do try it on. I get a bit sexy and I put my hand out and run it down her back, stroking like, trying to rouse her, but she's just dead inside............

59. Four Characters in Search of an Author: Scene 2

Now the elements are raging around the old coach as it wends its way towards an uncertain future. Our little group of voyagers are stunned by weariness and the oppressive dankness that has now spread like miasma through the stuffy interior. Fixed like frogs in amber, they lean or squat or slump in a variety of positions, lost in sleep or staring vacantly at the steamed-up windows. The soporific purring of the engine is occasionally broken by a knock or a bang or a crash as the coach goes over a hole or bump in the road, waking the travellers out of their stupor and allowing their wayward thoughts to roam over problems and secrets they would really rather forget about. The Stranger appears to be asleep. Flo sneaks a quick glance at him to see if he is still there and then almost as soon falls irresistibly back into her dream-world. He is bent forward now, as if in a trance. Everybody's heads seem to loll in a variety of angles as if under a spell.

Suddenly, one of the unavoidable roadworks that pepper our countryside with bottle-necks lifts the coach off the ground and lets it go heavily down, leaving everyone shaken and stirred. They all come to with a jolt. Road signs for Crawley, Haywards Heath, Hurstpierpoint, Henfield, Worthing, and Lewes loom through the rain in solemn procession — and Brighton at last throws down the gauntlet!

Flo

'Ere we are comin' past a place called Pease Pottage, would you believe? Makes me feel a bit peckish.......I'm glad it's not Pudding Lane, that's all I can say!

Oh, my gawd! That was a bump, that was. Thought we was

291

nearly coming off the road just then. Why this government don't make the roads up, I don't know. It's a disgrace. That's what it is....... Oh, my head! I do wish Mabel would stop bang-banging that old spade and pail of hers. Drivin' me up the creek, it is. If I tell her to stop it she'll only start hollerin' and wake the whole place up. That'd shake 'em out of their dreaming. The bus is bad enough — rockin' and rollin' all over the shot. No wonder I get me turns. Sometimes I think my heart's goin' to blow up like a balloon and burst. Taint no use goin' to see that old Dr. Glendale, neither. He just sits and looks at you and says: 'Well, Mrs. T. Which is it to be today – the pink or the white?' What on earth are you supposed to say to that? I always say the pink 'cos it tastes nicer, but I might just as well be drinking a strawberry milkshake for all the good it does me..............

Alf

Well, Alfie-boy! Here we are again, happy as can be, all good pals and jolly good company! Now then! You know what little Alfie's going to have, don't you? A nice swig of stout. Ah! Lovely. Let's have another. Cor, that aint 'alf good, mate. Have another, Alfie. I don't mind if I do, said the Colonel! Ta, ever so. ....

Now, then, Alfie, snuggle down. Have a kip. Close your tired old eyes and before you can say bob's your uncle, it'll be dear old Brighton, and just about opening-time. Yes, a nice little bit of shut-eye, eh? Get right off before that blasted kid starts her bawling. 'S a treat to have a bit o' peace and quiet...........

Yeah, 'Peace and Plenty'......now there's a bit of a lark for you. Always ends up at *The Bed of Roses* for a snifter. I just sit there and.............well, old Ma........I can see 'er laughin' like a jelly-fish..........now............about....Ma!.........Flo?........well..............she.... don't.... know................. nothing...............not really..............

Millie

I don't want nobody getting the idea that I don't think a lot of Eddie, 'cos I do. He's a good lad, he is. I've been real surprised since he's bin goin' up the gym. He's grown into a real good-looker, has Eddie. A proper Dirk Bogarde he is now and no mistake. He's done us all a power o' good in our house, I can tell you. What with me in the family way! Then there was the front room to be done up. Well — he done it, really. Made a good job of it 'n all. He's cleaned up our back yard. Got rid of all them old hutches and painted up Smutty's kennel. The place looks a treat, it does..............

It's nice him coming round our place for his meals. But really — him and his old books! You'd think he'd be studying to be Prime-Minister the way he's goin' on. When I look at him he reminds me all the time of Curly and I want to cry with it all. There's just one thing about me and Eddie though — I just can't bear 'im touchin' me. He looks after me like a nurse, he does. He's kind, like his ol' Dad. He even looks just like 'im. He's got them eyes, sort of gentle and yet strong. But he don't mean nothing to me like that. Still, he's good company taken all round. Makes me laugh — like the time I went round about his Ma kickin' the bucket. Well, I mean.! The way he poured out the tea was pathetic. I tell you something — he needs someone to look after 'im. 'S a good job Mum's around to get his supper, that's all I can say. It'll be better for 'im when he's joined the Navy. Somehow, though, I shall miss 'im when he's gone..............

Flo

I'll never ever forget what Alf done to Millie. He ignores her for nigh on seventeen year, and when he *does* notice her goes and slashes her hair off with a bread knife. It just aint normal, is it? *He* can't talk, neither, the way he was carryin' on with Ma next door. Don't think I'm siding with Millie 'cos I'm not. I mean, it's her own look-out if she can't take precautions. Fancy not knowin' who the father is. Just fancy, eh? How many blokes has she been with, I'd like to know. It don't bear thinkin' about..........

Mind you, I'm not so daft I don't hear rumours going about, neither. It's a wonder to me she aint had triplets by now, some of the louts she larks about with up the Purvis Bowl. That place is a den of iniquity, it is. Ought to be closed down.............

And what about Eddie? He's been keen on her for months. I don't know what they get up to when they go to the flicks, mind. Then there was that night his old Ma died. Just the right timing — six months now. And her comin' in after midnight too. I dunno though. Eddie's a good boy. He wouldn't get a gel into trouble and not marry her, would he?..................

I knew something was up when she come back from old Purvis's place. She looked really squiffy, if you ask me. And him supposed to 'ave mixed the drinks up. Now what sort of explanation is that? A nice little bit of hanky-panky if you ask me. Not that Effie Mudd on ironmongery might not be a bit cuckoo. She was the one what told me..............

Eddie

I got me suspicions about Curly. If I knew he'd put Millie in the family way I'd skin 'im alive, I'm tellin' you. Stands to reason I'd do anything for that gel, kid or no kid. I just think of her havin' to slave all day in that old button bazaar! Well! 'S enough to send you bonkers, aint it? And what's she got when she gets home of an evening with that mob to put up with? Take Alf! Used to be a nice sort o' bloke. Now look at him. Drinks like a fish, he does. He's let 'isself go ever since my old dad was killed. They was pals for years and years, them two. But boozin' aint no good to 'im. Leads old Flo a caper'n all! If it wasn't for Alf, she'd be all right. But one thing's for sure — he aint never been no father to the kids — not really........

You know, when I'm round there 'avin' me tea in their little back-kitchen, well — I get a feeling. I don't know why but I reckon Alf's sort of — I dunno! — desperate. He wants to tell me something, Get something off his chest. Maybe it's something I shouldn't know. Maybe it's something I'd rather not know. Not for my ears, like..........

I'll never forget that day he come home and found Millie was in the family way. He was like a wild animal. Way over the top, he was, like he felt guilty about it as well. That was the first time I realised he was a man with a secret. He scared poor old Millie out of her wits. Who knows that he didn't do something to that baby inside of her. Could come out a cripple or something. I just wish I'd got there sooner. What with Flo blubbing her eyes out in the front-room, and Millie sobbing her heart out, there wasn't much of 'em left to cry over..........

As for Mabel — well, when Flo saw Millie blubbing away and Mabel saw her mother blubbing away you couldn't blame her for wantin' to join in too. Now Mabel — she's a bright little kid. But she's gotta be careful she don't end up like Millie one o' these days. 'Cos her mum don't look after her. Let alone her dad. She's just a little soul without anywhere to go. I worry about her more than the others, if the truth was known. I don't know why but............

This blinkin' rain is getting on my wick. These weather-forecasters ought to 'ave their heads examined — temperatures in the eighties and all that crap. No wonder old Mother Baldock gets mud in her spuds. I should think old Dandy Crawford's best out of farming, the way things are. I wouldn't be a farmer for all the pee in China!........at least that's how Curly puts it......

Thinking of old Crawford makes me wonder about Curly. He's prop'ly put 'is foot in it, aint he? Must 'ave gone off 'is rocker to do a thing like that. He's a queer customer and no mistake. I don't envy 'im now with the coppers after 'im. I mean, you can't never 'ave a kip without the fear o' bein' nabbed. Taint my pigeon if he gets nicked. Still, if he can do it to one he can do to another. I seen 'im go up to blokes in the market just 'cos they cheeked him and deal out a fistful o' punches. Usually somebody 'd end up with a bloody nose or a black eye.........

Take that time over the Purvis Bowl, with all them Teds and Rockers. They was just itchin' for a fight and when wolves are in a pack they're dangerous, I can tell you. I pity the poor sucker who got mixed up in a razor fight. But get one of 'em on 'is own and he's as yellow as a lemon. That was the night I see Millie comin' out of No 3. What the 'ell was she doin' in a bombed-out house in the dark, eh?............

What gets me is these tales about her and Purvis. I ask you, what is a bloke supposed to think when he's told she's been mumchancin' about with an old geezer like him. Then, three months later, we hear she's got a bun in the oven! Stands to reason, the pay-off's gotta come sooner or later for somebody. There'll be fireworks if his financey finds out about it! Aggy Balcock, or whatever her name is. The whole place'll be hoppin' with coppers..............

Flo

I was just thinking about my Alf, the way he used to come over and fetch me of a Saturday night when we was walking out together. Usually we'd go up the Roxy if it was nippy. But on a nice summer's eve, we'd take a stroll over the bridge and have a wander around the City. I used to love it best of a Sunday — not a soul about, nowhere. Ever so quiet it was — no traffic nor nothing to worry ourselves about. Most likely, it'd be just me and Alf, arm-in-arm, and him saying soppy things in me ear. Sometimes, if we was lucky, there'd be a dark passageway we'd come across, and he'd push me into it and put his arms round me and we'd kiss and kiss. Oh, he was so strong and 'andsome, the way he used to look at me, and I'd melt—his eyes brown as chestnut.

Mind you, I knew what he had a mind to do. I tell you, I was knocked for six............

　　To look at him now, you wouldn't know him for the same man. I can't get over it sometimes, how he's changed. When I see 'im sitting there slobberin' over his tea, well — he knows what I'm thinkin' all right! I don't have to tell him...............

　　The way I see it, he went right overboard when old Jack died. Of course, I knew something was up when he give up the market work and went into the tannery. I mean, for a man to change his job at his time o' life — well! — you'd think he'd want his brains tested, wouldn't you, eh? After that, seems as if he went to pieces. He was all over Ma Carpenter and Eddie, he was. Didn't care two hoots about any of us. Oh, no! Just left us to sink or swim. *And* there was more to it than met the eye there. I had my eyes skinned, I can tell you. You can't keep much from a wronged woman, you can't...........

　　It was all about the time I got worked up over everything — sort of seized up inside. Was never the same after that. I just couldn't go on pretending I wanted him anymore, not to go with — you know what I mean! — like in the old days. Got so I couldn't have cared less if he hadn't come home at all. Always drunk, anyway, breathing his filthy breath all over me in bed. That's what hurt most. 'Cos I knew where he'd bin and who he'd bin with, and it hurt like hell that he didn't want *me* anymore. I kinda lost touch with everything. Went all numb and cold inside..............

Eddie

　　Just our flippin' luck to get rain. Comin' down in buckets, it is. Do you know, it's so blinkin' dark, the lights are full on in the shops and the houses. 'S like mid-bloody-winter, it is really. You can hear the swish-swish-swishing of the puddles under the tyres. Taint my idea of an 'oliday, not by a long chalk. Nowhere near like the time we went to Southend on the old *Golden Eagle* from Tower Bridge. We went right down the river, we did. Wapping, Greenwich, Woolwich, Tilbury — it was a real treat, I tell you. There was me and Ma, and me ole Dad and his pal, Alf, Oh! And there was Flo. Musta' bin the week before he 'ad his accident, it was, nigh-on nine year ago, or maybe a bit over. A real scorcher, it was. And me, well, I was just a nipper at the time. Dad was in a right good mood, laughing and joking about the old days, and Ma splitting her old sides thinking o' the things they used to say to each other. Talk about bringing the skelingtons out o' the ol' family cupboard!

O' course, Dad had to tell his tale about his old Auntie Moggie what 'ad the pony and trap so as she could fetch her own stuff from market, and how one day the old pony ran amuck in the middle of the stalls, knocked everything skew-ways, dragged the old jalopy up the street and tipped the old gel right bang-smack into a pile of sticky dates. Well, Ma shook like a great big jelly-fish and laughed till her eyes was red with tears. Yes, well! Them was the good old days — or so they say.............

Maybe they was. I dunno. Still, I'm not grumblin', not so as you'd notice. It would be nice to 'ave ole Ma back again, though, just so as she could lead off a bit at me, make me feel I was somebody, let me feel not so much on me lonesome, like.............

Anyway — now what the 'ell was I thinking about? Oh! — Yes! — you coulda baked a flipping cake on the deck that day we went to Southend. Poor Ma! Well, I tell you, she sweated like a sow in labour. There she was, wavin' her hanky about, which you'll admit, wasn't exactly the sensiblest thing to do, now was it? Puffing and blowing, she was, her being so fat an' all — fatter than old mother Baldock, I can tell you, and that's saying something. But somehow with Ma it was all over the place, not sort of fenced in where it should be, if you get me. You shoulda seen her in the Hall of Mirrors! Laugh! She nigh-on brought the roof down on top of us, what with her shakin' like a flippin' strawberry blancmange. He face was the right colour for it, that's for sure.............

What a day, though! Up and down the pier on the little old trains, round and round the Kursaal, me sucking peppermint rock and toffee-apples all day. Everything luverly, with the salty air blowing in your face — a real breeze off o' the old briny, it was, and the pong o' seaweed tickling your nose. When you got back to base, well, there was them stalls with piles and piles of little grey winkles you 'ad to wiggle out with a pin and souse 'em in vinegar. Then there was cockles and muscles — 'Ere! Eddie, me ol' cock! Stop worryin' so much about Curly and concentrate! You mean mussels, old son! Well, yes! And don't forget the shrimps.........

One day, me and Dad went off to Margate with our shrimping-nets. Ma stayed for a kip on the beach. Well, we just thought we'd give her a bit of a surprise for tea, see? Anyway, we got well on a pint o' the little blighters. We knew you 'ad to boil 'em so we got the old primus-stove and boiled 'em up. There was such a stinko that it woke Ma up. Not only that! The whole lot of the little sods had turned a sort of 'orrible brown colour. When I saw 'em, I started to blub like billy-ho. Well! Ma thought we'd gone barmy or something. She started 'ollerin' something awful, I can tell you. Called Dad I dunno what, and as for me, well — better not think about it, eh? What with the heat, she couldn't take no more larking about. So up gets me Dad and chucks the whole blinkin' lot back in the briny, primus-stove and all! That set Ma off yelling a few four-letter words and everybody coming round us to have a dekko at where the old stove sank. And you know what it's like when you're bawled at from close up, don't you? I mean, you can't hear a bleedin' thing that's bin said. Well, it was like that with Ma. And all the time she was goin' on about Dad being a right charley for not putting salt in with the little so-and-so's to keep 'em pink! Well! I mean to say! Fancy puttin' salt in with 'em when they must be full of salt already. A rare old shemozzle, it was, and Dad swearing it'd be the last time he'd ever go out with us again. And it was, too!........

Makes me think of her going off at me in the ward up at the 'ospital. Leadin' on at me like she never had nothing to do with bringing me into the world. As good as sayin' I hadn't got a father to me name. Like Millie's kid'll have no father to give it a name. I wish it'd bin me, that's all I can say..................

Millie

This is crazy, I know. I can't never stop thinking about my Curly. There's times when I hate him for what he done — going off and leaving me like that. It aint natural. Trust me to get taken in by his big ways, and him throwing himself around like a king-pin, talkin' big to everybody. I hate him, I tell you! I hate him, I do...........yes, I do, but.........

Oh, need him so bad. I want 'im that much it hurts. I need 'im to put his big arms round me and hold me tight. I want to feel his hands feeling me all over. I want him to kiss me, like the time I run away from the bomb-site like a scared rabbit. But I hadn't never made love before. He was so— you know what I mean —animal! I let him do things to me I never knew about before, but I wanted then, I can tell you. I felt like I was melting...........

Sometimes I lie awake in bed at night, all numb with wanting him, just waiting and waiting for him to come to me and hold me

298

and........and............

Then, when I wake up in the morning, I start hating him all over again. I hate him so much I could die.............

Then I feel something move inside me. Something ever so lightly moving, calling out to me, calling right up through my inside till it touches my heart and forces its way up and catches in my throat, and I feel faint and start to cry. And then, oh, yes, then, I want him so much. I just go on wanting and wanting till it hurts to want any more...............

And all I have left now? His kid and a diamond ring. That ring never leaves me. I wear it night and day. Sometimes I just sit and stare at it for hours and hours it seems. Watch it sparkling. Try to see things in it — a place, a face, perhaps. All the colours of the rainbow, when you turn it in the light. But then, that's how I feel about Curly and nothing 'll ever change that — 'cos I love my Curly.............

Alf

When I was a kid, no older 'n our Ron, we used to get up by Bushy Walk for a lark or two with the courtin' couples. We made a sort of den right in the middle of the bushes. We did it by clearing out all the old brambles and brushwood. Made a nice little hide-out where we could go for a quiet smoke. One afternoon — it was quite late — most people had gone home to supper — a courtin' couple came and sat on the bench right opposite us — young American army officer and one of our local wenches. Before long, he had his hand up her blouse, then up her skirt, and then – blimey! – in less than two shakes of a ram's tail, he was on top of her and going at her like there was no tomorrow. But there was a tomorrow, and a next day, and a next — sometimes different couples. In fact, we realised we had got quite a little show going for ourselves. We started charging for the 'entertainment'—tuppence a time the going rate. Practically the whole of our class had a dekko, sometimes two or three times. I can tell you, we learnt a thing or to that wasn't in our school books! No wonder I know how to please a woman, not that Flo cares much about it. Anyways, we made quite a little nest-egg in them days........

Now, why should that bring old Ma to mind, I wonder? Why her and not Flo? Maybe it's not so queer as you might think. I mean, Ma was Ma and Flo was Flo, the way I see it. Not that I can really talk of 'em in the same breath, mind you.............

Never 'ad much time for each other, they didn't. If it hadn't

299

'ave bin for old Jacko, I dare say they wouldn't have ever spoke from one year to the next. Oh, yes! I know Flo had a real soft spot for Jack. Used to think Ma was treating him something rotten. That's it, you see? Flo has a heart of her own, in her own sort of way, and so had Ma in her way too, but boy, they was different...........

Now Jack Carpenter, he was a real good sort o' chap. I can see a lot of him in young Eddie. Did his level best to give old Ma all the knick-knacks she wanted. Never mind that she never said as much as a thank-you to 'im, just 'cos he was Jack and no other reason............

Jack got on just fine in the market, what with his tips and his extras of a Christmas time, and never kept a cent to 'imself. As thick as anything with ol' Garville. They was like peas in a pod. Always talking together about something or other..........

Yes, got on fine all right, until — well — he got 'isself done in. We was real pals we was, and old Dandy Crawford was never yellin' and ollerin' about the place in them days. No! We worked like a team — and no stinginess about it, neither. I used to like the early mornings, too — going over the coffee-stall when we'd done with everything, just for a natter and a steaming mug of hot tea. Then came the day I'm thinking about and can't never forget, neither.............

You see, there was this-'ere bloody great girder come swinging down on a bloody great crane— and before you could see what was happening, Jacko was under it. Oh, Christ! There he was, staring up at it, swinging across over the sheds, and us just standing there, craning our necks to see it go, when — Oh! God help me!—in seconds, it was crashing down on top of us. I pushed Jacko out of the way. You see, I thought he was going to be clobbered, good and proper. Instead of that, the girder—Oh, Christ Almighty!—this bloody great girder crushed him. His legs all buckled up in knots. He yelled out like all the agony of the world was running through his bones—I tell you I can't never forget it. Never!—he was—it was horrible—so—horrible!—he was---sort of severed across the groin. And all the time, him yelling and screaming. I tell you, I won't never forget it. I won't. Never! I just had to stand there, helpless — useless — bloody useless. Like I was paralysed. I could see he'd had it, poor old bugger! He just had to go on yellin' at me and I had to just go on starin' at him — on and on starin' at him till I thought I'd go crazy...........

They said I'd killed him. Me! Alf Thompson! And the best friend Jack Carpenter ever had. They said I'd killed him. They said it was me what pushed him under! Christ! How was I to know, eh? They said he'd 'a' bin alive now if I hadn't pushed 'im. But how was I to know? I ask you! How was I to know I was killing him? You can't help doing what you do when it's got to be done — when it's an emergency like, now can you?.............

Old Police-Sergeant Paxton was on the case. If it hadn't been for him, well— I don't know where I should have bin — doing a stretch, most likely. He had brought little Louise to see the market. How she screamed! I can hear her now, sometimes. Just a pretty little girl screaming in front of all that blood. Screamed and screamed and screamed, she did! Nobody could stop her. She was carted off to the 'ospital and given a jab to keep her quiet. Must have bin a shock to 'er, for she never did speak a single word again. They never found out what happened to her, but she's grown into a beautiful young lady now........only she's never said a word from that day to this.......

At the inquest, I went all to pieces and couldn't give my evidence at first. I knew then what it was not to be able to find the words. Then I had to be brought home. Flo was out, so Paxton took me to his place. I remember he had quite a problem calming little Louise, and Dr. Glendale had to be called. All the time, my head was full of wailing and screaming and the sight of Jacko's blood running into the gutter, and the sight of Jacko lying there all twisted up and horrible, his face long and drawn like, drained so yellow you could see the black stubble on his chin like coal-dust. His eyes deep inside his head, sunken like, staring at me, his lips moving senselessly as if he was trying to say something, but no words came and I'll never know what he wanted to say to me now. All that blood, trickling down the gutter — Jacko's blood I helped to spill. That's why I can't never go round Paxton's place no more. I can't stand them red roses no more— nagging at me like the red blood of Jacko Carpenter..............

That's all I hear from morning till night — screaming, all the time — Jacko screaming, little Louise screaming. Then I come home to Flo hollerin', Mabel bawlin', screaming their guts out with it all, and there's me, in the middle, wanting to get the 'ell out of it, just for a bit of peace and quiet up at *The Bed of Roses*..............

One of these days, though, I'll have a word with our Ronnie...... find out how his lessons is goin' on. P'raps go down to 'ave a chin-wag with his teacher. And do you know what? Maybe I'll take Flo out for a fling some place. Get her singing a song or two like she done in the old days.............

Hey! Alfie-boy! What's this, eh? Feeling the old thirst coming

301

on, are we? Here we go! Good 'ealth! Alfie-boy!........ Ah! Perfick!..............
    I think I'll have a kip now............P'raps I'll......Oh, well........ Wake me up at opening-time! ....

Flo

    Funny how you go through life meeting up with people, aint it? I mean, maybe you don't know 'em at all from Adam. Maybe you'll never speak to 'em again. May be you brush up against 'em in the street and they knock your basket out of your hand and you're five minutes late because of it — and maybe those five minutes is all the world to you. Yet everybody goes on their own sweet way as if nothing had happened. So do you, except you're five minutes late and you get the sack or miss a bus that crashes with a lorry and half-a-dozen passengers are killed. Or maybe by being late you make somebody late, which makes them late and so on..........

    Well! You know, if my basket hadn't been knocked out of my hand, I might never have met Alf. I was late for work, see? He stopped to help me pick up the potatoes rolling all over the pavement. Getting under people's feet, they was. You see, Alf might never have stopped if I hadn't bin in a hurry to get home and he hadn't knocked my basket flying. Just goes to show, don't it? If I hadn't met him, I might never have had kids like Ron and Millie to look after, kids as plague you till you could scream. What's more, I might never have had to sit at home of an evening waiting for Alf to come. I might have been waiting for Jack Carpenter, maybe. I might have had a nice lad like Eddie for a son. He's grown into such a 'andsome lad, he has. No thanks to Ma, neither, the way she treated 'im. He'd be a credit to any mother, he would. Look at the way he come round and decorated our living-room after the fire. No end of time and trouble he took. Maybe it's because he's always had a soft spot for Mabel. Well! There's no surprise in that!..........

    However much Eddie did to put things right, he couldn't never bring back the photo of my Alf. I'll just have to get used to the idea of seeing him just as he is. Imagine the lovely young man he was. I'd like to know, though, does he still love me just a little? It aint easy when you're looking for the answer in a dream-book........

60. Under a Cloud!

Now the coach is passing that auspicious stone pillar on the London-to-Brighton road, announcing:

WELCOME TO BRIGHTON

Like the ancient heroes of old, our time-travellers have navigated the dangers of Scylla and Charybdis reasonably unscathed and have yet to discover what life holds for them on this fateful August Bank Holiday. As the intrepid band of hopefuls approach the sea, the winds whirl and swirl through the little streets of old Brighton town. The rain beats against the windows of the coach with such ferocity that the travellers shrink into their seats. A flash of lightning and a rumble of thunder greet them as they make their way down towards The Steine. Wild rivers of rain rush down the roadsides into bubbling drains. Whatever assaults this little band of lost souls had hoped to make on the pleasures of some or all of the Seven Deadly Sins that Brighton might offer them, it was a dead certainty that the spirits of our wanderers in this paradigm of Limbo would be considerably dampened, if not drowned, by the force of the storm.

Rudely awakened to the harsh reality that will face them in the hours to come, one by one, the weary passengers emerge from their day-dreams and slumbers, their musings and their meanderings. Gulpings, yawnings, sighings and snortings show that there is some semblance of life coming back to them as they crouch down behind the steamy windows of their labouring vehicle. Almost to a man, they wish they could put back the clock and find themselves once more at home, beside their own cosy firesides on this, the coldest of summer days.

As they rub the condensation from the windows of the coach and stare at the deserted streets, they see that there is no way out but forward and no way forward but straight into the eye of the storm. Now their mysterious author has given them the means to express their feelings in words, they must break free in their own way, and face the consequences of their actions.......

"Grandpa!"

"Yes, Ronnie, my lad."

"When I get to Brighton I'm going to paint you."

Mr. Lawton laughed a wheezy laugh and said:

"Like painting the town red, I suppose. Are you going to paint me black or a pale shade of grey, depending on which side of the bed I happened to get out of in this morning?"

Ron could not understand Grandpa ever being anything but the purest white as far as he was concerned, and said with passion:

"Oh, no! Grandpa! I'm going to paint you all the colours of the rainbow."

Ron could not see why the remark should be so amusing but it sent the old man into a series of coughings and splutterings and chucklings that were quite incomprehensible. At first his face was drawn, and bore a look of irritation. Then he smiled through his yellowing teeth, then opened his mouth wide and laughed and laughed. They were both laughing heartily as the coach drew slowly in to rain-sodden Brighton, laughing so much that Ron was jumping about in his seat with it all and Grandpa was shaking with delight. Taken all in all, they were the happiest couple in the coach.

"Where are we now, Grandad?"

"Just coming into the Old Steine, so you'd better be getting your tackle together else we shall be last off the coach, and you don't want that, do you?"

Ron jumped up on his seat and collected his bundle of swimming costume, towel, paints and picnic.

"Where shall we go?" he asked eagerly. "I mean, are there any rocks and things?"

"Not here, Ron. You can go to Black Rock, if you like. Plenty of rocks and cliffs up that way. We can take Mr. Volk's little railway if you want. Afterwards we can come back to the West Pier. The beach is nice and clean there and you can take a canoe out if the wind drops. We're going to have to shelter for a bit until this storm passes over, if it ever does."

As the coach turned down to the parking bays beyond the Aquarium, a freak storm exploded in the skies, deluging the whole town. Forked lightning streaked across the darkened horizon in blinding flashes and seemed to do a power-dive into the surging sea, only to be followed by a frightening clap of thunder right over the coach, that all but burst everybody's ear-drums. Then, more rumblings and grumblings over the sea. Gigantic waves lashed the promenade, stretching out like heavy-fingered hands to grasp the stoic tripper and soak him to the skin, pouring rain and scorn on mackintosh and umbrella. To many, this storm seemed as if it might be a sign of things to come.

Miss Baldock was beyond the limits of her patience. Twice on the road down, the coach had been forced to stop to allow a screaming Mabel to be taken behind a bush! Countless were the times the dear lady had been disturbed in her reveries by Mabel bang-bang-banging that wretched spade and pail in her ear. Happily, the child had refrained from bawling into deafness anyone within earshot of five feet, but now, if you please, she had begun to screech and scream with all the power her little lungs could muster as if to set up some opposition to the natural clash of celestial forces above the coach.

Things were made worse by everyone deciding to stay put until the rain stopped, if it ever did take it into its mind to pity the poor passengers in their hot and steamy mobile shelter. It seemed perfectly clear to Miss Baldock that they had all come down from London simply to sit about in a stuffy old bus, breathing germs over one another and staring helplessly at the belligerent sea. It would not be long before they all had to set off to London again. Well, not for anybody, ever again, was Agnes Baldock going to repeat the experience.

Sitting like this at such close quarters with a coach-load of rowdy tradesmen was not Agnes's idea of fun. Gabriel must be out of his mind. As for the rest, well — the rain would give them all a jolly good bath. They certainly needed it.

Nobody was prepared to leave the safety of the coach in the circumstances. They preferred to remain where they were — in the stifling, sweaty atmosphere to which by now they had become accustomed. No-one dared brave the storm and risk an attack of bronchitis or pneumonia. Even if the Vicar did choose to love the English climate till he died, she, Agnes Baldock, did not intend to follow him to a cold grave without a fight. Practicalities prevailed, however, since the driver announced in no uncertain terms that he had to lock the coach up for the day and if they didn't get up off their bloody backsides and evacuate the vehicle he would bloody-well drive back to the smoke without them! So our reluctant trippers fumbled, bumbled and grumbled and finally tumbled out into the wind and the rain.

When they looked round for the good-looking stranger, he had disappeared into thin air.

"Well I never!" said Flo. "I wouldn't like to meet *him* on a dark night. That's for sure!"

"No such luck, dearie!" said Effie sadly.

305

61. Tim Comes to Terms

Louise thrust herself forward into the gale and set off in the direction of the Palace Pier. The sight of the gloomy reflections in the pavements dampened her spirits. As she reached the Pier, she stopped in the shelter of a large bill-board announcing the 'Mystery' coach tours for the afternoon, but other more pressing thoughts beset her.

The promenade stretched out in bleak desolation, disappearing in great sprays of spume along towards Hove. Rivulets of rain pursued a hurried course along the gutters and went bubbling into over-filled drains. The waves dashed against the blue-painted railings, throwing wads of green-black sea-weed smack onto the flesh-coloured pavements. Out at sea, could be seen the white sail of a small dinghy, swinging from side to side, prow riding the waves. Louise watched it thoughtfully, and wondered and hoped.

After a time, she stepped out into the wind again and, finding it too fierce, she crossed over into the narrow alleys of the Lanes, still as yet deserted, and wandered in and out of the antique shops stuffed with bric-à-brac and curios of all kinds. Clearly imprinted on her mind was the image of a white sail in swirling grey seas. She discovered Zetland's Tea-shop, where she sat in sheltered ease, hardly touching her hot chocolate, thinking about how her life had changed since she had met Timothy, and remembering with some apprehension that, in a few weeks from now, she would be facing her throat operation at Guy's Hospital. She finished her coffee, paid her bill, and stepped out into East Street, which, although the time was only eleven-thirty on an August morning, displayed bright lights in every window, making everything glow with a kind of Christmas-like festivity that depressed her even more. She decided that a seat in one of those glass shelters that punctuate the promenade was far more preferable and, once settled in a corner, gave reign to her thoughts amidst the loneliness that gripped her heart till it hurt.

Louise was suddenly aware of a stir of voices, a cry from somewhere across the waves, though this could have only been in her imagination for the noise of the storm was considerable. Perhaps it was some sixth sense that told her that a drama was taking place that would affect the future pattern of her life forever.

Out at sea, only a few hundred yards or so from the rusty iron girders of the pier, a white sail emerged from the waves only to be swept up again amid the angry foam. Everyone's attention was now on the dinghy, being lifted up like an empty matchbox by the surging waves, only to disappear beneath the foam. In one last thrust, the vessel was thrown against the iron struts of the pier, crunched against it and disappeared again into the void below the waves. She knew that the storm-tossed seas were taking their toll, but she hoped and prayed that it should not be Timothy. A crowd gathered from nowhere, faces grimly set under the rain, silently turned towards the sinking craft.

She pointed to the dinghy as it writhed in the waters, with the solitary figure clinging to its hull, but the onlookers could only stare blankly back at her and shrug their shoulders.

Seconds passed like hours. Louise ran along the Promenade and crossed over to King's Parade in search of help. Unthinkingly, she flung open the door of a red telephone box, snatched up the receiver and dialled emergency services.

A disembodied voice answered from outer space:

"Which service please?"

Louise sought vainly to utter some sound as meaningful as she could make it, but her efforts were undecipherable and futile. Tears ran down her cheeks at the thought that she might lose the one person in the world who had shown her a glimpse of the primrose path of happiness.

"Hallo! Hallo! Are you there? Which service do you require?" came the voice again.

Dropping the receiver, she dashed into the street, falling straight into the arms of a smallish man and a plumpish woman. They spluttered with the shock of it.

"Where do you think you are going, young lady?" said the man gruffly. "I tell you, Cynthie! These young people! Really! They ought to be taught a few manners. I don't know what the country's coming to. Bumping into people like that ----," and then shouted into Louise's face: "Why don't you look where you're going?"

His mouth opened like a cod-fish as he saw the girl struggling with his wife, pulling at her arm, dragging her towards the telephone kiosk.

"Why, bless my soul! If it isn't Miss Paxton!"

Louise clutched at his arm, leaving the quivering Cynthia to recover of her own accord.

"Anything the matter?" said the little man, face twisting up into an unpleasant leer. "Why, look, Cynthie, she's crying. Now fancy that. Now, whatever would a nice young girl be crying for on an August Bank Holiday Monday, eh?"

Louise pointed at the sea, then at the crowd, then at the telephone, then at the sea again. In her face could be read so much love, so much fear. Her thoughts raced round in her head in the turmoil.

"Cynthie! Look! Must be an accident. Let's go and look."

He made to cross the road to join the crowd but Louise forced him back in her frenzy until he fell against the telephone kiosk. Weeping helplessly, she picked up the receiver again.

"Which service, please? Emergency Service. Hullo! Are you there?"

The little man, now in the clutches of what he thought to be a mad-woman, stuttered into the mouthpiece:

"I — er — excuse me — I — oh dear!"

"Hullo! Are you there?"

"Look here! There's a bit of a crisis down here. Girl — gone barmy, by the looks of it. Keeps pointing out to sea. Promenade — big crowd! Now, would you like to have my name for the newspapers?"

"Is the girl connected with the sailing-boat stranded beyond the pier, sir?" said the disembodied voice. "If so, help is on the way."

"Sailing-boat! Stranded! Where? Where?" he said, twisting up with the drama of it all. "Young man? Capsized boat? How thrilling! Fancy that, Cynthie! Boat sinking!"

Louise gripped his wrist till he winced and his little eyes almost popped out over his *pince-nez*.

"Ooh! You wicked girl! You're hurting my arm. Let go, I say."

Louise put her head in her hands and seemed to groan — a strange sound that came out of nowhere — a long seemingly never-ending utterance from deep inside her — a sound that was so distinct from any sound they had ever heard sent a disturbing shudder through the motionless Frank and Cynthia as they stood staring out to sea. They could not realise that they had inadvertently been present at a remarkable event — the beginnings of speech where speech had been denied for so long. Through some inexplicable power, amidst the emotion and terror of the drama, Louise had been granted a God-given chance to retrieve something of the world she had once known and so tragically lost. In her desperation, she thrust the little man from her and ran wildly away.

"There's gratitude for you, Cynthie," he said, brushing himself down. "They're not normal like the rest of us, these people."

Unaware that something momentous had happened, Louise gripped the blue-painted railings and stared out at the merciless rising and falling of the waves. Tim's face was just visible as the boat rolled over in the waves. He seemed to flounder. As Louise watched, so she prayed, urgently, passionately.

Suddenly, through all the noise of nature, she heard the first faint whirrings, increasing to a deafening roar, of a helicopter swooping down out of the clouds. For Louise, there was hope now in that grim grey morning. Nearby, stood a man dressed in tweeds, next to a slightly-built woman, her hand clasped tight in his. Louise came forward, anxiously gripping the rail. The woman heard the strange yearning voice from within and placed her hand on Louise's arm reassuringly.

"Thank God! Thank God!" exclaimed the woman, as the solitary figure was lifted out of the swirling waters and gently lowered onto the beach. Ambulance orderlies moved forward. Louise wanted to cry out with the relief of it all. Looking at the woman standing next to her, she realised with some surprise that she was not the only one with tears in her eyes.

As Timothy, wrapped in blankets, was carried up the beach on a stretcher, Mrs. Crawford moved forward and kissed him, holding him for a moment, grateful for his safe return to her. Facing his father for the first time since that fatal day in the market, Timothy found there were no words to express his feelings, confused as they were with remorse and guilt. Andrew Crawford, whose affections for his son normally extended to no more than the occasional handshake, now leaned over and held his son's hands in his with renewed affection.

Some hours later, when Timothy had been discharged from hospital, the family was once more reunited in the lounge of the Old Ship Hotel, where Mrs. Crawford had been staying while visiting her husband at the nursing home. She poured the tea and handed round the toasted tea-cakes.

"Dad! It's good to see you. Really good!" They stared at each other for a moment, deep in their thoughts. "I'm sorry, Dad. So sorry. I hurt you, I know. I was selfish about leaving home."

For a moment, Andrew Crawford was silent, searching for something appropriate to say. Words did not come easily to a man of his taciturn temperament.

"That's all right, my boy. You did what you thought best."

Timothy, like his father, had been so close to death. The experience served now as an unshakeable bond between them.

"Thoughts raced through my mind out there in the water," said Timothy after a long silence. "Everything seemed so clear to me

309

suddenly. I realised that maybe life would have been different for us all if I hadn't left home. Maybe —"

"Don't think about it, son. It's old history now."

"I've made a decision, Dad. I want to come back," said Timothy. "I don't want you to have to sell up the farm. You never liked the idea of retiring, did you? At your age, with years of farming behind you. What would you do stuck in a rest home in Weston-super-Mare, or in a bungalow in Peacehaven, far from the things you love best. You'd hate every moment of it— away from the old house, the cattle, the fields. If I come home you can retire just the same, if and when you want to. Mother wouldn't be happy anywhere else either. She knows every inch of the place. She'd be miserable if she didn't get a chance to grumble about all the jam-making and the cooking and the preserving — and someone special to worry about!"

As he spoke, Louise came through the swing doors and stood looking round the foyer. She was radiantly happy, and now that she had combed the gale out of her beautiful fair hair, she looked charm itself. She caught sight of them and smiled.

"But, I'm telling you," said Timothy to his father, " I shall not be coming home alone."

He stood up, put his arms round Louise and kissed her. They stood holding each other for a time, and then Timothy turned and said:

"Mother! Father! This is Louise. I'm going to marry her — that is, if she'll have me!"

Of course there was a great deal of kissing all round and a bottle of champagne was ordered. As Timothy was speaking softly to his mother and father, united now by this drama, Louise realised that something immensely important had transpired for all of them.

Timothy raised his glass by way of a toast: "To all our new beginnings!" he said.

With that, the young couple of tomorrow bade the old couple of yesterday farewell, leaving them to sort out their new world for themselves.

Timothy and Louise left the hotel and made their way towards the West Pier. The pale shadow of the moon began to appear in the deepening blue of the sky to the west, and Timothy, strolling along with his arm round Louise, fancied he could glimpse the first faint sparkle of the evening star. As they made their way to the end of the pier they heard the orchestra playing *Love is the Sweetest Thing,* a song which held a memory of happier days for his mother and father. Now, as he

310

and Louise gazed out to sea and heard the waves lapping gently against the pier, this treasured moment of music under moon and star seemed to symbolise for them both the realisation of a dream.

62. Casting Off a Councillor

Agnes Baldock was in no mood for jocularity. She glowered over her shandy with such a hotness of temper that the froth might well have evaporated but for the Councillor's conciliatory coolness. His calm obeisance brought to mind the lamb on its way to the slaughter-house, except that this was the *Irish House*.

Neither Agnes nor Gabriel was sure who was going to fire the fatal shot. Her intuition was just feminine enough for her to sense something was afoot. Agnes eyed the Councillor with something of an air of distrust and watched him gulping nervously at his whisky-and-soda. Regret filled her up to the very brim — regret that she had ever thought of coming on the outing to Brighton in the first place, regret that Gabriel had nothing whatsoever to do with her own private dream of marital bliss, regret that the sun was not disposed to shine upon her hopes for a secure future side-by-side with the proud messenger and promoter of public morals. She had the discomforting feeling that before long she was going to be tried and tested in some brutal way and that the force of that assault would be deadly to her self-esteem.

"I'm hungry," she announced emphatically.

They rose and made their way through the crowds of laughing, chattering trippers streaming down East Street. The rain had stopped, the wind had dropped, and the pavements gleamed in the dull grey light, enough encouragement to the scores of optimistic holiday-makers to emerge from hotels and guest-houses to fill up the bars, cafés and public houses. Everywhere there was an air of expectancy which annoyed Agnes the more. She scowled at queue after queue of eager rivals in search of lunch. The crowds, with their laughter and high spirits, made her as sour as an unripe lemon.

"You see! I told you so!" she said. "All you think about is pub-crawling. You just had to go and sit in that filthy hole with all those scruffy-looking layabouts, and this is what happens. We're forced to go without lunch. Not a table to be found at any price."

It seemed that, while Gabriel Purvis was indulging in pre-lunch drinks in that brief moment between noon and one-o'-clock, the whole of the population of London had flooded the Brighton streets and, together with the whole of Brighton, had deluged forth in their hundreds and thousands from countless cars, buses and coaches.

Miss Baldock grew steadily more acidulated as restaurant after restaurant dispelled any hope of ever getting anywhere near a table. In and out they went until the Councillor was almost loth to go up to a single head-waiter more, lest Agnes should make a public spectacle of them both. He watched his beloved's lips purse into a thin line of anger and frustration. If only her mouth would stay shut, Gabriel thought, I might have a bit of peace, and besides, talking to her about things would be easier.

After an hour, they arrived exhausted and irritable in the bright lights of East Street once more and ended up queueing with a group of bedraggled trippers outside Fuller's Tea-shop. When they did get a table and fiddled about with a prawn salad for half-an-hour they spoke not a word to each other. Agnes, for a moment at least, was beginning to relent, thawed out a little by the warmth of the coffee she was silently sipping. Her defiant mood was strengthened by the appearance of a large slice of Fuller's walnut cake with lashings of soft white icing. A strange tug-of-war was going on inside her. Her intuitive sense of doom made her set up her defences, yet at the same time had dampened her spirits.

"Well," mumbled the Councillor out of a blue gloom, "we're not all perfect."

"And what is *that* supposed to mean, I'd like to know," snapped Agnes.

The Councillor jumped. He had been thinking aloud. Agnes for her part wished she had not said anything at all.

"I mean, Agnes, we can all make mistakes."

"Mistakes?" queried Agnes. Her heart flipped over like a pancake.

"We can't help regretting things."

"Things? What things?" Then, with more sarcasm: "For instance?"

"Saying things, Agnes. Doing things that come back at you later and make you feel bad."

Her stomach rolled over and lay down with a thud. She hadn't expected the tables to be turned on her quite so brutally. All the way

312

down from London, Gabriel had seemed to expire slowly and resignedly, like a punctured tyre. Now, here, his spirit had gone out of him altogether.

"*That* doesn't sound like you, Gabriel," she said, attempting to infuse a note of scorn into her voice.

"It could happen to anyone, Agnes," he sighed. "The higher the flier the heavier the fall. And it hurts. Maybe it kills everything in you. Everything you ever stood for. It shrivels up and dies, Agnes, and you can't recognise yourself anymore."

"If you're going to go on about the problems of old age, Gabriel, this is not the place or the time. Really! What you need is a pep pill. Indulging in this revolting self-pity will get you nowhere with me. A man of your age! Really!"

"My age?" he said, looking up at her, frowning, not understanding. Then he turned to gaze out on the crowded street. The laughter and chatter of young holiday-makers filled him with a sense of foreboding. Councillor Joseph Gabriel Purvis suddenly, for the first time in his life, felt the pangs of loneliness and futility and knew that not all the Agnes's in the world could make things better. In fact, it looked as if things were going to get worse if he was to tell Agnes everything. He gave a deep sigh and gazed at her apprehensively.

"Agnes!" he said. "I've something to tell you."

Her bosom inflated like an angry hen's.

"Oh?" she said, roundly expectant.

"I can't marry you, Agnes."

She sagged like a couple of pricked balloons, and said, after a pause:

"I see! So that's it, is it? Can't marry me, indeed. *And* why not?"

His wrinkled hand ran through his white wispy hair. She would force him into a confession sooner or later.

"You can't marry me," she said, raising her voice to a quasi-fog-horn level: "You can't marry me. Well! May I remind you that the law will have something to say about *that*! A proposal of marriage isn't something you can get out of so easily, you know. Oh, no! It is not as simple as you think, Gabriel."

"It's no use, Agnes. We can't get married and there's an end to it. You'd never live down the scandal."

"Scandal?"

Miss Baldock seemed to levitate from her chair. "What

313

scandal?"

"I'm in trouble, Agnes. Something terrible has happened. I tell you, it is impossible. You can't marry me."

"Oh, I see! Now it's supposed to be *me* marrying *you*, is it? And why not? Why? Tell me that."

"Agnes! You're not going to like this at all. You see, there's been trouble over Millie Thompson. She's having a baby."

"Oh, Gabriel, we know that. The whole of Rothersey knows it. I fail to see what Millie Thompson's baby has to do with you, I do, really."

Councillor Purvis screwed up his nose into his eyes and wiped a crumpled handkerchief over his forehead.

"Look, Agnes!" he said quietly. "I don't have to go into details, do I? The police insist — "

"The police!" she gasped.

"Agnes! Don't keep repeating what I say. It's difficult enough to tell you as it is. Now, as I was telling you before you interrupted me, the police have insisted on my giving evidence in the Polenti case. I shall have to tell them everything."

"Everything?" she said, with an admixture of horror and curiosity. "But the case has nothing to do with you."

"It has everything to do with me. I was blackmailed, Agnes. Blackmailed, don't you see? You remember Donoghue, don't you? Well, he tried to get money out of me over Millie Thompson. The police planted a trap but he got away. Now, they're bringing the case against Polenti. Of course, he will be sentenced and the case will be closed in the hope that Donoghue will make an appearance, break cover again, if you like, when he thinks it's safe enough. Anyway, what I've been trying to say is — it'll all be in the papers."

Miss Baldock blenched and sat up, rigid in her chair with a constipated intensity, like a tortured figure in marble. All the air she had expired only a moment ago she now breathed back in a long swishing sound that told the Councillor that the lady was not pleased. Indeed, it was very likely that an explosion would shatter his world in a matter of seconds.

"In the papers?" she muttered with a remarkably restrained whisper. "You, Gabriel, in the papers!? You and that — that — harlot? That common little painted prostitute? And all this under my very nose. And you dare to ask me to marry you when you have got that nasty little whore with child? Why, you — you — you pig!"

314

The Councillor could never have believed Agnes to be so expressive in her use of English if he had not heard it with his own ears, as indeed had the whole restaurant!

"You pig! You pig!" she said again, rising to her full height now, in a frenzy of indignation.

Silence was everywhere pregnant with curiosity.

"You pig!" she hissed again, and then, her eyes closing up inside her head, her mouth creasing up into a thousand little lines of contempt, she said it again and again and again, louder and louder and louder:

"You pig! You pig! YOU PIG! **YOU PIG!"**

Miss Baldock succeeded in reducing the whole of our vast English vocabulary into one little three-letter word.

She strode out into the street, knocking a coat-stand over on her way. Two harmless silver-haired old ladies disappeared quite suddenly beneath its array of wet rain-coats and mackintoshes.

By the time Mr. Purvis had recovered enough to follow his beloved with an apology on his lips — and the waitress had recovered enough to follow Mr. Purvis with the bill — Miss Baldock had merged into the throng of trippers and the Councillor saw nothing more of her until his return to the coach that evening.

EPISODE THIRTEEN

Later that afternoon

Through the Storm

63. Mystery Tour

The coach climbed steadily up the steep road to Race Hill and cruised slowly along the ridge of the Downs on its way towards Falmer. Far below lay the endless grey expanse of sea and to the west lay the sprawling lines of houses, shops and squares that go to make up the town of Brighton, partially enveloped now in a cloak of sea-mist.

Millie did not attempt to look at the scene, choosing rather to stare ahead, vacantly. Eddie longed to put his arm round her and hold her close to him. Instead, he sat stiffly in his seat, bouncing with the movement of the wheels, wanting very much to take her hand in his, never once daring to intrude upon that impregnable insularity with which Millie had encircled herself. Eddie felt nothing but anguish, a strange tightness in his chest, as if he were suffocating. Nothing seemed to matter anymore, nothing, that is, except the way he felt about Millie, and he could do no more about that than fly.

The road twined in and out of the Downs, sinking into coombes darkened with cloud, rising once more to smooth grassland on the hill-tops at Ditchling Beacon, everywhere grey and gloomy as far as the eye could see. The coach turned slowly down the steep winding hill in the direction of Hurstpierpoint. Not one of the silent passengers saw any beauty in the sombre landscape with its bluish-grey-to-mauvish fields, its curious silver light across the low sky, and that strange hint of pink and green above the horizon to the west, though no doubt a Monet or a Turner would have made something memorable of it. The sight of this view made Millie immensely sad. Eddie wished they had stayed down in the town and gone to the pictures.

"Right, you lot!" said the driver. "Off you get. Time for teapots! Come on! Wakey-wakey!" A motley group of what appeared to be sleep-walkers stumbled out of the coach and shuffled across the car-park towards the tea-room, deserted now but for a few early hikers stranded by the storm and hoping for a lift back into town.

Millie would have gone straight back into the coach if Eddie hadn't taken her by the arm and led her into the urn-smelling warmth of the tea-room. They chose a table by the radiator. Tea came in the form of a plump platinum blonde with dangling ear-rings, brassy bangle bracelets, and a badge pinned above her right bosom announcing

Try Our Friendly Waitress' Service

"Blimey!" said Eddie. "They give it to you here on a plate, that's for sure. I could do with a good service!"

"Eddie Carpenter!" Millie exclaimed. "Do you mind! That aint the way to speak to a girl. Just mind your p's and 'q's, if you please."

"Sorry!" said Eddie. "Just one of Curly's jokes."

"There's no need to bring him into the conversation, either."

"Conversation!?" said Eddie huskily. "Call this a conversation? A conversation's between two people. I might just as well be talking to myself most of the time I'm out with you."

Cups and saucers clattered onto the plastic table-cloth and the largest blue enamel teapot Eddie had ever seen swooped overhead and was tipped dangerously up and down, splashing tea on Eddie's shirt-front.

"'Ere!" he said to the blonde. "What *is* this? A blinkin' christenin'?"

She glared at him, raised one of her two sets of eye-brows and said, in a surprisingly small Cockney voice: "Is that supposed to be funny?"

Eddie stared in turn into the tea-cup, then at the glittering paste jewellery and, for want of anything better to say, blurted out:

"Dinin' at the Ritz tonight, are we?"

She seemed to have an irresistible urge to hit him over the head with her elephantine teapot. She lifted it threateningly, brandishing it almost, but all she said was:

"Do you mind!" and flounced off for a refill.

"Sugar?" said Eddie to Millie.

"O' course! You bin eatin' at our place for six months and you don't even know that." She sighed irritably and stared at the other tea-drinkers.

"Cor!" he exclaimed, almost at the end of his tether: "Sufferin' catfish! What with you and 'er over there with the tea-urn! Proper pair, you are!"

"Oh! You bore me!" Then after a long pause she said quietly: " Do you hear things about Curly, up the market, then?"

"What's it to you?"

"I'm just askin', that's all" she said testily.

"All right! So I do! Let's drop the subject, shall we?"

She began running her finger over her diamond solitaire, over and over again. Eddie knew it was no use telling her anything because she wasn't listening anymore. Just as suddenly she broke in with:

"Funny how things turn out, aint it? Him on the run — me at home, waiting. Taint fair somehow."

Although Eddie realised Millie was thinking aloud, he touched her arm with his fingers, lightly, but she drew away with a quick nervous little movement.

"Millie," said Eddie desperately. "You can't go on like this no longer. It aint natural. I mean, what's goin' to become of you, eh love? What about your Mum and Dad?"

"What about 'em?" she said bitterly, all the time stirring her tea.

"Now, Millie! That aint nice."

She shrugged her shoulders and pouted, gazing round the room at the trippers in their Bermuda shorts and garish flowery shirts.

"What a day out!" she said. "Whoever coulda thought of a *Mystery Tour* but you. In this weather! Here we are, stuck right up here in the back-o'-beyond. We could just as well 'ave had a nice cuppa in the town and gone to the flicks. Instead o' that, we're crawling about out here in the cold and the wet. What did you say this place was called?"

"I dunno, do I! A 'Mystery Tour' is supposed to be mysterious. They never tell you where you're going till you get there, see? Wouldn't be no point in it."

"Well, there would with me. If they'd told me, it would still have been a mystery to me. It's a bloody mystery why I ever come down here with you in the first place. I shoulda stayed at home and washed out me smalls."

"Oh! You make me sick. I don't know what's come over you, I don't really. Like a bear wiv a sore 'ead, you are."

"Well! You brought me 'ere, didn't you? It was your brilliant idea. There aint a day goes by without you nag-nag-naggin' at me for somethin', and I've just about 'ad enough of it."

"Oh!" said Eddie. "So it's *me* gettin' at *you*, is it? I like that, I must say. I don't know how your Mum and Dad put up with you, I don't really!"

"Look who's talking! Mr. High-and-Mighty!" said Millie rising to the argument. "It don't take long for you to come mincing over to Mum every time you want a bellyful o' grub."

"You're changing the subject. Blimey! You got your fighting-irons on, aint you? Anyways, I aint quibbling about — "

"Oh, yes, you are! You're gettin at me all the time and you know it. 'Millie, what's going to 'appen to you?' 'Millie, what are you goin' to do when the kid comes?'"

"I never said any o' them things."

"Well you meant to, so there. I can read you like a book, Eddie Carpenter. I know what your game is. Anyway, why should you care? It aint your kid, is it?"

Eddie was never so angry as when Millie said that, so angry that he could have struck her.

"I don't bloody-well care who the 'ell's it is. It might have had any of a dozen blokes for its father as far as I can see, old pervert Purvis an' all."

For an instant, Millie's face turned white. Then, with a quick movement, she brought her hand smacking across Eddie's face with such a force that it surprised both of them into silence. She crumpled up in fits of sobbing. Through her sobs he fancied he heard her mumble something like: "I'll never ever forgive you for that, Eddie Carpenter!" But he couldn't be sure. He just couldn't be sure of anything any more.

They sat together in silence for what seemed an eternity, not daring to look into each other's eyes, drowned in a kind of deep shame and humiliation. To Eddie, the table had become, in a matter of seconds, an impenetrable wasteland.

After a long time, he looked up. Millie was staring vacantly at the plastic table-cloth, her eyes moist, her cheeks stained like a child's, and something touched Eddie's heart.

If only he could smash the barrier that separated them, smash it for good and all. But the memory of Curly was inviolable. Millie sat numbly against the wall and Eddie was helpless to do anything about it.

64. Old Man on the Beach

The wind was so strong it nearly blew Grandpa Lawton away altogether. He thrust his old head into the gale and pursued a breathless course towards the Palace Pier.

Ron struggled along impatiently, laden with swimming costume, paint-boxes and brushes, and bags of liquorice allsorts and lemon sherbets. He didn't intend to miss a thing, even if the wind and the rain were spoiling the holiday for him. He dared the waves as they came surging up, rising in great fountains of spray and splashing down over the promenade in ice-cold lakes. He took his spade and lunged at them like a modern Don Quixote. And all the time, he watched Grandpa out of the corner of his eye, watched him totter like a bent and brittle twig in the storm, saw his old eyes water in the wind. Ron felt the strangeness of youth run through his limbs.

All the morning long, the holiday crowds roamed the town, creeping into shop-doorways, slithering over shingle beaches, or sitting hopefully in quiet cafés, awaiting the final fulfilment of the BBC weather reports — "bright periods" and "temperatures rising to the eighties"!

Gradually, the gale *did* drop, the rain-clouds *did* disperse, the temperature *did* go up, and by half-past one everyone was waiting for a miracle — a miracle which was loth to manifest itself, in spite of the Vicar of St. Crispin's prayers.

For a long span, everywhere seemed covered in a cloak of mourning that closed over everyone and smelled of dampness. Yet a quiet note of anticipation crept through every hotel lounge and every public bar.

By a quarter-to-two, the atmosphere was tense. By two o'clock, nerves were frayed and the heat increasing. Was the BBC weather man a reliable sort of chap? Or was it all a devious ploy to persuade listeners to stay tuned and increase the ratings.

Well, as almost always happens, things changed just when everybody was about to give up and go off to the pictures. Yes, it really happened. The clouds parted. The sun blazed through. Joy was in every heart. Every heart, that is, except one. The little man from Worthing was strolling along the promenade with his wife.

"There'll be fog tonight, Cynthie, mark my words! We won't be able to see our hands in front of us and we'll be stuck out in the middle of nowhere for the night."

But by-and-large, everybody was little less than optimistic.

"Turned up trumps, they have," said Mrs. Thompson cryptically.

"Who have?" said Alf.

"The BBC, of course."

Alf shrugged his shoulders. Anybody would have thought they'd laid it on of their own accord, the way Flo was going on. He couldn't see any "of course" about it. She was in a funny kind of mood, one way and another. He could feel it, as sure as he was holding a pint of bitter in his hand. There was something going on in that head of hers and he didn't like it at all.

Meanwhile, Grandpa Lawton, on reaching the haven of the Palace Pier, had a fit of dizziness and was compelled to rest for a few moments in the shelter of the ticket-collector's kiosk. Ron would have gone on all by himself for two pins — that is, he would have done if he hadn't wanted Grandpa all to himself today. So he sat down too. Then he jumped up. Then he sat down. And just as soon jumped up again, all impatient to taste the pleasures in store for him on the end of the pier, and finally Grandpa was cajoled into fishing around in his pockets for sixpences.

Ron sped forward like a greyhound. In no time at all, he had circuited the pier, and was running back, puffing excitedly, and with the almost incomprehensible wheezings of a long-distance runner, he poured out a flow of information about pin-ball games, fortune-tellers, weight-machines, candy-floss, jellied eels, boys fishing for dabs and crabs, shrimpers, stacks and stacks of Brighton Rock and toffee apples. "It's ripping, Grandpa!" Ron shouted. Then he charged off, bent again on further explorations, while Grandpa laughed and laughed. He had done it all before, so long ago. Long, long ago.

In the Hall of Mirrors, Ron had fits over the way Grandpa changed shape.

"Look at your knobbly knees and spindly ankles," he said, laughing for all he was worth. "And your big balloon of a belly! Your head is no bigger than a cricket ball."

"Well," said Grandpa, "if it comes to that, what about your inflated bottom and weedy little chest! As for your head and ears — well! — they're as big as an elephant's."

Ron laughed and laughed and laughed. He stuck his tongue out till it filled his face in the mirror and crept up over his nose and eyes. He put up his fingers and saw them go to pieces. He screwed up his eyes till he really began to look like that mangled corpse, the thought of which had frightened him so much when he crept into Grandpa's house all alone. The more faces he made, the more he lost his original gaiety.

"We look a sight for sore eyes, we do!" said Grandpa.

This remark rankled in Ron's mind. He stopped laughing and stared almost clinically at the two grotesque forms before him. Here was quite a different Grandpa Lawton. Here was a Grandpa Lawton he had never seen before, a Grandpa with a cricket-ball for a head. Ron didn't care for what he saw.

They came out into the gloom of a grey day that was supposed to be a gay day, an English Bank holiday in August. The wind had

323

dropped now. The clouds were rising in the sky. The air seemed almost sultry.

"Let's go to the beach," announced Ron sullenly.

Everywhere now there was blue sky with just here and there a patch of cloud, reluctant to leave, reminding our travellers that nothing is ever perfect. And yet, if you looked long enough, the imperfection of the cloud-studded sky took on a beauty all its own. The sun shone hotly on the exultant crowds, who now flung off their clammy clothes and plunged headlong into the icy 'briny', flinging their arms to the gods, shouting and singing for joy, and vastly pretending, like the ancient Greeks, that this must surely be the gift of Jupiter to his children, even though the silken couch and bowl of grapes had been usurped by the common deck-chair and a large portion of fish and chips!

Grandpa purchased a pint of shrimps, some bread, some light ale for himself, and a bottle of coke and a portion of chips for Ron. They made their way back along the promenade in the direction of the West Pier.

After his snack, Ron pushed off to watch the antics of Punch and Judy, resplendent in their many-coloured costumes, Punch magnificently sly, cruel, scheming, lying. There was something about it that disturbed him. It somehow cast a shadow over the day, haunting him for a while with dark thoughts of deceit and betrayal. Later, settled comfortably beneath the shade of a smart green-and-yellow boat, drawn up on the beach, Ron and Grandpa chatted over their picnic.

"I bet you didn't get shrimps like these in the South Seas, Grandpa."

"Oh, yes we did, my boy. Great big fellers, they were, too. Big as my fist. Great big pink fellers, swimming around on the bottom of the ocean."

"Shrimps can't swim, can they?" said Ron.

"Well," said Grandpa, irritably, "you know what I mean."

Ron stopped chewing. He looked at the shrimps and said:

"Eddie says shrimps are brown when you catch them. It's the salt when you boil them that turns them pink. That's what Eddie says."

Mr. Lawton shook convulsively.

"Well, there's some as are pink and some as are brown. It's in the nature of things."

"Why?" asked Ron.

"That's life. I mean, what kind of a world would it be if everything was the same? Pink or brown, it's all the same to the shrimps."

"I know," said Ron, wrestling with his thoughts. "But, it's not the same to me, Grandpa. If I was black, I wouldn't be the same, would I? Stands to reason, you've got to stick to the truth. I'm white and shrimps are pink."

"Who said you are white? There is no such thing as a white human being. You are as pink as a shrimp, Ron. And a black man isn't black either. Not in Jamaica, he's not. He's all shades of brown."

"But Grandpa! You was never in Jamaica. Why, you said you was in Australia."

"Of course I was in Australia. Jamaica, too. It's all the same."

"But Grandpa! There's miles and miles between them. I learnt that at school. Anyway, you never said nothing about Jamaica before."

"Now, get on with your food and stop arguing the toss. I haven't come down here to argue the toss. Just get on with your grub." Ron had never seen kindly old Grandpa look so irritable before.

Ron finished his meal in silence, greatly troubled by what can only be described as a gnawing suspicion. In silence, too, he took out his paint-box and brushes, his brows knitting up from time to time with the turmoil of his thoughts. Slowly over the paper, there appeared a semblance of Grandpa Lawton, the jagged line of his nose and cheek-bones, the oldness of his head, not unlike a sketch by a primitive young Leonardo. Working carefully round his first sketch, he began to add light touches of colour, but, as the sun came out and grew strong in the sky, so Ron's vision of the old man on the beach began to change, became more mysterious through that freedom of expression which is so characteristic of child-art. But this was no ordinary portrait. Out of the Grandpa that Ron had known for so long there appeared another face, and its expression made him uneasy. He had inadvertently created a double image, and the secret 'second' self, common to all human beings but so rarely seen in all its falseness, was staring out at him from the picture. He was frightened by what he saw there.

"Got a tanner?" asked Ron sullenly. "I want to take a canoe out."

As he handed the sixpence to the attendant, Ron turned to look back at Mr. Lawton. He was sitting gazing down into the sands, and drawing pictures in them with his fingers, now wrinkled and arthritic. Perhaps he was looking for a vision too. Perhaps he was rooting around for a memory of a distant childhood not unlike Ron's own. Whatever it was, Ron wanted no part of it. All he could think about was getting out on the water, away from people. Other people were hell, and Ron just wanted a pleasant little spell of solitude to sort his thoughts out. He would be a very different kind of boy, when he returned to Laburnum Villas, from the one he set out as earlier in the day.

65. Caught Napping!

Alf and Flo stumbled out of the *Irish House* in as argumentative a mood as ever they could be in. True, Alf had had a pretty stiff session in the Public Bar. He was disgruntled and bored, and he could see that Flo was getting all worked up inside.

She's building up to something, he thought, as he struggled to get her and himself into some sort of holiday-spirit. But the effect of the alcohol seemed only to push his mood down to the very depths.

Yes, he thought, she's building up to something. She's ready for a flare-up. She's getting herself into one of her tizzies. He watched her furtively. There she was again, wringing her hands and twitching her nose nervously, and he knew something was up.

"Look here, ol' gel!" he said sheepishly. "What are you worrying about, eh? If it's Mabel, well, she's all right where she is, with them Marley girls."

"I wish I'd never let her go, that's what I wish," she said carelessly. The remark told Alf he was wrong about thinking Flo was worrying over Mabel. It was simply the way she spoke that told him. No! There was *some*thing. But what?

Alf decided that all he could do now was to continue the charade and wait for Flo to explode. Then maybe they could go back to the *Irish House* at opening-time.

"Now listen!" he said. "You grumble like billy-o when you've got her round your neck, and here you are growsin' 'cos you 'aven't. Taint logical. Stands to reason you can't be responsible all the blinkin' time."

"You can say that again, Alfred Thompson."

"Blimey! 'Ere we go!" said Alf. Whenever Flo called him by his full name like that, there was hell brewing up in the proverbial pot, and the lid was going to blow off any minute now.

"Well, who's kid is she, yours or mine?"

"Now, that'd be askin', wouldn't it?" Alf said, with sarcasm.

"Well, you're her father, so why don't you do something for a change. It's always me who's got to keep her in order, have her hanging round me all day. And all you do is booze with your so-called 'Peace and Plenty' cronies. It was just the same when Millie and Ron were nippers. You just drank yourself silly and left it all to me."

"Can't you ever stop naggin'? Like a bleeding air-raid siren, you are. Always wailing, day and night. Anybody'd think you was the only one what has troubles. Well, you aint, see? Not by 'alf, you aint."

At this point, just when they were passing Hannington's store in North Street, Flo started to twitch again. Without any warning whatsoever, she darted through the doorway and disappeared among the crowd of shoppers.

Alf followed miserably and set off on an aimless journey into the labyrinth of counters bearing haberdashery, toilet requisites, and underwear. Guilt gnawed at him remorselessly until his inside began a series of nauseous revolutions. His mind was a confused mess of memories mingled with regrets, tangled pangs of dread and anguish. Nothing seemed clear to him anymore. Nothing seemed to matter to him anymore.

When Flo finally returned to sanity, she might just think of looking for him. Then they could wander about until opening-time. They would go and have a drink, and another drink, and another, until they were incapable of thinking about themselves, incapable of remembering who they were or what they once meant to each other years ago.

Just at that moment he saw Timothy leaning over the jewellery counter. He felt somehow cheered by the possibility of conversation with a friendly face. When he came closer he realised it was not Timothy at all but the young man from the coach. Alf was tempted to speak but thought better of it. The incident somehow made him feel uneasy.

Through his muddled thoughts, Alf was aware of a disturbance. A long wailing cry penetrated his moment of self-pity — a cry that froze into his very marrow. He stopped and listened. There it was again — a long, anguished, almost demented howl. It came floating across the counters and cut right through Alf's inside, leaving him breathless. Panic gripped him. He began pushing violently through the silenced shoppers, everything suddenly clear in his brain, clearer than it had ever been, perhaps, and the sound of that cry ringing in his ears.

"Flo!" he shouted wildly. "Flo! Flo!"

A crowd had already gathered when he reached her. She was slumped on the floor, clutching something in her hands, and weeping silently. A man in a black suit was gripping her arm like a vice and saying:

"Come, madam! Explain yourself, or I shall be compelled to call the police!"

Before Alf knew what he was doing, he was pushing the man in black against the counter till his back must surely crack in two.

"Take your bloody hands off of my wife, you bastard! What have you done to her?"

His voice trembled with indignation. His eyes blazed with fury as they had not done for years. He flung the man aside and knelt beside Flo. She was still weeping, perhaps a little as a child would weep after losing something very precious. She still squatted on the floor, staring at the thing she was holding so desperately in her hands.

Alf couldn't bear it any longer. He felt his eyes grow moist as he looked at Flo, so cast down. He lifted her gently to her feet, up into the gloating faces around them.

"What's the matter, love?" he said, with unaccustomed gentleness.

She seemed so pathetic that he found it difficult to look at her.

"Now come on, ol' gel! You can tell your old Alf, eh?"

But Flo went on weeping, and the faces went on staring and gloating. When Alf saw them, he rounded on them and yelled with such a ferocity that they vanished into thin air.

The man in black recovered himself, straightening his coat and tie. There was, for a moment, a mood of stalemate which was suddenly broken by Alf taking the initiative:

"All right!" said Alf with a renewed firmness of voice. "How much for the things she took? How much?"

"That will be seven-and-sixpence-half-penny," the man replied with a phenomenal dose of dignity. "I suppose you realise the consequences of this sort of thing?" he added, threateningly.

"What do you mean, 'This sort of thing'?" shouted Alf. " Oh, yes, I know your type."

Alf counted out some coins and thrust them into the man-in-black's hand.

"Call the coppers, if you dare. You've got your money. The thing's bin paid for. But I'm not 'avin' the likes of you putting your

328

filthy paws over my wife, see? It probably aint the first time you fancied a customer, neither! Get 'em into your nice comfy office, do you? Make a nice little bargain? One bit of goods in exchange for another, eh? Well, not with *my* wife you don't. There's your money. It'll pay for your taxi to the 'ospital!"

Once outside, he handed Flo a handkerchief and said:

"Wipe your eyes, love, and think no more about it."

They turned down into the Lanes and were soon lost among the twisting alleys and streets, where Alf hoped they would not be followed, for he still felt the urge to look over his shoulder in case the police had been called in after all. It would be a fine kettle of fish if they were arrested on August Bank Holiday.

A number of coaches were lined up by the Palace Pier for the afternoon outings. Realising that it might be a risk to stay in the town for long in case Flo was planning something even more sensational, Alf pushed her on to one of the vehicles, which somehow seemed to be waiting there just for them — to take them off somewhere, anywhere away from the bustle of the town and the man in black. Alf chose two seats at the back of the coach and, when they had settled themselves snugly in, he lit a cigarette and put it between Flo's lips, something he had not done since their courting days. He put his arm round her and, with the other hand, eased a small packet from her clenched fingers.

"Baby's nappies!" he exclaimed incredulously. "And what's this? A Mickey Mouse rattle! Poor ol' gel! Whatever made you do a thing like that, eh?" In other circumstances he would have laughed at her and teased her.

There was a tenderness in his voice that Flo had not heard for many a year. She sank into his arms and sobbed her heart out. "Oh, Millie!" she cried through her tears. "My darlin' little Millie!"

66. Voices on the Pier

For most of our coaching party nothing could match an afternoon on that peninsula of pleasure — the Palace Pier at Brighton. Whilst experiencing the joys of being on board ship, they felt also the security of strolling on *terra firma*. Sixpence slapped down on the iron desk of the little man in the glass cabin, and then — away through the turnstile, down the wooden ramp to the amusement halls and arcades and cafés, the hundred-and-one slot-machines and the ghost-train screams and the candy-floss.

Mabel stuck a sticky paw into Lizzie Pomfrett's hand and promptly burst into tears. Somehow, her strands of her hair had curled round her toffee-apple in a sticky whirl. To the accompaniment of wailings, the apple was extricated and briskly cast into the sea — whereupon more squawkings and stampings of stubborn little feet brought forth another twopence and Mabel was satisfied. Then Lizzie and Iris and Effie, the girls from Marley's Stores, were at liberty to cackle away in a stream of trivial confidences. Their voices rose in rich round tones that drowned the ice-cream vendor into a muffled blasphemy.

After lunch they strolled along the promenade towards the West Pier. Sixpence and they were 'on deck' to enjoy the fun. What cries of delight! What laughter! Over the loud-speakers a voice with a specious Oxford accent plied them with seductive suggestions:

> *Afternoon and high teas are now being served in the*
> *Ocean Restaurant, ladies and gentlemen. The chef's*
> *speciality for today is beautiful fresh salmon mayonnaise,*
> *or delicious local-caught fried fillet of plaice and*
> *chipped potatoes. Hot-dogs, shell-fish of every kind, fresh*
> *fruit, and cups of tea are on sale at the end of the pier."*

The rhythmic movement of the waves on the beach below interfused with the delicately strangled strains of the ladies' orchestra provided the holiday-makers with that uniquely soporific nostalgia which plays such an essential part in English seaside sensations. The hypnotic strains of *The Maid of the Mountains, Desert Song* and *The Dancing Years* floated across the restaurant, accompaniment to the chatter of ladies in retirement and the incessant timpani of tea-cups, lingered for a while at windows, teasing the ears of elderly sunworshippers lounging in countless deck-chairs along the promenades and walkways of the beloved pier.

Out at the end of the pier, old men and young boys stood motionless with rod and line, patiently waiting for a catch, whilst nearby, the terrible triumvirate, Teddy Rogers, Freddy Higgins and Billy Watkins, cheered excitedly as they hoisted a crab from the swirling eddies below.

330

Everywhere was tranquil and quiet. Even the ladies' orchestra had taken the opportunity, between *Sleepy Lagoon* and *In a Monastery Garden,* to spend their *Pennies from Heaven!*

Beyond the pier could be heard the purr of a speed-boat. It came bearing the 'three plump graces' from Rothersey and was heading straight towards the pier, much to the consternation of its three passengers.

"Ooh! Ow! Eff! I'm goin' to fall in the drink if I don't look out!" cried Lizzie.

" 'Ere! Lizzie!" yelled Effie, "don't you 'ang onter me, 'ang onter 'er, else we'll all be fit for fryin' tonight!" Then she squealed again: "Ooh! Ooh! Oow! I do wish my Fred was 'ere!"

"Don't be daft, gel!" cried Iris. "If your fat Fred was on this 'ere boat, we'd all bleedin'-well sink, the way you fill 'im up with grub."

The boat lurched over a small tidal wave, hoisted the women into the air and deposited them in the bottom in a heap.

"Oh, Gawd! We'll be tipped out, mates. Sure as my name's Mudd, we'll all be tipped into the drink. Ow-oo-oo-ch! Sto-op!"

The Oxford Voice returned:

*Afternoon and high teas are now being served at popular prices. There are heaps of attractions and all kinds of games to be played at the south end of the pier.......and please, ladies and gentlemen, please do **not** throw your lighted cigarette ends on the wooden decks. Please do not throw.............*

The Voice was drowned by the resumed cheers of Teddy Rogers and Freddy Higgins as they hoisted another crab to the deck once more.

Meanwhile Lizzie and Effie, finding their sea-legs again, stood giggling and tittering outside the palmist's window:

All the Secrets of the Palm
YOUR FUTURE FORETOLD WITH AMAZING ACCURACY
Love   Money   Marriage   Success

331

"Not for me, Liz, gel! I've had more than my share of love and marriage after nigh on ten year, I can tell you — and it's cost me a darned sight more than half a dollar! It's as much as I can do to keep Fred off the bottle as it is."

"Oh! Don't be daft, Effie! For two-and-sixpence, you can go in there and find out if he's two-timing you over the house-keeping money. Find out if you're going to meet a dark, handsome stranger. Then you can give old Fred the boot."

The girls burst into the silent waiting-room and filled it with their laughter. A harassed-looking middle-aged man assumed a pinched expression, embarrassed at being discovered in this temple of intuition.

"Oh! I do feel daft," Lizzie sniggered. "I mean, what can Gypsy Rose Lee tell me I don't blinking-well know already. My bloke could never love nobody if he tried. All he thinks about is jumping on me every night; he aint got a bean to his name; he don't believe in getting wed; and his idea of success is running up a debt at the dog-racing!"

At that moment, Mabel started to grizzle. She was getting tired and missing her mother.

"Let's sing a song, shall we?" said Lizzie. They all began to squawk like a trio of parrots:

> *Mairzy doats and dozy doats*
> *And liddle lamsy divey*
> *A kiddley divey doo, wouldn't you?*

Very soon, sooner than everyone realised, or cared to realise, the afternoon began to draw into evening. The pier began to look deserted. The elderly had returned to their boarding-houses and one-room flatlets; the old fishermen had gone 'ashore' in search of the first thirst-quenching pint of the evening. Two of the remaining crab-fishing 'triumvirate' were straddling the iron girders by the landing-stage, talking confidences, and swinging their legs over the water below. One or two older couples strolled arm-in-arm along the promenade before going home to their supper.

High up over the pier-head, on the upper deck, just by the silver dome, a young man was kissing a girl. Effie shaded her eyes against the bright glare of the early evening sun.

"Why!" she said, "I do believe it's that young fellow what was on the coach. Now, you'd think he'd be a bit more private about it, wouldn't you? At least he's found 'is tongue, anyways. Never spoke a

332

word to anybody, and then he has the cheek to disappear just when we we was 'opin' for a bit o' slap and tickle to brighten up the day."

"Oh, Eff!" said Lizzie, giggling her head off. "You aren't 'alf a caution. Don't you mean 'Brighton'?"

"It looks like that Millie Thompson's got 'old of 'im. A fine how-d'ye-do, if you ask me."

"If you ask me, Eff, old gel," said Iris, "you need your peekers on. Can't you see she aint Millie Thompson. Why! That's the Paxton girl havin' bit o' nooky with Tim Crawford. Always thought 'e was a dark 'orse, that one. Looks as if something's up, there, eh?"

"Oh, you are awful" said Lizzie.

"Well, if I hadn't told you, it'd be all over Rothersey that Tim Crawford was having it off with Millie Thompson, now wouldn't it?"

"Well, I don't know what to think, to be honest. There's some daft things goin' on today that I can't fathom out."

The three muses were interrupted in their conversation by Effie going into a kind of fit. They all peered through their arched fingers into the bright sun and uttered a series of "Ah's", "Ah-ooh's."

"Ah-ooh! Innit luv'ly!"

"Ooh-ah! Innit nah-ice!

Surreptitiously, a multi-coloured beach ball had floated from under the fishing jetty and sailed gaily round the pier on the tide.

Close by was Ron in his little red canoe, rocking gently from side to side. He was full of thoughts about Grandpa, too full of them perhaps to realise what was going on. He sat up and let his hands touch the ripples of the water as they moved outward from the boat. Then he looked straight into the sun and saw the ball, like a mine floating in from the sea.

Ron paddled stealthily towards the ball, still black, shadowy, uninviting. He hesitated for an instant, then he gathered it up in his arms and saw suddenly all the reds and blues and greens and yellows in it and he smiled and clung to it triumphantly and immediately forgot about his troubles.

The music had stopped now. So had the voices of the announcer, the salesman, the fisher-boys, and the ice-cream man. In the distance, towards the entrance to the pier could be heard the singing of the three plump graces of Rothersey:

> *I do like to be beside the seaside*
> *I do like to be beside the sea*

Then, at last, there was silence, except for the gentle lapping of the water against the pier and the soft rushing sound as the lazy evening waves crept up the pebble beach and receded endlessly.

All three ladies squeezed through the turnstile, with Mabel in eo and were gone into the strolling promenaders, and with them went something of the joy and happiness that is itself the life of this glorious old pier. Now, coloured strings of fairy-lights lined the promenade for as far as the eye could see, and the silver domes and minarets of this relic of Victoriana gleamed above the gently-lapping waves.

Timothy and Louise were motionless, his arms about her, lips touching her cheek. They were the perfect image of human happiness caught in a timeless moment.

The sun slipped behind the Downs and the sea was liquid silver. Breakwaters jutted out into the bay like black needles, through streaks of sapphire and indigo, beyond the pier and to the west. Under a crescent moon shone the evening star in a translucent sky. For Timothy and Louise it was, as for all our travellers had they recognised it, a sign of new beginnings. For once there was hope in every heart.

67.   A Marriage of Convenience?

If Alf had taken the trouble to look on the front of the coach they happened to be travelling on, he would have seen that before long they would be arriving at:

> # DEVIL'S DYKE

There was no mystery about it. There on the panel over the driver's cab it was plain for all to see. But Alf hadn't seen it. He was far too busy paying up his three-and-sixpence just so that he and Flo could be left to themselves, hidden away in the back seat, on their way to anywhere out of the town.

On arrival at the tea-rooms, the last thing Alf and Flo expected was to see an unhappy Millie and a sullen Eddie sitting over a cold cup of tea. It could only be expected that, as the gods clearly decreed, Flo feeling as she did, and Millie, feeling as she did, fell into each other's arms and wept bitterly.

"Oh, Mum! Dear Mum!" cried Millie. "Oh-oo-oo-ooh!"

"Oh, my little Millie!" cried Flo, with an inappropriate turn of phrase. "Oh-oo-oo-ooh!"

And great was the deluge of salty water that flowed over the tea-cups at this unexpected reconciliation of mother and daughter.

"Crikey!" exclaimed Alf to Eddie. "Anybody'd think they'd never seen one anuvver before in their whole lives"

"P'raps they 'aven't — not like this," said Eddie, thoughtfully.

"What a carry on, this is!" said Alf.

"Nark it, will you?" said Eddie irritably.

"Here! Watch it, matey!" said Alf. "You're in a funny sort of mood, aint you?"

"So would you be if you'd bin told where to get off like I have."

"What do you mean? You and Millie had a tiff, have you?"

"Oh! For crying out loud! O' course we have. I shoulda thought you could see that a mile off. We aint even on speaking-terms. Don't know what's got into her, I don't really. Turned me down flat, she has. I've been askin' her for months."

"You mean," said Alf gaping wide, "you really want to get married to our Millie in 'er state of 'ealth?"

"What do you think?" said Eddie dejectedly. "I've been on at her for months, I tell you."

"Here! Hold on, ol' son!" said Alf in an accusing tone. "This kid! It wouldn't be yours by any chance, would it?"

That made Eddie boil. He stood up and waved his fist at Alf.

"You bloody-well watch what your saying, chum, because your goin' to end up in 'ospital if you're not careful."

"All right! Calm down! Calm down! I'm only askin' so don't get so bloody stroppy," Alf shouted.

It took Alf Thompson some time to get used to the idea that Eddie Carpenter was not the father and still wanted to get married to Millie, or as Flo put it: 'To be foster-father to some other bloke's kid.' When Alf did get used to it, which was with some difficulty considering his mild state of intoxication and his generally unsettled mind, he set to work on the turbulent and tear-stained Millie.

"Now look here, my gel!" said Alf, with the sensitivity of a sledge-hammer. "Tears or no tears, you're going to listen to your old Dad for a change. I've had just about enough of crying and snivvling for one day, what with you and your mother. And I'm the one what knows

335

best."

"Since when have you known what's best for *me* or anybody, I'd like to know?" said Millie petulantly.

"Now, that's enough of that, Millie," said Alf firmly. "Here you are, in your condition, with a good boy like Eddie who wants to marry you, kid or no kid, for better or worse, and it's a damned sight more likely for worse if you turn out to be a misery like your mother has. Now, there aint many lads around like Eddie, so you'd better start thinking again."

"He's only thinking of the kid," she said, pouting. "Wants to give it a name, he does. He's so moral, it's not true!"

"No, he aint," shouted Alf with an angry burst. "He could go and get hitched to any bit o' stuff off the streets if he just wanted a bit o' the old one-two! But he wants to marry *you*! Am I getting through to you, you silly little twit!"

"Here! Alf!" said Flo, suddenly coming to. "Don't you speak to Millie like that. Whatever next!"

Alf stuck his finger at her like a dagger.

"You! Pipe down!"

"Oh!" said Millie, waggling her head in her mother's hoity-toity fashion. "Quite the little dictator, aint we?"

"Shut your trap!" he shouted, getting to look quite dangerous. Turning to Flo, he said:

"I'll speak to Millie how I like, and don't you dare try to stop me. Keep out of this! Millie is marrying Eddie 'cos I say so. Is that clear? Why, what could be better that a fine strapping young feller-me-lad like Eddie for a son-in-law! He's a good lad, is Eddie. Been as good as a son to you and me, and don't you never forget it. Don't you go putting your spoke in the wheel when it's not wanted. I've just about had enough of you both for one day. Sitting there gibbering and blibbering like a pair of prize monkeys! I'm telling you for the last time: Millie is marrying Eddie, and the sooner the better for all of us."

Millie looked at Flo. Flo looked at Millie. Eyes as wide as saucers! They were so surprised by this uncharacteristic outburst that they forgot to cry. They gaped at each other, lost for words. Flo was so astonished that for a moment, she thought Alf was losing his mind. Far from it! He was, for the first time in years, in absolute command of the situation, and it was not long before they all realised it and began to accept it. He raised his hand and whistled to the bejewelled blonde to bring some more tea. She glided sparklingly across the floor and tripped on a stray rock-bun. The elephantine tea-pot soared into the air on the end of her plump pink arm. Marcasite glittered as she described a semicircle with her bosom, finally saving the situation on tip-toe, as if she were about to break into her own version of *Swan Lake.*

"We'd like some more tea," said Alf imperiously, and bring us a few tarts."

She scowled as Eddie suddenly broke into peels of laughter. He laughed till his sides ached.

"Do you mind!" she said, in her piping voice.

"I don't mind if I do," said Alf. "How about after closing-time!"

After that Eddie was jumping about in his chair, tears rolling down his cheeks, he was laughing so much.

The blonde hoisted the blue tea-pot high over their heads. Hot brown liquid poured copiously from the chipped spout and flooded four cups, surrounding them like small white islands, in a sea of tea. The pot swished over them like a great monster and was gone as suddenly as it had come. It vanished behind the extensive rear of the waitress as she turned to serve the next table. On her way back to the kitchen, she unceremoniously squashed a raspberry jam doughnut underfoot, just as a small boy bent to pick it up. When she had completed her precarious journey to the bar, they saw her sneak a gulp from a pint glass of lager hiding behind the counter. This sent Flo into fits of giggles, and soon even Millie couldn't resist a snigger or two. Before long, they were all the happiest people in the place. Laughing and giggling and sniggering and tittering for all they were worth. Then Eddie dared to put his arm round Millie and Alf put his arm round Flo, and that made Flo so happy that she burst into tears once more, which, of course, spread across the table. They cried so much the tears of years that Alf and Eddie had finally to put their cups to their mouths like nursemaids feeding a couple of babies.

"Cor, blimey! What a family, eh?" said Alf, shaking his head happily.

At last, Eddie got round to asking Alf how he and Flo got to the place.

"That's a long story, mate!"

"We're on a Mystery Tour," said Eddie.

"Where are we then?"

"Devil's Dyke. Look! It says so here." Eddie picked up a leaflet on the table. So fraught had been the recent emotional upheaval that nobody had noticed it."

337

"We've had enough of the Devil's work for one day, thanks very much." said Alf ruefully.

The guides started to circulate again, collecting up stray mystery-tourists. At the coaches, Alf took Eddie's arm and said: "You're coming with me, my lad. Millie can go with her mother in the other coach. I've had enough of them for one day. Anyway, I want to talk to you."

They turned to take a last look at the countryside around them. The sun shone orange from a cloudless evening sky, giving still some warmth to the Downs, which stretched out like smooth undulating velvet, rolling away into the distance towards Steyning and Chanctonbury Ring. Below and to the north was a green carpet of woodland and meadows. Everywhere was a picture of tranquillity. Alf sighed, pushed his hands deep into his trouser-pockets, and said:

"It does you good to get away for a bit, don't it? See how the other half lives, eh? Makes you understand things a little bit clearer. I mean, Laburnum Villas aint the whole bloody world, now, is it? There's a good deal more to see before we all kick the bucket, a good deal that's good and fine. That's why I'm glad Millie's going with you. You'll show her a fine new life, away from Rothersey, away from me and her mother. You'll give her a bit of self-respect, too. She's a good girl, really. Aint had much of a chance, you see. Only, she needs taking care of, like we all do."

He paused, staring down into the valley, now scene of the kind of peace and contentment that Alf had long forgotten until that moment. Eddie stood quietly brooding by his side.

"You know, Ed," said Alf pensively. "A thing or two has happened to me today. I had an electric shock that went through me from head to toe. Something as hasn't happened since your old Dad packed it in. Something as has set me on the move again. Fancy! All those years waiting for it to come. Honest, Ed, when your Dad died so sudden on us, well, it was a terrible thing. Why, him and me was kids together. Mates for life, we were. That is — till he found out about me and your Ma. I dunno! It was something you just can't explain. Me and her, I mean. Old Jack wasn't never angry with it. He just knew I'd failed him, like. I wasn't no friend of his no more. Not when I done what I done with his back turned. Christ! I'll never ever forget seeing him lying there. All twisted up in his own blood, just staring at me. Staring, he was. I just couldn't help thinking —"

"Alfie, boy!" said Eddie, quietly. "You don't have to go on

338

about it, you know. Dad wouldn't have wanted you to. He loved you more than anybody, did Dad. He just wouldn't want it, Alf."

"Yes, but can't you see, he — "

"Look Alf! I don't want to hear no more about it, see? He would have died whatever happened. It was only a matter of months."

"What d'you mean?"

"I mean, the doctors had it in for him, poor sod. He was done for by the medics."

"You mean old Jacko was — "

"Cancer. As thin as a bean-pole, he was, at the end."

"Yes, but, your Ma. How did she — "

"Oh, she knew all about it. Just wouldn't never give in to it, see? And Dad never knew she knew, neither. I suppose that was why she went on hollerin' at him, so as he'd never know she knew. Went on shoutin' and hollerin' even when the pain was twistin' him up in knots. Poor old bugger!"

Eddie stopped speaking, stared at Alf and then added as an afterthought:

"You know what I think? I think he done it on purpose. I think he threw himself under that girder. And you want to know something else? I think he was glad as hell you was there with him at the end, 'cos why? 'Cos he was terrified to be on his lonesome when the end came. He wanted to go with his best friend by his side. Don't you see?"

Alf broke into an irrepressible sob, so heartfelt that he could barely stand the pain of it. His eyes were full of tears so that the green hills grew smudged and the trees grew into one another, shapeless splodges on his vision.

Eddie took him by the arm and helped him onto the coach. As they turned down the road towards Brighton, a carpet of small lights twinkled like a sea of stars, but Alf could not see them. He had his own horizons.

68. A Cheap Day's Journey into Night

Long before the London coach was due to leave, Miss Baldock was sitting in her seat. From time to time, she quivered with indignation at the memory of the day's events, and breathed bitterness into the empty corners of the coach. A kind of tortured tightness gripped her bosom as if her brassiere was about to explode. No victim returned on whom she might vent her spleen. She made idle conjectures as to who would be the first to arrive, but then, glancing at her watch, she saw that she had at least an hour-and-a-half to go before the official time of departure. So she had ample opportunity to build up a temper. She could just sit tight and fume.

Agnes was obsessed now with a deep longing to get right away from Rothersey. Away from the dreadful people in whose company she must continue to endure the last three months of the year. Away from all that they stood for, which, except for her ex-beloved, was a great deal of nothing. The thought that, in an hour or so, she would be hemmed in by them on every side disgusted her, suffocated, as she would be, by their beery breath, persecuted by their lewd joking and their deafening songs.

No. This kind of life was definitely not for Agnes Baldock. As soon as the compensation money came through, she would be off and away, right out of sight and hearing of Laburnum Villas. When the arrangements for the sale of Mr. Lawton's effects was completed – the whole lot was not worth the price for taking it away—she would pack up her troubles in her old kit-bag and be off. But where? That was the question.

If it hadn't been for Frank and Cynthia she might never have had any hope at all of breaking away, but they had mentioned that the new owner of the little café in Worthing was already wanting to sell out. She had fallen for some beefy able-seaman from Portsmouth. One of her 'customers', so they said. Well, there might be hope yet for Agnes Baldock. It could certainly be said that she had much to offer! A cosy little business with a flat over the top was not to be sniffed at, especially with maritime 'prospects'!

As for that scoundrel, Gabriel, well! He could go and lick his own wounds for all she cared. Such goings-on, indeed! It was enough to turn the stomach of every decent-thinking person in Rothersey, if indeed there were any, which she doubted. Take the Thompson family — a load of thieves, prostitutes and drunkards. That's what they were. She would be mighty glad to see the backsides of that little lot. As common as dirt, they were. Not a scrap of decency or breeding about them. She could see it in their faces and their queer-shaped bodies — their eyes were so close together they nearly touched each other, their noses were snubbed like golf-balls, their ears stuck out like signposts, and their knees almost reached down to their ankles. If that was the state of their bodies, what must their minds be like? Ill-bred from the sewers, that's all that could be said about the Thompson litter.

Destiny decreed at that unfortunate moment in her thoughts that Ron Thompson should be the first to put his head on the block, without the protection of Grandpa Lawton. Indeed, Miss Baldock was astonished that the old man was nowhere to be seen. Perhaps, she mused, perhaps he has had a stroke or some sort of fit. Well! She would discover sooner or later. She pounced on her unsuspecting victim.

"It's high time somebody arrived," she said with severity. "And where is Mr. Lawton, might I ask?"

"I dunno!" answered Ron, glumly.

"Oh! I see!" she said, smirking viciously. "Lost our little sugar-daddy, have we?"

"What's it to you?" Ron replied miserably.

"Now, there's no need to be insolent, Ronald Thompson. I asked you a straightforward question and I expect a straightforward reply."

"Well, I'm giving you one, aint I?," he said with defiance. "I dunno, see? I dunno where he is. I dunno! I dunno!"

He began to shout into her pinched-looking face.

"How dare you speak to me in that fashion, you nasty little boy!" she said tetchily. "Anybody can see what you need — a jolly good hiding. That's what you need. Would do you a power of good. Knock some sense of what's right and what's wrong into you! A fat lot of good that sot of a father of yours is! And what's more, you're to stop messing about with Mr. Lawton, or I shall have something to say about it. It's not healthy for a boy of your age to be consorting with an old man of eighty. Listening to all those stories — or should I say — tales! Perhaps you understand that better, do you? Telling tales?"

She glared at him like a she-devil.

"What's it to you, you old bag?"

"How dare you call me names! I do not approve of young boys who tell lies. And still less do I approve of old men who tell tales." Her tone was insinuating when she reiterated: "I suppose you do know what I mean by 'telling tales'. I'll tell you a tale you won't forget for a long time. A tale that's not fiction, Ronald, but hard fact. A tale about an old man who tells lies, Ronald. Lies! Lies! Lies!"

Just like the flippin' Vicar, thought Ron. Everything in triplicate.

Ron began to get scared when he saw her mouth twitching as

she drew in breath through her nose. He expected her to breathe out fire like the dragon in one of his comics. He was even more alarmed as she seemed to inflate her bosom like a barrage-balloon. She was certainly loaded for firing! He knew he had to tread carefully.

It dawned on Ron that Miss Baldock had said something of importance to him — something he began to reflect upon. He gripped hard on the chromium rail protecting Miss Baldock from the open door. He gripped so hard he couldn't feel anything in his fingers anymore, they were so drained of blood.

"You mean," he said at last, "you mean that Grandpa never did all those things? He never did go to Australia? He never did sail in a wind-jammer? You mean, he......."

"Can you imagine a shrivelled-up old man like Mr. Lawton being a sailor on the high seas, or a lumber-jack in the outback? Why, he couldn't break a twig in two. He never set foot outside Rothersey. Never! He was born in Laburnum Villas and never left it till he was put in the Old People's Home."

Ronald started to whimper. Then the tears came, copiously. As the terrible moment of truth dawned on him, he began to sob pitifully. Suddenly he screwed up his face and screamed out:

"It's not true! It's not true! It's not true!"

Over and over he said it. He began pummelling his amazonian assailant with short sharp blows that took the wind out of her, it was so unexpected. She pursed her lips tightly and fought back. She caught Ronald in a clinch, fingers closing over his head, pulling his hair. All the time he was yelling at her:

"It's not true! It's not true!"

"Take your hands off me, you brat! You nasty little pig!"

Only another arrival could save the situation, and who better than the Vicar himself — arch-peacemaker and champion of 'Peace and Plenty'. There may not have been much peace in evidence but there was plenty of Miss Baldock showing by the time he arrived. Her skirt was practically up round her neck with the wriggling about of it all, and the seam of her blouse was split under the arm.

Ronald ceased punching, stood still, breathing hard, his face wet with tears. Then he ran to the front of the coach and crouched low in his seat.

Miss Baldock straightened herself out, as far as that were possible, though it might have been more appropriate to say that she rounded herself off. She had not finished with the wretched little

342

Ronald Thompson. She would make it so that he would not be able to sit down for the next six months.

The Vicar, having recovered from the shock of glimpsing Miss Baldock's plump pink knees, now addressed himself to her in more formal tones. He could see that Miss Baldock had hidden talents of which he had hitherto been unaware. He could now see what her erstwhile paramour, Councillor Purvis, admired in her. She was a fighter through and through. He had seen that at the 'Peace and Plenty' fiasco. 'Fight the good fight, with all thy might.' He remembered the ribald shouts of "Knock her in the knickers!" and "Bash her on the snitch!" and such phrases that had floated so gracefully on the air in the Village Hall on that inauspicious day in June.

"I'm sure our faiths do not divide us to such an extent that we might not join in a little gentle conversation together on our return journey," said the shiny-faced vicar with a sparkle in his eye.

"*This* seat is taken," the lady said firmly.

"Ah! Yes! Yes! Yes! I had almost forgotten. You lovebirds will be cooing to us soon enough. When's the happy day to be?"

Agnes did not reply. She plumped her basket down on the spare seat and stared out of the window at the blue sea, now darkening in the evening light, as her future was darkening, if she'd only known it. She was not to escape from Laburnum Villas so easily as all that. She had schemed to get what she wanted, but not even her conscience could pay the price her fate required of her. Sooner or later, she would come to grief. Perhaps she felt a twinge of a threat when Mr. Lawton at last climbed onto the coach and crept into the front seat next to Ron. The Vicar was in unusually high spirits in spite of the rebuff from Agnes. But no more so than the rest of the Thompsons, who arrived arm-in-arm, laughing and hugging each other.

Alf was preceded by a crate of ale and another of stout, much to Miss Baldock's dismay.

Soon, Mabel arrived with Effie and Iris and Lizzie. A spirit of gaiety filled the coach as they climbed on laden with tins of toffees, candy-floss, and bags of fried fish-and-chips.

Mabel, who had missed her mother all day without realising it, started to cry immediately she caught sight of her. She stood weeping in the aisle like a pathetic little waif. Mrs. Thompson, in the wake of the Hannington's episode, was feeling vulnerable and started to cry too. At that moment, each saw in the other an object of love — love that had had no way of expressing itself until now. Realising how much she had missed her little girl, she took Mabel up in her arms and hugged her as she had not done for many a month.

"Oh! My little sweetie!" she said. "Come and sit with your mummy and daddy." With all the twists and turns of the day, the exhausted Mabel was soon asleep in her mothers arms, and Flo, in her turn, was soon asleep in Alf's. Had Ron been in the mood to paint another portrait, he might have called it 'Family Reunion'. He glanced at the back of the coach to see if his 'Lone Stranger' had returned but there was no sign of him, nor would there be for the rest of the journey, which may account for the uninhibited high jinks of the girls from the button factory. Before long, they were joined by the girls from the Roxy, who had spent a rollicking time with the tannery boys. And now, in a matter of seconds, the whole coach was filled with raucous shouting and singing. They all intended to make the most of the return journey, for it was, after all, the last annual outing they would have with the residents of Laburnum Villas.

On the arrival of Councillor Purvis, Agnes looked the other way. She did not allow herself to be intimidated into offering to remove her basket from the spare seat. If she had only known it, however, the Councillor was both disturbed and relieved by her obvious expression of disgust. He felt the freer for it, and it was no surprise to Agnes when he sat himself down next to Lizzie from the bacon counter.

"Really! Squeezing himself in next to that brazen hussy!" muttered the affronted Miss Baldock.

Meanwhile, the driver was tapping his fingers on the steering-wheel, waiting for the nameless young man to appear. Effie had been looking everywhere for him and had come to the conclusion that he was the person they had spotted on the West Pier earlier in the afternoon and that he had decided to stay behind to enjoy what pleasures and delights an evening in Brighton might be inclined to offer. Effie was almost on the point of getting off the coach to join him she was so smitten and had to be forcibly restrained by her sister, Iris, who was cynical enough about men to recognise the futility of chasing after false hopes.

Before long, Lizzie had Councillor Purvis wrapped round her little finger — and a lot else, as far as Agnes could see. He was laughing and joking and even partaking of the alcoholic beverages proffered from time to time. Lizzie just had the knack. You could never be serious for five seconds with the luscious Lizzie, however you were feeling — and she knew all there was to know about feeling!

Much to Miss Baldock's dismay, by the time Tooting Bec was

reached, the whole coach was a riot. Tim and Louise were quiet enough with their own thoughts and their own kind of bliss. But the rest? Well! Effie and Iris were singing duets. Alf joined in with a few words he had picked up in the Army during the war. Eddie and Millie were asleep in each others arms and Lizzie had her arm round Joe Purvis, which looked very much as if she meant business! She waved a half-empty bottle of stout in the air and cried out: "Yippee!" as she gave the Councillor a beery kiss on the cheek, leaving behind a fine imprint of a pair of red lips. The Councillor, now close to being classified as 'blotto', began to sing a version of 'The Toreador's Song' from *Carmen,* the naughty words of which not even Alf Thompson had heard. Before long, Joe was the life of the party. Agnes Baldock was horrified, especially now that the Roxy girls were cavorting in the aisle with the tannery boys in a variety of highly suggestive dance movements that would certainly have been banned by the Lord Chancellor for obscenity. Then everybody began to chorus:

Knees up, Mother Brown!
Knees up, Mother Brown!
Ee-aye! Ee-aye! Ee-aye-oh!

The boys waggled their hips, the girls wobbled their bosoms. Miss Baldock closed her eyes and ears to it all.

Our weary but happy travellers finally disgorged at Laburnum Villas. Never had there been, nor would there be again, such tender farewells, such uninhibited and abandoned gaiety as on this special homecoming.

"What a day it's been!" said Alf joyously. "Cor! What a day!"

"You can say that again, mate," said Eddie. "You can say that for all of us." And he never meant anything more sincerely in his whole life.

Agnes Baldock had good reason to disagree, the way things turned out. On the pavement outside the Councillor Purvis's house lay the twisted remains of his precious television aerial. A violent gust of wind had whisked it off the chimney-stack and sent it crashing to the ground. In spite of his over-indulgence on the coach, he was clear-minded enough, even in his befuddled state, to recognise a warning of things to come.

❀

69. The Last Rose of Summer

Now that the great day was over, Louise began to worry over Uncle Walter. As she and Timothy let themselves quietly into the house, they sensed the uncanny emptiness of the place. She shivered slightly. Timothy, aware of her thoughts, put his arms round her and held her for a moment. Her fears were compounded by her regret at decision to go to Brighton in the first place. Uncle had wished it and she had reluctantly complied with that wish.

Hand-in-hand, Louise and Timothy mounted the stairs with foreboding. Uncle Walter lay on the bed with a stillness and silence that only the dead possess. Louise burst into tears and uttered that strange cry from deep within her. Whatever vain hope of seeing him again was dashed forever.

For one dread moment, they stood together, holding each other.

Beside the bed was a brilliant orange rose in a glass.

"Brazilian Wonder!" Timothy whispered. The rose seemed like a flag of truce, brightly and glowingly triumphant. To Timothy, it was the end of something more important than he knew, the last rose of Uncle Walter's summer. In the old man's expression there seemed to be the trace of a smile, the final approval, perhaps.

Timothy gazed at the rose thoughtfully, sadly, wonderingly, and asked himself how it was possible for him to have changed so much in six months at Laburnum Villas. He could not recognise himself for the same youth who had quarrelled with his father for the sake of an ideal, and argued with Uncle Walter over their favourite roses. He realised that his return to the farm was as vital to him as life itself. Things were going to be different from now on, for him and for Louise.

EPISODE FOURTEEN

New Year's Eve

A Light on the Horizon

70.   More Monkey Business

Mrs. Thompson was in a mood for gossip when Timothy called to take Mabel out on her last visit to the Lollipop Shop. He was carrying a bunch of bright purple and pink anemones which he handed to Flo.

"Anemones!" she exclaimed with surprise. "I wondered how they would come to me."

"Why? said Tim. "Were you expecting some?"

"Tim! I couldn't begin to explain. It was my dream, you see."

Tim leaned against the backdoor and stared at the kitchen in disarray.

"Getting packed up at last, Mrs. Thompson?"

"Good Lord, no! Haven't even thought about it."

"We're leaving tonight," he said. "We want to spend New Year's Day at the farm. It'll seem less like an end to everything and more of a beginning for us. Let us hope the stars look down on all of us with favour wherever we go."

"Oh!" said Mrs. Thompson, feigning polite regrets, "we *shall* miss you. Who's going to look after Mabel now? She won't be the same without you."

"Mabel's a very different young lady with or without me, Mrs. Thompson."

"She used to be a naughty little so-and-so, I can tell you. I couldn't never keep her in order, the little monkey. I don't know what's come over her, I don't really." She paused for a moment. Then flew off at a tangent in her usual butterfly way:

"Ere! Have you heard about the little bit o' monkey-business across the road here last week? The police found a flick-knife there with blood-stains on it. A nice how-d'ye-do, I must say. There's more to it than meets the eye, I can tell you!"

"I've been off the scene this week," said Tim. "Far too busy getting all our things packed and moved down to the farm."

True, there was something odd about the happenings at No 3. No-one ever took much notice of the old shell of a house, and certainly no-one for a moment thought it held any particularly sinister secret. All the more amazement, therefore, when everyone read the headline blazoned across the front page of the *Rothersey Clarion:*

| **GRUESOME MURDER AT LABURNUM VILLAS** |

The horrific discovery caused a sensation in the Borough. It had all started with Mrs. Thompson telling Millie to go and look for Mabel. Ron was practising his recorder for a surprise item the Vicar was getting up for New Year's Day. Ron refused to be disturbed. Ron was beginning to have a mind of his own.

Well, anyway, Millie was supposed to be looking for Mabel. She hunted high and low. She searched the doggy interior of Smutty's abode. She ransacked the cupboards and hutches in 'The Dumps', but nowhere could she find Mabel — not, that is, until she looked out of the front-room window and caught sight of her playing with her little monkey friend on the pavement outside the ever-open door of No 3. She had noticed Beppo going in and out of the house a few days before, whimpering wildly and clearly very upset indeed.

A number of people had reported seeing the monkey in strange places of late — outside the Purvis Gymnasium in Napoleon Avenue, for example. Later on, he was seen scampering out of the gentlemen's lavatory in the Public Gardens, and soon afterwards spotted picking at his fleas in the precincts of Rothersey Borough Market.

So here was Millie spying the wayward little Mabel on the pavement opposite, as large as life. As soon as Millie appeared, Beppo disappeared. Mabel began to squall: "I want Beppo. I want Beppo!". She had to be forcibly removed to the quietude of her bed.

Millie stood for a moment looking up at the torn face of the house and thought of that evening back in February when she had fled from Curly's arms. A sadness enveloped her as she stepped nervously through the ruined hall. She stood quite still, listening, hoping, hardly breathing. Everywhere was silent. Nothing moved.

"Curly!" she said almost in a whisper. "Curly! Is that you?"

There seemed to be no-one, yet she had a strange awareness of an eerie presence, closer than she realised! Her spine tingled and her heart beat faster. Fear caused a tightness in her neck as if a hand were closing round it and strangling her. She wanted to scream but her throat seemed to freeze. She stumbled and fell to the floor. Not six inches from her was a face. A pair of eyes stared out at her ghoulishly — whites turned yellowish in the half-light — eyes dead as stones. A large gash severed the top part of the skull and the greyish-white face was streaked with blood. The loathsome smell of death permeated the hall. Her hand accidentally brushed against the stiff, cold body. She screamed and fled to her mother's arms.

"Oh, Millie!" said Flo. "You shouldn't be having these shocks in your condition, dear."

Words cannot adequately describe the pandemonium that followed. The usual police enquiries — questions, questions, questions — and no answers, but news travels fast in a small community. Within a few days, the fated organ-grinder was identified and Ma Blackwood was called to confirm the evidence.

Pa had been dead a week now and nobody had ventured to suggest how it all might have happened.

"Do you think he was murdered?" said Mrs. Thompson to Timothy.

"Who can tell?"

"Whatever was he doing in the old house, I'd like to know. And who did that 'orrible knife thing belong to?"

"Another unanswerable question," said Tim. "After all, that monkey's been seen in the queerest places in the last few weeks. And the old man's most likely been with him at the time. Why was he hiding himself away? That's what I'd like to know. It's my view he was watching for somebody. Following them, maybe. And he wasn't quick enough to make a getaway. His face was a nasty mess. As to murder — well — it's my guess he died several hours after he was beaten up. Heart attack, I shouldn't be surprised. Or exposure."

Mabel began tugging at Timothy's arm.

"All right, duckie! Let's go."

At the Lollipop Shop they were greeted by a gang of boys disgorging from the doorway, licking their sticky fingers and shouting noisily. Inside the shop, all seemed tranquil enough. Tim and Mabel looked upon a rather harassed, paler, Ma Blackwood, though as far as she was concerned, Pa's death had not been so much of a loss as might be imagined. After all, their so-called marriage had been a farcical ploy that meant nothing to either of them — a little 'business deal' with the Mafia crowd. Nevertheless, his brutal departure from this life made her nervous.

"Hallo, my little darling!" she said in her thick accent. "What colour are we having today? Is it a red one?"

"Nope!"

"Blue, then?"

"Nope!"

"Well, my sweetie, that's all there is today."

"Chocolate!" announced Mabel to everybody's surprise, and pointing to a pile of Cadbury's.

"What's come over her? She's getting quite choosy, this young lady, " said Ma.

While Ma was leaning over the counter, something far more important caught Mabel's sharp little eye, something that brought joy to her heart. She clapped her hands with glee and began shouting: "Beppo! Beppo! Come to Mabel! Beppo! Come to Mabel!"

A leather thong attached to Beppo's chain protruded from under the counter. Mabel tugged at it with her strong little hands.

"Put that down!" screamed Ma in a terrifying voice. Timothy immediately saw another side to Ma Blackwood he had never experienced before.

"Put it down, you little wretch, you!" But it was too late. There in front of them was Beppo's little harness that Mabel knew so well, now covered in blood-stains.

Apart from hearing that Mabel had quite a tongue in her head, Ma Blackwood also learnt that Mabel had a good pair of lungs, for she screamed and screamed and screamed and screamed, and inadvertently attracted the attention of the local police, who promptly came to investigate. In the search, Beppo's battered little body was found dumped in a dustbin. It did not take a month of Sundays to put two and two together. The murder of Pa Blackwood, the outrageous slaughter of a defenceless animal and the discovery of his little harness underneath the counter of Ma Blackwood's shop counter, and then the finding of the vicious-looking knife, which apparently was similar to one seen in recent months by several local residents — all this seemed to point to one person, and that person was Curly Donoghue. It all tallied nicely with the statement of the Polenti ring-leader, who had liberally spilled the beans down at Rothersey Police station following his arrest.

By the time the police car arrived, the shop was shuttered and barred. A struggle followed a break-through from the rear of the shop next door, and before long, the place was a shambles of broken glass and crushed confectionery. An extensive collection of stolen property was forcibly removed. The Lollipop Shop was no more. From that moment, Ma Blackwood was permanently out of business. Together with her Polenti boys, she was invited to take tea at the police-station and was persuaded to enjoy whatever board-and-lodging the State could offer for the next five years. She was in for a long holiday. She would have plenty of time for sewing!

71. Trouble Brewing

Christmas Day had been warm and sunny and, ever since, everyone had been marvelling at the unpredictability of the English weather, just as they had done on almost every New Year's Eve since they could remember. As it happened, today, the skies were heavy-laden with snow clouds. Before too long, the little street would be shining and crystalline, conveniently dressed for a celebration and a wake at one and the same time.

There was nothing especially inspiring about this particular New Year's Eve, for, beneath the superficial *bonhomie,* there was a sadness at the impending mass departure from Laburnum Villas. The midnight chimes of Big Ben would herald for all the tenants of this little enclave a new beginning. With one or two notable exceptions, they would all be the proud or pained, thankful or nostalgic occupiers of a bright and gleaming Council flat, with a blue or a yellow or a green front door, a rubbish disposal unit, a smart tiled bathroom in mottled pink and grey, a view (depending on the direction in which the windows faced) of the Houses of Parliament and Battersea Power Station (both emitting a great deal of hot air) in the sprawling west, the Tower of London in the sprawling east, Elephant and Castle and Croydon to the sprawling south, and Golders Green and Crouch End to the sprawling north. Again, and with possibly one or two exceptions, they would all long to get back to the slum-security of the grimy old Victorian cul-de-sac they had known so intimately, to be absorbed once more in the complex rituals of its daily life, to feel the comforting proximity of the pub and the picture-house just round the corner, to sink blissfully back into anonymity and mental indolence that were in a curious way their wisdom and their strength. Some would have remembrances of things past. Some would have their dreams of a future in store. For others less fortunate, worn down by the travails of life, it would be simply a time of waiting. Every heart now was filled with that cloying sense of futility, of temporariness.

The occupants of the Villas, however, were by no means ready to set out on the last stretch of the road to their various destinies. The final seal would not and could not transform their lives until late that afternoon. The poltergeist of apathy had to be exorcised if they were to be saved from whatever it was the Good Lord thought they should be saved from. Accordingly, He raised His long finger with the calculated move of a chess-player and brought it down on the next defenceless pawn.

We must remember that the finger had already moved to some of our pawns: Ron, after all, had been cruelly brought to task on the question of faith and human frailty, and we cannot deny that it must surely be for his eternal good, though for the moment he is still smarting over it. The wound has not healed, and if we know Ron, it will require careful attention if he is to become the lad he could be if he would only try. As for Millie, her inviolable memory of Curly still lies strong within her, and no amount of rational persuasion to the contrary would make any difference to her feelings for him. Mabel, unaware of the changes that were surreptitiously taking place in her rapidly-maturing little body, had little or no interest now in lollipops. In fact, she had become quite a little show-off with her new craze for play-acting at school. There was Flo Thompson with the fear lurking in her mind of the two men intent on bringing down her house of sand. Agnes Baldock, now all but chastened, still nurtured a longing for some brutish oaf who might come to her out of a badly-written novelette. Some, like Joe Purvis and Curly Donoghue, had still to cross treacherous territory, but whatever might happen, there was no going back.

It would be easy for the plot of a novel to be contrived in such a way that the threads of the characters' lives could be tied neatly up into a convenient knot and the story completed. Should these characters be real people (and perhaps they are, though it is very unlikely, don't you think?), then we would want to follow their lives to that point where it is fitting to stop and say: 'These are the facts of the case. These are the people concerned. These are the particular joys they took pleasure in and the sorrows they endured. Now what may we infer from it all?' Well! We are almost at that point. We are aware that events are closing in on the people concerned, not because of some fictitious fabrication, but because life itself, as with all of us, is working out its own solution in its own relentless way.

The calm that spread through Laburnum Villas on this last day of the year possessed an ominous quality all its own. It was the calm that precedes the expression of high emotion, for there is still room for fear, anger, violence and remorse. The little street was coming to the end of its life. Before long it would be little more than a pile of rubble and the soul would have gone out of it. It was, above all, the terrible temporariness of everything that got under the skin.

Timothy returned from the Lollipop Shop with a very distressed Mabel, whose incessant crying for the loss of her friend, Beppo, made any conversation almost inaudible. His graphic account of the arrest of

353

Ma Blackwood and the rest of the Polenti gang gave Mrs. Thompson some exciting news to make a note of.

"Oh, well!" sighed Mrs. Thompson as Timothy prepared to take his leave of her. "Here today and gone tomorrow, as the saying is." This painful platitude might, by a more generous observer, be considered a gross rationalisation of the general predicament. It would least of all apply to Flo since she would, through sheer inefficiency and indolence, be the last to leave the Villas behind her.

"I shan't 'alf miss the ol' place. Nothing'll ever be the same, ever anymore. What *will* become of us all?"

In a matter of days, a fleet of removal vans had started to carry away the memories of a lifetime and deposit them without ceremony in the empty and as yet characterless spaces provided for them at the gleaming Rothersey Heights. Timothy had seen off their own van and Mrs. Crawford was helping Louise to clear the last of the cupboards and drawers. In less than an hour, Uncle Walter's possessions would be stowed away in the car.

Mrs. Crawford had been a tower of strength to Louise during the difficult months following her operation. At first it seemed that no-one could replace Uncle Walter in Louise's affections but in losing someone who had cared for her over the years with such wisdom and love, she had found a true friend in Timothy's mother. If Louise showed any signs of coming out of her protective shell, it was the growing affection she soon began to show for Mrs. Crawford. Timothy watched this increase and flourish like one of her old Uncle Walter's roses. Tim realised that, for once, he had taken the right decision in bringing his mother to stay at Laburnum Villas. Her friendship with her new-found ally had blossomed more than he could have ever hoped. They had spent many hours together, reminiscing, reading, and talking much of Timothy. As healing progressed, so Louise was able to articulate more successfully, though she might never fully recover her natural voice. Now, Mrs. Crawford was beginning to teach her willing pupil to read aloud and gradually, short conversations arose out of nowhere and faded into nowhere. Regular visits to the hospital for speech therapy had brought about the miracle of speech in Louise that Timothy had longed for from the first moment they met. Whilst this physical barrier was to some extent being resolved, the emotional hurdle remained almost insuperable. For years, she had lived an inexpressive life, giving little of herself to others, spending much of her time alone, feeling comfortable only in the gentle, caring companionship of Uncle Walter.

She grieved secretly at his loss, sitting for hours gazing out through the kitchen window at the little rose-garden that had now settled down to its winter sleep. Timothy had taken the best of Uncle's roses to plant in the garden at the farmhouse. By midsummer there would be an added blaze of Crimson Glory among his father's rose-beds.

"When you getting married, Tim?" said Mrs. Thompson, breaking brutally through his reverie.

"In the Spring, we hope. With the first daffodils. The garden is awash with them then — swathes of yellows, creams and whites, in infinite variety:

A host of golden daffodils;
Beside the lake, beneath the trees,
Fluttering and dancing in the breeze.

"You know — the stuff of poetry, but then so is love, come to that."

Mrs. Thompson was embarrassed by poetry and she always felt uncomfortable when people talked about love, so it was with a brisk change of subject that she continued:

"Poor old Mr. Paxton! One of the best, he was. What a year it's been, eh? I could write a book about it, I could. All that's gone on in this street, and I know only the half of it. I dreamed about a book once. I can see it now, as plain as can be. Just like the one I saw in a shop window once when me and Alf went up West — Charing Cross Road, I think it was. I never seen anything like it. Alf had to drag me away from it, but I tell you that book was so lovely I never forgot it. In my dream-book it said if you dream of a book bound in bright colours it meant you was going to be a writer, or something like that. Daft, isn't it? It'd be a lark if I ever wrote a book." She stopped speaking suddenly for she had the feeling she had said that before, a very long time ago.

"I think you'd write a good book, Mrs. Thompson. What you don't know about all the goings-on in Rothersey isn't worth the printing, so what you do know must be worth it. Why don't you try?"

"I couldn't put two words together, Tim. I aint got no education. You've been to a college, you have. It's different for you."

"Do you know something, Mrs. Thompson, I envy you."

"Envy? Whatever next!"

"Really, I do. I've been over-educated, don't you see? I

couldn't write to save my life. But you! You talk it all out of you. Why don't you put all your grouses and grumbles on paper. Write about what you feel inside. Don't worry about what other people think. Make Laburnum Villas come alive in words. Once you've moved, you'll have so many mod-cons in the kitchen, you won't know what to do with your time. Politicians and stars of stage and screen are doing it, so why not you."

"No. I couldn't, Tim. I'm just a nobody. Anyways, if I was to write all I know about the people round here, I'd be clapped in the clink, I would."

"Look! All you have to do is to answer a string of questions about your life and what you know about the Villas and the people who live here. How many people round you have a story to tell? There's Millie, Mabel, Ron, even Alf! Besides, there's Grandpa Lawton, there's Miss Baldock, there's Eddie, and Curly Donoghue. How many more people do you want to write about? Tell the story of how you feel about leaving. You don't have to be a star to write a book. The publisher finds someone else to write it for you these days!"

"Tim! You're flogging a dead horse. I aint got it in me. Everyone 'd laugh their flippin' 'eads off!"

"That's just it. Make them laugh if you like. Be natural. Be yourself. That's what you have to be, and you'll be a success. I'll read it for you and I'll tell you what I think."

"Why are you saying this to me, Tim? Nobody ever took that much interest in me before."

"That's because you let them take you over. You were always there to be leaned on. Now, you're going to be free, so why not try a bit of flying?"

"You know, anybody 'd think you'd got inside my dreams. P'raps I'll think about it."

"Oh, well! It never rains but it pours!"

"There you are, Mrs. Thompson! Another little story for your 'life and times of......', and you've already given yourself a working title."

"Have I?"

"*It Never Rains but it Pours.* How about that, eh?"

Flo's brain was suddenly teeming with titbits of gossip that came flooding back to her from her years at the Villas. She was so absorbed in her thoughts that she hardly heard Tim bidding her goodnight. When he had gone, she caught sight of her bunch of anemones on the draining-board and wondered how it was that Tim had come to choose the very flower of her dream. He was almost like a messenger from her world of dreams, a guardian angel come to her in her hour of need, like the young man she noticed standing by her in the Brighton shop. Then she remembered the men in dark suits. Flo could not know that Fate was preparing a frightening little story of its own that would give her plenty of ideas for a literary trip down memory lane!

72. Surprise Visit   No 1

Since it was New Year's Eve, there was an air of expectancy lurking in the nooks and crannies of Laburnum Villas. Mrs. Thompson was fussing over her party — for after a morning visit to the Rothersey Registry Office, Miss Millicent Flora Thompson had now become Mrs. Edward John Carpenter. Eddie was on leave before his first posting to Malta as a ship's engineer.

Ron had very little on his mind through the whole of the ceremony except his hopes of winning a scholarship for his painting of Grandpa Lawton on Brighton beach. After doing his fair share of standing in line to be photographed with the rest of the family, he had a strong urge to go off in search of the latest copy of *The Eagle* and then spend an hour or two at the flicks. As his big sister was embarrassingly larger than was usual for ninety-nine point nine per cent of brides on these occasions, it was not surprising that the Registrar's eyebrows practically hit the ceiling when confronted with the shapeless reality! What was worse, Ron and Mabel were made to stand right in the firing line for the photographs so as to provide some camouflage for the larger-than-life Millie.

Mrs. Thompson was opening a tin of pilchards in tomato sauce to fill the sandwiches with for the evening party. She was just thinking how nicely things had turned out for her and Alf, and for Millie and Eddie, too. Her thoughts were interrupted by a 'rap! rap! rap!' at the front door. 'Rap! rap! rap!' — sharper, like machine-gun fire.

She wasn't expecting visitors. The triple knock had a military note about it which told her that whoever was waiting there at her door was someone whose clutches she might have hoped to escape had the time been opportune. She hesitated, nervously wiped her perspiring palms on her apron, and crept silently through to the hall.

'Rap! rap! rap!' it came again.

Her heart pounded away. She felt a tremor of fear gripping her so hard that it took her breath away. Slowly she moved to the door. She heard voices on the other side.

'Rap! RAP! ra-ra-RAP!!!'

When she finally opened the door, she found herself face to face with two hefty men in Trilby hats and regulation raincoats.

A pair of thugs, she thought, and was about to slam the door in their faces when one of them drew a small card from his inside pocket and held it up to her nose.

"Good evening, madam. Police! We would like to ask you one or two questions. Mind if we come in for a moment?"

They did not wait to be asked. Mrs. Thompson led them through to the front room, gay with decorations from Christmas. The table was laid with all kinds of food, ready for the evening party of all parties, the last New Year's Eve of all her years at Laburnum Villas.

"Expecting company, are we?" said the man who asked all the questions.

"We're having a party tonight," she said lamely. Chill rivulets of blood flowed through her veins as she spoke.

"I see. For anyone in particular?

"Just family," she said quietly.

"Any — friends?" he asked in a knowing tone.

"Just family," she repeated hoarsely.

She could tell they knew she was frightened. She could feel them prodding her all over with their eyes, piercing the walls of her house, causing them to crumble about her as she stood helpless before them, nervously wringing her hands.

If they took her away before Alf came back from the pub she would die. And how long would they keep her? An hour? Two hours? All night perhaps? A week? Or even a month? Perhaps forever.

'Oh God!' she thought, 'don't let them take me away. Please don't let them take me away.'

So this was the nightmare of her house of sand. This was where she saw her whole life crumbling into the swirling river of disgrace and ignominy.

She wanted to blurt out her fuddled thoughts she wanted to say: "I didn't mean to do it. It was because of Millie, see? I'd been worrying meself sick over her. You know, her and the kid and that. Don't ask me why I did it. It just come over me. Please understand. I

358

just saw the nappies lying there on the counter. So I picked 'em up, see? I didn't mean it, but I said to meself: 'That's just what my Millie needs for the kiddie.' So I picked 'em up, see?"

The numbness came over her again.

"Mrs. Thompson!" said the inquisitor-man.

"I didn't mean to do it. Please don't take me away," she persisted.

The man looked blankly at her.

"Have you seen anything of Curly Donoghue?"

The question had no meaning for her.

"Donoghue, Mrs. Thompson."

"Donoghue! The dirty rotten louse!" she said, as if he were an irrelevance.

"Mrs. Thompson! I assume you know the full consequences of withholding information from the police and the penalties for harbouring a known criminal under your roof?"

"He aint here!" she said emphatically.

The silent man took out a long piece of paper and handed it to the inquisitor, who unfolded it and handed it to Flo, saying: "This is a search warrant."

"You aint searching *my* house, you aint. I'm respectable, I am. I've never had such a thing in my life."

The men went over the house all the same, inch by inch, delving into cupboards and wardrobes, looking under beds and behind curtains, groping around in "The Dumps", much to Smutty's annoyance for it was still his kingdom and there were these strangers poking about where they definitely weren't wanted. He growled and refused to be shifted.

Mrs. Thompson was sure they were searching for the stolen goods, even though she knew perfectly well there were none. She was filled with guilt. She felt the men would at any moment come stomping down the stairs with caseloads of stolen babies' nappies, maternity jackets and teddy bears she had inadvertently 'acquired' on her Brighton visit.

When they finally did come down, she was in a state of collapse. They were going to take her away and she would never be seen again. That was it. She would be clapped into handcuffs and frog-marched off to ten-year's hard-labour. Perhaps, she thought, that would not be such a change after all. She had done thirty years of it at the Villas. A fine start to the New Year, this was!

She began to snivel. She couldn't help herself. Her nose

359

started twitching and she could taste the salt in her tears as they ran down her face and into the sides of her mouth.

"I never meant to do it, I tell you." She clutched at the man's arms and sobbed.

"For crying out loud, Bill!" said the inquisitor man to the silent man. "We've got a right one here!"

"It's all right, lady. Don't upset yourself now. We're only doing our duty. Now you go back to your kitchen, and if you hear anything of Donoghue you're to let us know immediately. Do you understand?"

She nodded through her tears, not yet realising to what extent her fears had been unfounded. The two men stepped out onto the pavement and raised their hats politely.

"Happy New Year, madam! Sorry to have troubled you."

Flo leaned back against the wall of her hall and cried with the sheer relief of it all. Her dream house of sand had not crumbled about her. In reality, it would be the bulldozers that would one day destroy it, not some minor peccadillo in a Brighton department store. She had not been taken away after all, and surprisingly she did not faint.

Alf was enjoying his last pint over the newspaper when Flo arrived to lure him away to the Roxy Restaurant to attend Miss Baldock's farewell.

73. A Case in Point

A crowd was beginning to gather outside the magistrate's court. They were waiting for a glimpse of the hero of Rothersey, for it was practically certain that Councillor Joseph Gabriel Purvis would be acclaimed the man of the hour. So sure was this that the Vicar of St. Crispin's had taken over the Purvis Wind and Brass Ensemble and was now engaged in tuning them up to the right pitch. Great was the piping and wheezing and elephantine trumpeting as the odd collection of flute-players and horn-blowers came in with a cacophonic chord of defiance. It was Saturday afternoon and they would have much preferred watching West Ham beat the daylights out of Arsenal to waiting around for an old fogey of a borough councillor to come out and pontificate.

By now, everyone knew of the courage and determination shown by Councillor Joseph Gabriel Purvis in his relentless crusade against the Polenti gang, and especially the exposing of the evil in the heart of Gino Polenti. Since Polenti was unfortunate enough to be a foreigner, he was bound to be guilty and would be deported. Many of the foreigners settling in our country were devoid of morals and were only here to get what they wanted out of us. They had to go if they contravened our laws. Gino Polenti could not be tolerated in a fine English community like Rothersey, or so the Counsel for the Prosecution stated, and it was due to upstanding men of our age like Councillor Purvis that this should be so. Indeed, said Counsel for the Defence, the Borough had cause to be proud of such a man. His years of service to the public, his high principles, his outstanding courage in joining with the authorities in ridding the Borough of such an evil cancer, all this brought the Councillor added support. By word of mouth, his fame as champion of Rothersey spread even as far as Fleet Street and the columns of the national dailies.

Yet how much greater was his name honoured when the post-sentential news of the arrest of the Lollipop Gang became known. The idea was mooted that his name might just be included in the Queen's New Year Honours list. As Flo Thompson quaintly summed up his rapid rise to fame: "He'll be right for a gong before long, I'll be bound!"

Only one thing might have marred the Councillor's greatest hour — the question of his personal honour in respect of a certain 'Miss X', whom pretty well everybody knew was the deliciously curvaceous Millie Thompson. The matter would have still been cloaked in deep suspicion to this very day had not Gwendolen appeared from out of the Yorkshire Moors to testify as to his innocence and even virtuousness, if not virtuosity! She admitted that, on the night of the Councillor's successes at the meeting with the Committee on Juvenile Delinquency in February, she had been upstairs asleep and that no lights were on in the house when the Councillor had returned with 'Miss X'. She admitted she had come downstairs in a stupor and prepared alcoholic drinks— a strong gin-and-tonic for her father, a sherry for herself and a tonic water for Millie, further confessing she had not only mixed the drinks, she had also mixed them up! Nobody seemed to mind. In any case, with reference to the second visit to the Councillor's home in April, it had been made clear in Miss X's evidence in the witness box that the real father was being anxiously sought by the police.

The closing speech for the prosecution was so brilliant, so deftly expressed that the Councillor could not have hoped for a better one. It suited his campaign for popularity admirably. He was shown in a light

361

of impeccable integrity, a man of spirit and of honour, indeed, a gentleman. The speech ended by eliciting vociferous cries of triumph, everybody cheering him, and subsequently chairing him down the steps outside the court-room.

As he emerged into the cold sunlight, Gwendolen by his side, 'Angel Gabriel' Purvis felt a new man with a message inside him wildly gesticulating to be let out. Cheer upon cheer broke over the batteries of reporters, photographers and residents of Rothersey. The Vicar raised his baton. Instruments gleamed at the ready. The baton flicked and a grim, unsteady grunting noise came from the trombones, the rest of the brass following on the rocky path leading to the first bars of one of the more celebrated marches by Sousa. Everywhere, on this dark winter afternoon, the neon lights blazed forth the names of *The Purvis Recreation Centre* and *The Purvis Bowl*, calling the local youth to come and enjoy a bit of good clean fun, which, alas, was beginning to become quite unfashionable as the new decade was fast approaching.

The Councillor smiled triumphantly, waved his hand at the crowd, and for want of a better, emulated the Prime Minister's now hackneyed catch phrase: 'You never had it so good!'

"Peace and Plenty for Britain!" Joe Purvis — now 'The People's Man' — shouted deliriously.

"Hurray!" they shouted back. "Good old Joe!"

He turned to go down the steps to the waiting car, only to come face to face with 'Pixie' Calthrop.

"You win, Purvis. You win. But there's always a next time. You'll undoubtedly be tipped for mayor this time round in spite of your little misdemeanour."

"Thank you for your encouragement, however grudging, Calthrop," said Gabriel, smiling like a tormented sinner who has just discovered the secret of the good life. "It's what I've worked for all my life."

"Smiling damned villain!" muttered Calthrop.

With that exchange, Councillor Purvis took Gwendolen's arm and walked down the steps to his car, leaving the frustrated Calthrop with plenty to fume about.

"Come, Gwen! We must be off home. Our spanking new television set is arriving at five. We want to be in time to welcome it in, don't we?" The gleaming black monster was, however, never to be joined to its crumpled antenae. It was destined for a higher place in life than Laburnum Villas. In a few days it would be transported in all its

362

glory to the Councillor's tenth floor flat at Rothersey Heights.

Gabriel was proud of Gwendolen. Not such a bad girl after all. She had come to save his reputation, which had been in the greatest danger of ending in tatters. What was more to the point, she was a good cook, a neat little housekeeper, just what a man needed in his position. Exactly right for organising the entertainment in the Mayor's Parlour. And, joy of joys, he would remain unhampered by the restrictions of married life with a formidable lady of his acquaintance. Next year, he thought, I shall be living in a splendid flat (he had contrived to secure the show-flat!) with a fine view of the Houses of Parliament, and, who knows, the chance of a quick shake of the Royal Hand!

For the rest of Rothersey, the case was over. Polenti was to be sentenced and now everybody could look forward to the new life. With the unlimited magnanimity of a working-class community, they would forgive and quickly forget. "Poor bugger!" they would say, in sympathy with the underdog. And that would be the end of that, at least until Curly Donoghue turned up.

74. A Sticky Situation

After the worst of the wedding circus had run its course, Ron found a lucky moment when he could play truant from the family kissy-kissy displays on the steps of the Registry Office and slink away to see what antics Laurel and Hardy and Tom and Jerry were getting up to in the children's afternoon film show at the Palaseum. After a whole hour of violence and mayhem, Ron reluctantly made his way to the Roxy, this time not to his fantasy world of adventure but to the very real world of cream buns and chocolate cake.

"Well! Here comes our little genius," said Alf as Ron pushed through the glass doors. "Here's our little clever-dick himself."

"That's right!" said Flo, feigning her hoity-toity manner. Since she no longer carried a burden of guilt on her shoulders, she could enter freely into the party spirit. "*Now* you're talking real nice to him. The moment he's got a hundred quid in the bank. Thinking how much you can cadge off of 'im, are you?"

"No, I aint!" said Alf, raising his eyebrows like a latter-day George Robey. "I was thinking what a nifty couple o' nits we must be to give birth to this 'ere kid what can play that bloody tin-whistle and

363

daub hisself up with paint so as you wouldn't know 'im from a bit o' Marley's best lino."

"It's not a tin-whistle, dad. It's a piccolo."

"Just as well might be a piccalilli as far as I can see. Anyway, I thought you played that record thing."

"Recorder, Dad."

"How many blinkin' instruments do you play then?"

"Now don't get on to the lad," said Flo in a conciliatory tone. "This is supposed to be a celebration, not one of your 'Peace and Plenty' larks!" She looked round for any sign of a waitress.

"Cor, blimey! They aint 'arf slow in 'ere. Where's my welsh rabbit?"

By the time Ron's beans-on-toast arrived they were in great danger of suffering from over-exposure and had turned an unhealthy chocolate colour. As for the welsh rarebit, it looked anything but rare, and there was certainly nothing Welsh about it.

""It's numb with cold, it is," Flo complained. "It's probably got a dose o' that mixed-in-me-toeses most likely! I'll put in on the chair here so nobody sees it and take it home for Smutty. He'll eat any old rubbish."

Ron sniggered and crunched up one of his dried-up beans like a nut.

"Well," said Alf, coming up with a bright suggestion. "Call old Mother Balls-up over and kick her up the fanny. That'll warm things up a sight."

"Alf Thompson!" said Flo. "I'm not one for complaining in public."

"Well, you do enough of it at home, so why not here?"

"Well! Taint nice to complain. It's bad manners."

"Why don't you send it back, then? Tell old Ballcock to stuff it up her jumper," said Alf. "If there's any room! And stop bloody-well carping, both of you. Gets on my wick, it does."

Flo made a great show of pouring out fresh tea for everyone, for she caught sight of Miss Baldock bearing down on them. She was on safari, in search of her usual table.

"This table's reserved," Agnes announced in an intimidating tone.

"Well, we got here first," said Alf, equally emphatically.

"There's no need to be rude, Mr. Thompson," she muttered, pulling out a piece of cardboard from under the Thompson's tray. "Can't you read? It says: NO SERVICE!"

"Well! Well! Well!" Alf tittered, rubbing his stubbly chin. "It's three against one, then."

With a few steely glares and glances, the Lady Manageress strode off and no-one had the gumption to complain to her.

"Silly old bitch!" Alf muttered under his breath. "She's getting so big her boots won't fit no more."

Flo scraped her welsh rarebit onto a paper serviette and placed it furtively on the spare chair.

"I'll take it home for Smutty," she said.

This farce was interrupted by the arrival of Timothy and Mabel.

"Look at this, Ron, my lad," said Tim. "You're in the news. See for yourself."

He held out a copy of the *Rothersey Clarion*, open at page six and showing the headline:

'Old Man on the Beach' wins £100 prize

An Exhibition of works by young water-colour artists was opened yesterday at the Rothersey Art Gallery by the Minister for the Arts. The prize of £100, together with a scholarship to the Rothersey School of Art, went this year to fourteen-year-old Ronald Thompson of Laburnum Villas, Rothersey, for his study of an old man on a beach. The unusual gradation of tone and the adventurous style of the piece show this young artist to be in possession of a considerable talent. It was revealed this morning that the painting has been purchased by an anonymous buyer for the sum of £50.

Flo looked at Ron. Ron looked at Tim. Alf looked at Flo. In a flash, Ron was being patted and kissed and cuddled and hugged until he blushed a bright scarlet.

"Feel a proper nit, I do," he said.

As the first-house audience started to trickle through the glass doors into the auditorium, Alf rose to pay the bill. No sooner had they left the table than Miss Baldock was at their heels to reserve it for herself. She grimaced as she surveyed the wondrous confusion before her. Everywhere was crumbs and stickiness. She called the waitress over and told her to clear it all away immediately and to bring her tea from the kitchen, her last meal at the Roxy. Tomorrow she would be in Worthing, starting out on a new adventure.

Lunchtime customers were beginning now to thin out. Business was on the up-and-up and it was all due to Agnes. She remembered those words of Andrew Crawford about having a place of her own and how she could make a mint of money with her experience. Well! That was precisely what she had arranged to do. In a few hours she would be gone, out of this smelly hole and into the fresh sea-side air of Sussex.

When she sat down, which was with about as much delicacy as a hippopotamus, Agnes felt an uncomfortable squelch beneath her—something warm and sticky — spread out over her ample behind like soft plasticine. Her cry of horror attracted many pairs of eyes as they fell upon her rear quarters and saw a squadgy mass of yellow glue-like substance squashed as flat as a pancake.

It did not take Ron very long to snigger. Then Alf. Then Flo. Then Tim. Even now-not-so-little Mabel, began to giggle with glee and jump about like a plump little bean. The whole restaurant clientele seemed to have been liberally sprayed with laughing gas.

Miss Baldock had never been so humiliated in all her life, and on her last day too. This was all she needed to undermine her authority—impaled on one of her own welsh-rarebits! She scowled till her face almost cracked into little pieces. The situation was saved only by the timely arrival of the Rev. Curtis, who had come to add his ration of praise for Ron's artistic triumph.

Later that afternoon, Agnes was required to make an appearance at the Roxy Manager's office. There, she was presented with a pair of electroplated fish-servers as a parting gift. Nodding a specious approval and scanning the row of unsmiling faces, she found it difficult to believe that she would be missed one iota. As the clock of St. Crispin's struck its cracked and mournful five, it seemed to be her parting knell. She collected up her things from her office and prepared to say good-riddance to the restaurant of the Roxy Picture House. This was the end of a phase in the life of Agnes Baldock, or at any rate, almost the end.

EPISODE FIFTEEN

Early Afternoon

Unexpected Visitors

75. Surprise Visit   No 2

Alf, Flo and Mabel returned home to get on with the preparations for the wedding party their own way. Timothy announced that he had some shopping to do, and whispered to Ron that he wanted to have a word with him. They crossed the road and disappeared into Marley's Stores where Tim purchased a bar of chocolate and some fresh fruit. On the way out, he said to Ron: "Got five minutes to spare, Ron?"

"What for?" he said, guardedly.

"Thought we might take a short stroll together."

"What for?"

"Well," said Tim, realising the difficulties involved, "it *is* the last time I shall see you, for quite a long time anyway. So what's five minutes to us?"

"Okeedoke!" — which meant: 'No! I don't want to talk to boring adults' and 'Yes! Only if I have to.'

Timothy launched into the attack. It wasn't going to be easy, that was for sure.

"You've done very well, Ron. Your Mum and Dad must be really proud of you."

"I s'pose so," said Ron, diffidently.

"Oh, they are, Ron! As proud as peacocks, they are. You can see it a mile off."

"Maybe!" said Ron, thoughtfully.

"Well, can't you feel it, Ron?"

"Oh, I s'pose so."

"Of course you can, Ron. You've made wonderful strides with your painting. I wish I could have done it at your age, or any other age, come to that. And think, Ron! You've not only won a scholarship to Art School, there's actually someone around who believes in you enough to slap down fifty pounds just like that. Now isn't that something to be proud of?"

"I s'pose so," he said flatly, "but I can't feel it. It's all too sudden, like. When I did that painting I never thought about prizes and things."

"Of course you didn't. You just sat down and got on with it. And when it was finished what did you do?"

"Went out in a canoe."

"Then what?"

"I found a beach-ball floating in the sea. All colours, it was.

368

Smashing! When I got home I did a painting of it, too."

"There you are, you see? Even a beach-ball can give you inspiration."

"What's inspiration?"

"You do ask some questions, don't you?" said Tim, running his fingers through his hair in a despairing gesture, as they sauntered along under the trees in the pale sun of a winter's afternoon.

"I suppose," Tim said, "inspiration is something that makes you feel it's good to be alive — something that makes you so full of joy that you want to go and pick up your paint-brushes and paint it out of your system. Did you feel like that when you painted Grandpa?"

"Oh, *him*!" said Ron with a scowl. "We don't have to bring *him* into it, do we?"

"We are not talking about *him*, Ron. We're talking about *you*!"

"O.K. So we're talking about me! So what?"

"Go on, then," said Tim. "Tell me how you felt, then."

"Well," said Ron, with some hesitation, "I just felt peculiar, that's all. I just went all funny inside and I knew I wanted to paint Grandpa. That's all."

"How did you get the haunting expression in the eyes? How did you come to see him in that way?"

"My art teacher says it was more artifice than art. I don't know what that means but I daresay it means something rotten!"

"The very best that can be said about artifice is that at least you know how to get round problems. You don't want to listen too much to other people's opinions. After all, you are the one who won the prize."

"Well, I just saw Grandpa as I always knew him, and then I saw something else I'd never seen before. Another Grandpa Lawton. So I painted two different Grandpas in the same face. I just saw something else."

"What else?"

""Oh," said Ron, irritably. "What you askin' me all these questions for? It's like a blinkin' third degree!" His emotion was making him forget his grammar again.

"No, go on, Ron. What was it you saw?"

"I told you. It was like looking at two people in the same face. One I knew, and one I didn't want to know."

Almost before Ronald realised where they were going, he and Timothy were walking over the cinder drive of the house in Napoleon Avenue.

"'Ere! What's your game, then?" said Ron abruptly. "I'm not goin' in there. That's the Old People's Home. I'm not goin' in, I tell you."

"Ron!" said Tim firmly. "I've only got to leave a few grapes and some chocolate and then we can go home together."

"I aint going in."

Ron thought that he might make up some excuse and run for it.

"Don't be so silly, Ron. You won't bump into Grandpa, don't worry. He's up in his room, in bed. Probably asleep. He had an exhausting day yesterday."

Ron meekly followed Timothy up the steps and into the hall. A coal fire was smoking blackly in the grate, the smoke pervading the adjoining rooms and staircase. He was just about to slip out when Tim motioned him into the lounge.

"Wait there, while I take these things up to Grandpa."

Ron sauntered reluctantly into the large and spacious room, with its chintzy armchairs and sofa. When Tim came downstairs, however, Ron was waiting for him in the hall.

"But — but I don't understand," he said excitedly.

"Don't you, Ron," said Timothy in a teasing tone of voice.

"I just don't understand how *my* painting got in *there*!"

They went into the lounge. Ron's portrait of Grandpa, in a gilt frame, was hanging on the wall over the Victorian white marble fireplace.

"It's all very simple, really," said Tim.

"You mean. said Ron, remembering the *Rothersey Clarion* article, "you mean Grandpa actually went and bought my painting?"

"He did" said Tim. "And what's more, he's presented it to the Home. It will always hang there, Ron. Your picture, for everyone to see."

"Golly!"said Ron, wide-eyed with wonder. Then he asked almost in a whisper:

"Can I see Grandpa?"

"If you really want to, Ron. You can go to him now. Only for a few minutes, mind! He's very tired, poor old chap. It was quite a strain for him to get up to the exhibition yesterday. We arranged it all quite amicably with the organisers. The painting will be returned for a special viewing next week, when Grandpa is better. Who knows, perhaps you will be invited too."

Ron's visit to Grandpa was brief. The old man was pale and

worn out. He lay weakly in his bed, hardly seeming to breathe, and as still as a corpse. Just a slight turning of the head and the faintest of smiles told Ron that there was still a spark of life left to mark their final reconciliation. But the old man's eyes held a strange distant look, as if he were already journeying to another gallery in the sky. It would be the last time Ron would see him.

76. Surprise Visit No 3

No sooner had Agnes Baldock packed Mr. Lawton's last bundles off to the Old People's Home than she began to feel an atmosphere of decay about the house. She hadn't realised until the old chap left how much a part of the place he had been. And now that she had barely seen the last barrow-load of junk being wheeled off up the road, little twinges of remorse wriggled their way through the tiniest of fissures in her hardening heart. But only momentarily! The immediacy of her departure left her in no doubt whatsoever as to the rightness and justness of her actions. Seeing the bareness of the old man's living-room, shorn of its former dinginess and squalor, she was convinced that whatever her motives may have been, it had all been for the best. She had saved him from a fate worse than death, or so she wanted to believe.

The sound of her own feet as they clomped over the bare boards made her lonelier than ever. She mused with some rancour on the fact that she had never been successfully assimilated into this tightly-knit little community. She had, to the last, remained a 'foreigner'. Nothing would have induced her to embark upon the long descent to the mean averageness of people like the Thompsons. Why! When she conversed with the Thompsons and the Carpenters she might just as well have attempted to talk to the Man in the Moon for all the understanding there was between them. Yes, she was a foreigner in her own land. At least in Worthing she would be among her own sort, people of breeding and manners, retired people with money, taste and respectability.

It was just as she was putting her toothpaste and other toiletries in her vanity-case that she was startled by a knock at the back door. Then she realised that Frank and Cynthia were calling for goodbyes. She closed her case and went to open the door. The blood drained from her face when she saw who her visitor was.

"Evenin', Aggie, me old dear!"

"You!" she gasped.

"Surprised, are you?"

She stood speechless for what seemed an age. As she tried to close the door in his face, a strong arm came up and a clenched fist pushed her violently back into the kitchen.

"Well? Aren't you goin' to ask me in, Aggie, darlin'?"

"Get out of my house!" she spluttered.

"Here! Now that aint very 'ospitable-like, is it? Don't you want to give your old boy-friend a goodbye kiss?"

"Get out of here, Donoghue. Get— out— of — my —house, do you hear me? I'll call the police if you don't."

"Now how d'you suppose you're going to do that, eh, my darlin'? Anyway, I'm here to look after you, see? Seein' as how you bin so *nice* to me in the past, like. Never forget a good turn, I don't."

He jerked himself away from the door and lurched towards her aggressively. He ran his hands down over his thighs as if he were cleaning his palms. She watched his fingers opening and closing with the frustration of it.

"No!" she gasped. "No! Please don't!"

With a violent thrust that took all her wind away, he pushed her against the cupboard and ran his hands over her shoulders, pressing the whole length of his body against her.

"Why don't you give me a bash over the ear-'ole. Cop me one on the kisser, Aggie. Come on!"

His voice was quiet and insinuating as if he meant business. With a sudden shout straight at her face, loud enough to make her wince, he breathed hard at her, gripping her blouse and rubbing his hands over her bosom to frighten her. Then he spat into her face with all the venom of a viper.

"You scared, are you, Aggie? Bloody scared, are you?" he said hoarsely. "You aint got no 'Dandy' Crawford to protect you now, have you, me old sweetie? And you're as scared as hell. Scared I'm goin' to push you over and do something you've been wanting for years."

He thrust at her brutally and she fell heavily to the floor, her face contorted with fear and loathing.

When she felt his hand between her legs and smelt the unwashed flesh of his body, she began kicking out at him with all her strength but he overpowered her, pinning her to the floor.

"You bloody old bitch!" he shouted, almost in a scream of anguish. " You ruined my life, you old cow! Think you can order me around, do you? Well, I'll show you something you aint seen before, as good as you'll ever get. I'm telling you, you bitch!"

He struck her brutally across the face. Once, twice and once again. A tiny drop of blood oozed from the corner of her mouth. He was crazy with his own power as he sat astride her, his thighs gripping her like a vice, his fists forcing her down till she felt the very breath go out of her.

Her ears thrummed with fear. Her brain whirled round and round till she grew faint. Yet, suddenly, all her rapidly diluting strength seemed to coagulate into a whirling mass of disgust and loathing for this monster that was ravishing her body and devouring her soul. She felt the unshaven stubble of his beard against her face.

In one last desperate effort, she clasped the folds of his leather jacket like a frenzied heroine of Greek tragedy. Her fingernails tore at his flesh. She bit hard into his neck. In a supreme physical spasm, she thrust him from her. As she did so, her hand came against the black hardness of the iron poker lying on the hearth. Gripping it with all her strength, she brought it crashing down over his back. He yelled out in agony and clutched his spine, his face contorted into shapelessness, as it had been on that fatal day when Agnes had brought about the first stage of his downfall. He writhed on the floor, while she wielded her instrument of chastisement over and over again, striking him with blows on thighs, on arms, on back, till his very bones seemed to crack. She was purging her own soul as much as his. She was whipping out her sin and cleansing herself of the filth of the world that lay before her. She was a high priestess thrashing a penitent.

Curly cried out for mercy, like a young child, a cry most terrible to her ears, a cry from the wilderness of despair and hopelessness. In a moment, he was gone — out through the door into the darkness.

Agnes did not know how long she had been unconscious, but when she came to, Frank and Cynthia were helping her to her feet with a flood of sensational comment and their customary shallow sympathy. The trickle of blood had dried on her chin and as she sat flopped in a chair, Frank patting her cheeks and Cynthia bathing her wounds, she looked more like a boxer resting in his corner between bouts than a departing tenant of Laburnum villas.

"Oooh! What a nasty gash, Cynthie! Be careful you don't make it bleed all over the place. Poor Agnes! Attacked in her own house like this."

He spoke these words with about as much feeling as a bull-dog has for a cat, and Agnes, in her hypersensitive state, heard it and registered it.

"Never mind!" he went on, "we'll soon get you to the Police Station and then we can get the whole story out of you. We'll feel better then, won't we?"

Miss Baldock was not now so stupefied that she did not notice the revealing change of pronoun. She knew perfectly well that all these two were interested in was sensation and the publicity that attended it. A nice picture of them both on the front page of the Sunday papers, that's all they were after.

With an effort, she rose to her feet and announced that she was better already, and certainly had not the slightest intention of going to the Police Station with *them* or anybody else for that matter. *She* had a train to catch.

Straightening her tweed costume, she adjusted her under-garments, and surmised that the pleasure 'Lucy Locket' had derived from her leather-jacketed dispatch-rider must have been an entirely literary one, as fictitious as Donoghue's virility was, as spurious as her own vision of what sex was all about.

You would think we could finish this sorry chapter of the Agnes Baldock story, but people like Frank and Cynthia are hard to get rid of. They just won't let go.

"Why, Agnes, dear, if we hadn't been so persistent you might have been raped and ravished in your own kitchen. Just think of it."

Agnes was trying not to.

"And if we hadn't kept on knocking at the front door— well! if Cynthie hadn't slipped round the back and found you lying on the floor, dead to the world — there's no telling what would have happened. You would have been a gonner."

"I don't care what it seemed like to you," said Agnes rashly, "I don't care, do you hear? There's no need to gloat over the thing, is there? It's people like you that cause half the trouble in this world, with your leering and gloating and poking about in search of sensation. Always looking for trouble in somebody else's life, always wheedling out nice little scraps of gossip, always poking your noses in where your not wanted. I know your type. We get plenty of them at the restaurant, enough to know what troublemakers you are. Now just leave me alone."

Frank and Cynthia were thunderstruck.

"Well!" gasped Cynthia, her mouth twisted up as if she just swallowed a pint of vinegar.

"Well!" Frank spluttered, affronted beyond measure. "And after all we've done for you. We've befriended you. We've given you hospitality. We've found you business contacts in Worthing. We've —"

"LEAVE ME ALONE!!!" shouted Agnes. I'm *not* going to the Police Station. I've had enough sensation for one day. I'm tired, do you hear? Tired! Tired! Tired! Tired of this house. Tired of Rothersey. Tired of you. I'm leaving on that train tonight and no-one's going to stop me."

"Cynthia!" said Frank. "Let's get out of this demented woman's way. There's no point in carrying on with this vulgar discourse."

As they walked off up the street, Agnes overheard them indulging in a veritable sludge of sympathy:

"Poor dear! Quite beside herself! Shouldn't be surprised if she's a bit off her rocker. You never know where you are with these old bats. What she wants is a good man. She'll never get one the way *she's* going about it. Let her stew in her own juice, that's what I say."

Having so dismissed Agnes Baldock from their minds, they could go and enjoy the thriller at the Roxy, unaware that real drama, sensation and violence were abroad in Rothersey tonight.

In a strange way, Agnes already felt a different woman. Different, that is, from the woman she had been a few hours earlier. In the space of that short time, she had suffered humiliation and degradation. Pride had been purged from her soul, so had wrath, so had avarice, so had lust, so had envy and covetousness. She felt a new being, a new Agnes Baldock. Clearly, it would be some months before the chrysalis would give birth to the butterfly, but, in a curious way, she felt reborn, renewed in spirit, even in the very teeth of fate.

As she turned the key in the lock for the last time, and looked up and down the little world of Laburnum Villas, she knew it was of brief duration. Hardly had she left than the cranes and bulldozers would come swooping in to demolish it, and with it would go her dreams of quite a different future than the one she was now embarking upon. Not without some regrets, she stopped opposite Gabriel's house, with its bay-windows and its Brussels lace curtains. Yes, she stopped, but only for one brief moment of sadness. Then she turned the corner and was gone forever from the Villas.

77. Surprise Visit No 4

Ron wandered out into the High Street with its brightly-lit shop-windows. The happy crowds sauntering past the gaudily illuminated Town Hall filled him with loneliness and depression, the luxury of which was cut short by the sudden appearance of the Rev. Daniel Curtis from the late afternoon shadows, like some mysterious messenger from outer space.

"Come with me, young Ronald!" said the Vicar, who happened (through an arrangement with Timothy) to be passing by just at that moment. "I've something special to show you."

"What for? Why?" said Ron, suspiciously.

Somehow, the euphoria of his recent success had begun to pall and he found himself sinking into inexplicable gloom brought on by thoughts of a happy past with Grandpa Lawton and an uncertain future with not a friend he could really call his own.

"It's not about 'what for' and 'why'," said Rev. Curtis. " Just come along with me and you'll see for yourself."

"Is it a present?"

"You could say that."

"Where are we going?"

"You'll see. I have a call to make at St. George's. It won't take long, I promise you."

"Churches are boring," Ron said, looking downcast.

Ignoring the protest, the Vicar led Ron out along the bustling High Street and soon they were passing by the Palaseum, in the direction of Rothersey Bridge. Turning down a side road, the Vicar unlocked a wrought iron gate in the wall and led Ron up a flight of steps to a tall, heavy-looking door which he opened with a large key.

"Come on in, Ron. I have to leave a letter here for the Vicar."

Ron paused, feeling a mixture of reluctance and apprehension.

"Now, do come along, Ronald. This is a House of God, you know, not the headmaster's office! Everyone is welcome here. Now, sit down and make yourself comfortable! I have another appointment later, so we mustn't be too long."

Ron perched himself on the edge of a long oak bench and looked round the vestry at the rows of hymn-books lining the walls. The panelling made the room dark and dismal. It had the aspect of a torture chamber he had seen in a horror film once. Now he came to think of it, the old flea-pit of a Roxy Picture House, in Ron's opinion, was an absolute palace, compared to this, and no mistake!

"There's a story about this place which might just interest you," said Mr. Curtis. "It's about a little girl called Amy, whose father, Old Dorrit, had lost all his money through bad business dealings and ended by being sent to a prison for debtors."

"You can't go to prison just because you owe money."

"Oh yes, you can, Ron. Especially if it's other people's money you owe. *Neither a borrower nor a lender be!* Shakespeare wrote that. He says it's the best way to lose your friends, and we don't want to do that, do we? Just remember to look after your prize money. Money is like water, Ron. It disappears through your fingers in no time."

"Shakespeare's boring."

"Shakespeare tells you what life is all about — how to distinguish right from wrong, how to deal with life when things get difficult. Anyway, this Amy dearly loved her father, as every child should, though unfortunately it isn't always the case these days. The war changed all that."

"She should be so lucky. My father doesn't even know I exist."

"I'm sure that's not true, Ron, if you only knew. *Honour thy father and thy mother*, so the saying goes in the Bible. This story tells us a lot about money, and honour come to that, Ron. It also tells us a lot about real love. Amy—Little Dorrit, as everyone affectionately called her— loved her father and he loved her, but when he got into debt, love didn't save him from prison. Love did help though. She eventually met a gentleman called Arthur Clennam, who grew to love her so much that he wanted to marry her."

"There you are, you see. It turned out all right for her. Nobody loves me. I'm different."

"You are certainly different, Ron. But it wasn't as simple as all that. Life never is. Love and money are not the whole picture. The little things in life are important, too. *Always be thankful for small mercies.* There you are! That's another good saying. Sometimes we are more fortunate than we realise. After all, look what Grandpa Lawton's tin of sweets led to — a £100 prize and a scholarship."

"What happened next?" asked Ron, mildly interested. He was beginning to think that all this was mysteriously relevant in some way.

" In this case," the Vicar went on, "the old father was lucky enough to inherit a fortune, which should have been a great joy to his family, but it all went to their heads and they became arrogant and selfish. You see, life is a series of rewards and punishments. The

377

wicked usually suffer for their wickedness— at least they seem to in literature, if not always in life— and sometimes even the good are caught up in the wickedness of others, too. Now, through bad advice, the kindly Arthur lost all his money, and, through a fraudulent deceit, his inheritance too. By a trick of fate, he found himself in the self-same prison that Little Dorrit's father had been confined to. Little Dorrit's family now had so much wealth in their pockets, they just did not know how to handle it. When she later discovered how destitute and sick her dear friend, Arthur was, she nursed him back to health. That's how he grew to love her so much—through kindness and selflessness. The trouble was, he could not say how much he loved her in case she should think he was more interested in her fortune."

"That's silly. If I had money, I wouldn't let no-one—" [*he paused to correct himself*] " — anyone get the better of me, especially a girl. My Mum says they're all money-grabbers. She says you can read all about it in the papers."

"Don't you believe it, Ron. You just have to make sure who your real friends are. It's love that makes the world go round, not money. Money is useful to us, but it cannot make people love us. It has to be hard-earned, like your well-deserved prize-money."

"I think love is silly. Didn't she have no — any pride?" said Ron, getting quite involved with the story.

"Well, Little Dorrit was showing her true feelings for someone she loved. She was being true to herself. That's what you must be, Ronald. Make the most of life's opportunities. Now, this is the very church which Amy — Little Dorrit — was christened in, and said her prayers in on Sundays, and eventually married in. I'll show you the altar where she made her marriage vows and where true love triumphed in the end. Come with me."

He opened a door into the chancel. Ron cautiously stepped in. At the touch of a switch, the whole of the nave was flooded with light. Ron gasped. He had never been in a church before. He gazed with astonishment at the richly decorated plaster ceiling with its festoons of drapery and happy smiling cherubs.

"Now there's a work of art for you — made by craftsmen well over two hundred years ago."

They climbed a flight of stairs to the gallery.

"Look, Ron! You can almost touch the angels here." The Vicar led him along the gallery to a vast organ, sat down at the console, switched on the power and opened a book of Bach's *Toccatas and*

Fugues.

Ron climbed up excitedly onto the bench, his legs dangling over the pedals.

"What are all those things?" asked Ron, pointing to the confusing array of organ stops.

"These all control the kind of sounds you want to make. Give me your hand and I'll put your fingers in position. Now, press down evenly. Firmly though, or you won't play all the notes."

A shiver went up Ron's neck at the sheer volume of sound that a simple chord could make, reverberating high up round the swirling cherubs on the ceiling.

"There you are! You ought to take some lessons, Ron. See here, on the music, it tells me if the music is loud or soft. I'll play you something, if you like."

The first chords reverberated through the church and Ron realised that his piccolo and recorder were no match for an instrument that could flood such a vast space with resounding music the like of which he could never have imagined.

On the way out, Ron caught sight of a painting. It was of an old man he seemed somehow to recognise, though he had never set eyes on it in his life.

"This beautiful painting was done in the seventeenth century," said the Vicar. "A long time ago, Ron. But how real it still looks today. You can see the great prophet, Moses. There is real knowledge in that face."

As Ron looked up in wonderment at the wise old face of Moses and the majestic flowing robes, he saw something there that stayed with him for the rest of his life—something he could not recognise at that moment, a glory and a grandeur that was mysteriously meaningful, something which made him feel that even he, little Ron Thompson, could belong to a life that was immeasurably greater than himself.

Back in the vestry, Mr. Curtis went to a cupboard in the corner and took out a brown paper parcel.

"Open this when you get home, Ronald."

As they came out into the glare of the street lights, the Vicar handed Ron a coloured postcard of the painting of Moses and a paperback copy of *Great Expectations.*

"There you are, Ron. Charles Dickens wrote this story about a young lad called Pip, not unlike yourself, though I hope you don't meet a young lady as arrogant as the one in the story. He has to learn the hard way about the power of money and the value of true love. It all turns out happily in the end. You should read Dickens, Ron. No writer other than Shakespeare knew his fellow-man better. Read as much as you can now, Ron. You'll find it's a very enjoyable way to learn about human nature and the ways of the world. Remember, Ron, 'There are more things in heaven and earth than this world dreams of.' Shakespeare wrote something of the sort."

As he turned into the Villas, Ron felt, contrary to Mr. Curtis's assurances, that his world was falling apart. His feeling of wonderment seemed to vanish, and gloom suddenly enveloped him. Somehow he couldn't see himself being capable of matching up to all these fine things he had seen and heard. The memory of Eddie, all done up to the nines with his fancy suit and carnation buttonhole, and Millie standing there, camouflaged by her pink maternity coat, with the baby kicking about inside her demanding to be let loose on the world—it just didn't add up. All this was confused with images of plaster cherubs on ceilings, strange and wonderful music ringing in his ears, and the unforgettable face of an old man in flowing robes gazing down at him, a face not unlike Grandpa Lawton's, now he came to think of it. It all made his prize money and scholarship seem so unimportant.

As to the antics of Tom and Jerry at the Palaseum— well! they had quite gone out of his head. He sighed joylessly as the sound of revellers at Millie and Eddie's's celebration party could be heard all down the little street. When his mother opened the door she greeted him in her usual harsh tone:

"Where've you bin all this time? 'Pon my word, boy!"

Ron noticed his mother had been crying.

Life suddenly seemed to him trivial and pointless.

EPISODE SIXTEEN

Later the same evening

New Year Resolutions!

78. Surprise Visit   No 5

Flo wiped her tears quickly away as Eddie and Millie arrived. Millie was far too worried about her baby to see the redness in her mother's eyes, but Eddie saw it. Glancing at his newly-acquired wife, as she sat resting her legs in the front room, she seemed to him so ungainly. He had missed seeing her shapely figure, that he had first put his arm round at the Purvis Bowl on St. Valentine's Night, and he wouldn't have that pleasure again until his next leave.

"Now then, Mum, ol' gel! You don't have to upset yourself about our Millie. She's right as rain." He watched her solemn expression and the diffidence of her manner, and laughed nervously.

"I can see it as plain as daylight," said Millie. "The little so-and-so will make up its mind to turn up just when I'm getting into the party spirit."

She looked round the kitchen at the platefuls of food her mother had prepared.

"It's a right ol' bun-fight, this is."

"Don't start moaning now, Millie," said Eddie. "We've only been married a few hours."

"There's no need to go on at me. You may have married me for me money but that don't mean to say you can carry on as if you was the Aga Khan."

"Oh, crikey!" said Eddie, and burst into song:

> *Here we are again,*
> *Happy as can be,*
> *All good pals*
> *And jolly good company.*

Millie made a false grimace. Then they began laughing. Alf came in just in time to join in the chorus. He had enough drink inside him to float the *Queen Mary*. Mabel, however, took no notice of these trivialities, intent as she was on Smutty's needs, and crept in on the scene bearing Smutty's drinking-bowl.

"Smutty wants a drink!" she announced, standing on tiptoe and pouring the muddy contents into the sink. "A proper drink!" It was not long before she had her way and Smutty was lapping up a bowlful of warm beer. Even better, he was granted special dispensation and allowed to enter the forbidden precincts of the front room, where he might partake of a good things that adorned the table, now laden with all manner of sandwiches, jellies, trifles, and a bowl of boiled rice decorated with dollops of strawberry jam. Alf presided over the drinks at one end of the table, armed as he was with a comic bottle-opener given to him by a friend from the tannery, though it is not the sort of thing the Vicar might have appreciated.

In next to no time, the whole company was filled with the festive spirit. Smutty was ensconced in one corner with Mabel, whose large plate of quivering raspberry jelly set him barking when it wobbled. Ron was engaged in a competition with Teddy Rogers and Billy Watkins as to which of them could cram the most food into their mouths without swallowing. Teddy, after succeeding beyond all the limits of human expectation, finished by getting a jab in the ribs from Billy and showering the piano keys with a coagulated mess of splodge. How Flo grumbled! Then she began to smile. Then she began to laugh. Then she began to cry tears of happiness.

Eddie and Alf were getting steadily tighter as Millie and Flo continued to replenish everyone's glasses and plates. They were interrupted by Alf demanding a performance from Flo on the piano.

"Oooh! I couldn't!" she said as coyly as she could manage. "That thing hasn't been played for ages."

They all gathered round the piano for a sing-song. Flo began to play. The room was filled with such a clattering and a plinking and a twanging as no-one had ever heard outside the Purvis Band!

"The notes won't play," said Flo, relief mingled with disappointment.

"Sounds like somebody tripping up on a pile of old tin-cans, it does. What a shindy!" said Alf.

"Well!" said Flo. "You did ask me to play."

"If I was in a skiffle group I could get a better sound out of a washboard!"

On opening the top of the piano, Eddie feigned a comic splutter and said:

"Sufferin' cats! There aint 'alf a stinko in 'ere!"

He drew out a rush bag.

"Hey! I used to have a rush bag like this," said Alf. "So this is where it's been hiding itself."

Eddie thrust his hand in and pulled out a box of rouge. Next came some face-lotion, mascara, lipsticks, cold creams, talc, and a dozen other confections.

"Here!" gasped Millie. "That's my make-up! How did it — ?"
She caught sight of Freddy Higgins in cahoots with Billy and Ron.
"Why, Ron Thompson! You little devil, you."

Had so much time not elapsed since the original prank, Millie might have been more upset, but now she hardly cared for all these cosmetics. Her other face had gone forever under a liberal application of vanishing cream!

Ron disappeared under the table with his two stalwarts and remained there, giggling for all they were worth, while Eddie extracted about a pound of moth-balls from between the hammers of the piano. At last Flo began to play the old tunes and the house was filled with rough tuneless grunts and wailings and warblings. *Red sails in the sunset, Goodnight, Sweetheart, Roll out the Barrel* and other native songs.

"I want my song," cried Mabel.

"Oh! Mabel wants her song. Come on everyone."

So everyone was happy to turn into a Max Bygraves for a moment:

> *When you come to the end of a lollipop*
> *To the end, to the end of a lollipop,......*

And Mabel's favourite part:

> *Gilly-o, golly-o, I love my lolly-o,*
> *Down to the very last lick*
> *But what can you do with it*
> *When you are through with it?*
> *All you have left is the stick!*

Ron sang with such gusto that he was compelled to retire to the bathroom, where he lost in a matter of minutes the results of a solid hour of stuffing himself in a regurgitated stream of raspberry jelly, trifle and pilchard sandwiches. He had come to the end of *his* lollipop all right! It is very likely that he will never go near another sweet-shop again.

While Ron was learning to be a man, Millie slipped out to make a pot of tea, leaving the company to their singing.

> *When you come to the end of a lollipop*

sang the heavenly choir with tears of joy and elation:

> *Plop goes your heart!*—

and plop went Ron's stomach again! He breathed a sigh of relief and wiped the cold sweat from his forehead. He could hear Millie going down the hall and he thought he heard the back door open in the kitchen below. Mabel was singing her song at the time. A proper little Vera Lynn she was turning out to be.

As Millie put her hand up to switch on the kitchen light, she dropped the plate she was carrying and gripped hard on the kitchen door. She thought she was going to faint from fright, but she managed to steel herself enough to close the door quietly behind her, shutting away the din of singing in the front room. She leant back against the wall and took a deep breath. The silhouette of a man showed blackly against the dim darkness of the window. She switched on the light to find, as she expected, that it was Curly. He was unshaven, his leather jacket covered in grime, his jeans soiled and torn. Millie, big with his child, moved slowly over to the table and began to spread butter and pilchard and tomato paste on the bread.

"So it's you, is it," she said in a harsh tone that surprised her.

There was a long pause while she arranged the sandwiches on the plate. Curly watched her like a hawk. He was staring at the sandwiches too.

"Well? Where've you been?" she went on. "Aint you got no tongue in your head?"

She spoke harshly, yes, but there was a tiny tremor in her voice. She heard it, and so did Curly. Almost ashamed under the glare of the light, he put his hand over his eyes. His thoughts went back to that day in February when he had first held her in his arms, and that April night when he made love to her. They had given themselves to each other. It had been perhaps the only moment of such passion in his life, though he had not realised it until now. He looked at her shapeless figure and knew that before very long Millie would be giving birth to his child, and he was filled with remorse.

"Don't look at me like that, Millie," he said at last. "Please, love."

"Oh! So you've got a tongue in your head, have you?"

She sighed, stopped cutting the bread and put down the knife. She spoke to him like a mother speaking to her truant child.

"And how else am I supposed to look at you, I'd like to know. The way you treated me. Whatever were you thinking of, going off like that, leaving me to face the music? Here I've been, all on me lonesome, and you going off and doing those terrible things, instead of just settling

385

down like every other self-respecting bloke. I mean, however could you do it, eh? You can't have no heart inside of you to do a thing like that. Why, if the truth was known, I was probably the only girl who ever really loved you, and most likely the only one now who ever will, the way things are going for you. It aint right, that's all."

He stared miserably at the food on the table and she realised he could not have eaten for a long time. When she handed the sandwiches to him, he grabbed them almost like a wild animal. She poured him a beer and watched him push the food into his mouth with his fingers, chewing ravenously between gulps of beer.

"I loved you like nobody I ever loved, Curly," she said. She was struggling against her tears. "It aint right, that's all. Now I'm married to Eddie, it aint no use harping on it. We're both dead and buried, you and me. And if you don't get out of here quick, Eddie'll kill you if he sees you. So take this and go."

She handed him a ten-shilling note out of the housekeeping money in the kitchen drawer. She'd fix it with her mother later. Now a wave of nausea came over her and she gripped the edge of the table to steady herself. Tears could no longer be held back. They came in floods as she began to sob.

"Oh, Curly! Oh Curly!" she cried.

He moved forward to comfort her. She sprang back convulsively. Frantically, she picked up the bread-knife. He retreated, frightened at the power of her emotion, her face twisted with anguish, tears streaming.

"I aint goin to touch you, Millie, darlin'. I aint goin' to touch you, love."

His voice cracked with the intensity of his feelings. Millie heard it, flung down the knife, remembering in her misery the self-same knife in her father's hand on that terrifying day in July. She fell into Curly's arms and wept. They held each other and wept together, while the sound of the singing and jollity filtered through from the party in the next room. She could never have known how tender he could be as he was now. It made everything all the harder to bear. Their love was never greater than now and their souls were being ripped to shreds.

After a while, they drew apart, both knowing full well the futility of things as they were now. He stood looking down at her, miserably, tenderly, but Millie also saw the look of desperation in his eyes.

"What are you going to do?" she said.

"I gotta get going, Millie. I need money."

"I gave you that ten bob."

"Taint enough, Millie. I need big stuff, so as I can make it to Ireland. Maybe take my old Ma with me. Get her away from all this. Lie low for a while."

"I aint got no money, Curly," said Millie, desperately.

It did not take her long however to realise that Curly had his eye on her diamond ring. It was not that he was looking at it that hurt, it was the way he looked that caught her heart. Seeing that this was the last and final sacrifice she had to make, she drew the ring from her finger and placed it in the palm of his hand. It was the last memento of their love. As he took it, her heart went with it, and the wound it left behind would take many years to heal. If they hadn't heard voices in the hall, she would have seen him weep at the shame of it all. As it was, he kissed her for the last time, slipped quickly into the darkness, and out of her life.

In the back alley, he leant against the wall and wept like a child who weeps for something it has killed. The windows of Laburnum Villas were dark and empty as his own heart was dark and empty, so empty that it pained him as he strove to keep back the abundance of love which surged up within hm. He clutched the ring in his clenched fist, and bitterness and remorse spread through him like a cancer. He cried out into the darkness.

Eddie discovered Millie lying on the kitchen floor in a state of collapse. She was holding her stomach and groaning. He held her gently in his arms and called for Alf to fetch Timothy Crawford round and then to hurry for Dr. Glendale.

"It's all right, love. Don't cry, love. Everything's going to be all right. You'll see."

He knelt beside her, running his fingers through her hair, lightly kissing her, speaking to her in soothing tones. Eddie realised when he saw the back door ajar and the empty glass on the edge of the table that Donoghue must have brazenly entered their home. Who else could it have been? He knew that if Millie was to be happy he had to keep Curly out of her way, though he was not to know that, whilst the physical bond between Millie and Curly had been severed for good, the emotional wound would, for Millie, take some time to heal.

Eddie knew he had to teach Curly a lesson. It was now or never, if his marriage to Millie was to be a lasting affair. With this in his mind, he left Millie in Timothy's capable hands and set forth into the night on a crusade in which Curly would somehow have to be brought low.

79. Ah, Sweet Mystery of Life

Alf was too much out of his wits to even think about paying a call at *The Bed of Roses*, for the turn of events weighed greatly on his mind. He sped up the street in quest of the elusive Dr. Glendale, leaving behind a strife-torn household of neurotics: Flo rushing about like a madwoman, tucking Millie into bed with a rare surfeit of attention that would have outdone any midwife, whilst Timothy lurked about in close watch like a crouching cat waiting for a mouse to pop out of its hole! Mabel, oblivious of the enormity of this event, assumed all the responsibility of the major-domo by clearing some of the dirty plates and glasses from the front-room with an efficiency beyond her years that would have surprised everyone had they been in a state to remark upon it. Ron and his company of 'English worthies' cleared *off*, rather than *away*, forsaking Mabel only after they had cleared *up* what food was left.

"Let's have a dollar's-worth of flicks," suggested Teddy Rogers. So they left the emotional chaos of No 4 for the more exciting prospects that Rothersey High Street could afford. Outside the Roxy Picture House, a green ghoulish figure with bulging red eyes dripping with blood, and long twisted strangler's fingers, glowered over them from the house-high poster.

"Cor!" gasped Freddy Higgins. "Let's have a go."

"Gee-whizz!" said Billy Watkins. "What a lark, eh?"

Ron made a face.

"What's the matter with old sour-puss?" said Teddy.

"He's scared, that's what he is," said Billy, sneering lightheartedly.

They all began jeering at Ron and poking him in the ribs.

A grim little queue began to form up in spite of the first few specks of snow. The pavements glistened freshly and breath came cloudily from clenched teeth. Soon, the queue began stamping their feet.

"Look!" cried Billy. "It's snowing!" He began jumping about with excitement. "It's snowing. Oh, boy! Oh, boy! Oh, boy!"

"We'll be able to make snowballs when we come out" said Freddy. Let's get in the queue. Quick! *Vampire in Soho*: 'By popular request!' Smashing!"

"I've seen it twice over," said Ron glumly. "It aint much cop. It's just a re-run for the New year. I couldn't sit through that crap all over again."

Freddy, Billy and Teddy would not be deterred from their vicarious pleasure and Ron left them to play havoc with the Roxy queue of horror-fiends. He wandered off in the direction of the Palaseum, where he found an even longer queue waiting to savour the delights of sunny Italy with *Romeo and Juliet.* He hung about in the snow, gazing vaguely at the posters and thinking it was probably a slushy love-story like *A Kiss in Time.*

"Queueing in all seats," shouted the commissionaire, clapping his woolly-gloved hands with the cold. "Three-and-six to the right. Four-and-six to the left. Queuing at all prices."

Ron looked at him with surprise. If it wasn't the same geezer that used to be at the Roxy.

"Crikey!" said Ron. "Frankenstein again! Been promoted, have we?"

The commissionaire looked down at Ron and announced in an unnecessarily loud, stern voice:

"QUEUEING ALL PRICES! ARE YOU BLOODY-WELL DEAF, SONNY?"

He wandered pompously over to address the queue:

"These damned kids. They think they can twist you round their little finger, they do. I bin in this cinema lark for ten year and I aint never seen a polite one amongst the lot of 'em. It's just the same up the Roxy. Get away with murder, they do. Proper little know-alls with it. Over-educated, that's the trouble. Little angels at 'ome. Little bastards when they're looking for a buckshee ticket."

By the time he had wandered back, Ron was fishing around for money. The commissionaire thrust his corpulence at him menacingly:

" 'Ere, you! Don't I know you from somewhere?"

Immediately, Ron felt guilt spreading over him like cold porridge. He began to walk off towards the Town Hall.

" 'Ere!" came the shout again. Ron turned sheepishly. He suddenly felt depressed again. Everything was wrong about things. His prize money, his scholarship — everything!

"Aint you that Thompson kid?" said the man, screwing up his face with the sheer mental exercise of it.

"What's it to you?" said Ron.

389

"Proper little clever-dick, aint you?"

" What d'you mean?"

"Oh! Answering back are we, now we're in the papers? Right little VIP, aint we?"

"Look here!" said Ron on the defensive. "If you want to pick a row with me, wait till I'm your size — which I hope I never will be!"

"None o' your sauce, my lad. D'you want to see the bloody film or don't you? Make up your mind. I can't stand here gossiping to you all night. I've got important work to do, I have."

"Anybody'd think you were the blinkin' manager!"

"I'll 'ave none of your lip, my son. Never you mind what I am. Get in there and shut your trap. I'll let you in for nix, seeing as 'ow it's New Year's Eve and you're such a smart-aleck."

After he had explained to the suspicious usherette that he really was a close personal friend of the commissionaire, Ron was thankful to be allowed to wander into the warm, welcoming half-light of the auditorium. He felt as if the bottom of his world had dropped out, and he couldn't tell why. He sat in the smart plush seat, miserably alone. He was convinced that there was no-one in the whole world who gave him even a second thought. He might just as well have been born an orphan. There was no way out. He would spend the rest of his life unwanted and friendless.

After the first scenes of the hustle and bustle of sunny Verona, Ron began to sense that Shakespeare wasn't such a bad sort of bloke after all. The valiant Mercutio fought with a fury that filled Ron with admiration, and the enraged Montagues and Capulets struck him as being parents who really cared about their children for a change. For the first time, he began to notice the soaring, romantic music and it made his heart take a flip. When Juliet appeared on her balcony and spoke strange and wonderful words, Ron was transported. She was so beautiful. A strange feeling came over him that brought new emotions to the surface. He began to listen intently:

> *Spread thy close curtain love-performing night,*
> *That runaway eyes may wink, and Romeo*
> *Leap to these arms, untalk'd of and unseen.....*
> *Give me my Romeo, and when he shall die,*
> *Take him and cut him out in the stars,*
> *And he will make the face of heaven so fine,*
> *That all the world will be in love with night....*

These were strange words to him indeed. He could did not understand them but, being the artist he was, he could sense the meaning of them. The scene was imprinted on his mind and stayed with him for weeks afterwards. Gone were the times when he could sit through yet another *Vampire in Soho*, though he began to realise that there had been more to *A Kiss in Time* than met the eye! One thing was certain — things would never after this be quite the same between him and Teddy, Billy and Freddy.

As he came out into the street, he felt the sadness of everything again: the futility of life ahead, living as he did in the grim mediocrity of Laburnum Villas. It was the same old story. Whenever he grew tired of it, he would seek out the nearest cinema and sink into the back-row seat to forget it all. But there was always an end to every film, however many times he saw the programme round. Life always seemed ten times more unbearable than before. He had parted company with painting and the excitement of the exhibition. Now, all that seemed behind him. He sank into gloom and despondency. Even the thought of being an uncle had lost its first glamour. As he pushed out through the swing doors, he realised he was just stupid, little, less-than-ordinary Ron Thompson, plain and simple. Nothing more than that. It hurt him terribly. He could never aspire to the stature of a romantic Romeo or a dashing Mercutio. The drabness of Rothersey High Street seemed very far removed from the loveliness of Verona.

"Hullo!" said a voice. It was a light voice, and it startled him out of himself. A girl in a navy-blue school overcoat and hat stood on the pavement in the snow. She smiled at him in a way he had never seen Millie or any other girl smile.

"Hallo!" said Ron, straight-faced and unsure of himself.

"Did you enjoy the film?" she asked, almost disinterestedly.

"Nor arf!" said Ron shiftily.

"What does that mean?"

"Well — what do you think?"

"I don't know. By 'half' I suppose you mean a lot!"

They stood on the snowy pavement and shivered..

"You haven't much to say for yourself, have you?"

"Not when I haven't got nothing to say."

"You don't speak English very well, either."

"What's it to you?"

"Nothing to *me*. It's not me who has to worry." Then with a toss of the head, she changed the direction of the conversation:

391

"Did you like Juliet?

"Smashing!" said Ron. "Did you?"

"Oh. I always like her part. We're the same age, you see."

"The same age? Come off it! Why, I bet you're no more than fourteen."

"Nor was Juliet."

"Her? Fourteen? Don't make me laugh."

"Well, it's true. I thought everyone knew that."

"Do you have Romeos climbing up to your balcony then?" said Ron, sniggering.

"They'd have a job. We live on the tenth floor."

"Where?"

"Rothersey Mansions."

"Where's that when you're at home?"

"It's next to the new block by the station."

"Cor! Rothersey Heights! That's where we're moving to in the New Year."

"We'll be neighbours then. What's your name."

"Ron."

"Ron what?"

"Blimey! You don't half ask a lot of questions, don't you? What's yours?"

"Priscilla!"

Ron laughed.

"Priscilla? What a name to go to bed with!" He'd heard his mother use the phrase.

"Who's asking you to go to bed with it?" she asked with a straight face and a twinkle in her eye.

They giggled. Ron had never thought of that. She smiled at him again in a way that made him lower his eyes.

"However do you manage with a monniker like that?"

"You do use some funny words. What's your other name?"

"I aint got no other name." He had never thought about his name before and felt ashamed at its ordinariness.

"I shall call you Ronald," she said almost proudly.

"How can you put up with Priscilla? What's it for short? Prissy or Silly?"

"That's an old chestnut. People make cracks like that everyday."

"You *are* a bit prissy, aren't you?"

"Maybe, but I'm not half so silly as you are!"

"Look here!" said Ron, testily. "I aint going to stand here and be insulted by the likes of you. Got better things to do with my time."

He made to go but she took him by the arm.

"Don't be like that, Ronald. What's your other name?"

"Thompson."

"Not *the* Ronald Thompson? The boy who won the painting competition?"

"That's right!" he said quietly, rubbing the toe of his shoe in the snow.

"Gosh!" she said with obvious admiration. "That's wonderful. Really wonderful! My father's a painter."

"What's he paint? Window-frames?"

"There's no need to be so snooty about it, just because you've won a competition. If you must know, he teaches at Rothersey Art School."

"That's where I'm going," said Ron with surprise. "I got a scholarship to go there."

"Would you like to meet him?"

"What, now?"

"No, silly! Tomorrow. For tea."

"Oh, I dunno! We're moving out tomorrow" said Ron modestly. "He won't want to meet me anyway."

"Of course he will, when I tell him about you. Besides, as from tomorrow we'll be neighbours. *I* want you to come, and if I want you to come, he'll be ever so nice to you. He loves me."

"What about your mother?"

"Dead!"

"Oh, sorry!" he said, surprised by her abruptness.

"Nothing to be sorry about. She died when I was born."

"You mean, you never had a mother at all?"

"No. I wish I had. Have you got a mother?"

"Nor arf!" he said, half-proud and half ashamed.

"Perhaps I shall meet her one day."

"You wouldn't want to meet her."

"Why ever not?"

"Always grumbling, she is."

"That's because she loves you. Just like my father with me."

"It's cold," announced Ron emphatically.

"Well, there's no need to stand here, is there? You can see me home if you like."

"See you home?"

"It's the usual thing when boy meets girl."

Ron hadn't thought about *that* before either. He began thinking hard about Eddie and Millie and came to realise a few things he had never thought of before. The maturing man in Ron, the boy, was demanding to be set free.

"Okeedoke!" he said.

They turned down the High Street towards the station and Ron remembered that he hadn't walked over that stretch of territory since he had met the Vicar and visited Grandpa Lawton in hospital.

"Look here!" he said. "Haven't you got some other name? I can't call you Prissy or even Silly. I'd laugh, I would."

"You can call me Bill, if you like."

"That's a boy's name. I'm not calling you that."

"Short for Wilhelmina."

"They certainly had it in for you when you were christened, didn't they?"

She tossed her head again and made a special effort to explain:

"My mother was Dutch. It was her second name, after the Queen of the Netherlands."

"What was her first?"

"Elsa."

"Elsa!" said Ron with relief. "That's what I shall call you. Elsa!"

"I'm not sure my father will like that. You see, it was his special name for her," she said, taking his hand in hers as they trudged through the thickening snow.

"I don't care what your father thinks. That's what I'm going to call you." And as an afterthought he said cautiously: "I like the sound of your mother. D'you think she would have liked me too?"

When they reached the new flats, Ron inspected them with the air of a property speculator.

"Aren't you going to kiss me goodnight?" she said almost coquettishly.

"Kiss you?" Ron was horrified. "Whatever for?"

"It is the done thing, I believe. You know! Boy meets girl, boy kisses girl! Don't you remember in the film? 'Farewell, farewell, one kiss and I'll descend.'"

"Descend where?" said the frightened Ronald.

"No! No!" she insisted. "That's what Romeo said. Not very romantic, are you. I mean, you're not exactly the sort of lover that would sweep a girl off her feet with a single kiss."

"All right, then," said Ron, trembling a little with apprehension. "One kiss, that's all."

He stood gaping at her, hopping from one foot to the other. He had, as yet, no aspirations of being another Romeo.

"Well, come on then," she said. "I can't wait here all night."

Ron looked at her again as if she were the original serpent in the Garden of Eden. Then he leaned forward and kissed her roughly on the cheek. He felt the softness of her skin against his lips and experienced things he had never known before.

In a moment he was rushing off through the snow as fast as his feet could carry him, his body aglow, his head spinning like a top.

"See you tomorrow for tea," she shouted. Ronald ran all the way home. When he got there, he found that he was at last an uncle, and a very grown-up one at that.

Later, as he was climbing into bed, he caught sight of the brown paper parcel Mr. Curtis had handed to him at the church. Unwrapping it, he found a book and a note inside.

Dear Ron,

I want to give you something very dear to me. My father gave me the book when I was a boy, and I'd like you very much to have it. You will see that it is in very good condition. He taught me early in life to look after my books. Even the dust-wrapper is intact. Not a tear in it. I can tell you, if you were to damage it you would knock a good deal off the value.

I wish you every success with your studies.

> *Yours sincerely,   Rev. Daniel Curtis*

P.S. As I have no heirs, I have arranged with my solicitor for a sum of money to be put in trust for you until you come of age. This money will help you in your chosen career when the time comes. Remember 'Little Dorrit'!"

The volume was a first edition mint copy of *Tarzan of the Apes*. Ron looked at it almost disinterestedly, trying to come to terms with the fact that he would almost certainly never read it, though once upon a time, in his early Roxy Picture House days, he would have given his very soul for one. He placed the picture postcard of Moses against the table-lamp by his bed, and turning on his side, his head cradled in his arms, he stared at it for a long time until his eyelids closed and he sank into another land of dreams, quite different to the ones of his fast disappearing childhood. After all, in an hour or so, it would be New Year's Day, and he was going to have tea with a very special girl.

80.   Curly's Last Performance

The young people of Rothersey went arm-in-arm towards the music and the dancing on this last night of the year. They surged over the snow-covered pavements, past the queues at the Palaseum, those lines of beings pinched with the cold, beings of another generation, of a new world.

Gone the wartime austerity. Gone the fear of bombs and doodlebugs. Gone the painful separations from loved-ones. It was out with the old ways, in with the new. Out with austerity and *ersatz*: in with New Look and G-Plan furniture. Out with ration books and clothes coupons, in with bananas and chocolate and ice-cream. Out with the carbolic soap and soda crystals, in with washing powders and launderettes. Out with the palais-glide and the hokey-kokey, in with jive and rock-and-roll.

The straggling queue of picture-goers had not yet, it seemed, changed with the times. They were silently taking their turn not only to enjoy the horrors of vampires and stranglers but to immerse themselves in the disappearing black-and-white world of the Ealing comedies and dramas. They would at least, as Mrs. Thompson used to say, 'be in the warm, dearie.' And very cosy it would be, too, with a monster sitting in the next seat, devouring half a pound of chocolate nut crunch and a bagful of lemon sherbets!

Hundreds of Rothersey youth were pouring through the stately portals of *The Purvis Bowl* with nothing on their minds but a bit of fun. It was the perennial moment of optimism when all seemed right with the world. There would be plenty of clutching and hugging, twisting and wriggling on Councillor Purvis's newly-installed dance-floor. There would be kissing and canoodling in corners, and, for the older generation, still a chance for bit of saucy rib-tickling, twittering to

396

tangos and chuckling to cha-cha-cha's.

A sandwich-man moved slowly along the queue ever hopeful of converts from *Vampire in Soho,* reminding them in blood-red lettering:

Prepare to Meet
The Wrath to Come

Curly Donoghue had been on the run now for six months, sleeping rough, keeping out of sight in the daytime, scrounging whatever he could under cover of darkness.

Everything had gone wrong for Curly ever since Gino got himself arrested with the fifty pounds in his dirty little hand — the 'blood-money' Curly owed Ma carpenter for Millie's ring On this cold December night, he crept nimbly along under the shadow of the overhanging trees which ran the length of the Public Gardens. If he could make his way across the bridge without being seen, he could lose himself in the maze of Soho streets, and make contact with the link-man who was to get him across to Ireland. Millie's ring would be more than enough to pay him for his services and Curly didn't care if he arrived penniless as long as he remained a free man, free from the ever-tightening power of the law.

On the other side of the road, he saw the darkened windows of Ma Blackwood's shop. It set him thinking about what he had done to Pa.

Stupid old bugger! [he thought]. Shadowing him day and night. Turning up in the queerest places, always with that stinking monkey of his, picking at its fleas, watching for him with its evil little eyes.

He'd have wrung its neck if only he could have caught the little vermin in time.

But no! The silly little sod had to run up a drain-pipe and cringe there while he threw rocks at it.

All right! So Curly had been lurking around No. 3, but only in the hope of seeing Millie, just so he could get to telling her how he felt about her. What else could he do till he got his hands on some of that dough!

Curly remembered the night he saw the monkey playing about on the pavement outside No 3. The dirty little flea-bag was always around when Pa Blackwood was up to something — like when he was stalking him in the Public Gardens. Curly cornered it and crashed its head to a pulp, though still its little eyes kept staring at him. If only he hadn't dropped his flick-knife in the rubble, he would have used it on the old man. He needed to be taught a lesson he wouldn't forget in a hurry!

Curly had laughed to see the old man's eyes turn in their sockets as he slipped softly round the wall of the house. He was scared. Dead scared! Curly lunged at him, brought his knee up under the old man's crutch, made him double up with the pain of it, Crushed his face into the rough stones till the blood came, twisted it like a lemon on a squeezer, till the flesh wept blood and the old man's breath became hoarse with gasping and spitting. Curly kicked at his bones till they cracked and splintered, knocked him into a senseless pulp like a quivering jelly-fish. How was he to know the ol' geezer would snuff it?

Such were Curly's thoughts as he made his way by the railings of the Public Gardens. On reaching St. Crispin's, he darted across the road into the shadows of the shop doorways. He glanced at an advertisement for one of the better-known brands of beer which showed a healthy rugged youth with a shock of fair hair just like Curly's, laughing eyes, smiling mouth revealing a fine set of white teeth — the perfect vision of what he most wanted to be: a strapping, vigorous, virile, athletic idol for all the girls to fight over.

Next to the poster was another, this time of a girl with rosy cheeks, and her long hair blowing out in the wind. She was throwing her head backwards and laughing with that 'Come and get me' laugh, just like the beautiful girl he had seen that night at her window, the girl he had dreamed about so many times since.......

It didn't take Curly more than a split second to see the top of a policeman's helmet appear up over the wall across the road. He leapt down into the alley which led to the foot-bridge over the railway. With a little luck, he would be able to reach the back of the Purvis Bowl just across from Ma Blackwood's place.

For a moment he stopped, breathless, beneath an elm, shabby with the grime of centuries. He was startled by a rustling noise and was astonished to find his old mother stooping over a bin, obviously going about her business of totting. There she was, fishing about for scraps, and it filled Curly with a feeling he had not had for many a year, a feeling for her that went beyond the bounds of logic, for in this creature-of-the-night Curly had once seen only an object of hatred. Now he felt something that hurt him more than hatred, something near to pity. The futility of his situation dawned upon him, for in that timeless look of pity

398

he saw reflected in those bright bead-like eyes a part of himself which was irredeemable. He saw also, mirrored in those eyes, his approaching doom. Without knowing why, he thrust the precious ring into her hand, enclosing its brilliance in her grimy palm. That strange look between them of complete recognition had more love in it than they could ever know.

"Ma!" he said. "Pack it in, will you? The coppers are coming. Get out of here, for God's sake, else they'll clap you inside!"

The policeman paused for a moment, just at the end of the alley, peered into the half-light, and then began sauntering slowly towards Curly at the steady but determined pace of a coffin-bearer. At that moment, Eddie came running up behind, shouting, waving his arms. They spotted the dim outlines of Curly and Ma Donoghue beneath the elm-tree and began sprinting towards them.

"Begone with you," she whispered, the glint fading from her gaze. "And God bless you, boyo!"

Eddie's eyes had been too keen not to recognise Curly's familiar silhouette as he sped along the alley towards the footbridge. Leaping forward past the old woman he raced off in hot pursuit of his quarry. Ma Donoghue, pretending to rummage round in the bottom of the bin, suddenly gathered up its contents in her arms, whisked round, and slung it full in the constable's face. She fell on him amidst the confusion of stinking garbage, arms flailing. Shouting what unholy obscenities she could muster, she began kicking with her old boots for all she was worth.

The stairs of the footbridge clattered with the sound of heavy boots on iron as Eddie gave chase and hurtled after Curly, up and round and up and round, taking two steps at a single leap. Once at the top, Eddie gained ground. Lunging forward, he caught hold of Curly's belt and brought him thumping down on the unforgiving metal-plated floor. Below, trains passed by noisily, hissing, steaming, clanking, chugging, while Eddie and Curly were locked in a struggle. Curly cupped his hand over Eddie's chin and, little by little, he forced Eddie's head through the criss-cross iron bars of the fencing on the side of the bridge. With all his strength, he began to thrust Eddie's neck down against the sharp blade of metal, drawing blood, and Eddie knew that in less than a minute he would be not far away from being suffocated. He began to give out agonised gasps. With a quick jerk, he brought his knee up like a piston and punched the blood out of Curly's groin. Releasing his grip, Curly gave a yell of pain. Eddie began lashing out with swingeing blows that bruised Curly's ego almost more than his body. He struggled to his feet and ran off along the bridge again, just as a train passed underneath sending up a billowing cloud of smoke that hid him from sight.

Eddie heard the noise of Curly's boots clattering off in the direction of the Purvis Bowl. He rose to his feet shakily, then, staggering a little for an instant, he chased Curly into the glittering lights of Rothersey High Street. The cinema queue had melted away, the messenger of doom had gone up west with his sandwich-boards, the pleasure-seeking crowds of local youths and their girls were by now enjoying the festivities. Eddie raced after Curly, past the protesting commissionaire, through the crowded foyer, on and out through the emergency doors. Fired by his crusading zeal to teach Curly a lesson he would never forget, Eddie followed, determined to fight to the bitter end to save Millie's honour.

The high fire escape coiled up the outside wall to the penthouse offices of the Purvis Bowl. Up went Curly, like a flash, leaping almost effortlessly. Eddie, breathless, straining to the limits, his thighs and buttocks aching, climbed higher and higher into the darkness, tempered as it was by the glow of neon lights from the advertisements on the sides of the buildings below. His head was swimming when he reached the open parapet at the top. Curly was poised dangerously on the edge of it, swaying from side to side like a maddened animal in a fight to the death. At the bottom of a sixty-foot drop, lay the glass domes of the Purvis Bowl, like two enormous orange moons.

The silver glint of a knife-blade showed up in Curly's fist, the same knife perhaps that he had used to fell Andrew Crawford. It flashed dangerously as Eddie, panting for breath, stood poised to attack. Fear struck sharp into Eddie's guts as he sought to regain his lost wind. He was fighting not only for his breath, but his life too, and he was doing it for the love of Millie.

"Don't be a fool, Curly!" he muttered.

Curly sneered and snarled like a panther. Eddie feigned several blows to put Curly off his guard. Curly struck out suddenly, viciously, with the urgency of a desperate man. They circled round each other like a pair of tigers set to kill.

Curly leapt forward and caught Eddie's wrist in a grip of steel, held him for an instant, then he lunged at Eddie with the knife and sent the blade slitting down Eddie's thigh, making him cry out in agony. Eddie's blood was up, just as Curly's was and he fought with a ferocity that would have surprised even Curly if he had been capable of

400

reasonable thought. Curly, still gripping the blood-stained knife in his fist, brought it down over Eddie's eyes. Eddie put up his hands, catching Curly by both wrists, blanched, gasped, and prayed. Sweat streamed down over his face as they stood there on the edge of the parapet, locked in the grip of a vice, the struggle now of two equal forces, matching each other with strength and will, equal, that is, except for endurance. Curly's life had been one of hardship and toughness, Eddie's softened by the comforts of home. Therein lay the solution to the struggle, for Eddie, finally unable to hold his grip, sagged from sheer exhaustion, his breast filled with that dread only felt by those who recognise the immanence of death. He let go of Curly's wrists and collapsed onto the rooftop. Curly, froze for a moment in horror, high over the festivities of New Year revels. His face contorted with fear, he swayed precariously over the abyss.

"Eddie! Eddie" he gasped.

In the fraction of a second that followed, they looked at each other with fear almost bordering on affection, for their worlds were falling asunder and could never be put together again.

Curly, losing his balance, swayed backwards and with a hoarse scream, let out a terrified cry:

"Millie!" — and plunged full sixty foot into the void. His arms and legs splayed out as he smashed through the splintering glass of the dome and hit the floor of the Purvis Bowl another thirty feet below.

For an instant there was a grim silence. Music, dancing, revelling ceased. The roar of the festivities faded to a silence of dread and horror, only to be followed by the screaming of the girls and the shouting of the boys as they realised the enormity of the event and fought to get clear of the the shattered glass and the crumpled carnage of flesh and bone that was once Curly Donoghue.

So ended everyone's high hopes of a Happy New Year's Eve. When the police arrived, they found Eddie unconscious, high up on the parapet, his leg streaming with blood from the knife-wound. The clock on St. Crispin's Church struck midnight. Everywhere, bells hooters and horns welcomed in the New Year and the London streets were full of cheering crowds. They had good reason. They had hope! It was the first day of January l960. The last decade of the old order, with all its trials and tribulations, was over.

81. The Venus Child

By the time the ambulance delivered Eddie home from the hospital, Millie had given birth to another little lollipop kid. As usual, Dr. Glendale remained conspicuously absent in spite of Alf's appeals to his sense of duty, not that this was any surprise at all to Flo, who having prepared herself for once for the oncoming event, knew only too well that G.P.'s like Dr. Glendale were only fit for curing things you could better cure yourself with a hot toddy or a dose of Friar's Balsam.

Upstairs, Timothy was clearing up the bowls and the jugs and the soiled cloths. If his medical career ended there, in that tiny bedroom of No 4, it would have all been worthwhile. His thoughts now lay on more distant horizons, far removed from clinics and out-patient departments. Here, in the tight little room, packed with its ornaments and its trinkets and its souvenirs, its faded posters of Elvis, the glass bowlful of buttons, here was the inexplicable beauty of the first squawkings of infancy. Once it was accustomed to the temper of the room, with its smell of humanity and its curse of Adam, the little intruder settled down to its first sleep, this tiny child of Venus, dozing at its mother's breast.

Mrs. Thompson was still smarting at Eddie's surprising disappearance at the very moment of crisis and , when he came limping in, anxious to hear news of Millie, he found his new mother-in-law wearing her battle-irons.

"Well, it's 'ere!" she announced coldly, "and a fat lot you care! Gallivantin' off without as much as a sailor's farewell! A fine how-d'you-do, I must say. Leavin' your wife when she's abed with child!" However, the recounting of Curly Donoghue's decline and fall put her in quite a different frame of mind.

"May the Good Lord save us!" she said, which was a fine thing coming from someone who hadn't been inside a church since she was married, and only then on sufferance because she thought it was the proper thing to do. "Curly Donoghue! In this house! Right under our noses!"

"That's right! Came to see our Millie."

"Why! The dirty rotten little — "

"Now, don't go off about him and Millie. It wasn't nothing to do with her. She aint interested in him no more. Wouldn't be no use anyway, now, him being where he is!"

Eddie looked gloomily into the fire as it sparked up the

chimney, a tone of infinite sadness touching his grey-blue eyes as he sighed.

"What a business, eh? Me and him! We was pals, we was. Known 'im ever since we was kids. I can't understand it, Flo. Him turning on me like that. Must have had a devil in him somewhere. He couldn't never get it out of hisself, like. I didn't mean to do him no harm. I just wanted him to stay away from Millie, that's all."

There were tears in his eyes, and Flo realised that something much more than a battle of strength had taken place, something she was incapable of explaining.

"He was a good bloke, really," Eddie went on, falteringly. "He just didn't know how to get along with his mates. Couldn't never take life as it comes. Always trying to make something out of it that wasn't meant for him. I shouldn't have chased after him, I suppose, 'cos it made the police suspicious and then all hell was let loose. But I just didn't want Millie to get hurt no more."

It was gradually dawning on Flo that Eddie was in some way trying to justify himself, but for what?

"Is Curly dead?" she asked, cautiously. "Have you gone and done something, Eddie?"

She looked at him as he drooped over the fire, his face intense, its paleness warmed by the glow of the red-hot coals. Flo saw in his tearful eyes all the pain that a broken friendship can possibly bring.

"Oh, Flo! What have I done?" He stared at the dying embers, almost in shame, and burst into a fit of sobbing that nearly broke Flo's heart. "What have I done, Flo?"

There being no answer to such a question, they sat quietly together for quite some time.

"Eddie," she said, almost inaudibly, "before you go up to Millie I want to tell you something. Stay a minute."

She began wrestling with her words, striving to say something so simple in itself yet so difficult to express.

"You see, Ed — you and me, well! — we've got a lot in common. Our situations, I mean."

Flo had never known what it meant to be tactful, but now, for the first time in ages, she realised that a whole world of happiness depended on her ability to convey to Eddie the true significance of her feelings and her thoughts.

"It's funny how one dies and another's born," she mused. "I've often wondered about it, I have. All that business about the soul and that. You know what I mean. There's Curly dying like that, just at the moment his kid's being born into the world he's left behind, and he'll never set on eyes on the poor little blighter."

Eddie waited, sitting silently by her, listening and trying to see where she was leading.

"What I mean to say is, it must mean something to somebody up there in the clouds, else – oh! I dunno! We'd all be in the flippin' zoo, wouldn't we?"

Eddie nodded.

"Yes," she went on, "you and me — we've got a lot to be thankful for, one way and another. Like having to bring up somebody else's kid just as if it was your own!"

"I don't get you," said Eddie, frowning. Then, jumping up in consternation, he said:

"You mean — you, Millie — Millie — !" He couldn't get the words out for fear they might be true.

Flo waved her hand almost with an air of futility.

"No, no!" she sighed. "Millie's my kid through and through. Can't you see that? As like as two peas in a pod, we are."

Then Flo looked straight into Eddie's eyes.

"I'm talking about Mabel."

"Mabel!" gasped Eddie. "You mean Mabel aint — "

"That's about it, son. Our Mabel aint our'n. Leastways mine!"

For a moment, Eddie was stunned.

"Well" he said, lamely. "There aint no way of telling how things really are with folk, eh?"

Flo remained tense, bent as she was on her task of bringing order out of confusion. Eddie was shocked.

"How could you bring up somebody else's kid, just like that? I mean, was she an orphan?"

"Mabel was no orphan, Eddie. She's Alf's kid."

"Oh!" said Eddie, quietly uncomprehending. "Alf's kid."

"Couldn't you never tell?" said Flo.

"Well, she *is* a bit different, I s'pose. Though I do see a resemblance somewhere, but it aint Alf."

Flo paused, and added: "There's something else, too."

"Something else?"

"Eddie! Maybe you're not going to like this, but I have to tell you something you may not want to hear, and if I don't tell you now, I'll never find the guts to say it again. Seeing as how you being father to a

404

kid that aint your'n."

Eddie waited.

"Eddie," said Flo, "Mabel — well — Mabel — you see, she's Alf's kid all right, but she — well — she belonged to your Ma!"

If anyone ever gave the appearance of being hit with a sledge-hammer in a clap of thunder, Eddie did. He sat on the edge of his chair and gaped.

"Christ Almighty!" he said in a hoarse voice. "You mean to say Ma was Mabel's ma too? You mean Mabel and me — well! Blimey! She's my kid sister!"

"I know what you're thinking, Ed, but don't blame your mother. It's all over long ago."

"What do you mean 'blame'? You don't know what you're bleeding-well saying. How could she — I mean, her and Alf — how could they?"

"Oh, Eddie, lad, I know it's difficult for you. Remember the time your Dad was killed and your Ma went into hospital with a nervous breakdown? You was just a kid and you had to give up your school and go out to work? Well — she didn't go in 'cos she was cut up about your Dad. She went in 'cos she was having Mabel, see? And what's more, your Ma didn't want her, neither. She was goin' to put her in a home for unwanted kids. At her age, she wasn't one to have howling brats round the place. Well, Alf was pretty cut up about Jack and I was pretty cut up about Alf. I didn't never have to suffer so much as I did then."

"But you, knowing that Alf and Ma — I mean, how could you?"

"It wasn't easy then, Eddie," she said, hoping to stop him from saying something he regretted, "no more'n it's easy now. With Alf taking to drink, me twisted up with the misery of it all, and Ron just a youngster at the time. No, Eddie, it wasn't easy."

"All right!" Eddie almost shouted in his indignation. "All right! But what about me, eh? What about me?" He dug his fingers into his chest savagely. "Don't I have no rights? Here I am, nineteen flippin' years old, and I don't even know I've got a kid sister. Christ Almighty! What a flamin' balls-up! Didn't you have no bleeding self-respect? Didn't you turn round and tell Alf to eff off? Talk about history repeating itself! Didn't you — "

"Oh! Didn't I, didn't I, didn't I!" said Flo angrily. "Look here, Eddie, son. Do you think I liked it anymore than you do now? I just had to put up with it, the same as you are going to have to put up with it. The only thing is, you went into with your eyes open, and that's a thing to be thankful for, I can tell you, my lad. Alf had to an' all with Millie. Why the 'ell do you think he nigh on did her in for good when he knew she was going to have that kid, eh? It takes a load of courage to face up to the truth, Eddie, and the sooner you bring yourself to do it, the better it'll be for all of us. And when you've done that, you can go on doing it for the rest of your life. When Ma palmed Mabel off onto us, she took to drink. When Jacko died, Alf took to it too. It was the end of your Ma. She just couldn't face the facts. Living's a difficult business when you can't forget your past, when things keep gnawing away inside of you. Millie needs you more than you know. And I'll tell you another thing, son. Have a child of your own — the two of you — and seal the knot. It'll make all the difference. As to our Millie, well, I couldn't wish her a finer lad for a husband than you. So up you go, lad, and give your little daughter her first kiss. My God, she'll need a father like you, with Curly's blood in her. "

Eddie looked tortured and pale. He stood inert, almost powerless, as he pondered Flo's timely words. Then he flung his arms round Flo and hugged her till she cried.

When he left her to her thoughts and the peace of the kitchen, Flo sat in the warm glow of the fire, feeling proud of a job well-done. Little by little, the fire made her drowsy. 'Eddie is a very long time up there with Millie.' Flo was sinking into sleep and taking up her butterfly net and sweeping it round in the happy haven of her own world of dreams. Her house of sand was firm against the storms of life. Now, she knew in her dreaming that all was well, all was so very well, and that, before long, she would be holding in her arms, a little grand-daughter, and be thankful.

82. Goodbye to All That!

As Louise and Mrs. Crawford packed the last of the luggage into the boot of the car, Timothy stretched his aching back and gazed round at the grimy old houses he had come to know so intimately over the last six months.

The gas-lights, surely among the last in London, shone and hissed like harvest moons and sent shafts of light through the gaping windows of No 3, only to be dissipated in the shadows of its ruined walls. Out in the street, there was a silence like that of a deserted village where once were the voices of men, and now only spirits lurked lost and lonely. Soon, Laburnum Villas would be nothing but a pile of debris, brick torn from brick, slate from timbers, until nothing remained but a few twisted drainpipes and gaping sewers. There would be no blue plaque to commemorate those who once were its heart and soul. With the terrible urgency of modern progress, Alf's ideal world of 'Peace and Plenty' would bring about changes as remorseless as they were necessary.

Save for the lighted windows of No 4, the little houses were in darkness, gloomily ochred by the glow of the gas-lights. The windows possessed that darkness of a temporary absence while the tenant has slipped out for a packet of cigarettes or for a last hour or two of nerve-wracking horror at the Roxy. It was the darkness of Time, touching this little world with his finger and passing on, the darkness of departing souls from Limbo.

Tim stood at the door of No 5 Laburnum Villas and surveyed the scene before him., He was, for a moment, filled with a nostalgia for the place that belied his feelings of 'cheerfulness and healthful ease' — a phrase that Louise had found in her poetry reading that satisfied him now that providence had designed a blue-print for his future life.

He realised that the lives of every one of the residents of this miniature enclave were, in their own special way, changed. They had been, like characters in a play, 'translated'. Even the Thompson family, who after all had been as set in their ways as a row of custard tarts, were now softening up and adapting to the new world that was not of their making.

Theirs was not the spirit of the explorer or the adventurer, though Ronald would make up for all of them, given the chance. Even Mabel, one day, would vindicate her former precociousness in favour of marriage, though there too were indications of an as yet unidentifiable talent for the histrionic.

There is no doubt at all that the last year had witnessed many changes of heart and mind among the occupants of this little world. They had undergone a transformation that had in some way purged them of their fecklessness, swept away the vanity of human life and replaced it with humble endeavour. Eddie would have at one time given his life to become a successful pigeon-fancier, whilst Millie had yearned for stardom under the hypnotic spell of Elvis.

It seemed now that everyone who emerged from the Villas into the new age would have to start learning how to live all over again.

407

There were, of course, other considerations. Curly had no means of finding answers to life's problems because nobody had taught him how to live his life in the first place. Ma and Pa Blackwood had followed the same false path. Ma Carpenter had gone so far as to fight a duel with her own soul. In an over-crowded world there was plenty of room for despair, for grievance, for selfishness, for revenge. Things rarely happen exactly as we would wish. Someone, somewhere, somehow, passes us and touches our lives, however lightly, like a traveller who asks the time and causes you to miss your connection. The least we can hope for is a smile across the compartment of our train as it hurtles towards journey's end. Such thoughts filled Timothy with an unfathomable sense of loss.

As for the Thompson family, they went their own ways and found a kind of happiness, each to his or her own degree. Timothy's remarks must have had some effect on Flo, for after a few years, an amusing little book entitled *The Trouble with Millie, or, It Never Rains but it Pours!* by Florence Mildred Thompson, appeared in the bookshops. It was modestly reviewed for its freshness and originality as a tale told in its own simple way of the joys and sorrows, the trials and tribulation, of a small community in a south London borough. In time, it was to become a miniature classic of its kind, the personal reminiscences of an older way of life than the young could know or care about today.

As for Mabel, who would have connected her, years hence, with the actress, Mirabel Thompson and her sensational performance as Major Barbara in Shaw's play at the Vaudeville Theatre. After all, she had held the stage at 'The Dumps' for long enough, though there is no doubt her performances had not been greatly admired by Smutty.

The windows of Councillor Purvis, Grandpa Lawton and the Paxtons now hid no secrets. It seemed to Timothy therefore fitting that the Thompsons should remain in sole possession of the Villas for the last night of the last decade of the year.

One final look round and Timothy jumped into the car, Louise sitting beside him, his mother in the back seat, hemmed in by boxes and suitcases. They drove slowly out of Laburnum Villas and for the last time followed the familiar route home.

Turning away from Rothersey Bridge and the Palaseum and the boarded-up Lollipop Shop and St. Crispin's Church, they passed a dozen other places they had come to know so well. Over the crossing where Grandpa had fallen, past the Town Hall with its bright brass door-knobs polished so conscientiously by Flo Thompson, past the Old People's Home in Napoleon Avenue, past the Day Nursery which Mabel had long since outgrown, past the Roxy Picture House, past the Hospital, and on to the Cathedral. Here, Timothy pulled in to the side of the road.

"I'll be back in a moment," he said, and dived down into the long dark tunnel under the railway. At the bottom, he came out among the old familiar piles of crates and boxes. The stale, heady odour of decaying remains of vegetables, struck his nostrils almost as forcefully as Uncle Walter's 'Crimson Glory'. As he moved among the stands, he reread the names of farmers and traders he had known and talked to in the old days. 'John Garville', he read. How he had missed those countless visits to his godfather's stand, with little Miss Violet Finch sitting in her glass-cabin like a precious prairie bloom. He could hear her laughter as she deftly managed her double entries. He recalled the pleasant daily visits to the amiable Miss Trencher's English Breakfast Rooms — the smells of bacon and eggs and fresh toast, and the spirited din of conversation. He came suddenly upon the stand that looked, by now, much in need of a coat of paint. *Andrew Crawford & Son.* He ran his hands over the paintwork, the lettering now chipped, barely visible. He opened the door and climbed up, standing in the place from which his father loved to preside. On his right rose the great stone buttresses of the Cathedral, deep in shadow, and above, the tower stood fair and square in the moonlight, the hands of the clock gleaming silver.

As on that last fatal visit to the Market, all time seemed timeless, and for an instant, fused into a single moment of happiness. It seemed only yesterday he had suffered one of the most brutal humiliations of his life and walked out, so he had thought, for ever, on a world which he now knew meant everything to him. It was as if Laburnum Villas had never existed. As he sauntered up through the tunnel again, he felt joy in his heart. The Cathedral clock struck midnight as he climbed back into the car. He heard the sound of bells ringing from the City churches across the river to herald in the new decade.

409

EPILOGUE

New Year's Day 1960

How It All Ended

83. Daffodil Dawn

Driving for an hour through the clear moonlit lines of shops and houses of the East End, Timothy and his mother, accompanied by Louise, at last reached the open countryside above the estuary. The river shone like silver ribbon as it swerved and unravelled majestically on its way to the North Sea. London lights shone everywhere like a firmament of stars.

Turning down into a small winding lane, lined with willows pointing jaggedly at the moon, they passed the two old yew-trees at the end of the garden, standing like sentinels against the indigo sky. Timothy drove slowly round, past the bunching shed, the granary, and the barn, and drew up by the back door to find his father, now recovered from his wounds, standing at the kitchen door, enveloped in a welcoming orange halo of light.

In the morning, Timothy came down early to find his mother laying the table for breakfast. They sat together, drinking coffee and recalling the events of the last months that had so changed their lives. It was one of those intimate moments between mother and son that now encouraged Jane Crawford to speak more openly on a subject that had much troubled her for many years and which she had never allowed herself to mention to a soul. She looked at Timothy anxiously.

"Timothy, I want to talk to you about your father — that is, your father and me — how the rift between us came about. It all started at the Covent Garden Association dinner-dance. You see, your father was angry with me for wearing a new dress for the occasion. He said I was extravagant. I thought he would be pleased. Instead, he humiliated me in front of our friends and market colleagues. In fact, after that, he would fly into rages at the slightest thing. I could not seem to put a foot right. I remember the evening was terribly unhappy. I cried a lot and John Garville was perfectly sweet to me. Your father went off to the bar and I stayed a lot of the time with John.

"In the succeeding weeks, I saw a good deal of John. Whenever your father had one of his angry fits, I would telephone John and it all invariably ended with my going up to town. We usually had lunch at his club. One particularly bad day, your father was so jealous that he struck me across the face. I cried so much. I was desperate you see. If it hadn't been that I loved you so much, I would have left home for good. I did not know what to do. In the end, I rang John and he drove down and took me back to London. He put me up at his flat for the night, until we could decide how to put things right. There was never anything untoward between us, you understand, but your father thought otherwise and threatened me with divorce. His friendship with John ceased and it was only after some years that, for business reasons, he began to tolerate John.

"Another bone of contention was John's interest in your future. He was always very fond of you and, as your god-father, took a great interest in your education and welfare. This was why he left you monies in trust to mature on your twenty-first birthday. This was kept a secret from your father for obvious reasons. Only I and John knew about it. Eventually, your father discovered it through a mistake of the bank. Letters were misdirected and the whole thing came out, with all the attendant ructions. The matter was not mentioned again until you had the argument with your father in the market in February.

"Why I am telling you this is because, since your father's convalescence, we have come to an understanding. The whole drama of his *contretemps* with Curly Donoghue has taken its toll. He is a much more complaisant man than he was, more secure within himself, and I think he regrets his unreasonable attitude towards us all.

"So now you are home again and you have brought us a beautiful and charming future daughter-in-law. You have changed too. You are still my own Timothy, but I can see now you are your own man, too, and I like that in you. I do want so much happiness for you both. Bless you!"

This tale struck Timothy with considerable emotional force. He leant across the table and took his mother's hands in his. It is true that tears were shed a little, tears of relief rather than gratitude. He stood up and kissed her lightly on the forehead. There were no words to express their feelings. There was no need.

Louise came downstairs, looking radiant, a picture of happiness itself. Leaving his mother and father to prepare the breakfast, Timothy led Louise out into the snow and the chill daffodil light of dawn, and showed her the secret places of his childhood, the hideaways and woodland walks that were his joy and boyish delight. They followed along the furrows of the Nine-acres, through woods white with snow, over the watercress-meadows, now thick with a coating of ice, and along the banks of the stream, lined with bull-rushes and willows.

As they came to the top of the hill, they saw below them, the old brick farmhouse which lay nestling in the hollow in a circle of green laurel and yew. Timothy took Louise in his arms and kissed her. Soon it would be spring and they would be married. The woods would be aglow with daffodils and bluebells, primroses and snowdrops, flowers of aspiration. Then Timothy would begin again, begin to build on the things he had learnt while he had been away, during his time of compromise.

As they turned into the yard, Ray, the driver, came to meet them. He had looked after the farm during Andrew Crawford's convalescence. Now, things had to change.

"So you're back, then," he said in a dead tone of voice.

"Yes, Ray, and glad to be, too."

"There's some as is and some as 's not," he said, with his eyes firmly fixed on the ground.

"What do you mean by that?" said Tim, embarrassed in front of Louise.

"I means, Master Tim, I means there's plenty o' work to be done round here. No time for loafers and book-worms." In the contemptuous tone of voice, it was plain to see this would be the last time he would ever call anybody 'Master'.

"Point taken, Ray," Tim said, trying to keep his temper between covers. "But as father has given me a free hand to make whatever changes I like, there are bound to be some you won't agree with. Everything will work out, you'll see."

"So he's given you a free hand, has he?"

"Yes and the first thing I'm going to do is to spruce up our market image. I'm going into partnership with my god-father, John Garville, on the market-gardening side. There's a lot of talk about freezing vegetables now and selling in the new supermarkets. It could prove to be big business. As well as that, I'm going to renovate the old stables and bring in a livery facility. There's plenty of call for it round here, especially for the children."

"Come off it, Tim. You couldn't sit your arse on a horse to save your life." Timothy knew Ray was doing his best to show him up in front of Louise.

"I'm going to have a damned good try," Tim replied angrily.

"So what happens to me, then."

"That, Ray, is up to you. Either you're with me or against me."

"I've only ever taken orders from your father."

The implication of the remark was clear enough to Timothy. It made him realise that he would be travelling a hard road if he had to manage his father and Ray at the same time. Their old master-minion

414

relationship would be impossible to break. He considered his father sufficiently amenable, and therefore agreeable to change, but Ray's old-world intransigence could prove to be a serious threat if the merger with John Garville was to prosper. Nothing is ever perfect, even in a world that has seemingly changed for the better. With Louise by his side, he was as sure of success as he ever could be. The question of Ray had troubled Timothy during the whole of those few disastrous weeks in the market, and now it had once more come to challenge him. He would be forced to throw down the gauntlet and confront him, knowing full well that this could open a whole Pandora's box of troubles with his now quiescent father.

As Ray strode off up the lane, Tim frowned. Louise, the pacifier, began laughing at him a little. She could see he was rattled by Ray's attitude. Just for a moment, a shadow passed over him and his expression changed momentarily as if he were annoyed with her. She smiled at him so disarmingly that he began to laugh too.

"There you are!" she said. "That's more like it." He kissed her.

"I love you, darling Louise. How extraordinary it is that we, two wandering souls in this wilderness of life, have found each other. How happy we shall be, my dearest Louise!"

Timothy, who had started by wanting to cure the ills of others, had ended by curing his own. As for Louise, well, to say that the restoration of the faculty of speech must surely be considered a miracle is, in part, to deny the skills of surgeons and psychiatrists who helped it to come about. Over the last months, Timothy and his mother had seen Louise grow in confidence and, instead of her silent and solitary readings of poetry under Uncle Walter's care, she and Timothy could now enjoy those moments together in all their completeness. Timothy's initiative in helping to restore Louise's voice had been no mean feat; he had given her the essential confidence to break free of her bonds and burst into flower like one of Uncle Walter's fragrant summer roses.

The next morning, just before breakfast, Louise came down to the hall and slipped a small notebook into Timothy's pocket.

"I love you, too," she whispered, "with all my heart."

Timothy stood up, took her in his arms and held her close to him. Later, in his study, he opened the book to find poems Louise had begun writing soon after her first meeting with him on that momentous day in February, verses that mapped out the landscape of her increasing love over the months of their friendship. *Poems from Louise* was only the beginning of a whole new world for her which would one day attract the notice of a London publisher.

After some minutes, they heard Mrs. Crawford calling out to them that breakfast was on the table. Timothy and Louise came in to the welcoming warmth of the farmhouse kitchen. Mother and father were sitting at the table. Their restored, though measured, affection for each other made everything seem as near perfect as this world can dare to promise. In the centre of the table was a fine bowl of early spring flowers.

"Look, Timothy!" said his father, with a twinkle in his eye. "Daffodils from the Scilly Isles. I've ordered another consignment for the market this year. Rather a good idea of mine, don't you think?"

84. The End of the Affair!

For Miss Agnes Baldock, it was a case of 'off with the old and on with the new'. Her arrival in Worthing coincided with the sale of premises in Montague Place, a charming side-street adjoining the sea-front. A viewing of the accommodation convinced her that this was the very place she had dreamed of. With the purchase completed, she could now begin the task of planning the refurbishment of 'The Laburnum Tree Tea-Rooms', or what would, among the locals, come to be known as 'Aggie's Place'. Its proximity to the pier, the Lido and the busy shops along Montague Street made it an ideal place to meet, and soon it developed into a thriving dating venue for singles hoping to become doubles!

In the course of time, a beguiling young Irishman by the name of Mick began to frequent the establishment. This Mick turned out to be a sea captain with a yacht called 'The Saucy Skipper' and was a great attraction for ladies like Agnes who were footloose and fancy free and had an unfulfilled wish to form an attachment with any available young man in sight! The ladies, in turn, held a powerful attraction for Mick, especially if of a certain age, substantially proportioned, and not too short on the spondoolicks, as the Irish say.

Even after Agnes discovered the truth about Mick — even when 'The Saucy Skipper' turned out to be, after some secret probing by Agnes, not a boat but a night-spot for sailors on leave in Portsmouth — even if his dashing uniform *did* turn out to be no more than bogus fancy dress — even then, she still forgave him and, as a result, in spite of all the rash of forgivings that inevitably followed, she found at last the perfect compromise in her choice of a life-companion.

As for Joe Purvis, well! He had a gleaming new pent-house apartment, a balcony with views of the Mother of Parliaments, and a knighthood to go with it. Perhaps in the not too distant future he might be granted a seat in the Upper House, should the call come for him to occupy such an elevated perch. He dreamed of the day when, with Gwendolen sitting in the Public Gallery, he might rise with pride to deliver his maiden speech and astound their Lordships with his quaint eloquence.

A month into the new decade, the little close of Laburnum Villas was razed to the ground. The flattened area was reduced to a sea of mud by the heavy rains. Ugly hoardings heralded the new age with a network of graffiti of dubious literary ingenuity. Posters warning of 'The End of the World' were overpowered by a huge black and yellow announcement:

Keep up with the times!

Visit the fabulous

WONDERLAND TELEVISION STORE

to be opened on this site on 1st May 1960 by

The Mayor of Rothersey
Cllr **Sir Joseph Gabriel Purvis** KBE

For the residents of Rothersey, the old way of life had gone for ever. For the former occupants of Laburnum Villas, at the very least, there would be the prospect of new beginnings — south of the river.

BEHIND THE SCENES

1. *South of the River*: Preparing the Ground

Fact and Fantasy

The best times for us children in my generation were spent on our Essex farm in the halcyon years before the Second World War. My father, Frank James Thorogood and his brother, Herbert Gill Thorogood, had inherited the family business on the death of my grandfather in 1935, so my sister, Mary, and I grew up alongside an extended family of five cousins.

Every Christmas, my Aunt Emma gave me books of adventure stories: Edgar Rice Burroughs' *Tarzan* books, Osa Johnson's exciting accounts of her journeys into the heart of Africa and the jungles of Sumatra, D. H. Lawrence's *Twilight in Italy* and *Mornings in Mexico,* and T. E. Lawrence's *Seven Pillars of Wisdom.* I owe much to Aunt Emma, who did a great deal to encourage a fantasy-image of myself as a precocious global adventurer in my early years — something I never became, at least not on a world-wide scale. The last book she gave me was Thor Heyerdahl's *Kon-Tiki,* which came out in 1950, when I was already twenty-three years old! At that point, because my fantasies showed no sign of becoming realities, she gave up, but she had by then already inadvertently established in my mind the thought that the world of the imagination was possibly a richer and more desirable place than the real world.

As an incorrigible young romantic, I regularly raided Mother's bookshelves, delving into her precious cloth-bound collection of Mary Webb first editions, and frequently sneaking a peek at Elizabeth Goudge's *Green Dolphin Country*, Margaret Mitchell's *Gone With the Wind*, and a liberal supply of novels by H.E. Bates, Vicki Baum, John Buchan, Pearl Buck, Warwick Deeping, Phillip Gibbs, Howard Spring, Dornford Yates, and the surprising appearance, one day, of Radcliffe Hall's *The Well of Loneliness.*

To prepare for my Oxford School Certificate examinations, I had to be purged of all these literary excesses by a good cleansing diet of Shakespeare, Jane Austen, Dickens, Thackeray, the Brontës, Galsworthy and Arnold Bennett. From this experience I became a life-long admirer of Thackeray' *Vanity Fair.* I still enjoy its skilful interplay of comic and serious. I continually marvel at the way in which great historical moments are set against brilliant ironic narrative and graphic accounts of the folly and vanity of society.

From my earliest years my parents had little choice but to indulge me in my passion for the cinema, largely, I think, because of my frequent bouts of ill-health, which prevented me from joining in the usual childhood games and pursuits, and I could, like Ron Thompson in *South of the River,* consequently follow my filmic fantasies unfettered. Black and white films jostled for position with the more up-to-date Eastmancolour and 'cinemascope' productions, Ealing Comedies, Hollywood technicolour extravaganzas and fast-moving Westerns. Sometimes I would see a programme twice round, thus doubly delaying the abrupt return to the reality of ill-health and school homework. I still have no trouble at all in sitting right through to the credits with old favourites like *The Lavender Hill Mob, The Wicked Lady, Kind Hearts and Coronets, The Thirty-Nine Steps, Dangerous Moonlight,* and *Rebecca.*

Inevitably, the time came in my late teens when I would break the mould and seek out the attractions that London could offer. The second-hand bookshops in the Charing Cross Road led me astray more often than not, sometimes extravagantly, for I rarely went home without a book to add to my collection. I discovered 'belles lettres', read Logan Pearsall Smith, Cyril Connolly, Harold Acton and the Sitwells. I spent late nights at theatre clubs watching 'absurd' plays by Picasso (*Désir Attrappée par le Queue*) and Ionesco. I read Freud and Jung, Kafka and Sartre, Mauriac (*Le Désert de l'Amour*) and Proust, and searched through the bookshops of London and Paris in my insatiable hunger for self-knowledge.

It was during the time as a student in Paris in 1949 that my innocence came to an abrupt end with the accidental discovery, on the Left Bank, of unexpurgated editions of Frank Harris's *My Life and Loves,* Henry Miller's *Tropic of Cancer* and James Joyce's *Ulysses,* all of which, so I was told, were listed as banned books on the Papal Index — the Pope's 'forbidden reading' list! Within a few years of my fall from grace, Penguin Books would publish the much-awaited explicit

421

edition of D. H. Lawrence's *Lady Chatterley's Lover*. The coming of a new 'Permissive Society' with its consequent increase in sexual licence was by no means light-years away.

Changing Times

For many families, the war changed little of the old attitudes and way of life. In some respects, austerity held back social advancement, especially for the younger generation. With demobilisation of the armed forces, it was increasingly difficult to find work and, until rationing ended in 1954, there could be little improvement in the economic life of the country. Father still carried on the family business in more or less the same way, though tractors were replacing horses. The old pre-war trains still rumbled and thundered over the arches of the Borough Market. The age of steam had not entirely disappeared.

In 1953, the pageantry and show of the Coronation of Queen Elizabeth II (the splendour of which Ron missed by being confined to bed with an attack of influenza) brought a refreshing sense of national identity and a renewal of interest in our history and heritage. My sister and I, in company with our friend Bunty, sat up all night on the pavement in St. James's Street and had a 'front-seat' view. Millions of people throughout the world were able to watch the complete ceremony and procession on television. Today, we think nothing of the whole world watching the Olympics in Australia or Mexico, but the filming and televising of the Coronation was a remarkable technical achievement for its time.

By the end of the decade, England was at last free of wartime restrictions, London was regaining its old spirit, a new confidence was returning, and a fresh global image had come about through the Festival of Britain in 1951, with its resultant expansion of the arts. Rapid advances in technological and scientific research during the war years had brought about remarkable improvements in medical treatment and care. Hire purchase (especially of televisions) and mortgages for first-time home-buyers became the chosen options for thousands of young couples. Social life was more relaxed and, following the ending of food and clothes rationing, the High Street shops were stacked with goods for shoppers eager to sample the ever-widening range of new items. Now, the hot-water bottle was replaced by the electric blanket. There were food-mixers, washing machines and launderettes, nylon and terylene, G-Plan furniture and Pyrex dishes.

In the face of this cultural change, we (like the Thompsons) continued to sing round the piano our parents' favourite songs like 'Goodnight, Sweetheart' and 'I do Like to be Beside the Seaside' as well as the wartime favourites, 'Run, Rabbit Run' and 'We'll Hang Out Our Washing on the Siegfried Line', and songs made famous by Vera Lynn ('The Forces' Sweetheart'), 'We'll Meet Again' and 'A Nightingale Sang in Berkeley Square', though Ivor Novello's timeless tunes, beloved of our favourite Aunt Cissie (soprano), had a very strong place in our musical evenings at the farm.

Whilst my mother instilled in me a love of reading and music, my father gave me a passion for the theatre. He was a devotee of 'Variety' in all its forms and we were taken many times to the Stratford Empire, the Ilford Hippodrome and sometimes grander venues like the Palladium to see Cockney performers such as Billy Russell, Max Miller, Tessie O'Shea, Bud Flanagan ('Underneath the Arches') and the rest of the 'Crazy Gang'. If Father felt flush enough, we would all have dinner at the Trocadero in Shaftesbury Avenue as a special treat.

The older performers held the musical stage for quite a time until quick-step, fox-trot, palais glide and hokey-kokey gave way to bebop, skiffle and 'rock and roll'. Along came Elvis Presley with 'Love Me Tender', and the Chordettes with 'Lollipop'. A galaxy of British stars of stage and screen — a constant source of comfort to the likes of Millie Thompson — including Tommy Steele, Shirley Bassey, Cleo Laine and Alma Cogan, formed the vanguard to a thriving world of British entertainment.

The next decade opened with Max Bygraves catching the flavour of the times with his rendering of 'When You Come to the End of a Lollipop', which was to delight end-of-the-pier audiences during many a summer season at our coastal resorts. It was not to be long, however, before sentimental 'lollipops' were ousted by the more robust

'Yellow Submarine'. 'The Beatles', with their new style of popular song, were destined to turn the musical world upside down and kill off the Fifties and all they stood for — or almost.

An End and a Beginning

In November 1959, my father died. Our life on the farm, like that of the residents of Laburnum Villas soon afterwards, came to an abrupt end. In the course of time, my mother and sister, Mary, had to leave the farm and went to live near old friends in Sussex.

One day in the summer of 1962, after an interview for a teaching post in London, I found myself wandering through the old familiar streets of Southwark. I rediscovered the 'dark tunnel' under the railway and ambled through the alleyways and yards of the Borough Market. After visiting the Cathedral, I sauntered on down Borough High Street, past Miss Davis's breakfast rooms (the 'Miss Trencher' of the story), and found Little Dorrit's church of St. George the Martyr. The plaster cherubs decorating the high ceiling were crying out for a coat of white paint. The organist was practising a voluntary for the Sunday service. I paused for a while, expecting to cast my eyes over the painting of Moses that would inspire Ron to carry on with his art course, but it was nowhere to be seen. I sat for a time meditating on the old days in the Borough. I felt sad for a moment. Then I had a sudden flash of inspiration. I went straight home to Kensington and began to write in long-hand the first 'scenes' for Episode One. But that was all nearly half a century ago.

2. *South of the River*: Devising the Plot

It is, perhaps, unwise for an author to admit to influences, but all authors are certainly subject to them and hopefully are, in the course of time, able to transmute them into a personal style of their own.

I began writing *South of the River* in 1963. To some extent it was a sentimental journey; an attempt to grasp the fading features of an era before they disappeared altogether. I had been to a party to celebrate the launch of the new and much-publicised television serial, *Coronation Street*. The concept of a story about a community living in a street whose life centred on the local public house was appealing. However, not being given to propping up the bar on a nightly basis, I did not choose to include a pub scene in *South of the River,* though my character, Alf Thompson, spends a great deal of his free time with his drinking companions at 'The Bed of Roses' and very often comes home the worse for wear!

Instead of the usual chapters, I have 'episodes' divided into short descriptive and narrative 'scenes', with a style of dialogue such as might occur in a radio or television serial — like the scene in which young Ron Thompson comes face-to-face with first love. I made the time fit into the span of a year — the last of the decade and, coincidentally, the last in the life of Laburnum Villas.

A first novel tends to be a highly elaborate affair, especially if it turns out to be autobiographical — and it usually does. I think, in a way, I wanted to write a fairy tale in which the good suffer at the hands of the bad, the bad suffer at the hands of the good, virtue triumphs in the end, and everybody lives happily ever after. So I settled for a kind of folk-tale with a classical twist in the form of a 'moment of truth' after which the characters are transformed and have to undergo a final test before they are allowed to enjoy the fruits of happiness.

This formality was counterbalanced by the extensive use of colloquial language, including many of the *clichés* that characterise everyday speech, but I failed to comply with T. S. Eliot's demand for 'the common word without vulgarity' since the expletive is a common feature in the vocabulary of three of my characters.

There was, at this time, a vogue for 'local colour' in literature and the theatre. Throughout the 1940s and 1950s, London street life formed the background for successful novels like Michael Sadleir's *Fanny By Gaslight* (1940), Richard Llewellyn's *None But the Lonely Heart* (1943), and Norman Collins' *London Belongs to Me* (1945), though Graham Greene chose Brighton as the more sensational setting for *Brighton*

Rock.

Eventually, East End Cockneys were brought to the fashionable West End — and centre-stage, too. In 1957, Loewe composed the music for *My Fair Lady*, based on Shaw's *Pygmalion*, the story of a Covent Garden Market flower-girl, Eliza Doolittle, whose discovery by a professor of phonetics leads to an elaborate scheme to eradicate her Cockney accent and pass her off as a society debutante. Tommy Steele starred successfully in a long run of the musical, *Half a Sixpence*, an adaptation of a novel by H. G. Wells. Later, Frank Norman produced Lionel Bart's *Fings Aint What They Used to Be* (1960), to be followed by *Oliver* (1961), Bart's highly successful musical adaptation of the Dickens novel. In another decade or two, such social types would become the bedrock of television 'soap operas' like *EastEnders*.

When I was scribbling down the first ideas for *South of the River* I happened to be reading Wordsworth's *Preface* to the *Lyrical Ballads* for a literature seminar I was running. One passage had some bearing on what I was about to write. Wordsworth's intention was 'to choose incidents and situations from common life and to relate and describe them throughout, as far as possible, in a selection of language really used by men and, at the same time, to throw over them a certain colouring of imagination, whereby ordinary things should be presented to the mind in an unusual way.....' Though taken out of context, this seemed to point to a possible method for me to approach my first novel. Indeed, there appeared to be no alternative if I was to write about Cockney characters in a small London community.

In Episodes One to Eleven I would show my characters to be the victims not only of their economic, social and cultural circumstances, but their own weaknesses, condemned as they are to wander aimlessly in an environment that, in spite of the trauma of war, had hardly altered since pre-war days.

In Episode Twelve I would take my characters away from their normal surroundings and put them down in an unfamiliar place — a paradigm of Limbo, perhaps — in inclement conditions, where they would all experience some moment of truth, a testing ground where they would have an opportunity to explore their emotions, fears and frustrations, away from the tensions and distractions of the daily round and common task. I would let them see the error of their ways, give them a chance to express their inner thoughts by means of interior monologue. In the last two Episodes I would expect them to prove themselves by undergoing some kind of test or trial that would bring them absolution, and even some degree of happiness in the end.

The works of modern-day authors are not necessarily capable of being read aloud as would have been the case in Victorian times. The novels of Charles Dickens, with their episodic structure and their clearly-defined characters and situations, are perfect vehicles for his undoubted histrionic powers as an actor. His choice of vocabulary and inventive literary devices, even his unconventional system of punctuation, make his writings eminently suitable for performance.

It is said that all authors have a 'voice' of their very own because they 'hear' the words as they write them. A character in a novel develops 'his' or 'her' own way of speaking to the reader and that makes Dickens different to Thackeray, and George Eliot different to Virginia Woolf. So my characters would have to speak to me through *my* 'voice' and, through that voice, come alive in the mind of you, the reader. But first I would have to find that voice.

Secondly, as to punctuation, I decided to adopt Dickens' method of combining the contemporary grammatical conventions with additional punctuation to act as 'performer's marks' — to indicate pauses of varying lengths, suggestions for irony, and aids to express a whole gamut of feelings. So in effect, a comma or a colon could serve as a 'stage direction'.

3. *South of the River*: Inventing the characters

On leaving school, I joined the family business in the Borough Market in London, where, like my character, Timothy Crawford, I had an opportunity to observe the comings and goings of market life and learn how to get on with a variety of social types and classes. Since the story is set in the London suburbs of Rotherhithe, Bermondsey and Southwark (collectively, the Rothersey of the story), some of my characters are Cockneys, who could just about be genuine enough to have been born within the sound of Bow Bells across the river to the north.

Agnes Baldock is ostensibly upstanding , leads a blameless life of strict routine and is quick to criticise faults in others, though she has a softer humane side when faced with Ron Thompson's tears. She is one of the new de-classed members of society brought about by post-war social changes. We are not told where she came from but we sense that she had perhaps lived in more affluent circumstances in the past. She was lonely and without prospects, like the rest of the occupants of Laburnum Villas.

Ma Blackwood, I suppose, does bear some resemblance to one or other of the formidable bunch of 'ladies' who regularly held up the bar at *The Rovers Return* in the early black-and-white days of *Coronation Street*, though she probably has more in common with the residents of Albert Square of the future *EastEnders*.

The pickpocketing gangs of today are no less vicious than they were in the days of Fagin. Ma's clutch of petty thieves and their under-the-counter activities make an ironic contrast to the innocence of her boisterous little customers, and it was, after all, little Mabel who trapped her in the end.

In **Ma Carpenter**'s case, her bark was worse than her bite, as Eddie well understood. She could be thought heartless in giving her baby daughter away to the feckless Flo, but Mabel probably had a better chance of making a go of life in the Thompson household in spite of being 'brought up by hand' as Dickens calls it. At least in the end, she finds a loving brother in **Eddie Carpenter**, who makes up for his mother's shortcomings by marrying Millie, baby and all. Ma and Eddie are both complete fabrications but I imagine their like could have been seen in almost any East End pub in the 1950s.

Andrew Crawford has absolutely nothing that in the slightest way resembles my father, who wanted only the best for me and gave me the finest liberal education a boy could ever hope for at Brentwood School and Trinity College, Dublin. He was greatly loved by all who knew him for his gentle nature and wry sense of humour. As I was an only son, like Timothy Crawford, Father would have dearly wished me

428

to continue with the family farm, but with my older cousins already ahead of me, there seemed little chance of following in his footsteps.

Timothy's struggle to rise out of the comparatively comfortable life on the farm and face the world head on does have some parallel with events in my own life, but thank heaven I never had such a devastating argument with my father as he had with his. Father did have a temperamental Scottish farmer friend who was given to occasional outbursts from time to time so I used him as my model for Andrew Crawford. However, though I borrowed the name Crawford for Andrew and Jane, it has no connection with our friendly neighbours of the same name who lived at the farm on the hill beyond our watercress meadows. I remember one of the sons had a racing green MG motor-car, which I envied as a young boy.

On the occasional Saturday evening, Father would take us to the Capitol Cinema in Upminster, where we sat in our regular seats in the so-called 'Dress Circle'. The Crawfords once impressed us by turning up in evening attire after a smart early supper with friends. The nearest we got to high life in London was the grand twenty-first birthday party which Father gave for me at the famous Holborn Restaurant. He had hoped to book Frascati's (where Andrew and Jane Crawford held their wedding reception in *South of the River)* but it was not available. My sister Mary and her friends, who had missed her celebration because of the Blitz in 1940, joined the two hundred guests, many of whom were father's friends from the Borough Market and the Covent Garden Market Association.

My father was, I think, disappointed with me for not following in his footsteps, but with my three cousins already in line for the business, he accepted the situation. He was, I think, also proud of me, and later came to realise that I was achieving my potential more satisfactorily in my post as a lecturer in English literature and language.

Jane Crawford is a complete fabrication, though her close bond with Timothy is a fair copy of my own relationship with my mother. We had a great deal in common, especially music and a love of books.

Timothy Crawford, like Agnes Baldock, is an 'intruder' into the tight little community of Laburnum Villas. Whereas Agnes bullies her victims along, Timothy's methods are more subtle, especially with

429

Millie, Ron, Mabel and Flo, but in the case of Louise, he helps to bring about a cure. He is a motivator, a manipulator, a catalyst, as well as a protector. He is, above all, a good listener. He has, too, a shadow personality — someone who stands in for him when he is engaged in trying to make something of his own life — the mysterious young man on the coach to Brighton. He also has an assistant in the Vicar of St. Crispin, who steps in when needed. Whilst the incidents in Timothy's life do have some similarity to my own in some respects, his story has little bearing on my own experience.

Curly Donoghue is a complete invention. He is the only character in *South of the River* whose first name is directly taken from *Coronation Street*, but as a character he is the antithesis of his namesake in the television serial. As to my choice of 'Donoghue', it happened that the concert pianist , Peter Donohue (*sic*), had just taken Moscow by storm with his brilliant performance of Tchaikovsky's famous concerto, and we heard the admiring crowds on the wireless calling for 'Pee-taire Do-no-hew!' with a very gutteral throat-clearing Russian 'h'! So it was that, by a very remote coincidence, 'Curly Donoghue' was born.

John Garville, Timothy's godfather, is very loosely based on my godfather, Joseph Boyes Lee, who, with his brother, John, carried on their father's business as potato merchants in the Borough Market and farmed land at Yeldham in Essex. I chose to place him at Finchingfield, the perfect Essex village. The brothers became, over the years, two of my father's most devoted friends. Joe had a fine baritone voice and was much in demand in the Croydon area for his performances in Gilbert and Sullivan operettas. He was frequently asked to sing 'Take a Pair of Sparkling Eyes'. On a recent walk round Southwark, I was touched to rediscover the location of my godfather's old business premises tucked away beneath the railway arches. The firm's brown painted board is still there. John Garville is similar only in his love of music, but the details of his relationships in the novel are an invention and bear no relation to my own godfather's life.

Freddy Higgins and Councillor Purvis's daughter, **Gwendolen**, are names linked to a terrifying incident that occurred during the Second World War. I was sixteen years old at the time. In my school holidays I sang in Rainham Church choir on Sunday mornings. On my way to church, I was in the habit of calling in to see our house-help, Gwen, and her family. One particular Sunday, I left their house as usual, but had hardly gone a hundred yards down the road when an ear-splitting explosion blew me off my bicycle. The tremendous blast threw me against a wire fence and I was badly bruised. A V2 rocket had made a direct hit on the house I had left only a few minutes before. Gwen's husband, Ted Bull, and their small baby, were killed instantly, and the house totally destroyed. The same thing happened to a family called Higgins a few weeks later only a mile or two away. Like **Gwendolen Purvis**, Gwen was an accomplished cook and great help to us all, but she was badly wounded and didn't come back to us again.

Louise might be said to be almost entirely invented. I never knew anyone with her particular disability, though there was the case of a young bride, Winnie Gill, whose husband was drowned in *The Titanic* disaster. On hearing the tragic news, she became so severely traumatised that she lost her voice completely. Twenty years later, on accidentally falling down a flight of stairs, she screamed and, from that moment, her voice returned.

Louise's engagement to Timothy, as friends who know me well have suggested, may possibly be the fictional fulfilment of my own broken engagement in 1957. A beautiful fair-haired girl named Elizabeth came into my life, whom my parents hoped would succeed in bringing their 'prodigal son' home to the fold at last, as happens to Timothy in *South of the River.*

Walter Paxton, the gentle and considerate uncle to Louise, is an affectionate portrait of my step-grandfather, with whom I had many interesting conversations about his life in the police force. I stayed with him and my grandmother for eleven weeks as an evacuee during the Blitz Dovercourt, on the Essex coast, was a tranquil little seaside resort until nearby Harwich became the victim of a string of bombings by the Germans in the early 1940s. It became so dangerous that I was sent back home to the Thames Valley which, at that time, was enjoying a brief lull in hostilities.

Priscella (Elsa) was based on a Dutch girl I used to know. She had very fair hair, bright blue eyes and a smiling face. She loved to come to the farm, particularly for Mother's traditional Sunday afternoon teas. She had the strange habit of disappearing from time to time, only to be found later lying on the ground (for a full hour sometimes) in among my father's favourite roses. She liked to dream away, gazing up at the prize blooms silhouetted against the sky — a true romantic.

Councillor Purvis and **Agnes Baldock** are complete figments of the imagination, but how I enjoyed inventing them! The original image of them came to me suddenly as I began writing their first 'scene' together. I remembered a clever caricature sketch I had once seen of Sir William and Lady Wilde (parents of Oscar) by Harry Furniss, depicting from the rear view the ebullient Lady Wilde, over-powering and broad-beamed, beside the diminutive, wispy-haired, womanising Sir William.

Whilst I envisaged Joe Purvis as of beanpole appearance, with wispy grey hair and a tendency to *embonpoint*, I saw Agnes in sturdier mould, standing fair and square in her brown brogues. Both Agnes and Councillor Purvis are lonely, united in their separateness by secret longings that for different reasons are never consummated because they are both attracted to more youthful *liaisons.* The Councillor settles for celibacy and Agnes accepts a rather one-sided compromise.

Alf Thompson's life is dominated by the old ways and his memories of the war years. The working-class custom of having a 'mate' to whom you were loyal almost to the death, would never betray, would stand by in times of difficulty, is shown in the friendships between Alf and **Jack Carpenter**, as much as between Eddie and Curly. Whereas Curly broke every rule in the book and paid for his disloyalty, Alf, haunted by memories of his wrong-doings, suffers for his betrayal of Jack and has to live with his guilt. Luckily for him he finds a way out through his emotional 'confession' to Eddie.

Mabel was the name of my first 'girl friend' at my little elementary school. She didn't like her name so I called her 'Em'. The incident concerning the coal in Mabel's panties comes from a rebellious moment in my sister Mary's childhood, though the 'Inky' episode, which ended by destroying Flo's treasured photograph of Alf and Jack Carpenter, is connected with an identical incident in my mother's childhood and happened while she was staying with her grandparents at Albury Farm, Cheshunt.

Many of the scenes with the Thompson children, Mabel, Ron and

Millie, are drawn from real life stories floating round and about our family. I didn't have to look very far for inspiration.

Councillor Calthrop was based on father's first cousin, Uncle Sidney Boyton Thorogood, but unlike the pompous Calthrop, dear old Uncle Sid was every child's dream for a favourite uncle. I once saw his wife, Aunt Mabel, at a family wedding, dressed in a diaphanous mauve frock and a wide-brimmed hat of lavender Honiton lace. I cannot remember her in any other way now. Uncle invariably wore a smart yellow and grey checked suit made of an expensive West of England cloth. Early every morning, Tuesday to Friday, he would travel on the train from Southend up to Stratford Market, where he reigned supreme as the sole proprietor of 'S. B. Thorogood', fruiterer and purveyor of farm produce. As children we were amused to learn that he used to keep a crate of champagne under the bed for what he called 'emergencies'.

Millie Thompson is a thoroughly modern Millie. She comes from a variety of sources. There was Iris, for example, one of our live-in maids, who left us to do war-work in a button factory. My sister Mary still has the large biscuit tin filled with hundreds of buttons of all shapes and sizes, which provides the family with an endless supply for any occasion. There is, however, no similarity of character at all between the gentle Iris we loved as children and the starry-eyed, trend-setting Millie.

There is a striking contrast between Millie's wish to identify with the new 'culture' and her father Alf Thompson's habit of clinging to the old ways. Like many people in the early 1950's, the Thompson family, closeted in their little cul-de-sac, with all their economic limitations, carried on to a certain degree with the old traditional pursuits at a time when most of society in the towns and cities was being transformed by the coming of television and mass-culture, though only 42,000 households owned a television in 1951.

Ron Thompson escaped from the drab life of the underprivileged child into the fantasy world of the cinema, which continued to flourish, as the popular form of entertainment long after television came in. Ron was the name of my best friend at elementary school. I suppose Ron, Em and I were all about eight years of age at the time.

'Ron' of *South of the River*, on the other hand, had not the

433

advantage of a liberal access to books that I had in my youth. He made a virtue of necessity by immersing himself in the fantasy-world created for him by Grandpa Lawton. After Grandpa died, the Vicar of St. Crispin's was called upon to encourage Ron's awareness of books and music.

Ron's education came through his imagination, with any additional guidance he could gain from his friendship with Grandpa Lawton. I put a lot of myself into Ron. Like him, I fantasised over stories of faraway places, in my case, with the help of Arthur Ransome's *Swallows and Amazons*, R. M. Ballantyne's *The Coral Island* and H. De Vere Stacpoole's *The Blue Lagoon*. But there was a difference. Ron had Grandpa Lawton: I had Aunt Emma!

4. *South of the River*: Then and Now

The Borough

Borough High Street has still something of the same bustling atmosphere of my time there in the late 1940s. Most of the smaller shops have escaped the notice of local planners and so have survived the threat of developers and their bulldozers.

At the western end of the Street, the church of St. George the Martyr marks the limit of my old territory, whilst at the other end, where the traffic crosses over to London Bridge, stands Southwark Cathedral, now dwarfed by hideously tall skyscrapers on the north side of the river. To the southeast, lie Bermondsey and Rotherhithe. I was able to spend a nostalgic morning a few months ago with the Southwark Local History Librarian, who kindly displayed for me a wealth of fascinating photographic and documentary evidence of the district's past.

The Borough Market, where I worked in the family business for two years on leaving school, and where Agnes Baldock and Curly, the vicious market porter, almost came to blows, has become a favourite venue for the young. The old market offices and holdings have mostly

434

been turned into smart restaurants and wine bars. Even the Cathedral has a pleasant coffee house of its own, and countless tourists wander idly through the Market on their way to Southwark Cathedral.

On occasion, after we had finished the business of the day and deposited the takings safely in the Market branch of the local bank, I would go down to Bermondsey and Rotherhithe with Bill, our amiable lorry-driver (the antithesis of the sarcastic, resentful Ray in *South of the River*), to collect manure for the farm from several of the costermongers' stables. This is where I first discovered the idea for Laburnum Villas, for close by was a little enclave of run-down Victorian terraced houses known as Balin Place, now sadly re-developed.

The name 'Laburnum Villas' was a natural progression from places called after trees or flowers — Acacia Avenue, Rose Walk, Primrose Hill, and so on. There is a Laburnum Close in London's East End and a Laburnum Road in South London. Laburnum, whilst being one of the most beautiful of trees, with its pendulous yellow blossoms, has a brief spring flowering all its own. It is also poisonous. Ironically, the vengeful Curly Donoghue is standing underneath the tree when he catches sight of the beautiful Louise combing her hair by her bedroom window.

Napoleon Avenue and Lupin Lane are, as far as I know, pure fictions, at least in Southwark and Bermondsey. However, I did discover in my copy of *London A to Z* recently a Napoleon Road in Clapton (East London) and a Lupin Close in Tulse Hill (South London).

Essex

Rural Essex has not changed quite as much as today's media image would suggest. My sister and I can still enjoy a nostalgic trip back to our old haunts and revive memories of our childhood on the family farms now managed by later generations of Thorogoods.

Albyns, our seventeenth-century Essex farm-house, complete with its barn and stables, is happily still intact. The Thorogood line, like

435

other dynastic farming families in the south of the county, such as the Crawfords, Gunary's, Pouparts and Vellacotts, continued to flourish through the war-time years and after, but with the threat of cheaper foreign produce, fresh ways and means had to be found through bulk deals with the new supermarkets and more profitable agency and commission opportunities. Once a rich market garden for such produce as runner beans, peas, lettuce, radishes, beetroot, and fine 'champagne' rhubarb (all neatly packed and displayed for market in specially stamped *S. Thorogood & Sons* sacks and boxes), the Albyns farmland has now become the Hornchurch Country Park and is administered by the Havering Borough Council.

My choice of Little Warley, a charming village near Brentwood, for the setting of Andrew Crawford's farm probably arose from my father's intention of buying a house there to get us away from the intensive bombing of the Thames Valley during the Blitz. I used to enjoy a solitary Sunday afternoon amble round the country lanes there when I was a schoolboy at Brentwood.

The Roxy Picture House is a composite of a number of 'flea-pits' I frequented as a child, run-down places like the old 'Laurie' in Romford Market Place, where I spent many happy hours with The Marx Brothers, Charlie Chaplin, The Three Stooges, and countless cartoons featuring Popeye and Olive Oyl, Mickey and Minnie Mouse, Goofy and Pluto, the floppy-eared hound. Among the smarter trends in cinema design were the swish 'Havana' in Romford High Street, from which I created the Palaseum (a portmanteau of 'Palace' and 'Coliseum', two West End theatres much loved by my father).

Brighton

The Brighton of fifty years ago, where the residents of Laburnum Villas suffered a sea-change in their lives, has largely disappeared. Though the Palace Pier, now known as 'Brighton Pier', continues to attract the young to sample its fruit machines and hot-dog stands, it has, for me at least, lost something of its old charm.

On a happier note, The Old Ship Hotel, where Timothy and his father were finally reconciled, still thrives today. Masts of yachts now dance about in the breeze that blows across the modern Marina. The once-flourishing antiques emporia in the Lanes have mostly moved out in favour of silversmiths, jewellers, and pedlars of souvenirs and trinkets. Zetland's tea shop, where Louise came to realise how much she loved Timothy, closed many years ago and could never be replaced by anything comparable. Hanningtons, the famous department store, where Flo Thompson literally 'came to grief', was sold and split up into separate stores and boutiques.

Saddest of all, the West Pier, where Effie Mudd and Lizzie Pomfrett spent their idyllic afternoon with little Mabel, became the subject of controversy and intrigue. Whilst patiently waiting to arise like Venus from the waves, the old lady crumpled, cracked into pieces and collapsed into the sea. Her remains caught fire one night — mysteriously, it seems — bringing crowds of onlookers to mourn her tragic end.

In the misty recesses of memory I think I can remember a novel on our bookshelves at home entitled, *The West Pier*, by Patrick Hamilton, one of Mother's favourite authors. Perhaps, when I have a yen to revisit one of my former book-hunting haunts in the Charing Cross Road, I might just find a copy — and thumb through its pages for old time's sake. But then, the booksellers of my acquaintance have all gone now.

Sometimes, I imagine I am back in the Ocean Restaurant of my childhood, happy in the company of Mother, Father, and sister, Mary, and I fancy I can hear the plaintive strains of tea-time music floating across time.

Bramber, Sussex, January 2005

5. Diary of Events for the 1950s

1950   General Election Labour returned to power without a majority.
India declared independent republic within the British Commonwealth
McCarthy Committee inquisition on Un-American activities
William Cooper's *Scenes from Provincial Life* published
Scottish Nationalists stole Coronation Stone of Scone
Venus Observed: Christopher Fry's verse-play

1951   General Election Conservatives returned under Churchill.
Durham County Council applied 'Closed Shop' principle for its employees
Fraudulent Mediums Act. Repeal of Witchcraft Act 1735
Guy Burgess and Donald McLean defected to Russia
Dock Strike in Britain
Festival of Britain opened by King George VI
Census in Britain the first since 1931
Introduction of Health Service charges split Labour Party
42,000 households owned television sets (most hired a set)
'X' Certificate for films unsuitable for under-16's
The Browning Version by Terence Rattigan
The Lavender Hill Mob (B/W film)
Dickens' *Great Expectations* (B/W film) with Richard Attenborough and Martita Hunt
Dickens' *Oliver Twist* (B/W film) Alec Guinness as Fagin
American musical *South Pacific*
The Archers, BBC Radio serial
80 acres of London compulsorily purchased for re-development

1952   Accession of Queen Elizabeth II
Identity cards abolished
Agatha Christie's *The Mousetrap,* longest running play in the history of English theatre, opens at the Ambassadors Theatre, London
Myxomatosis first used in Britain to destroy rabbits

438

1st British atomic bomb exploded Monte Bello Islands
First hydrogen bomb exploded by USA at Eniwetok Atoll
Contraceptive pill first made
Farewell journey of last London tram
Television in Scotland
Abolition of 'Utility' goods system

1953 Death of Queen Mary, aged 85
Fighting in Indo-China. Rioting in Pakistan
Coup d'état in Iran
Coronation of Elizabeth II televised
First atomic shell tested in Nevada
Myxomatosis epidemic
Smog in London.
Disastrous North Sea floods (also in Holland)
Casino Royale, Ian Fleming's first James Bond novel

1954 Food rationing ends
Landlord and Tenant Act giving security of tenure to
occupying tenants
Influx of West Indian immigrants
Cyprus — conflict between Greeks and Turks
Revolution in Guatemala
John Keats: the Living year (Gittings)
Doctor in the House, film with Dirk Bogarde
Lucky Jim: a novel by Kingsley Amis
World-wide concern about atomic fall-out
Shakespeare's *Romeo and Juliet*: a film by Renato Castellani

1955 Rebellion in Argentina and general strike
Hostilities in China
Winston Churchill resigned
Waiting for Godot, play by Samuel Beckett
Credit Squeeze to control inflation

1956 Elvis Presley: *Rock N' Roll* (HMV)
Terrorism in Cyprus
CND protest march Aldermaston
Dickens' *David Copperfield* on television

1957 Treaty of Rome to set up Common Market

Racial Violence in Little Rock USA
Loewe's *My Fair Lady*
Harold Macmillan succeeds Anthony Eden
First British hydrogen bomb exploded, Christmas Island
The Entertainer, play John Osborne at Royal Court Theatre
Saturday Night and Sunday Morning   Alan Sillitoe's novel
Room at the Top, John Braine's novel
Fings Aint Wot they Used to Be   Lionel Bart's musical
Epidemic Asian influenza

1958   Prince Charles became Prince of Wales
Empire Day renamed Commonwealth Day
Singapore gained independence
Civil strife in Lebanon
Notting Hill race riots
Russia launched *Sputnik 1*
John Betjeman, *Collected Poems*
Alaska became 49th state of U.S.A
Boris Pasternak, *Dr Zhivago*
C.P. Snow's novel, *The Conscience of the Rich*
Carve Her Name with Pride, film of wartime spy, Yvette
Szabo
Race riots in Notting Hill and Nottingham
USA launched *Explorer* 1,2,3 and 4.   USA *Pioneer* 1,2 and 3
Reports of Yeti (Abominable Snowman)
Agricultural production stepped up in China
Mon Oncle, film satire with Jacques Tati
Your Life in Their Hands, TV series about hospital treatment
Space exploration with U.S.A. 'Explorer' (first earth satellite)
and Russian Sputnik III
Last steam locomotive manufactured at Crewe

1959   General Election: Conservative government returned to power
under Macmillan: 'You never had it so good!'
Obscene Publications Act
Shelagh Delaney, *A Taste of Honey*
Iona and Peter Opie, *The Lore and Language of School-
children*

440

Elvis Presley: *A Date with Elvis* (RCA)
Colin MacInnes, 'teenage problem' novel, *Absolute Beginners*
Arnold Wesker's play, *Roots*
Look Back in Anger, film with Richard Burton
The Horse's Mouth, film with Alec Guinness
First British experimental surgery unit at Hammersmith Hospital
Uprising in Tibet. Army revolt in Iraq
Civil war in Belgian Congo
Le Rhinocéros Eugene Ionesco
Alfred Hitchcock's film thriller, *Psycho*
Paperbacks increasingly popular
Two monkeys recovered from space. Moon probes

1960 Marriage of Princess Margaret to Anthony Armstrong-Jones
Brezhnev made President of Russia
United Arab Republic National Assembly
African states granted independence: Cameroons, Ghana, Nigeria etc.
Belgian Congo independence followed by civil war
John Kennedy, first Roman Catholic President USA
Robert Bolt's play, *A Man for All Seasons*
Harold Pinter's play, *The Caretaker*
D. H. Lawrence's novel, *Lady Chatterley's Lover* (Penguin Books)
BBC White City Television Centre opened
Stiletto heels in fashion
Alfred Hitchcock's thriller, *Psycho*
Film version of Lionel Bart's musical *Fings Aint Wot They Used to Be*
Farthing ceased to be legal tender. New one pound note issued.
US communications satellites, Echo I
Russian satellite, Sputnik V, launched. Two dogs on board
Earthquakes in Morocco and Chile. Typhoon in Hong Kong
Polaris submarines in Holy Loch

References to Songs Quoted in the Text

1. Red Sails in the Sunset   p 95
   Lyrics by Jimmy Kennedy. Music by Hugh Williams. Copyright by The Peter Maurice Music Co. Ltd. Featured by Anona Winn. Also sung by Suzette Tarri.

2. Ah, Sweet Mystery of Life   p 95
   Lyrics by Rida Johnson Young. Music by Victor Herbert (1859-1924) Made famous by Hollywood film-star Jeanette Macdonald

3. Give us a Bash at the Bangers and Mash   p 96
   Author and composer unknown

4. The Cornish Floral Dance   p 139
   Lyrics and music by Kate Moss. Published 1911. Made famous by baritone, Peter Dawson. Originally a 'Furry Dance' associated with the Cornish village of Helston. Traditionally played by brass bands.

5. Run, Rabbit, Run   p 145
   Words by Noel Gay and Ralph Butler. Music by Noel Gay. Copyright by Noel Gay Music Co. Ltd. (1939). No. NOMC 115. From the musical show, *The Little Dog Laughed.* Featured by Billy Cotton and his Band.

6. Keep the Home Fires Burning   p 145
   Popular song from the First World War. Lyrics by Lena Ford. Music by Ivor Novello. 1915 Publisher not traced, possibly Keith, Prowse.

7. We'll Meet Again   p 146
   Words and music by Ross Parker and Hughie Charles. Copyright by The Irwin Dash Music Co. Ltd. (1939) No. IDP 346 Broadcast by Henry Hall and his Orchestra. Made famous by Vera Lynn

8. Oh, You're a Great Big Wonderful Baby   p 146
   Neither author nor composer listed on Internet

442

9. Rudolph, the Red-nosed Reindeer   p 159
   Lyrics by Robert May. Music by Johnny Marks c. 1949
   Publisher not traced.

10. Goodnight, Sweetheart   p 191
    Words and music by Ray Noble, Jimmy Campbell and Reg Connelly.
    Copyright by Campbell, Connelly & Co. Ltd. (1931) Featured by
    Jack Payne and his BBC Dance Orchestra.

11. Mairzy Doats and Dozy Doats   p 332
    Words and music by Milton Drake, Al Hoffman and Jererny
    Livingstone.
    Copyright Miller Music Corporation (1943) No. F & D Ltd. 21302
    Another version by Al Trace (see Internet) Made popular by Bing
    Crosby. 'Mares eat oats and does eat oats and little lambs eat ivy. A
    kid'll eat ivy too. Wouldn't you?'

12. Knees up, Mother Brown! p 345
    Listed on Internet as 'Traditional' with author, composer, and
    publisher unknown.

13. Here We Are Again   p 382
    Author, composer, publisher not listed on Internet.

14. When You Come to the End of a Lollipop   p 384
    Words and Music by Al Hoffman and Dick Manning. Copyright by
    Topper Music Publishing Corp. (1960) Copyright by Rogers Music
    Ltd. 1960. Recorded by Max Bygraves on Decca Records.